MASTER OF SHADOWS

"Angela doesn't hold anything back. Anyone who is a Mage-verse fan is going to love this new addition."

—*Night Owl Reviews*

MASTER OF SMOKE

"Knight's clever and comedic seventh Mageverse paranormal . . . follows a passionate romance between an unwilling female werewolf and an amnesiac Sidhe warrior containing the spirit of a great cat, set against a complex series background incorporating vampires, witches, alien spirits, and the legend of King Arthur . . . The result is a successful mix of magic, romance, humor, and mind-blowing sex."

—*Publishers Weekly*

"If you enjoy a paranormal series with a healthy dose of erotica, enough wit to lighten the mood, battles of good vs. evil, and a new twist on an old story line, then what are you waiting for? Enter the world of Mageverse—I promise, once you get in, you won't want to go back!"

—*Night Owl Reviews*

MASTER OF FIRE

"A fantastic book . . . The story was fresh and new and exciting . . . Sure to keep the reader on the edge of her seat. Ms. Knight has outdone herself . . . [She] has created some of the hottest sex scenes known to man. The sexual chemistry between Logan and Giada is out of this world . . . Not to mention, the ending is sure to leave you craving the next book."

—*The Romance Studio*

continued . . .

"A great addition to the Mageverse series . . . Most enjoyable."
—*Book Binge*

MASTER OF DRAGONS

"Many thanks to Angela Knight for keeping this series sexy and unique."
—*Romance Reader at Heart*

MASTER OF SWORDS

"Fabulous . . . A terrific romantic fantasy that spins the Arthurian legend into a different, unique direction."
—*Midwest Book Review*

MASTER OF WOLVES

"Grandmaster of the paranormal romantic suspense."
—*Midwest Book Review*

MASTER OF THE MOON

"The author has certainly gotten inventive with her Mageverse series, and there's no denying it is something different among the current glut of paranormal books."
—*RT Book Reviews*

MASTER OF THE NIGHT

"A terrific paranormal romantic suspense thriller that never slows down until the final confrontation between good and evil. The action-packed story line moves at a fast clip."
—*Midwest Book Review*

WARRIOR

"A wonderful science fiction romantic suspense."
—*Genre Go Round Reviews*

MASTER
of
DARKNESS

ANGELA KNIGHT

BERKLEY SENSATION, NEW YORK

THE BERKLEY PUBLISHING GROUP
Published by the Penguin Group
Penguin Group (USA) Inc.
375 Hudson Street, New York, New York 10014, USA

Penguin Group (Canada), 90 Eglinton Avenue East, Suite 700, Toronto, Ontario M4P 2Y3, Canada
(a division of Pearson Penguin Canada Inc.) • Penguin Books Ltd., 80 Strand, London WC2R 0RL,
England • Penguin Group Ireland, 25 St. Stephen's Green, Dublin 2, Ireland (a division of Penguin
Books Ltd.) • Penguin Group (Australia), 250 Camberwell Road, Camberwell, Victoria 3124, Australia
(a division of Pearson Australia Group Pty. Ltd.) • Penguin Books India Pvt. Ltd., 11 Community
Centre, Panchsheel Park, New Delhi—110 017, India • Penguin Group (NZ), 67 Apollo Drive,
Rosedale, Auckland 0632, New Zealand (a division of Pearson New Zealand Ltd.) • Penguin Books
(South Africa) (Pty.) Ltd., 24 Sturdee Avenue, Rosebank, Johannesburg 2196, South Africa

Penguin Books Ltd., Registered Offices: 80 Strand, London WC2R 0RL, England

This is a work of fiction. Names, characters, places, and incidents either are the product of the author's
imagination or are used fictitiously, and any resemblance to actual persons, living or dead, business
establishments, events, or locales is entirely coincidental. The publisher does not have any control over
and does not assume any responsibility for author or third-party websites or their content.

MASTER OF DARKNESS

A Berkley Sensation Book / published by arrangement with the author

PUBLISHING HISTORY
Berkley Sensation mass-market / August 2012

Copyright © 2012 by Angela Knight.
Excerpt from "Enforcer" from *Unbound* by Angela Knight copyright © 2013 by Angela Knight.
Cover art by Gene Mollica. Hand lettering by Ron Zinn.
Cover design by George Long.

ISBN: 978-0-425-24793-8

BERKLEY SENSATION®
Berkley Sensation Books are published by The Berkley Publishing Group,
a division of Penguin Group (USA) Inc.,
375 Hudson Street, New York, New York 10014.
BERKLEY SENSATION® is a registered trademark of Penguin Group (USA) Inc.
The "B" design is a trademark of Penguin Group (USA) Inc.

PRINTED IN THE UNITED STATES OF AMERICA

10 9 8 7 6 5 4 3 2 1

ALWAYS LEARNING   PEARSON

3 1561 00284 3690

ACKNOWLEDGMENTS

As always, I had a lot of help on this book.

Virginia Ettel, my dear Bookdragon, did troubleshooting on my giant snake, originally far too fat and un-snakey. Author and Gaelic speaker Eileen Gormley kept Finvarra from sounding like a Lucky Charms commercial. Shelby Morgen (aka the Queen of Porn, the Mistress of Darkness, and She Who You Don't Want to Sing to You) kept me from collapsing into a whimpering heap of self-doubt. Sandy (aka Camille Anthony) helped me avoid a nasty anticlimax. Kate Douglas, Markeeta Karland, and my beloved friend Diane Whiteside spotted assorted plot holes, typos, and logic problems.

My agent, Jessica Faust, provided encouragement and suggestions in the book's early stages. Congratulations to her and her husband on their new baby boy, Ryland.

Thanks, as always, to my patient editor Cindy Hwang, without whom I would have no career. Her assistant, associate editor Leis Pederson, is always willing to help with my latest crisis. Thanks, Leis.

I also want to dedicate this, the ninth and last book of the Mageverse series, to my sister, Angela Patterson. She has always been my dearest friend and cheerleader, even in the days when I was struggling to get something, *anything*, published. She will never know how much that meant to me. Her husband, Chuck, has been a source of warm encouragement and the occasional cackling laugh. (Sometimes at my expense.) He and Angela love being grandparents more than anyone I have ever seen. As well they should, with grandbabies Princess Naomi and the Bonny Princes, Charles, William, Richard, and Henry.

Most of all I want to thank my loving (and beloved) parents. My mother, Gayle Lee, encouraged me to become a writer from the time I was nine and wrote "The Mouse Who Went to the Moon." Her unstinting praise made me believe I could actually *do* this. My father, home builder Paul Lee, taught me the meaning of dedication, hard work, and craftsmanship, characteristics I have tried to bring to my writing.

As always, I want to thank my husband, Michael, who is still the loving heart of every hero I've ever written. My son, Anthony, and his friend, James Berg, provided meals and housecleaning when I was too busy writing to do either. They are much appreciated.

Last, but certainly not least, I want to dedicate this book to *you*, my readers, who have stuck with me through the Mageverse series. I hope that you will enjoy the coming books in my new Familiars trilogy. Thank you for reading!

ANGELA KNIGHT

ONE

William Justice arched against the mattress like a man being tortured on a rack, his hips rolling upward as he braced his big feet on the bed. Breathing in pumping pants, he ground his head back into the pillow and growled. The low rumble didn't sound human.

An erection curved high over his taut abdomen, hard as a blade, flushed dark and thick with need. A single bead of pre-come clung to the curving tip of his velvet glans. He sucked in a deeper breath, making the long shaft dance. The drop broke free, hit his belly, and rolled into his navel.

Dropping his hips to the bed, he went still, dark lashes fanning his cheeks as his eyes flicked behind his closed lids, tracking the dream that tormented him.

One big hand fell into the sheets, curled into a fist around a handful of twisted cotton, and gripped hard. A bead of sweat rolled down the thick curve of his biceps, drawing a shining trail as it worked its way along the contours of muscle.

As always, he dreamed of Miranda Drake. Miranda, with eyes the vivid gold of sunlight-shot amber, and a mane of hair as red as fox fur. Her breasts looked intriguingly full beneath the soft cotton T-shirts she favored, usually with some snarky phrase scrawled across the front. Snug blue jeans drew attention to her long runner's legs and delightfully curvy ass.

Justice had never seen her naked anywhere except his dreams. These days, that was damned near every time he fell asleep. Sometimes he dreamed her nipples were the color of peaches on the sweet cream curves of her breasts, or candy pink, or soft, dusky rose. But in every single dream, her scent intoxicated him with its rich, erotic promise as she reached for him with a wicked, witchy smile.

Never mind that the real Miranda treated him with a cool, distant professionalism that made it plain he was her bodyguard. And that was all.

All he was. All he'd ever be.

"Dammit, Miranda." Lips peeling off his teeth, Justice growled, the sound deepening to become a bestial rumble. "Miranda!"

Magic flashed. Blazing sparks engulfed him in azure energy. The glowing outline of Justice's big body grew even bigger, muscles bulging thicker, swelling along lengthening bones. Fingernails curved into claws, shredding the sheet he still gripped. A silken tide of sable fur raced across his body, thickening over chest and groin just as his short hair lengthened into a thick, black mane that extended halfway down his back.

Justice woke with a jerk, pointed ears flattening against his skull. "Fuck," he growled through the sharp teeth filling his long muzzle. With a disgusted growl, he rolled out of the king bed that was now too short for him, leaving behind shredded navy sheets.

Third time this week he'd wrecked the bed. That damned witch was driving him insane.

Justice stalked on clawed toes to the stained glass window, jerked the latch up, and swung the window wide. Fall air gusted into his face, cool and damp with the woody smell of decaying leaves. Judging by the angle of the sun, it was early afternoon. They'd started keeping Magekind hours, he and Miranda, sleeping during the day and going on missions at night.

You did that when you worked with vampires.

Bracing his hands on the window frame, he stared out across the elegant cityscape of castles, chateaus, and villas that surrounded Miranda's cottage. Towering walls of marble and granite shone in the afternoon sun, surrounded by trees gone orange and gold with autumn. Topiary knights and ladies danced and jousted between the gilded oaks, swaying in the afternoon breeze.

Avalon.

An enchanted city built by witches on a world that was the other-dimensional twin to Earth, Avalon inhabited a universe where magic was a natural force, like magnetism or gravity. You could use that power to build a house—or turn into a werewolf.

Two months ago, Justice had agreed to serve as the bodyguard Miranda desperately needed. Her father had sworn to kill her, and he was more than capable of carrying out the threat. Even King Arthur and his vampire Knights of the Round Table weren't enough protection.

Not against Warlock, immortal wizard, werewolf, and all-around son of a bitch.

Justice wasn't sure he was good enough protection either, especially given this damned sexual obsession he'd developed. Bodyguards did not become obsessed with the bodies they guarded. Not and keep their clients alive.

Yeah, that did it. Looking down, Justice saw that the thought of Miranda in danger had indeed killed his hard-on. He swung the window closed, turned to brace his back against the cool wall, and tried not to remember the dream.

So of course he remembered it anyway. Miranda, naked on her knees, offering him the smooth, perfect peach of her ass. Her witchy eyes shimmered as she smiled at him over one slim, pale shoulder. Her oval face reminded him of an Art Deco goddess, with its delicate strength and long Roman nose. Dusky rose lips curved in a white and wicked smile, seductive as Eve's. Her gleaming hair cascaded around her shoulders in a thousand shades, from fox-fur to antique gold, and her round, pretty tits danced as she moved. Her pink nipples seemed to beg for the swirl of his tongue and the rake of his teeth. Her slick sex pouted at him from the soft, fiery curls between her spread thighs. Ready for his aching cock . . .

Which promptly stirred and began to rise again, unfurling with the hot flood of arousal through his veins.

"You're killing me," Justice told the dream, raking both hands through his thick werewolf mane in pure frustration.

Dammit, it wasn't as if she were in her Burning Moon. The Dire Wolf equivalent of heat struck fertile werewolf females once a year. During that month, their bodies produced clouds of pheromones that drove every male around insane with need. Justice's obsession would be understandable if he'd spent weeks drinking that seductive scent. Only Miranda wasn't *in* her Moon. The crazed heat he felt was purely his own creation. Meanwhile, she treated him with the unwavering good manners of a lady of the Chosen, a werewolf aristocrat who could trace her lineage back fifteen centuries. God knew what had inspired the erotic nymph of his dreams. It certainly had nothing to do with reality.

Dammit, he shouldn't even be thinking about this. If he didn't stay on his clawed toes, she didn't have a prayer against Warlock.

Protecting people was what Justice did. It was what he was. Even becoming a werewolf hadn't changed that. He damned well wouldn't let it.

I am not going to let Miranda's luscious peach ass distract me from keeping her alive.

Miranda Drake dreamed of her mother's death.

On some level, she knew it was a dream; she'd had this particular nightmare so many times, even her unconscious mind recognized it. Yet repetition hadn't blunted its power to suck her into horror.

She screamed at herself not to open the door, but the dream Miranda did it anyway. Just as on that night three months ago, Gerald Drake stood on the other side—seven and a half feet of enraged, fully transformed werewolf. Snarling, her stepfather stormed into the house, slamming the door behind him.

Miranda backed away, her heart in her throat. He'd been beating her and her mother ever since she could remember. She knew this one was going to be bad.

"You utter fool!" Baring the knife length of his fangs, Gerald backhanded her before she could block the blow. She slammed into the wall with a crash that rattled the foyer paintings as she fell flat on her ass. "You betrayed your people." His voice rose to a roar. "You betrayed your god!"

Miranda shook her ringing head as she fought to scramble to her feet. She had to get away before he hit her again.

"Gerald, wait!" Joelle Drake darted between them, raising her hands in supplication. "Miranda has done nothing to betray anyone, much less Warlock!"

He seemed to swell in his rage, towering over the fragile figure of his wife. "Don't you dare lie to me, you stupid cunt! Calista Norman called—she told me all about what you did. How could you let Miranda anywhere near a Knight of the Round Table? You knew she'd talk!"

Calista, you bitch, Miranda thought, steadying herself against the wall as the room rotated slowly around her. Stars flashed in her vision. He'd given her a concussion.

Again.

"We had no idea the knight would be there." Joelle spoke in a desperate rush, trying to get through to him before he killed them both. "The ladies were holding a Grieving for Joan Devon, and . . ."

"Joan Devon!" Gerald mocked her in a high, singsong voice. "Why do you think Joan's husband is dead, moron? She gave him up to the knights! Just like she"—he pointed a curving talon at Miranda— "gave up Warlock!"

"No, no, you're wrong!" Joelle wrung her hands and darted a frantic glance at Miranda. "She told them nothing. Did you, darling?"

"Not a damn thing." Miranda forced herself to meet her stepfather's furious yellow gaze without flinching. "The woman tried to give me a communication spell, but Mother knocked it out of my hand and told her to stay away from me. So we left."

Gerald's long muzzle twitched, drawing in her scent.

Oh, shit, *Miranda thought.* I should have talked around it. He'll know I'm going to contact . . .

"You lie!" He sprang at her, knocking Joelle aside with a sweep of one furry arm. Miranda skittered back, calling her magic as she retreated from his snapping jaws. The Shift raced over her body in a wave of fur as muscle and bone contorted like soft clay in the grip of her power.

"You dare change?" As she met his frenzied gaze, she realized he'd lost control completely. Gerald intended to kill her this time. "You dare fight me? You dare?"

Fear iced her veins, but she made herself sneer. She was tired of cowering before the bastard Warlock had appointed her guardian. "Oh, I dare. And if I get a chance to talk to Belle again, I'm going to tell her everything."

"Then I'll have to see you don't get that chance, you traitorous bitch!" He drew back a clawed hand, obviously intending to rip out her throat.

Joelle threw herself between her daughter and the blow. "Ger—"

His claws ripped into Joelle's face before she could get the rest of the word out of her mouth. She flew sideways, her body slamming into the base of the stairs with a crash. Something snapped with a crack that seemed to echo in Miranda's skull. "Mother!" Forgetting her stepfather, she crossed the room in one leap, landing beside her mother in a coiling crouch. It was even worse than she'd feared. Joelle's head lay at an impossible angle, the life draining from her eyes.

Oh, God. I finally got my mother killed, *Miranda*

thought numbly. She started to snatch Joelle into her arms, only to hesitate, afraid she'd somehow hurt her mother even worse. "Call 911!"

"It's too late." Gerald sounded utterly indifferent. It was no pose, either; he really didn't give a damn. "She broke her neck. She's dead." He bared his teeth, stalking toward Miranda on clawed feet. Grabbing a fistful of her mane, he hauled her away from Joelle's body as he drew back for another open-handed swipe of his claws. "And I'm not done with you."

He didn't notice the short sword his stepdaughter conjured into the hand held down by her side. He damned well did notice when she rammed it into his chest.

Miranda's lips peeled off her teeth. "Well, I'm done with you!"

"Miranda?" *The female voice breathed into her mind.*

She jerked the blade out of Gerald's chest, and her stepfather fell onto his knees, gagging in agony. Emotionless as an executioner, Miranda took his head with one swing of her sword.

"Miranda?" *The voice called again.*

He won't be healing that, she thought.

Miranda jolted awake, sweating, her body trembling in waves. She sat up and buried her head in her hands as tears rolled hot and fat down her cheeks.

"Miranda? Dammit, girl, answer your cell! We need you now!"

Jolted from her misery, she looked up. She'd thought the feminine voice was some new wrinkle in that god-awful dream, but now she realized it was Belle, using magic to touch her mind.

Miranda grabbed for the enchanted cell phone on the cherry nightstand. Reaching into another witch's consciousness took a hell of a lot of power, especially when one witch was on Mortal Earth and the other was in the Mageverse city of Avalon. It was much more efficient to use a cell spelled for inter-dimensional communication. "Belle? I'm here."

"Finally," her friend said, sounding relieved. "I need you and Justice. Now."

A minute and a half later, Miranda strode down the hall to Justice's door. He was already up; she could hear him pacing. *Must be in wolf form*, she thought, listening to the click of claws on the bedroom's hardwood floor.

Breathing in, Miranda caught the seductive male scent of an aroused Alpha Dire Wolf. And remembered his size, his strength, the tempting power of his hard warrior's body.

Which was exactly why she needed to stay the hell away from him, no matter how sexy he was. The very last thing she needed in her life was another Alpha werewolf. *Just look what happened to Mom*, she told the nipples that stood in tight peaks behind the lace of her bra. *Besides, Belle needs us.* It was night in Pakistan, and Dad's pet monsters had come out to play.

Miranda gave the door a businesslike rap of her knuckles. "Justice?"

After an instant of startled silence, he laughed. "Ah, sorry. I didn't even know you were out there. Some bodyguard, huh?"

Actually, he was a pretty damned good bodyguard. He'd killed the werewolf assassins that had jumped them in Paris last month, along with the other assorted killers before and after that. She'd be dead a dozen times over if not for Justice.

Miranda cleared her throat. "Belle just called me. She needs us. Apparently the Knights of the Round Table got in a fight with some monster Warlock dreamed up."

"But it's still daylight." Being vampires, the knights slept during the day.

"Not in Pakistan."

"What the hell is going on in Pakistan?"

"One of the witches is dying. Belle said she's trying to hold on long enough to tell us about a vision she's had about us. I gather it's pretty damned important."

"She had a vision about *us?* Crap. Why?"

"Don't know, but we'd better haul ass. And Belle says we need full armor, so I've got to conjure yours." Miranda already wore her own suit of interlocking plate. The bullet-proof steel was engraved with spells that made it feel as weightless as silk, though it could protect against damn near any impact and most magical blasts. A silhouette of a dragon's head was enameled in red across the breastplate. Arthur Pendragon had ordered Miranda and Justice to wear his personal heraldic symbol as protection against friendly fire. Magekind warriors had a tendency to think any werewolf was the enemy. All too often, they were right.

"Give me a minute," Justice said through the door. "I've got to change."

Miranda felt the explosion of magic as he Shifted. Clothing rustled, then the door swung wide.

Oh, my.

Working to keep her expression cool, she took in Justice's broad, bare chest, faded jeans, and big bare feet. The way he held the door open made his biceps bunch until they looked the size of grapefruit. Sparks of werewolf magic still flickered in his black eyes, a remnant of his transformation.

Miranda liked to tell herself that William Justice had a thug's face, between his broad cheekbones, square jaw, and aggressive nose. Thick black brows slashed over deep-set ebony eyes. Cop's eyes, watchful, assessing, maybe even a little paranoid.

She could resist all that. Really. She'd be just fine if it weren't for his mouth. Wide, curled in a wicked grin more often than not, with a full lower lip she really wanted to bite. Just hard enough to make those obsidian eyes go all hot.

Then she'd run her hands down the powerful lines of his chest, exploring every thick contour, tracing her fingers through the soft curls that covered that chest, following the tempting line of sable hair that dove behind his zipper, pointing the way to . . .

Alpha werewolf, Miranda reminded herself sternly, jerking her eyes away.

"Uh, Miranda?" he asked in that velvet rumble of his.

Licking her dry lips, she forced herself to meet Justice's night-dark gaze without letting her eyes drift downward. She was *not* going to follow that maddening line of hair . . . "Yeah?"

"I need that armor. You did say we've got to hurry."

"Oh. Uh, right." Reaching for the energy of the Mage-verse roiling invisibly around them, Miranda concentrated and began to spin magic into steel.

Seconds later, Justice's jeans had been replaced by armor that matched her own. Somehow all that ornate gleaming metal only emphasized his strength, drawing attention to the elegant V of his torso as it swept down to narrow hips and long runner's legs.

There was nothing muscle-bound about him; he fought with speed and agility, as ruthless and loyal in her defense as the wolf he was. *If he were human, I'd be in love with him by now.* She instantly banished the thought, afraid it would show on her face.

Luckily, Justice didn't notice her preoccupation. He was too intent on the sword she'd conjured for him, a length of steel designed for magical combat, its enchanted edge as sharp as a straight razor.

Eying the weapon's broad blade, Justice swung it with a skillful rotation of his wrist, testing its weight and balance. He gave her a brisk, approving nod through the open visor of his helm. "This looks good. Let's gate."

"Miranda?" Belle's communication spell reverberated in her mind. *"Daliya won't last much longer. If you don't get here in the next five minutes . . ."*

"We're on the way." Miranda shot a laser-thin stream of magic into the air. The point flared blue and bright, expanding as she fed it more power, until it became a rippling opening in the air. The magical portal cut across the dimensions to Mortal Earth—the home of six billion humans with no idea thirty thousand werewolves lived among them.

Justice led the way through the gate, wary and protective as always. Miranda drew her own sword and stepped after him. At least with his delightful ass covered in steel, she was less likely to drool at it.

He stopped so suddenly on the other side of the gate, she had to sidestep to avoid running him through. "Dammit, Justice, what the . . ." Then she got a good look at what had stopped him in his tracks.

The blasted ruins of a city square lay before them, buildings blazing against the night sky. Tumbled bricks lay in piles between chunks of broken cement spiked with rebar, as blackened wooden beams jutted like the fingers of charred skeletons.

Magekind agents moved fearlessly among the burning wreckage. Witches cast spells to snuff the flames as vampires dug survivors free of the rubble, then handed them off to healers for treatment of their injuries.

"Jesus, Dad *has* been busy." Miranda's feet were planted in something sticky. Flipping her helm's visor up, she glanced down to discover she stood in a puddle of drying blood. Grimacing, she stepped out of it and sent out a mental call. *"Belle?"*

"Behind you," the witch called.

Turning, she and Justice found they'd gated into the mouth of a filthy alley. Belle and Tristan knelt on the trash-littered ground, a woman in armor lying between them. Moving closer, Miranda realized the witch was curled protectively around a man's decapitated head, one hand stroking its bloody cheek. Her despairing grief was so intense, it filled Miranda's Direkind nose with the scent of sweetness gone acrid, like burning roses.

Miranda hurried toward them, armored boots sending gravel bouncing across the alley. Justice followed more slowly, checking the alley for whatever had felled the woman and her lover.

The dying witch lifted her head at their approach. Her eyes met Miranda's, glazed with suffering and approaching death. Had she been a victim of a werewolf bite?

Miranda sheathed her sword and dropped to her knees beside Belle.

Justice moved to hover protectively over them, eyes scanning from one end of the alley to the other. Nothing would sneak up on them with him on guard. Miranda could concentrate on the victim. Sending a wave of magic rolling over the woman, she searched for lethal punctures. The magic in werewolf bites sent Magekind victims into fatal anaphylactic shock; only Miranda's Direkind healing spells could save them. But since she couldn't be everywhere at once, she'd concocted a vaccine a couple of weeks ago and administered it to every fighter in Avalon.

Frowning, Miranda glanced at Belle. The blond witch's pretty face looked soot-smeared and exhausted in the frame of her open visor, and she smelled of blood, smoke, and grief. "What happened? I thought I vaccinated everybody. Did it wear off?"

Without answering, Belle bent closer to the fallen woman. "They're here, Daliya. You can tell them what you saw."

"Good . . . Good." The Maja lifted a shaking gauntleted hand.

Miranda took it automatically. "Are you bitten anywhere? My magic . . ."

"You cannot heal what kills me." The woman sucked in a rattling breath, obviously struggling for strength. They'd taken off her helmet, exposing lovely Pakistani features and huge dark eyes. Her black hair pooled around her head in a lake of ebony silk that gleamed in the firelight. "And I don't . . . want you to." She stopped to pant.

"That's her husband," Tristan explained gruffly, nodding to the head. "They were Truebonded."

Miranda grimaced, understanding at last. The Truebond psychic link was pulling the Maja into death after her mate. Actually, it was surprising she was still alive at all. Truebonded couples usually died within minutes of each other.

"Daliya fought to survive long enough to see you," Belle

explained, a rasp to her normally musical French accent, as if she'd breathed in too much smoke—or fought back tears. "She's had a vision involving you and Justice, and she says she has to tell you about it."

"Wolf." The dying Maja lifted her free hand toward Justice as if it took all her strength. "Wolf, I must speak . . . to you, too."

He hesitated, obviously surprised, then sheathed his sword and dropped to his knees to take the witch's hand.

The moment he touched her, light exploded in the depths of Daliya's black pupils. Feeble fingers clamped around Miranda's so hard, she almost yelped in surprise.

The witch began to chant in a feverish cadence, her musical voice much louder than it should be, as if an alien power had taken over her dying vocal chords. "Listen! Seek the Mother of Fairies as she folds enchanted steel into blades she fills with the souls of lost gods."

Daliya's black eyes flicked from Miranda's face to Justice's, magic sparking in her pupils like fireworks. "She waits in her forge for the hero wolf to come for Merlin's Blade. Then will the Hunter Prince be free—then will he rule in bloody vengeance or bend his knee to his spirit's feral king."

Her fingers tightened on Miranda's until the steel of both their gauntlets creaked under the strain. "It will take the daughter of evil and a master of darkness to lead the night world into the light. If they do fail, humanity will drown in blood under the white wolf's heel, and the crows will feast."

The Maja fell silent, panting as if she'd run a marathon, her last desperate strength visibly draining like water from a broken pitcher. Her dark eyes began to cloud in death. "Find the Mother at her forge, or Avalon . . . dies. Warlock will kill the . . . world. Magekind. Humans. Direkind. All will feed the ravens. All will die."

Her gaze slid away from Miranda's to seek her husband's head. She released Miranda's hand to touch pale, bloody lips with fingers that shook. "Wait for me, Kadir.

Now I come." Daliya's lips twitched as if to smile, despite the tear that rolled down one dark cheek. "Yes, yes . . . I'm always . . . late."

Her hand dropped to the pavement as her magic swirled away with her life, escaping back to its source in the Mageverse.

TWO

Silence fell with Daliya's death, heavy as a lead weight.

"Belle. God, Belle . . ." Tristan leaned across the fallen couple and kissed his lover with sudden, desperate hunger. She kissed him back just as fiercely, a single tear trickling down her face, her armored fingers stroking his face.

The naked love in that kiss made Miranda's chest ache. She tried to pull her gaze away and give them some privacy, but there was something about all that raw emotion that was hypnotic. She'd never seen a kiss so ferocious with pain and need, born not in desire, but in the awareness that death could strip them from each other.

Belle and Tristan were Truebonded just like Daliya and Kadir; the death of one would kill the other. Yet watching that kiss, Miranda realized neither would want it any other way.

Envy struck like a punch in the stomach. She'd never known that kind of love. Her mother had chased chimeras of it, only to find abuse and death.

Miranda glanced across Daliya's body at Justice. He, too, watched the couple kiss, the same helpless longing she felt in his ebony eyes. She jerked her burning gaze away and dragged an armored hand across her face to wipe away the tears. She had no idea if she was crying for Daliya . . . or herself. "Dammit. Dammit, what was that about? Who's the Mother of Fairies?"

Justice lowered the woman's limp hand to ground, giving it an oddly tender pat before settling back on his booted heels. He slid one arm around Miranda's shoulders, drawing her closer. Astonished, she looked up at him.

As if realizing the intimacy of the gesture, he straightened away so quickly his gauntlet scraped against her armored back. Clearing his throat, he looked over at Tristan, who'd finally broken the kiss. "And what the hell is Merlin's Blade?"

"Damned if we know." The vampire's deep voice sounded gruff, and his eyes shone as if he'd shed a tear or two himself. "Neither of us has ever heard of the Mother of Fairies or Merlin's Blade. I'd think she was talking about Excalibur, but Arthur never lets that sword out of his sight." A smile twitched the corners of Tristan's lips. "I think he sleeps with it."

Miranda and Justice exchanged a frown. Tristan had been a vampire Knight of the Round Table for fifteen hundred years, while Belle had been a Maja for more than a thousand. Between the two of them, they knew damn near everything there was to know about magic. Anything or anyone they'd never heard of was going to be a bitch to find.

"What happened to them?" Justice turned his attention to the two Magekind corpses. His intense, professional gaze reminded Miranda he'd been a homicide cop before somebody bit him. "Who took that vampire's head? And where's the rest of his body?"

Belle sat back on her heels and sighed. "Warlock's got himself a couple of new Beasts."

"*Two* of them?" Miranda demanded, appalled. It had been all they could do to kill the last one.

Justice winced. "Oh, fuck."

"Fuck is right." Tristan picked up the vampire's head, cradling it in a big, surprisingly gentle hand. "Kadir was one of our best agents. He worked deep cover for five years gaining the trust of those Sword of Allah assholes . . ."

Justice frowned. "Those are the terrorists who tried to buy the Russian nuke last year, right?"

"Yeah, same bunch. Kadir's the reason they didn't succeed. He had them thinking he was God's gift to jihad, even as he sabotaged every plot they put together. Whenever they'd start catching on, Daliya would cast a spell to make them forget their suspicions."

"Too bad she couldn't make the fuckers quit trying to blow up the planet." Belle opened her mouth, and Justice waved a hand. "Yeah, yeah, I know. Doesn't work like that."

Once a belief became deeply engrained in someone's brain—particularly a religion-based obsession like jihad—you couldn't erase it no matter how you tried. Too many associations with other memories that would eventually bring it back to the surface. You had to either change the mortal's mind by old-fashioned persuasion. Or kill him.

Arthur and his Magekind didn't believe in killing any mortal unless there was no choice at all. Even terrorists.

"So how did Kadir die?" Miranda asked.

The knight looked up, the curl of his upper lip revealing one fang. "Warlock's pet fucker ate him. Literally ate him. Poor bastard was halfway down the snake's throat when we got here. We were only able to save his head."

Justice stared at his friend, his stomach knotting in revulsion. "Warlock must have recruited himself a pair of bugfuck crazy serial killers. Sane werewolves don't eat people." When you became Direkind, you kept whatever moral compass you had to begin with. You might take a bite out of someone who pissed you off, but you didn't actually *eat* them. "And did you say 'snake'?" He'd loathed snakes since he'd damn near stepped on a copperhead when he was nine.

"Yeah. Some kind of cobra, but sure as hell not anything

you'd see in nature. Had to be sixty, maybe seventy feet long, three feet around. The other Beast was a werewolf centaur the size of a truck. Built like a Clydesdale, armored from head to tail. Carried the biggest damned battle-axe I have ever seen."

"Damn," Miranda muttered. "That sounds nastier than the first one." Warlock's original monster had looked like a cross between a wolf and a grizzly bear. The creature also sucked down magical blasts like a kid guzzling Red Bull.

"These bastards were definitely nastier," Tristan agreed. "They ambushed Kadir—I think he was on his way to some terrorist planning session. Daliya was back at the couple's home, but she sensed the attack through their Truebond. She alerted Gwen and gated to help, but by then the snake was already swallowing Kadir. We arrived a minute or two later, but there was nothing any of us could do."

"Christ." Justice winced, remembering some of the homicides he'd worked. The anguish of the victim's wives had haunted him worse than the murders themselves. At least the dead had stopped suffering by the time he arrived. "I hope you made those bastards pay."

"We gave it our best shot." Tristan's brooding green eyes dropped down to Kadir's face, and he returned the head to the protective circle of Daliya's body. "The entire Round Table tore into them with everything we had. Our blade attacks bounced right off their shields . . ."

"And our blasts were worse than useless," Belle said grimly. "Just like Warlock's first monster, they drank our magic and got stronger."

"We trashed six blocks of Mirpur City before we finally made them gate for home." Tristan pulled off his helm and raked his hand through his hair, pulling it from its tight warrior's queue to fall in disordered, sweaty strands. He looked tired, his face smeared with dirt and blood. "Had to bring in a hundred extra witches for crowd control when the fight brought the Pakistanis out to investigate. That damned centaur trampled six people and cut a three-year-old girl in two."

"Oh, my God." Miranda recoiled, her expression sick. "Why?"

"I think he was just pissed off. He killed that kid the way you'd swat a fly." Tristan's green eyes narrowed in fury, a muscle jerking in his jaw as he ground his teeth. "But it backfired on him, because Arthur lost his mind. You know how he gets whenever a child is hurt. Tore into the bastard so hard, he actually beat his way through the fucker's magical shield. Excalibur must have just overwhelmed the spell. Bloodied the centaur badly."

Justice grinned in genuine pleasure. "Good for him."

"We all cut lose then, whaling away until the sons of bitches lost their nerve and gated for home." He curled his lip. "Apparently they can dish it out, but they don't like taking it."

"The civilians still paid the price." Belle dragged her shoulders back and winced, putting a hand on her arm as if it ached. If anything, she looked dirtier and more exhausted than her partner. "We've had our hands full putting out fires and healing the wounded ever since."

Miranda glanced up. "I gather the Beasts kept you from tracking where their dimensional gate went." The Majae had been trying to locate Warlock's lair for months now, with no luck at all.

"Per usual. We have *got* to figure out how to punch through that jamming spell of theirs."

"How did you explain all this to the Pakistanis?" Justice asked.

"The usual suspects." Belle shrugged. "Team of suicide bombers hit the neighborhood. We changed everybody's memories to match the story. And made damned sure we wiped every camera phone for blocks around."

"Sure as hell don't want that little fight going viral," Tristan agreed. "All we need is for something like that to hit CNN, and we're all fucked."

"Why didn't Arthur call me in to help?" Justice asked in frustration. "Immune to magic, remember?" One of the joys of being a werewolf.

Unfortunately, that immunity meant his magic was limited to shape-shifting. Miranda and her psychotic father, Warlock, were the only Dire Wolves who could cast spells, which meant they were also vulnerable to magical attacks.

And now there were these new Beasts. Out there among the humans, eating people and blowing shit up. A snake, for God's sake.

"You're more useful making sure nothing happens to Miranda." Displaying a forearm, Tristan gave Miranda a tired smile. A set of bloody fang marks punctured his gauntlet. "The centaur got its teeth into me, but your vaccine really works. Otherwise I'd be dead now."

"My pleasure." Her voice dropped to a mutter. "I just wish I knew how long that spell is going to last. I don't want somebody dying because it took me too long to make more vaccine."

"Miranda, we don't know when—or even if—it's going to wear off," Belle told her. "You need to let your psychic batteries recharge a little longer before you start working on a new batch."

As usual, the witch was right. Preparing enough of the magical drug to vaccinate the city had left Miranda frighteningly weak. She'd barely been able to move for days. Justice had ended up waiting on her hand and foot.

Not that he'd minded. God, he was such a sucker.

"Then I shouldn't have wasted all that magic on building my new house last week." Miranda chewed her ridiculously tempting lower lip. Justice dragged his gaze away. "That was stupid."

"Well, *I* don't consider it a waste." Tristan's grin suggested he was trying to distract her from her obvious guilt trip. "It did get you and Justice out of *our* house." They'd been Belle's guests for three weeks, until Miranda had finished conjuring the cottage. "Don't get me wrong, I like you two, but once in a while I'd really like to have sex on the . . ."

Belle looked up at her lover. She didn't say a word, but he carefully shut his mouth without finishing the sentence.

"I didn't notice you held back all that much." Justice grinned, just as willing to play *Let's distract Miranda.* "I felt like a contestant on *Knights of the Round Table Gone Wild.*"

Tristan hit him lightly on one armored shoulder. It clanked. "You're just jealous, furball."

Jealous, me? Watching Tris and Belle flirt, kiss and steal surreptitious little caresses? While he hadn't dared lay one fuzzy finger on Miranda? *Like the Big Bad Wolf at a barbecue festival.*

Justice glanced over at Miranda, to find her watching him wearing an odd expression, part longing, part fear. *Of me? Why the hell would she be afraid of me? And why longing, for God's sake . . . ?*

Before Justice could consider that puzzle, an empty soft drink can bounced and rattled its way across the alley. He glanced around, instantly wary.

The woman who'd kicked the Coke can strolled toward them, a big video camera balanced on one shoulder. Yet none of the others seemed to notice.

Taking a deep breath, Justice recognized the ozone reek of magic. *She's protected by some kind of spell. Probably an invisibility shield.*

Magic didn't affect Justice, so he saw right through the shield, but the others had no idea she was there. He looked away as if he hadn't seen her either, his mind working furiously. *Since when do TV reporters work spells?*

There was no question she *was* a reporter, given the camera. While you could shoot video with a cell phone these days, professional equipment was a lot bigger and more elaborate. Just like the camera she was carrying.

Plus, she had the kind of stunning looks typical of female cable news reporters: a heart-shaped face, striking violet eyes, and curling hair the gleaming black of a raven's wing. Snatching another glance, he decided he recognized her. *Brenda? Brenna? Something like that.*

But he'd thought TV news reporters traveled with an entourage, especially in this part of the world. A cameraman, a sound guy, a producer, a translator, and at least a couple of bodyguards. This girl appeared to be alone. Which was dangerous as hell in fundamentalist Pakistan, especially for a woman who looked like that.

What is she, nuts?

Justice's protective instincts stirred. *You've already got your hands full with one beautiful, endangered woman, dumbass,* he reminded himself. *You sure as hell don't need another one.* Besides, with her power, the reporter could probably twitch her nose and make jihadis compose sonnets to her eyebrows.

Yet despite her admittedly stunning beauty, she didn't make him feel anything like the kind of elemental lust Miranda inspired. It was like comparing a firecracker to a lightning bolt.

Anyway, this chick is a reporter. Even as a human cop, Justice had never liked reporters. In his former-cop's experience, they lived to stir shit up. Lacking actual shit to stir, they'd create imaginary shit and stir that. Now that he was one of the world's tiniest minorities—Magical Americans— he *really* didn't like reporters. And that little spell-casting bimbo intended to put them all on CNN?

I don't think so, baby. But what am I going to do about you?

Justice watched from the corner of one eye as the reporter moved around them with her camera, shooting away. She turned to say something to her left shoulder and absently pushed a black curl behind one ear. One *pointed* ear. Justice put the ear together with the invisibility spell. *Holy hell, the reporter's Sidhe.*

The Sidhe were basically mankind's cousins, an ancient race of magic-using humans who inhabited Mageverse Earth. Their kingdom lay on the other side of the planet from Avalon; their king, Llyr Galatyn, was one of Arthur's more important allies.

What the hell is a fairy doing in Pakistan? We're broadcasting the news to Neverland now?

And what was that moving around on her other shoulder, the one *not* occupied by the camera? He couldn't quite make it out, since its bottom half was the same green as her silk blouse, while the rest matched the building behind her. In fact, he could see the pattern of the brick slide across the whatsit as it moved. Had to be alive.

A quick inward breath brought him the scaly aroma of reptile blended with the ozone tang of magic and the woman's natural feminine scent. Some kind of enchanted lizard? Like a magical chameleon, maybe?

"Do you recognize these guys?" she asked it. She was talking to a *lizard*?

"The big fella is Tristan, one of the Knights of the Round Table," the chameleon said in an Irish accent as thick as mud—and about that clear. "The blond one is La Belle Coeur, what they call a Court Seducer. Don't know who the redhead is, or the other fella, but . . . *He's starin' at us.*"

Her head jerked around so fast she should have given herself whiplash. The CNN Fairy met Justice's gaze, her violet eyes going round with horror. The camera vanished from her shoulder in an explosion of sparks as she whirled to run.

Justice grabbed for his own magic and leaped, shifting to Dire Wolf as he dove over Tristan's head. He was distantly aware of his companions' astounded shouts, but he didn't stop to explain.

He grabbed the Sidhe woman by one arm as his clawed feet hit the pavement. Jerking her to a halt, Justice glowered down at her from seven feet of muscle, fur, and fangs. "Oh, no you don't, News Fairy. Where the hell did the camera go? Bring it back *now*, or . . ."

"Let her go!" The leprechaun lizard Shifted into a dead ringer for a Gila monster, its body short and muscular, with a stubby tail and short 'gator legs. It was obviously a hell of a lot more agile than the real reptile, because it launched itself through the air like a flying squirrel. Landing on Justice's astonished head, it started ripping at him with claws like box cutters. "Get your hands off her or you'll be diggin' me out of your face!"

Justice barely grabbed the little beast in time to save his eyes. It screamed incomprehensible Irish curses as he dragged it off his head. It was surprisingly strong for something that weighed less than a house cat.

Justice had to fight to hang on as the lizard lashed back and forth in his grip, all four stubby legs clawing the air, tail beating his forearm hard enough to bruise. "Leave my Branwyn alone, gobshite!"

He jerked the little beast close enough to get a good look at his much, much longer teeth. "Stop it, or we'll find out if you really are magically delicious."

"Cac ar oineach!" The lizard snarled, its eyes narrowed to vicious, glowing slits.

"Don't hurt him!" the girl yelled, leaping up to grab Justice's arm, trying to wrench his lizard-gripping hand away from his jaws. "You can have the camera, just don't eat Fin!" Her eyes were wide with pleading, her lip trembling as she hung from his massive forearm, booted feet kicking a foot from the ground.

Justice's rage faded in the face of her genuine fear. "I'm not going to eat your lizard, all right? Just tell him to quit . . ."

A fireball splashed against the side of his head. Astonished, he turned just as Fin huffed another green flame baseball into his eyes. "Get away from her, or you'll get seconds!" the lizard howled.

"I don't care," Justice snarled, "because *I am immune to magic.*"

"Are your balls immune to teeth then? Because I'll bite the bleeding bollix off you!"

"Try it, you scaly little shit, and you'll end up a pair of boots!"

"Please don't hurt him!" Tears spilled down the girl's face as she braced both feet against his ribs and hauled on his arm for all she was worth. Being Sidhe, she was much stronger than she looked.

"Then tell him to keep his teeth to himself," Justice snapped, though he was starting to feel like a bully, "or I swear to God, I'll dropkick his scaly little ass right over the rainbow."

"*Téigh trasna ort féin*," the lizard spat.

Justice decided it was just as well he didn't speak Gaelic.

"Fin, you're not helping!" Branwyn cried, and started to sob. "Please, mister, please!"

"All right!" He lowered his arm until her feet touched the ground. When he handed her the lizard, Fin promptly Shifted back to his original form—he looked a bit like a miniature Chinese dragon—and shot up her arm to wrap his long, limber body around her neck.

The creature glared at him from the shelter of long black curls. "Lay one hand on my girl, you hairy skanger, and you'll be spitting teeth." No longer camouflaged, Fin's scales shone green in the illumination cast by the burning square beyond the alley. They had an iridescent sheen, streaks of violet and gold rippling as he moved. A bright red frill ran the length of his back from his golden eyes to the tip of his long tail. More frills adorned the tail tip, as long and delicate as feathers.

"All right, I gave back your scaly leprechaun," Justice told the fairy, ignoring Fin's dire Gaelic curses. "Now, where's the camera?"

She clutched her friend protectively close and glared at him. "Oh, all . . ."

"Justice," Miranda interrupted, edging closer as she spoke in the careful tone people use with schizophrenics, "who are you talking to?"

"This sneaking little fairy reporter and her pet reptile . . ." He winced as realization hit. "Both of whom are still hidden behind an invisibility spell."

Which meant Miranda, Tristan, and Belle just saw him have a screaming row with empty air. No wonder they were looking at him like a candidate for electroshock.

He glowered down at the reporter. "Drop the shield, Tinker Bell. And give me that damned camera before I forget I'm one of the good guys."

"Oh, yeah, you're just a fuzzy Prince Charming, you

are!" The reporter's voice dripped sarcasm—along with a sudden brogue almost as thick as the lizard's. "Picking on poor Finvarra. You ought to be ashamed of . . ."

He stuck out a palm and snapped his clawed fingers. "Camera and spell. Now, Tink."

The scent of magic disappeared, then flared again as the video camera popped back into view. She handed it over with visible reluctance and a growled "And *don't* call me Tinker Bell!"

"Think you're a hard man now?" The lizard sneered. His frilled tail snapped in contempt. "Tosser."

"Bite me, Lucky Charms."

"I tried, Scooby Doo, but the fleas beat me to it."

"That's Branwyn Donovan." Miranda stared at the reporter before turning an outraged glare on Justice. "You threatened to *eat* Branwyn Donovan? What next, Anderson Cooper à la mode? What's wrong with you?"

"I didn't threaten to eat the damned reporter," Justice gritted. "I threatened to eat her lizard. Which I gave back, despite being seriously provoked. Look, Miranda, she's been shooting video of us from behind an invisibility spell. Do you *want* to be on CNN?"

"I don't work for CNN," Branwyn announced with icy dignity. "I report for DCN. We have better ratings."

"Wipe that camera's memory card," Tristan told Belle in a cold voice. The Magekind were damned serious about making sure video of their activities never hit the air.

"It's as good as wiped." Belle gave Justice an approving nod. "Good work spotting her before she outed every one of us."

"I'm not going to out you, dammit!" Branwyn planted her fists on her hips and glared at the witch, who paused in the act of casting her spell, magic shedding bright sparks around her hands. "I'm Sidhe. I don't want the mortals to know magic exists any more than you do. They'd either burn me at the stake or dissect me like a frog."

"So why shoot video of us if you weren't going to run

it?" Tristan lifted a skeptical blond brow. "How stupid do you think we are?"

Branwyn transferred her glare to him, not in the least intimidated by fifteen hundred years' worth of legendary, pissed-off knight. "I was going to show it to my brother. I wanted him to see what those . . . *creatures* are doing to those who don't have a prayer of defending themselves."

Conal Donovan was the owner of DCN, as well as one of the richest men on the planet. He had fingers in so many pies, he should own his own bakery—and probably did. *Figures he'd be magic*, Justice thought.

Tristan looked her over, frowning. "What creatures are we talking about?"

She looked impatient. "You know perfectly well. That Budweiser Clydesdale thing and the giant snake that ate that poor vampire." Her voice dropped to a mutter, and a tear rolled down her face. "And I *liked* Kadir, dammit. He didn't deserve to die like that."

"How do you know Kadir?" Belle eyed her. "And why do you care?"

"How could I not care? Those bastards killed half a dozen people and a three-year-old. They've got to be stopped. Kadir tried. God, he gave it everything he had. He blasted the hell out of that snake with his AK-47, but the bullets just bounced off it. Then it bit him and . . ." She closed her eyes and shuddered. "I'm going to hear that scream in my nightmares until the day I die."

And if I don't get my hands on that axe of Daliya's, Justice thought grimly, *Kadir won't be the only one Warlock and his bastards kill.*

THREE

"Watching Kadir die must have been hideous." Miranda studied the reporter with sympathetic eyes.

Branwyn shrugged. "I cover the Mideast. Hideous tragedies are pretty much my beat. This was worse." She raked a hand through her hair, the gesture weary with defeat and frustration. "His wife gated in right after the snake started swallowing him. I've never seen anyone fight so hard to save someone else. She hurled blasts that should have fried that creature into Moo Shu Monster. It just soaked up her magic and kept right on eating him. And there was nothing I could do but shoot video and cry so hard I could barely see through the viewfinder." Her voice dropped to a mutter. "I felt so damned useless."

The lizard emerged from her hair and curled his long neck around to look into her face, the frill folded flat against his head. "Cop on to yourself, Bran. You've a snowball's chance in hell against a monster like that. Even with me amplifyin' your abilities, that thing would have sucked up your attacks the way it did the witch's—and you along with 'em."

"He's right." Reluctant sympathy softened Belle's tone. "Those things ate every spell we threw at them. If you'd tried to intervene, you'd have ended up as dead as Daliya."

Miranda moved a step closer, drawing the reporter's attention. "Look, Daliya had a vision before she died. She said someone called the Mother of Fairies has a magical weapon we need to stop Warlock. If we don't get our hands on Merlin's Blade, Daliya predicted that everyone—human, Magekind, and Direkind—*everyone* is going to die. Do you have any idea where we'd find this Mother of Fairies?"

The reporter nodded slowly, her reluctance obvious. "I know what she said. I was shooting vid the first time she had the vision."

"So what does it mean, Branwyn?"

The Sidhe stayed silent about two seconds too long. Justice's cop instincts began to clamor. *Warning, warning, incoming lie . . .*

"I've never heard of any Merlin's Blade."

"That wasn't the question." Justice gave Branwyn his best I'm-the-Law-Don't-Lie-to-Me stare. Never mind that they'd taken his badge. "She asked if you knew the Mother of Fairies."

Branwyn looked him right in the eye. "No."

He folded his arms and turned up the heat on his glare. "I thought you wanted to stop Warlock's killers from preying on the innocent. Or was that just bullshit?"

The tip of Finvarra's tail twitched, iridescent frills flicking. "You pay an unannounced call on the Mother, and she'll feed you a Scooby Snack you won't forget."

"Let us worry about that, Lucky Charms. Well, Branwyn?"

"Aren't you tired of doing nothing while people die?" Belle's cool tone gave the question such acidic bite, even Justice hid a wince.

"Branwyn, help us," Miranda urged softly, playing good cop to Belle's bad cop like a pro. "Please."

The reporter threw up her hands in surrender. "Look, I really don't have any idea how to find the Mother. She doesn't exactly hand out business cards. Conal would know if anyone does."

The lizard gave his frill a dismissive flick. "Good luck convincin' him. He wants nothing to do with Magekind, or your war with the werewolves." He gave Justice a twisted, toothy grin. "It's none of our bleedin' business."

"You really think that once Warlock murders Arthur and his knights, he'll leave you Sidhe alone?" Miranda snorted. "Yeah, right. Warlock hates anyone or anything with power he doesn't control. He'll be hunting fairies the day after Avalon burns."

"It's better to become our allies now than wait until it's too late for any of us," Tristan put in. "If you help us find Merlin's Blade, we can stop Warlock and save a great many lives. Yours included."

Finvarra sniffed. "Maybe you can stop Warlock. Or maybe that poor witch was out of her tree and talking shite to all the little angels."

Miranda met the lizard's cynical gaze. "We won't know until we try. I'm willing to give it everything I've got." Power blazed up in her eyes with a glow like leaping flame. "And I've got plenty."

Finvarra studied her a moment before he grunted and retreated back under Branwyn's hair. "Eh. Might as well," he told the reporter as he curled around her neck. "Otherwise they'll show up at Conal's gaff, make bits of his bodyguards, and blow the feckin' shite out of his security cameras."

Tristan gave him a smile tinged with menace. "Yeah, that *is* pretty much what we'd do."

The lizard sniffed and flicked his tail. "Stick it up your hole, Vlad."

Across the alley, on the roof five stories above their heads, Andrew Vance watched the Magekind, the werewolf traitors, and the fairy bitch. Straightening from his crouch, the big man padded silently toward the drainpipe on the building's opposite side. He needed to put some distance between him and the enemy if he didn't want them to sense the dimensional gate he was about to open.

Warlock would want to know about this.

Minutes later, Vance stepped through the gate into a dim stone passageway as a buzzing crack echoed off the granite. Warlock was giving his whip a workout. No surprise, considering the failure of Vance's fellow Bastards.

The answering howl sounded like Jack Ferraro. The little weasel had no tolerance for pain. Tom Addison made much less noise under the lash; Hell, Vance suspected the sick fuck actually enjoyed it. Though when he chose, Warlock could make even Addison scream like a fourteen-year-old girl.

The general had a real talent for torture. It was a gift Vance appreciated, being no slouch himself.

Following the crackling pops of his master's whip, he strode down the snaking stone tunnel that led deeper into the mountain. Warlock had dug a whole network of caves within the Blue Ridge Mountains, so deep that the ancient rock itself shielded his magic from detection. Here he could do as it suited him, and no one could stop him.

Especially not his three Bastards.

Vance found Warlock working over his fellow slaves in the huge cavern he thought of as the Womb. Vance had been reborn in the great stone cave two months back, entering a whole new existence of magic, power . . . and sweet, sweet blood. A world that suited him, especially considering how his old life had imploded.

He'd been on death row when Warlock found him, following his conviction on charges he'd murdered a family of Afghan civilians. Actually, he'd killed one too few of them: the twelve-year-old boy who'd survived to blab.

Never mind that his so-called "victims" had it coming. Vance was a reasonable man, but they'd pushed him too far. He'd returned the boy's sister when he'd finished with her, but nooo, that wasn't good enough for them. The bitch's mother had gone whining to his boss at Winston

Civilian Security, accusing Vance of kidnapping and raping a child.

A child, my ass. She'd been fourteen. Afghans married them off at that age.

If the kid's mother had kept her mouth shut, Vance wouldn't have been forced to make an example out of them all. Otherwise, every civilian contractor would have been in danger from uppity Afghans.

He'd only been protecting his fellow Americans. And look at the treatment he'd received: his name dragged through the dirt on every cable news show. They'd dug up his dishonorable discharge from the Marines, even interviewed his former captain, who'd called him a psychopath and a disgrace to the uniform.

Once he ruled at Warlock's side, that little bastard was going to pay for running his mouth.

The General snarled something vicious, and Vance hastily jolted back to the present. It wasn't wise to give Warlock anything less than one hundred percent of your attention. You had to cater to that impressive ego if you wanted to keep your ass in one piece. Which was why Vance called him "General," when he held no actual military rank.

Blatant flattery, but Warlock ate it up every time.

Vance paused, making sure his booted feet were well outside the inlaid silver circle on the stone floor. Viking runes were cut deeply into the rock, maintaining the spell that held the two Bastards hanging helplessly in midair, waiting for the next flaying stroke of the whip.

They were in human form now: Ferraro, a thin, elegant blond who'd once used his pretty face to seduce four wealthy women into marriage. Within a year or so of each honeymoon, he'd kill the bride, always contriving to make her death look like an accident. Warlock had gotten to him just hours before the cops had.

Addison was bigger, though not as tall as Vance. In human form, he was balding, with a long, bony face, a beak of a nose, and a beefy body on the verge of running to fat. He still bore the childhood scars his mother had once liked to inflict with a box cutter every time he'd stepped out of line. That ended the day he turned sixteen and realized he was bigger than she was.

He'd promptly taken the blade away and used it to slit her throat.

Over the next twenty years, Addison used that same box cutter on forty-five women, as he murdered his way across the United States. He was in the middle of a Manhattan killing spree when the NYPD finally caught him and threw his ass in jail.

Luckily for Addison, news reports of his vicious artistry captured Warlock's attention, and the General spirited him out of his cell—and turned him into a real monster.

Too bad the General was less pleased with his recruits' more recent performance.

"One!" the wizard roared, pacing around the circle's perimeter, flicking his whip in vicious cracks. "All the power I gave you, all the training, and the two of you were only able to kill one of them!"

"Milord, Arthur brought the whole Round Table and their most powerful wit—" Ferraro broke off with a shriek as his stupid protest earned him another vicious slash of the energy whip. *Moron.*

Though the Bastards could feed on Magekind magic—especially once it was filtered by the shielding spell—they had no resistance at all to Warlock's power. And if you pissed him off enough, he'd flay the skin from your back, order you to heal yourself with a Shift, and flay you all over again. Which was the treatment the two would probably get once Warlock heard Vance's report on their assorted fuckups.

Addison had taken too long to swallow that Pak vampire, deliberately spinning out the killing to make it as agonizing as possible. Though women were his preferred victims, he was sadistic enough to torture anybody, any time he got the chance. But that's what you got when you recruited a serial killer.

And then there was Ferraro, a sociopath with no con-

cept of loyalty whatsoever. Vance knew veteran fighters
who would have made far better Bastards than either idiot,
but when he'd suggested as much, the General's claws had
made clear just how little he liked having his judgment
questioned.

Vance had learned his lesson: follow orders and keep
your mouth shut, no matter how flawed the battle plan.

Just like Iraq all over again.

In this case, Addison's tastes had indeed proven to be a
liability. He'd been so stuffed with the vampire's corpse,
he'd been too slow when the knights arrived. What's worse,
they'd been driven into a holy frenzy as they fought to rescue the vampire's body.

Ferraro, meanwhile, hadn't managed to kill any of the
enemy at all. Frustrated, knowing the punishment that
awaited him back at the Caverns, he'd trampled every gawk-
ing Pakistani he could, then cut somebody's kid in half.

If he'd had a little discipline, left the civilians alone and
kept his mind on business, maybe he could have killed one
of the Magekind. Instead he'd driven Arthur into a rage
and barely escaped with his life.

Still, it had been interesting to watch the Celt in action
as Excalibur's magic cut right through Ferraro's shields.
Arthur was a skilled and cunning swordsman; given time,
he would have sliced up the stupid fuck like a Virginia ham
if Ferraro hadn't fled for his life.

Despite the knowledge of swordsmanship Warlock's
magic had given them all, Ferraro was simply no match for
the Celt's fifteen centuries of skill. He'd had to take to his
heels.

Vance would love to try his luck against Arthur. After
all, he was a soldier, not a serial killer or con man. He
knew how to fight, not just butcher whores and sucker rich
widows.

"Vance, I do hope you have something interesting to
tell me."

He jerked his head up at the sound of Warlock's lethal
purr. The Dire Wolf's fur was so white it seemed to glow

almost as bright as his savage orange eyes. The General was eight feet tall, but the effect made him look even bigger, like a brawny, vicious cross between a polar bear and a prehistoric wolf. With a jerk of a clawed hand, Warlock snapped his whip, lash burning white-hot with magic.

Vance suppressed his instinct to step back. Knowing any sign of fear would only piss his master off, he lifted his chin. "Actually, General, I've learned something I think you'll find very interesting indeed."

The cat strolled into Conal Donovan's office, white paws soundless on the gleaming Macassar ebony hardwood. Floor-to-ceiling bookshelves lined half the room's curve, stuffed with leather-bound volumes on every subject from physics to magic, along with a great many books on contract law.

Here and there stood elegant mahogany racks displaying Conal's collection of ancient weapons: swords, axes, and daggers from all over the planet. There were even a few blades from Earth's Mageverse twin—gifts from grateful expat Sidhe whom Conal had helped in one way or another. The ancient enchanted steel breathed fairy magic into the air, giving it the tang of ozone and alien power.

"Got a psychic call from Fin," the cat said. "Everything's goin' according to plan."

"Fin can be efficient when he chooses to be." Essus clicked his sharp beak as Danu meandered across the impressive width of the room. "Too bad he chooses to be so rarely."

The cat reached the desk that sprawled across the western end of the office. Gathering herself, she sprang to the desktop in a single neat bound. Essus had to admit she moved well, considering her bulk. Though to be honest, a great deal of her apparent size was fur: long, silky, and white enough to blind. Everyone—human and Changeling—considered her beautiful.

Essus privately thought his own flaming plumage was

much more impressive, particularly when one considered
his tail, which almost brushed the floor when he sat on his
padded steel perch.

He took great pride in his tail.

"They're gonna gate over as soon as Tristan and his lady
see to the bodies and consult Arthur," the cat continued.
She had a definite Southern accent, Georgia audible in its
drawling vowels and dropped gs. "I think they're really
waitin' for sunset here, though. Otherwise Tristan would
pass out soon as he stepped through the gate." Danu
sniffed. "Vampires and that Daysleep a' theirs."

She padded over to the contract Conal had left unsigned
while he considered its implications. "I wish the kids had
that kind of power. It'd be nice if they could just walk
through dimensional doorways whenever they wanted to
come home. No airports. No customs." Her curling lip
revealed the tip of one fang. "No cat carriers."

Pausing, Danu glanced over the Portalnet contract,
grunted, and plopped her furry rump down on its top sheet.
"Tell Conal to go over the fine print on this thing with a
jeweler's loupe. I don't like the beady little eyes on that
Portalnet CEO. Reminds me of a rat looking for a loose
chunk of Gouda. We don't want him thinking Conal's his
own personal Brie."

Lifting her left hind leg, she proceeded to lazily wash
her backside with a long pink tongue.

"Must you?" Essus flicked his tail feathers and turned
his head away; he had no desire to see her nether regions.
"And get off that desk. You know Conal hates it when you
shed on his papers. All those wretched cat hairs."

Danu looked from her backside and sniffed. "Hmph. I
wonder who leaves long red feathers everywhere? Could it
be a canary with delusions of grandeur?"

Ignoring the insult, Essus pushed off from his perch to
fly a quick circuit of the office, wing tips brushing the
leather spines of Conal's books. He landed lightly on his
perch again, now facing the semicircular window that took
up half the room.

The streets of Atlanta spread out like a private kingdom thirty stories below, a stunning sunset painting the skyscrapers in golden light.

"For the record, Conal is fully aware of Carson Greendale's cheese-eating tendencies," he told the cat. "Greendale isn't nearly as smart as he thinks he is. On the other hand, he does have ten million subscribers across three states."

Danu rumbled something that might have been a purr. "Well, I suppose that makes up for the beady eyes."

"Besides, Conal will snap his fat rat neck if Greendale gets out of line—figuratively, of course." Stretching his great wings wide, Essus shook his powerful shoulders before settling his feathers neatly again. A red pinfeather drifted downward. He ignored it, deciding he'd talk the boy into taking him out for a flight. All this talk of rats was making him hungry. "And get off that desk before Conal has to take a Dustbuster to it."

Danu gave him a cool look from pale sapphire eyes. "That's why we have a cleanin' crew. I'm only givin' 'em job security." She gave her furry butt a considering look and lowered her leg. Flopping back with boneless grace, she stretched to her full length and rolled around on the contract, no doubt to make her opinion clear to Conal.

Apparently satisfied with the quantity of shed hair, Danu sat up and folded her paws neatly beneath her body until she resembled a football of white fur. Only her tail tip moved, flicking in restless twitches. "She told me there's gonna be trouble, Essus. We may have to fight."

"You're not the only one who talks to Her. I know exactly what's coming." The phoenix eagle flexed his dagger-sharp talons on the perch. "It should be most entertaining."

Danu rumbled a growl. "Assumin' we live through it."

Concentrating on the image Finvarra's magic had created in her mind, Miranda spun a blast of power into a dimensional gate. Branwyn was the first through, Fin riding one shoulder. Her precious camera occupied the other; Belle had agreed not to erase the video so Branwyn could show it to Conal.

Belle, Justice, and the knight followed. They didn't draw their weapons—quite—but they were ready for any potential ambush. Justice had returned to human form, on the grounds that a seven-foot Dire Wolf was a bit too much of a threat, considering they needed Donovan's cooperation.

Once everyone was safely across, Miranda stepped through herself and let the gate collapse.

They stood at one end of a cavernous oval gym lined with top-end weight machines and expensive treadmills. One wall was dominated by rows of monitors, all playing programming from every cable news station, as well as their broadcast counterparts. A larger central flat screen displayed an earnest anchor speaking over the winged DCN logo.

"Ah!" a female voice shouted, drawing their attention to a fencing strip at the opposite end of the room just as a slender figure threw herself into an elegant lunge. Her blade met her opponent's with the scraping rattle of steel on steel.

The big man immediately went on the offensive, driving her backward with a series of furious attacks. She retreated with quick, sure steps, her body balanced for attack or defense as she parried with precise flicks of her foil. Her weapon licked out in search of the man's chest. Blade met blade in fierce metallic beats.

"Not bad," Tristan murmured beside Miranda, watching with professional interest. "She's got good speed, but he's one hell of a lot stronger. Not to mention damned big."

"Yeah, he's a bit of a bull." Branwyn absently stroked Fin's scaled head. "And he's got one hell of a reach. You think he's too far away to hit you—and then he flies into that long, long lunge and nails you anyway."

"You know, I don't think I'd mind getting nailed by that guy." Miranda smiled in wicked appreciation. "He does have a really nice . . . lunge."

She glanced back, meaning to share a feminine grin with Belle. Instead she encountered a flash of anger in Justice's narrowed ebony eyes. He glanced away, a muscle flexing in his jaw.

Miranda rocked back on her heels, jolted by the confused stew of her own reactions: anger at his jealousy when they weren't even dating; an abused woman's fear of an angry man's retaliation . . .

. . . And a wave of purely female satisfaction.

Strangely, it was the satisfaction that was strongest. *Do I want him to be jealous of me?*

Maybe she did. Warlock had never been jealous of her mother, mostly because he'd never really given a damn about Joelle one way or the other. Her mother, on the other hand, had loved the sorcerer almost as much as she'd feared him.

At least Justice feels something for me beyond that infuriating sense of duty.

Miranda frowned. Infuriating? His sense of duty kept her alive.

Besides, he's an Alpha werewolf.

That thought would have sent her into full emotional retreat a month ago. Now it barely registered, as if it was more habit than reality. Still, Justice was definitely an Alpha . . .

"*Allez!*" With that traditional French fencer battle cry, the man lunged, broad chest precisely centered over his powerful thighs, his body extending with perfect form and furious strength. His opponent missed the parry, and the plastic tip of his foil hit her chest so hard, the blade bent like a bow.

"Touché." The woman tapped her chest, acknowledging the point.

"That makes it four to five." Conal Donovan straightened and dragged off his protective mesh fencing mask, revealing a darkly handsome face gleaming with sweat. He gave his sister a smile. "And you made me work for it."

"Thanks." The woman took off her own mask, revealing shoulder-length hair dyed so vivid a violet, it almost glowed.

"Love the hair, sis!" Branwyn called, before adding to the others, "She likes to make damn sure everyone can tell us apart."

"That's because people keep trying to kill you," Fin grumbled, poking his scaly muzzle out of her hair.

"Bran!" Aislyn's mask and foil hit the floor with clattering thumps. Racing across the gym, she flung herself into her twin's arms. Miranda realized Branwyn was right; she wouldn't have been able to tell the two apart if not for that outrageous hair.

Aislyn drew back, her smile blinding in its radiant joy. "I thought you were in Pakistan, playing hide-and-seek with those Sword of Allah jerks."

"I was. I ran into some Magekind . . . friends." Branwyn released her to walk into her brother's open arms. "They gated us all to Atlanta. They've got something they need to talk to you about, Conal."

"Oh?" The big Sidhe eyed the foursome warily as he gave Branwyn a hard hug. Then, as if removing her from harm's way, he pushed her gently aside.

Conal Donovan was an inch or so taller than Justice, and his padded fencing jacket made him look even broader. The traditional white knickers should have looked silly on a twenty-first-century male, but they only accented the power of his strong legs.

He'd tied his black hair back in a thick tail that swayed as he studied his guests. Miranda suspected he wore it long to camouflage his pointed ears. The sense of Alpha masculinity that surrounded him was so thick, he could have been Direkind. "What's this about?"

"We're looking for information, and we hope you can help," Tristan told him, his own smile edged in warning: *Don't start anything or we'll finish it.*

Branwyn performed hasty introductions. Miranda tensed as Conal's brilliant eyes narrowed. Like his sisters, he didn't radiate the kind of raw mystical power she'd come to associate with the Sidhe she'd met in Avalon. Not surprising, since Branwyn had admitted she and her siblings were half-human. Still, there was an air of danger around him that told her Conal would make a very bad enemy.

"So what brings a Knight of the Round Table and one of Arthur's most powerful witches to my door?" Conal walked over to a wall shelf and grabbed one of the white towels stacked there. As he wiped the sweat from his face, his easy smile didn't get anywhere near his eyes. His irises were the same striking amethyst as his sisters', but on him, the color looked a bit alien—and forbidding as hell.

Tristan watched him right back. "We're looking for someone called the Mother of Fairies. Your sister suggested we ask you about that."

Conal's gaze shot to Branwyn's face. Only for an instant, but something in his expression made the reporter flinch ever so slightly. Miranda tensed, wondering if he "disciplined" his sister in the Chosen sense of the word.

"Before you chew me out, I want you to see this." Branwyn hurried to the nearest flat screen. Miranda relaxed; despite that wince, she didn't sound afraid of her brother. "I shot this video in Mirpur an hour ago." The reporter started plugging her camera's video and audio cables into the monitor's input jacks.

"I gather you're still working on the terrorism piece." Conal joined her at the monitor and leaned one shoulder against the wall as he prepared to watch.

"Yeah." With the others gathering around, Branwyn pulled out a small remote and pointed it at the camera to cue her video. "I've been shadowing a Magekind vampire named Kadir al Hamad for the past couple of weeks. He was undercover with the Sword of Allah . . ."

"What?" Tristan straightened as if somebody had goosed him with a Taser. "Do you have any idea what those bastards would have done to you if you'd been caught? *Both* of you?"

"She knows, Vlad." Finvarra leaped onto a nearby treadmill's safety rail. Wrapping his tail around the bar, he sat back on his haunches, forepaws folded. Given their long, agile toes, they looked more like hands than paws. "Why do you think she takes the chances she does? She's not a fecking eejit."

"Too damn many people in the Middle East see those terrorist bastards as heroes." Branwyn's jaw rolled as if she ground her teeth, and her brilliant Sidhe eyes narrowed. "I'm going to show them what their 'heroes' are like when they don't know a camera's around."

"While I make sure the gobshites don't see us or the camera." Fin's mouth curled into a grin that bared needle teeth. "Magic is a handy thing."

It had better be, Miranda thought. *Or we're all screwed.*

FOUR

"You do have a way with a spell, Fin." Branwyn walked over to give the lizard's scaly head a stroke. He closed his eyes in a delight that was almost feline. She looked over at Justice, Miranda, Belle, and Tristan, her full lips tightening. "Watching those bastards gloat about killing Moslems who don't believe exactly the same thing they do . . . The jokes they tell about the innocents they blow to pieces . . ." She shook her head. " 'Seventy-two virgins' my ass. It's got nothing to do with religion. It's all about power."

"The virgin thing never made sense to me anyway." Tristan waggled his blond brows in an obvious attempt to lighten the mood. "Do you know how much trouble even one virgin is? Give me a woman with a little experience." He exchanged a wicked smile with Belle.

Justice frowned at Branwyn, his protective instincts evidently aroused. "You do realize when this story of yours hits the air, the Sword of Allah is going to come after you."

"They can try. I've a talent for keepin' her alive." Finvarra twitched his frilled tail.

"You'd better." Conal contemplated his sister as if he

didn't particularly like what he saw. "I'm seriously considering hiring a bodyguard anyway."

Justice snorted. "Bodyguard, hell. What you need is Superman. Get somebody bulletproof between her and that death wish."

"I do not have a death wish," Branwyn told him with icy dignity.

Miranda frowned as Justice gave the Sidhe the same you-need-protection glare he so often gave her. *What's he doing? He's* my *bodyguard, dammit . . .*

Realization struck her, stinging like a slap. *Am I jealous? Of an Alpha Werewolf? Oh, hell, no. I'm not that stupid. If he wants to chase fairies, let him.*

". . . The world is overpopulated with assholes," Branwyn was saying. "I'm just trying to document them. One pucker at a time."

Justice's grin was distinctly feral. "I find nine-mil slugs work pretty well."

"I prefer to do my shooting with a camera. Less mess afterward. Speaking of cameras . . ." She hit play. "As I said, I was trailing Kadir to a meeting with his cell . . ."

They watched as the Pakistani agent took a right at a four-way intersection surrounded by tall, blocky buildings—a hotel, a couple of restaurants with signs written in flowing Arabic script, one or two impressive-looking villas. It was the middle of the night, and other than a lone pickup rumbling by, there was no traffic at all. Kadir strode down the dark street with a vampire's fearless stride, only to pause in mid-step, head lifting, dark gaze searching the shadows. The microphone picked up an odd sliding rustle, followed by a long, menacing hiss.

The camera's view spun sickeningly to an alley between a hotel and a restaurant. A massive shape moved in the darkness, moonlight glinting on steel. Something blue glowed in the darkness, and hooves rang on the pavement, striking sparks.

The cobra shot from the alley like a runaway train, hissing, eyes burning red against the black gleam of its scales.

Its body was easily three feet in diameter; there was no way to tell how long it was. It flashed toward Kadir, scales raking over the pavement with a gritty rasp. Its jaws gaped wide, fangs the length of a man's forearm catching the moonlight.

"Holy God," Justice murmured in horror. "That fucking thing is huge."

"And a hell of a lot faster than you'd think," Tristan told him.

Kadir leaped aside, avoiding the snake with a bullfighter's grace as he swung his AK-47 off his shoulder. He fired in a series of thundering bursts that raked the huge snake's length as it plowed past.

The Beast's scales flared blue, sending Kadir's bullets ricocheting harmlessly. The snake whipped around and reared over the vampire, its hood spreading wide, the cream scales of its endless belly shining like porcelain.

Kadir opened up on it again, this time aiming for its eyes. Something blue shone between them, an oval light, possibly some kind of gemstone, embedded right in the center of its skull. Light flared from the stone, and the slugs ricocheted off into the night.

The vampire danced back, ducking the flying bullets. Glaring up at the towering snake, he spat something in his native Potwari that was obviously a disgusted curse.

Hooves thundered on pavement, a backbeat for a long, chilling howl. Kadir spun, dark eyes widening as he aimed his weapon at the newest threat.

An enormous centaur exploded from the alley, all muscular power and lethal intent. The thing looked as though someone had crossed a Clydesdale with a demon from a video game. The torso fused with the horse body didn't look human—it was too broad, all exaggerated slabs of muscle covered in jutting plate armor that made it appear even more alien. The creature's armored gauntlets were tipped in dagger claws, and it carried a battle-axe that looked as if it could fell a California redwood.

Adding to the menacing effect, the Beast's armor was

engraved with runes cut into the thick steel. Long spikes jutted from the creature's armored chest, forelegs, and dinner plate–sized hooves, ready to impale anyone who got too close.

The centaur's helm had no visor, presumably to accommodate that wolf muzzle. His canines were so long, they protruded from his upper and lower jaws like tusks even when his mouth was closed. Orange eyes glowed from the beast's lupine head, with another blue gem embedded between them. Pointed ears lay flat against its skull as it snarled, lips lifting to display those vicious teeth.

"Evil-looking bastard." Conal frowned, shooting a worried look at his sister. He plainly didn't like the thought of Branwyn getting so close to either monster.

"And in his case, looks are not deceiving," she told him. Aislyn moved over to loop a comforting arm around her waist and give her a quick hug. "I felt like I was trapped in a nightmare. Even though none of them could see me, I was scared out of my mind."

"You had reason to be." Justice eyed Conal as if to make sure her brother got the point. "You could have been trampled or crushed without them knowing you were even there."

And once again, Miranda felt a prickle of pure green jealousy. She ground her teeth and tried to ignore it.

Kadir opened fire, but flares of blue energy bounced his bullets into the dark. The centaur charged, axe lifted as it howled out a challenge.

The AK-47 clicked on an empty magazine. Kadir grabbed the rifle by its no-doubt burning barrel and swung its heavy stock at the onrushing Beast. The centaur reared, and the swing slammed into its armored ribs, only to rebound harmlessly. That enormous axe descended in a blur of bright steel.

The Pakistani vampire swore and leaped aside, barely avoiding the lethal blade.

Kadir had just drawn the rifle back for another try when he saw the snake rear to strike. He threw himself into a roll that barely avoided the reptile's plunging dive. Its head alone was damn near the length of his entire body.

"He did know how to fight," Conal mused, watching with brooding pity. "But there's no way he could take both those monsters. Not unarmed." He looked at Tristan. "Why the hell didn't he have one of those magic swords you types carry instead of that useless rifle?"

Tristan shrugged. "Kadir was armed for combat in Mirpur City. He'd expected to fight men, not monsters."

The centaur's massive hooves swung over the vampire's head, preparing to stomp Kadir into jelly. The Pakistani leaped in a bound no mortal could have matched, avoiding the plunging hooves. He hit the ground rolling, made it to his feet, spotted the snake lifting its hooded head, and jumped ten feet straight up . . .

Too late. Before he could tuck his legs out of its path, the snake's fangs caught his left thigh, punching deep to pump deadly venom into the muscle. Kadir screamed as his body whipped through the air, dangling from the Beast's mouth. Clamping down, the reptile began chewing, driving still more venom into the vampire. Cursing, Kadir swung his rifle in a clumsy arc at the thing's head.

The snake reared high into the air—and dropped him. He fell fifteen feet to hit the pavement hard, right on his head and shoulders. Obviously stunned, barely conscious, he lay in a heap as the snake slithered around his body, opened its jaws, and swooped down to engulf his legs. It could have swallowed his head first, but that would have meant a faster kill as the vampire suffocated. The monster plainly wanted Kadir to suffer.

And he did, shrieking in agony as the snake began swallowing him in a series of lunging gulps.

Eyes helplessly locked on the video, Miranda made an involuntary sound of pain. Justice moved up behind her, not quite touching. She leaned into him, accepting the gesture of comfort. *Wish we weren't wearing armor.*

And then she thought, *What the hell am I doing?*

Miranda straightened with a jerk. She thought she heard Justice sigh, but when she looked back, his handsome face was expressionless.

On the screen, Daliya leaped through a dimensional gate, wearing full armor, a sword in her hand. Kadir screamed again, and her head jerked toward the sound, her dark eyes going wide and desperate.

She shrieked something in Potwari and charged the snake, her weapon blazing with magic as she started trying to hack the monster in two so she could free her mate. More gates sparked open around them as the Knights of the Round Table and the most powerful witches in Avalon arrived, summoned by Daliya when she'd sensed her husband's danger.

Too late.

Branwyn clicked the remote, stopping the video as the vampires converged on the snake, still in the act of swallowing Kadir. "And that's as much of it as I can stand to watch."

In the end, Tristan told Conal, he was the one who took Kadir's head. "Daliya begged me," the knight explained, his voice gruff with pity. "Most of her husband was down the snake's throat at that point, and she said she could feel the venom dissolving his muscle tissue. He was paralyzed by then, but vampires are pretty fucking tough, and he just wouldn't die. She couldn't stand to feel him suffering any longer."

"We tried everything we could think of, but we couldn't get him out of that snake." Belle scrubbed her hands over her face. Her eyes were red. "Even Excalibur bounced right off those damned scales. And our blasts only made the Beast stronger."

"Then the centaur killed that child, and Arthur went after him," Tristan said. "While the two Beasts were distracted, I saved the only part of Kadir I could. The monsters finally gated off to wherever the hell they go. Belle and I carried Daliya and Kadir's head into the alley while

Arthur led the cleanup crew putting out the fires and healing the wounded. The ones they could save, anyway."

His expression brooding, the knight stared at the monitor. The video was frozen on a close-up of the Pakistani witch's horrified face. "Daliya started babbling about mothers and fairies and somebody called the Huntsman . . ."

"No, it was the Hunter Prince," Miranda corrected. She'd memorized Daliya's prophecy, concentrating on every word as the witch spoke it. With that kind of magic, everything could turn on phrasing.

Tristan nodded. "That's right, it was the Hunter Prince. Not that any of it made much sense, even after I listened to her recite the thing half a dozen times."

"The Mother," Branwyn put in. "She was definitely talking about the Mother, Conal." She pointed the remote at the camera, fast-forwarding through the carnage. "I shot this after Daliya went down."

The video jumped to a close-up of the Maja's bloody, shock-dazed face. Her voice sounded almost dreamy as she chanted in English, ". . . and the crows will feast. Seek the Mother of Fairies as she folds enchanted steel into blades she fills with the souls of lost gods. She waits in her forge for the hero wolf to come for Merlin's Blade. Then will the Hunter Prince be free—then will he rule in bloody vengeance or bend his knee to his spirit's feral king. But mark me well—it will take the daughter of evil and a master of darkness to lead the night world into the light. If they do fail, humanity will drown in blood under the white wolf's heel, and the crows will feast. Seek the Mother of Fairies at her . . ."

"She kept saying the same thing over and over," Branwyn said. "Like the vision was on loop or something."

"I agree with Bran." Aislyn frowned at the screen, one hand rubbing her sister's bowed back in comforting circles. "She's definitely talking about the Mother."

Conal paused so long, Miranda knew he agreed with the twins. "Maybe she did see the Mother," he admitted finally, "but that doesn't mean the Mother is going to want a Knight of the Round Table showing up at her door. This isn't our fight."

"So you're just going to stand around and do nothing, even though this Mother of yours may have the key to defeating Warlock?" Tristan glared. "Thanks a fuckin' heap, Conal."

"Meanwhile, humans are going to die in droves," Justice pointed out. "Fifteen Magekind agents have fallen, and so have more than a dozen werewolves. How long do you think we can fight a war involving this kind of magic without somebody shooting cell phone video none of us wants on FOX?"

"Let us talk to her." Miranda moved closer to Conal, hoping to get through his stubborn resistance. "Let us at least try. We're running out of options."

"Look, I don't want Warlock running things any more than you do, but you still don't want to show up at the Mother's forge unannounced." Conal rubbed a hand back and forth across his square jaw. The long tail of his hair swayed with the movement. "That's a good way to get extremely dead."

Belle eyed him. "So what do you suggest?"

He sighed and threw up his hands in a gesture of disgusted surrender. "I'll call her and explain the situation." Jerking open the Velcro fastenings of his fencing jacket, Conal shrugged out of the protective garment and tossed it across a nearby weight bench. The sweat-damp white T-shirt he'd worn beneath it clung to his powerful chest. "Then it's up to her. I . . ."

The door to the gym banged open. The twins jumped. Miranda spun, reaching for her magic, aware of Justice, Tristan, Belle, and Conal tensing to fight.

"The wards!" a woman called in a voice as Southern as pecan pie. "Somethin's probin' the wards!"

"And it's evil," a male voice added, so powerful and resonant with authority it reminded Justice of Morgan Freeman the time he'd played God.

Yet nothing human came through the door.

A white, long-haired cat galloped in, following what Justice first mistook for the biggest freaking parrot he'd ever seen. The bird's plumage was bright scarlet, gold, and orange, its tail a blazing swath of color as it winged into the room.

The bird landed on Conal's shoulder, and Justice realized it was in fact an eagle. Or some kind of predatory bird, anyway; it had a raptor's beak and claws that looked like it could disembowel a deer. Magic glowed in its savage golden eyes.

"Where in the hell did you get a phoenix eagle?" Tristan stared at the huge bird with wary respect.

"He didn't 'get' me anywhere," the eagle said in that Freeman rumble. "I got him."

The cat leaped into Aislyn's arms, visibly shivering. "Oh, who cares, you big ol' feather duster? We have problems! That thing will eat us all!"

"What 'thing'?" Justice asked.

Miranda knew damned well they wouldn't like the answer.

The two bodyguards lay dead in a wide splatter of drying blood on the pavement outside the DCN Corporate Center. One corpse still gripped his gun. Judging by the scent of gunpowder wafting from the barrel, Justice thought he'd gotten off at least one shot.

Not that it had done him a damned bit of good. Both mortals had been bitten by something with one hell of a lot of teeth—and a much bigger set of jaws than any werewolf's.

"The snake didn't do this." Justice knelt beside Tristan, Belle, and Miranda, as all of them studied the ragged wounds. One man had been bitten almost in two, while the other had bled out after a bite amputated his thigh. "No snake has this many teeth."

"If it had been the cobra, it probably would have eaten them both." Tristan rose and drew his sword, his eyes flicking restlessly over their surroundings. "Though considering these bastards are Shifters, I guess it could be the same monster in a different form."

"The magical signature doesn't feel the same." Miranda frowned thoughtfully down at the corpses. "But that may not mean much."

"Scent's not the same either." Justice inhaled again, once more picking up a trace of oily musk under the reek of drying blood. "Does smell reptilian, though."

"Don't you dare leave those girls, Conal Donovan!" Belle snapped into her cell phone as she paced around the corpses. She and Tristan had persuaded the Sidhe to remain in the building's penthouse, guarding his sisters and the trio of enchanted animals they called "familiars."

The cat was positive the DCN Center was under attack by something nasty. Apparently she'd been downstairs, begging a treat from her favorite feline-loving guard, when the security cameras caught something big moving through the dark outside. Danu had magically summoned Essus and taken the elevator up to Conal's penthouse. Meanwhile the guards went out to investigate.

Where they promptly got themselves killed.

"We'll find the Beast who did this," Belle assured Conal. "Arthur told me he'll send reinforcements as soon as they finish the cleanup in Mirpur."

She stopped her pacing to listen, then shook her head. "No, I've put an invisibility spell over the scene. The police won't be called unless you call them. Which I wouldn't suggest you do until we're sure the killer isn't hanging around waiting to eat a few cops."

Miranda spotted something on the pavement and stepped away from the bodies. Bending, she examined the smeared brown shape that looked like blood. "Is this a print?"

Justice joined her, leaving Tristan hovering protectively beside Belle. "Looks that way."

"What the hell made it—the world's biggest chicken?"

"We don't get that lucky." It did look a little like a bird track, assuming the bird was the size of an elephant. The print consisted of a pair of foot-long claws in the shape of a V, adjoining something that resembled a curled thumb . . .

Somebody screamed. A high female shriek, ringing with the distilled terror of a woman facing her worst nightmare. Something roared.

And the scream cut off.

Justice and Miranda exchanged a single flashing glance, and raced toward the sound of the woman's despairing cry. Belle and Tristan sprinted after them. Justice knew a good bodyguard would get his client to safety before worrying about anybody else, but Miranda wasn't the type to hide when an innocent was in danger.

He also knew he didn't have time to argue with her, not when two men had just been slaughtered, and a woman was out there being attacked by God knew what. Besides, they might need Miranda's magic to fight whatever monster her father had conjured now.

So Justice ran, reaching for the Mageverse as he went, drawing on its thundering power. Magic flooded into his every cell, searing flesh and muscle, jerking bone into impossible shapes, sending fur in a rippling tide across his body. A firestorm of pain blazed in after the magic. He clenched his teeth against a rising howl.

One stride later the pain was gone, and he was seven feet tall, bounding along on powerful wolf legs.

Miranda matched him leap for leap, having Shifted at the same time. Her thick fur was the color of a fox's pelt on a long, cleanly muscled body. Even in wolf form, he found her beautiful, her body sweetly curved beneath its armor, almost delicate next to his powerful bulk.

Somewhere behind them came the ringing thud of armored boots as the two Magekind agents ran after them faster than any human—but not as fast as a pair of werewolves.

They shot around the corner side by side, only to slide to a stop in astonishment and horror at what they saw.

A freaking dinosaur lifted its head from the corpse of a woman who lay in a splattered pool of blood. Half the body was gone. The monster had taken the woman's head off like a child biting into a chocolate bunny.

They were too late.

The Beast had to be fifteen feet tall as it balanced on two clawed legs over the woman's corpse, a thick, counterbalancing tail whipping in the air behind it. It was covered in bright green feathers that clashed with the orange blaze of its eyes as it spread stubby wings over the woman's pitiful corpse. Its bloody jaws gaped, revealing a set of teeth that put Justice's to shame. The fucker looked like it could bite somebody in half like a Dorito. It had certainly taken a chunk out of that poor woman.

Right in the center of its head blazed that damned blue stone.

The Beast threw back its head and roared. The sound was still echoing off the surrounding buildings when the thing leaped over the corpse to dart toward them in long, bounding strides.

"This way!" Justice grabbed Miranda's hand and whirled to race up the block, darting down one alley and up another, along a third and a fourth. Leading the Beast away from the busy section of town, looking for somewhere it would be less likely to find someone it could eat or take hostage.

The sound of the creature's pounding footsteps receded; it was having a hard time getting through the narrow alleys Justice had chosen.

Not that alley, too wide. No, not that one, not long enough. There!

He found what he was looking for in a pair of blocky redbrick office buildings; judging by the fading scents, the workers at both had knocked off for the day.

Perfect.

They needed to hem the big bastard in, give him less room to use his teeth and claws. The narrow alley between the two buildings looked perfect for the ambush Justice had in mind.

Risky. God, it was risky, but if he could just strike fast enough, he might be able to end this before another innocent died.

"Got a plan?" Miranda shouted as she galloped into the alley after him. She carried a battle-axe she must have conjured as she ran. "Because I don't have a clue."

"We kick its ass." He jerked his chin toward the roof. "I'm going to hit it from up there . . ."

". . . While I distract it from down here." She lifted the axe and bared her wolfish teeth in something that definitely wasn't a smile.

"Or we could do it the other way." His every instinct yowled in protest at the idea of letting Miranda run that kind of risk. But if he could just catch the Beast off guard before it could raise that spell-shield, maybe he could kill it.

Before it killed anybody else.

Thud thud thud. The dinosaur's footsteps, coming closer.

Miranda snorted, looking toward the alley entrance. "I doubt I could hit Super Chicken hard enough to behead it, even in Dire Wolf form. You can. That makes me the decoy."

Her courage made his throat tighten. Before he could talk himself out of it, Justice snatched her against him, despite the armor both of them wore. He expected Miranda to jerk away again. Maybe even slap him. Instead she stared up into his face, eyes fierce with determination. "I can do it, Justice. I *will* do it."

"I know." He ached to kiss her.

Heat flared in her eyes, as if she shared that helpless longing. She started to rise on her toes, only to drop back to her heels again. "Muzzles." Her upper lip curled in eloquent disgust.

Justice laughed. She was right; werewolf heads just weren't suited to kissing. "Don't get killed."

He turned and leaped for the wall of the shorter of the two buildings, hitting it halfway up. Digging his claws into the soft brick, he swarmed upward, fast as a furry Spider-Man.

When he reached its flat roof, he looked down and held out a hand. Miranda gestured, sending a stream of magic toward him. An even bigger axe condensed in his palm. He grinned and gave her a nod—she'd given him exactly what he needed—then crouched behind the roof's low parapet. And prayed.

Thud thud THUD THUD.

The dinosaur appeared at the alley's entrance, a savage chainsaw growl rumbling from toothy jaws. Its gem blazed at them, blue with Warlock's magic.

Miranda did a mocking little dance in the middle of the alley. "Hey, Super Chicken!" She hefted the axe in both hands like a baseball bat. "I got your secret recipe right here!"

The creature roared again. Justice decided it was supposed to be a raptor, though he'd read somewhere that a real velociraptor was only about the size of a German shepherd. This feathered bastard was damn near as big as a T. rex, a good thirty feet from snout to tail tip.

Which was actually a good thing, considering the alley was only a few feet wider than the Beast's barrel chest.

Miranda raised her axe and charged, bellowing a battle cry. The blade exploded into a blaze of magical flame.

You do know how to get a guy's attention, Justice thought.

The beast roared again and thundered into a run. The roof shook under Justice with its pounding strides.

Holy Jesus, let us survive this, he prayed, and threw himself off the building.

Justice landed on the Beast's slick, feathered back, caught his balance, and lifted the axe to hack into its spine.

Before he could swing the weapon, the monster reared, roaring like a grizzly, short wings beating as its feathered tail whipped from side to side. Its head snaked around on that long neck and darted at him, toothy jaws open wide.

FIVE

Justice hadn't realized just how damned slick feathers were, particularly when the creature he stood on bucked like a rodeo bull. One clawed foot slipped, and the axe hit the creature's shoulder instead of its spine.

And bounced right off in a burst of familiar blue light.

Crap. That was the same spell that had protected the other two bastards.

The fanged head shot toward him on its long, snaking neck. He jerked back. Dagger-length teeth snapped two inches from his face with a blast of breath that stank of blood and meat. "Jesus, Super Chicken, eat a crate of Tic Tacs."

Another vicious snap. Justice tightened his clawed grip on the bouncing, slippery back and sought a better angle for a swing. Drawing the big weapon back, he hacked downward with all his magical strength. A blue glow burst around the axe, sending it rebounding with such force, it almost knocked him right off his perch.

Shitpissfuck.

Digging his clawed toes deeper, he bobbed around like a boxer to avoid Super Chicken's snapping attempts to bite his axe arm off. Before the raptor could try for another chomp, its eyes widened. Snaking around with a shrill squeal of rage, it drove its toothy snout down between its legs.

Miranda leaped away, narrowly avoiding its strike as she brandished her axe. "Spielberg wants his costume back, cockbag!"

Super Chicken leaped after her in a feline pounce. The sudden heave of its back flipped Justice off his perch. He clawed empty air, falling. Feathered ribs flashed by. He grabbed a fistful of plumage and scrambled up the thing's side again. Roaring in annoyance, the raptor threw itself at the nearest wall, trying to squash him like a spider.

"Shit!" Justice leaped straight up, twisting with a furious wrench of his body. The beast smashed into the building just below his feet. Brick shattered, the whole structure shaking with the impact. Justice hit the wall so hard he saw stars, felt himself falling, and clamped all four sets of claws into the rough surface. The axe went flying. Sucking in a breath tasting of brick dust, Justice cursed and watched it tumble.

An armored hand flashed up and caught the spinning blade right out of the air. "Need help?" Tristan called, and tossed the weapon back as if it were a tennis ball.

Justice managed to catch the axe without losing his grip on the wall. "Sure as hell do." He grinned down at his friend in relief.

"Sorry it took us so long to catch up." Tristan backpedaled, swinging his sword at Super Chicken's muzzle. It snapped at him with a squealing snort.

Beside Tristan, Belle feinted at the massive head with her own blade, and it jerked back, huffing in irritation. "I called Mirpur." Which probably explained the delay in their arrival. "Twenty or so Dire Wolves just hit Arthur's people. He doesn't expect them to give the Knights any real trouble, but they won't be able to give us reinforcements until they get rid of the wolves. Otherwise the bastards'll eat the civilians."

Shit. They were going to have to take care of Super Chicken on their own.

The raptor hesitated, red eyes rolling as if trying to figure out who to bite first. Damned if it didn't remind Justice of a girl contemplating a box of chocolates.

Mmm. Crunchy with a creamy blood center.

While the Beast concentrated on the Magekind agents, Miranda ran between its muscular legs and swung her axe hard, right at its belly. As she'd expected, the blade rebounded harmlessly, but in the instant of impact, blue glowing runes danced across its scales.

As she'd hoped, Miranda recognized that spell. It was the same one etched on Warlock's armor.

The monster's huge head darted down at her again, bloody jaws wide, magical gem blazing. She leaped away, glimpsed a clawed foot swinging her way, and barely ducked the kick before it could take her head off. *If I just had ten seconds to concentrate, I could work out a counter spell . . .*

Super Chicken's gemstone pulsed blue, and a voice rolled from it, deep, menacing. A familiar resonant baritone that seemed to throb with power.

Warlock's voice.

"You turncoat little slut." The gem's blaze intensified, and Miranda could sense her father's malevolent attention burning down on her. "Spreading your legs for Arthur now? It'll gain you nothing. You'll still die in screaming agony."

She wanted to yell a denial, to tell the bastard— finally!—what kind of monster he really was. But her body wouldn't obey. It wanted only to curl up in a ball, like a mouse quivering in the grass. Her instincts shrieked in panic as Super Chicken's head tilted with vicious interest.

A gesture she recognized. Warlock used to look at her with precisely that tilt to his head.

Suddenly Miranda was four years old again, running through a stone cavern lit only by her father's blazing, lethal magic. Burning hair filled her nose with a nauseating stench. She could actually smell the reek of it, like an olfactory ghost. Her mouth filled with bile.

"I wonder how you'll taste?" Warlock rumbled with the Beast's mouth. "I think I'll find out."

As if in slow motion, Miranda watched those huge jaws gape, plunging toward her. Her brain shrieked at her body to dive aside, but her feet felt welded to the pavement.

Which was when a furry armored shape plummeted down out of the sky: Justice, leaping right over the Beast's head. His golden eyes were wide, and stark terror twisted his lupine lips, but not for himself.

He's afraid for me.

No one but her mother had ever given a damn if she lived or died.

Justice's big body slammed into Miranda like a defensive end sacking a quarterback, tumbling her tail over ears out of the Beast's path. The world spun, armor scraping and clanking as she skidded across the pavement.

Justice shot to his feet, squarely between her and the Beast. He gathered himself to leap clear. "Miranda, move! Get the hell out of the . . ."

The Beast's jaws closed over Justice's chest the instant before he could throw himself aside, snatching him right off his feet. Justice howled in agony. A lacy plume of blood arced from the thing's teeth as they clamped into his armored chest. Blue light flared as the raptor absorbed the protective spells on the steel. The metal gave beneath the crushing fangs, and the dinosaur jerked Justice into the air, high over Miranda's head. She screamed as massive jaws ground down hard, crushing through the steel.

It's killing him!

She couldn't let him die. Not Justice. Not the only man who'd ever honestly given a damn about her. She remembered the curve of his arm around her waist, his muscular body holding her close, somehow feeling warm even through his armor.

Oh, hell no. You're not eating him, you son of a bitch.

Forgetting her fear for herself, Miranda leaped to her feet and charged, howling the shield counter spell she composed on the spot. A second pulse of magic conjured a pole arm, the ten-foot oak shaft tipped by a viciously barbed head. She aimed it at the center of the Beast's scaled breast, right where the heart should be.

The raptor sneered down at her around Justice's bleeding, struggling body, contempt in its tiny orange eyes, its gemstone burning blue and bright. *It doesn't realize it just lost its shield.*

Miranda hit Super Chicken at a dead run, all her strength and weight propelling her spear thrust. Blue light flared as the weapon hit the shield—and exploded through it as if ripping into a sheet of wrapping paper.

The spear embedded itself in the raptor's breast, penetrating scales, slicing through muscle and shattering bone. The Beast roared in shocked agony, and Justice tumbled from its jaws.

He hit the ground with an armored clatter, blood spraying, limbs sprawled wide. Every instinct demanded Miranda run to him, but she knew the raptor wasn't dead yet.

"Die, you bastard!" And she blasted every erg of power she could drag from the Mageverse into her palms. The spell seared her skin as it blasted up the pole arm like a lightning bolt. The rune-marked wood flared, bright as a torch.

Super Chicken reeled, squealing. Its blue gem flashed and went dark as, protective shield shattered, it could no longer absorb her magic. Werewolf magic exploded around it, and the creature's massive weight vanished off the pole arm. The raptor became a wolf in a rain of blue sparks and fell hard. Thrown off-balance as her victim Shifted, Miranda staggered and dropped to one knee.

The huge blond animal hit the ground beside her like a

sack of concrete, yelping as it struck the pavement. Before she could pounce, the werewolf rolled to his feet.

Dammit, dammit, dammit. The bastard's Shift had healed the lethal wound she'd inflicted. Snarling, the wolf took a threatening step toward her . . .

"Think again, you bastard!" Tristan charged up the alley toward them, his sword lifted for a decapitating swing.

The werewolf took one look and ran, yelping, tail tucked tight to its furry haunches. Bellowing battle cries, Belle and the knight raced after it, enchanted weapons trailing sparks through the darkness.

Miranda tossed the useless pole arm aside and whirled, eyes desperately seeking Justice. He lay in an armored heap on the dirty alley pavement. Unmoving. Her heart turned into a block of dry ice.

She raced to his side, casting a spell to strip away his armor so she could examine him. Dropping to her knees, Miranda spread her hands, sending her magic questing over his still, furry body.

He was alive. Barely.

Her eyes closed in a quick prayer of thanksgiving, then snapped open to catalogue the damage. It wasn't as bad as it could have been—the chest plate had given him some protection from those vicious jaws. Still, Super Chicken's teeth had bitten into Justice's torso in a V-shape, breaking ribs and puncturing at least one lung, judging from the bubbling sound when he breathed. Blood rolled from the deep, ragged injuries to pool on the filthy pavement.

So much blood.

If he could only Shift, his wounds would heal, just as the Beast had recovered from her pole arm attack. But Justice was unconscious—probably as a result of a head injury, which was yet another worry. Until he woke, he couldn't transform. And if he lost too much blood, he'd die, werewolf or not.

Miranda bit her lip, fighting panic. Normally she'd simply heal him herself, but his Direkind immunity to magic meant that wasn't possible. "Justice, wake up!"

He didn't even flick an ear.

Did she dare shake him? No, if he had a head or spinal injury, jarring him might kill him on the spot. "Justice, you need to Shift. Human, wolf, dog . . . Hell, I don't care. Just Shift! Please!"

No response. His lids remained closed as blood pulsed from his wounds, widening the pool around his body into a sticky scarlet lake. It soaked Miranda's fur as she knelt beside him, drowning her werewolf senses in its copper reek. Miranda ignored the choking stench and stared at him.

How do you make someone Shift?

She remembered her own first transformation with nightmare clarity. She'd been only fifteen, painfully aware that if her magic escaped her control, it would incinerate her like a match. And her magic was very, very powerful, even then.

The Direkind lost fully a fifth of their children to magic gone rogue. The Mageverse's energy transformed some and devoured others, and there was no way to tell who would live and who would die. As a result, both teenagers and their Dire Wolf parents viewed that initial transformation with helpless dread.

Unfortunately, it wasn't something you could refuse to do. Shifting was one of the body's deep, driving instincts, like giving birth. You Transformed whether you wanted to or not . . .

She'd huddled in the sweaty sheets of her bed that night, racking shivers alternating with waves of heat that felt as though she stood in the threshold of a crematorium.

Already burning.

Her skin itched so savagely, it was all she could do not to claw her flesh bloody. Cramps twisted her muscles into merciless knots, a precursor to the transformation. Yet as bad as the suffering was, her cold terror was worse.

I don't want to die. *That thought chased its own tail*

through her mind, repeating over and over until she wanted to scream in terror and despair. She wondered if anyone would care if they walked in to find nothing but ashes in her bed . . .

Gerald wouldn't give a damn. Warlock would be irritated that sixteen years of plotting had come to nothing.

And her mother . . .

The bedroom door flew open. Joelle Drake strode in, pale as fresh snow, shoulders squared with a determination that was so painfully rare for her. Though she'd suffered under her husband's fists for years, Joelle considered it her duty as a Chosen aristocrat to endure in silence. Yet now, as she looked down on her daughter's helpless terror, her eyes shone with love—and a fierce courage Miranda had never known she possessed. "Shift with me." It was a demand, delivered in a strong, sure voice that left no room for the possibility of death.

And her mother transformed, Dire Wolf magic blazing in the darkened room in a blinding sheet of azure energy.

Miranda felt that magic lick at hers, plumes of energy reaching into the pulsing core of her power, coaxing it hotter, brighter.

Until, like a burning fuse hitting a stack of TNT, Joelle's magic detonated her own. Merlin's ancient spell flashed through bone, muscle, and flesh, Shifting every cell. For the first time, Miranda felt the full power of the Mageverse in all its violent glory. She'd never see herself the same way again.

The explosion of magic faded slowly like a dying star as pain drained into weary peace. She felt as if she stood on a silent mountaintop, snow drifting cool and soothing over her stretched, burning skin.

Miranda met Joelle's golden wolf gaze, saw the pride and relief in those glowing irises. Usually when her mother Shifted, Joelle towered over Miranda. Now they stood eye to eye.

Miranda realized that her own pointed ears almost

brushed the ceiling, and thick, sharp talons tipped her red-furred fingers as she balanced on clawed feet.

She'd survived. She'd become a Dire Wolf instead of a screaming torch.

Feeling every bit as desperate and terrified as she'd been then, Miranda stared down at Justice. Her magic couldn't affect him directly, but what if she could drag him into Shifting by transforming herself?

It might not work—but considering that the alternative was to sit and watch him die, she was damned well going to give it her best shot.

Miranda reached into the Mageverse, calling the magic, dragging it deep like a drowning woman sucking in air. And breathed it out again over Justice's still, bloody body. His jaws gaped as he sprawled in the spreading pool of blood, his tongue lolling between his teeth in a way that reminded her uncomfortably of a dog that had been hit by a car.

Don't you dare die, William Justice. God, please don't leave me alone like this.

Miranda let her eyes lose focus as she stared at him— and saw *it*. The core of his magic burned deep inside his brain like a pilot light in a furnace.

There. Yes, that!

Desperate hope flooding her, she drew in still more energy and blew it out again. Her bones began to ache, a fiery itch spreading across her skin. A silent warning that she'd better use the power she called if she didn't want it to turn on her.

Deep within Justice, energy sparked, a flicker of his power responding to hers. So she pulled on the Mageverse with all her strength, breathing it over him like a hot wind.

Dangerous. Fuck, this is dangerous. If I stoke the magic too high, it could escape my control and fry me like bacon. And Justice could end up caught in the fire.

But if she didn't take the risk, he was dead. That was simply not an option. If not for Justice's courageous rescue when she'd frozen, she'd be the one dying now. She'd rather burn herself than abandon him.

So Miranda went right on dragging energy out of the Mageverse, building her magic into a seductive blaze, until Justice's power began to flicker and burn in response.

Don't die, dammit. Don't you dare die.

Well, Justice thought, *I fucked that up.*

Actually, it wasn't exactly a thought, more a faint awareness as he floated in a darkness that got darker with every ticking second. On some dim level, he knew he was dying.

Memories flashed through his mind like stuttering images illuminated by a strobe lamp. The Beast lunging at Miranda, preparing to bite her in two. Justice, leaping over the monster's head to knock her off her feet and send her rolling to safety.

Hot breath stinking of rotting meat rolled over his head. Justice looked up—and saw the Beast's toothy maw looming over him.

He'd tried to dive clear, but the monster snatched him right off his feet and bit down. Even with his armor, his ribs crunched like bread sticks in an explosion of white-hot agony.

Screaming, Justice had grabbed the thing's jaws in both hands and tried to lever them the fuck off him. And then . . .

Nothing.

Oh, Christ, did it eat me? Am I a decapitated head like that poor vampire bastard? *There really should have been a lot more terror behind that thought. Instead, all he felt was numb.*

Shift. I've got to Shift.

If there was any hope at all, that was it.

He tried to reach into the Mageverse and draw on its energy so he could transform and heal. Its life-giving magic refused to respond. He could only float in the cold, numbing dark, scrabbling with his fading strength for the power he needed.

Dying.

"Justice?" The voice was faint, scarcely a whisper. He heard it only because there was no other sound at all in the black chill.

Except it was no longer quite as black as it had been. Something glowed blue in the distance, moving toward him. The voice came again, stronger now. "Justice? Justice, where are you?"

Miranda.

He reached for her. "I'm here! Miranda, I'm here . . ."

She shot out of the dark like a comet, a blue blaze of light so brilliant, she made his eyes ache. For a moment he thought Miranda was going to barrel right into him—but then she slammed to a stop a foot away, as if running head-on into an invisible barrier.

He stared at her in hungry amazement.

She was gloriously naked. Her body shone against the nothingness like an erotic fairy sketched in lines of blue werewolf magic. Her breasts and hips curved, lush and sensual, nipples drawn into tight, shining cobalt points. Her hair curled around her shoulders in strands of sapphire light. "Justice, you've got to change!" Her voice reverberated in his mind as though his brain were a tuning fork, ringing with her mental touch. "You're dying."

"I know that, dammit. I can't reach my magic."

"You can." She flattened one hand on the barrier that separated them. "You have to—you're fading in front of me. And I can't heal you because you're immune to my magic!"

Yet she'd still managed to touch his consciousness. How the hell . . .

"Change!" As he watched, she began to blaze, brighter and brighter, magic flaring around her with furious intensity. "Reach for the magic, Justice. Come back to me, dammit."

He strained, clawing for the power, but it refused to respond.

"Come on, Justice!"

"I'm trying, dammit!"

"Try harder!" She had grown so bright, it was like staring into the sun.

Fear stirred—not for himself, but for her. "Miranda, you're pulling too much magic. You're going to burn." He'd seen it happen to a Dire Wolf who'd shifted one too many times during a fight. The man had blazed hot like that, only to vanish into blowing ash. "Stop!"

"No!" she shouted back, even as he recoiled from the sheer blazing heat of her power. "We're both going to make it, or neither of us will!"

"Dammit, Miranda!" Frustrated fury sparked in his brain. He hadn't sacrificed himself to that fucking monster for Miranda to commit suicide by magic.

He flung his will out into the darkness. At first there was no response, only the same chill nothingness he'd felt all along. But he was fucked if he'd take that for an answer. Not if it meant Miranda would cook herself. "Come on!" he howled into the darkness. "Damn you, let me shift!"

And the Mageverse answered his bellow of will, pouring into his cold, dying body, blazing through his cells with the familiar pain of transformation . . .

"Yes!" Miranda cried, joy and tears in her reverberating mental voice. "That's it! Come back to me!"

Justice opened his eyes. Miranda bent over him, human again, dressed in jeans and a T-shirt instead of blood-smeared armor. Fading magical sparks still lit her eyes, a remnant of the transformation. "Justice!" she breathed. "Oh, God, Bill, you did it! You shifted!"

It was the first time she'd ever called him by his first name.

Before he could yell the question boiling in his furious brain—What the hell did you think you were doing?—her mouth covered his, fierce and hot and sweet.

He froze, astonished as a fifteen-year-old getting his first kiss from his first crush. *God, her lips are soft.*

His arms swept up to wrap around her and drag her close. He wore nothing but the jeans he'd had on when the morning began, and he moaned against her mouth. She felt just as good as he'd always thought she would. She was tall and slender, and her breasts, full and lush, pressed against his bare chest.

He could get drunk on the taste of Miranda. Licking tenderly at her lips, Justice tugged the plump lower one between his teeth, and slid his tongue deep for a slow, swirling sample. It made him imagine the flavor of more erogenous places, and he remembered the way she'd looked, naked and ablaze with magic. "You taste like an April thunderstorm," he murmured against her mouth. "Ozone and raindrops."

She drew away, her gaze suddenly somber. "And you taste like blood."

Miranda slid off him and rose to her feet, then reached down to help him up with effortless Direkind strength. He staggered, utterly drained.

Glancing down, he took stock of his body. The lethal punctures had vanished. The only sign of his near-fatal injury was the pool of blood that surrounded their feet. *God, I need a bath . . .*

"It worked." Miranda smiled wearily up at him. "I got you to Shift."

Which reminded him. "And you damned near killed yourself in the process. What the fuck did you think you were doing?"

She gave him a long, steady look. "Saving your life, Bill." Turning on one booted heel, she stalked off. "Let's go find the others."

SIX

Ungrateful bastard. Miranda strode toward the DCN building, pointedly ignoring her bodyguard. *Damned near killed
myself bringing him back from the dead, and all he can do
is bitch.*

And kiss.

That *had* been one hell of a kiss. His mouth had moved
on hers with such skill, she'd found herself wondering what
else he could do with it.

Not that she intended to find out. Despite her momen-
tary joy at saving his ass, Bill Justice was still an Alpha
Werewolf. A fact she'd do well to remember.

Though he had saved her from being eaten by Warlock
in the guise of that damned monster of his . . .

Yeah, and I saved him back, Miranda told herself
staunchly. *We're even.*

Not even close, her conscience retorted. *He almost
ended up* eaten.

Shut up, dammit.

When they reached the DCN Center, they found Tristan

leaning against a light pole, his armored arms wrapped around Belle.

Conal and his sisters stood nearby over the body of that poor woman Super Chicken had murdered. They were talking to an older lady Miranda didn't recognize.

Despite the two-inch heels on her boots, the newcomer appeared less than five feet tall. Middle-aged, perhaps twenty pounds overweight, she wore blue jeans and a tight sweater that called attention to her impressive bust line. Her straight, fine hair fell past her hips, dyed a shade of neon green so vivid, it clashed with Aislyn's violet bob.

Adding to the rainbow effect, Conal's huge red bird perched on his shoulder, its flaming tail spilling down his back. Aislyn cuddled the fat white cat with the Southern accent as Branwyn absently stroked Fin's head. All six of them—Sidhe and familiar alike—watched the strange woman with obvious awe.

Who the hell is that?

The two Magekind agents turned as Miranda and Justice joined them.

"There you are. You had me worried, Fuzzball." Tristan slapped Justice lightly on the shoulder. "But Belle swore Miranda would get you to Shift. And as usual, she was right."

"I don't suppose you killed Super Chicken," Miranda asked.

"No. Ended up chasing the furry bastard halfway across Atlanta, though." Tristan grimaced in disgust. "He gave us the slip."

"We were about to gate back to help you when I sensed you Shift." Belle gave Miranda a wicked little grin. "Somehow I got the feeling you wouldn't appreciate being interrupted."

Feeling her cheeks go hot in a redhead's blush, Miranda gestured toward the stranger with Conal and his sisters. "What's going on? Who's the human?" She pitched her voice too low for the newcomer to hear; the woman didn't give off even a whiff of power.

Until she turned and *looked* at them. The raw magic in her gaze seemed to burn right into Miranda's brain.

Whatever else she is, that *is definitely not human. She's even more powerful than Warlock.*

Panic blasted Miranda as the strange woman's gaze reduced her to the frozen immobility of a rabbit cowering in a hawk's shadow. She could barely breathe as every instinct howled in incoherent animal panic.

But as she fought to keep the terror from her face, a wave of magic rolled through her consciousness, warm and compassionate as a mother's touch. The fear melted away like ice in the heat of August.

Miranda jolted back to full awareness with small, warm hands cupping her face. Blinking, she focused on the woman who was suddenly inches away, holding her in a kind, maternal gaze.

Nobody would call her pretty. There was too much strength in the strong-boned features, too many years in the crow's-feet around those iridescent eyes. Yet somehow she had a wild kind of beauty, like sunrise over the face of the desert.

Miranda swallowed. Her throat felt raw, as if from unvoiced screams. "Why the hell did I think you were human?"

"Because I chose to seem so." Her voice was surprisingly deep, with a curious accent Miranda didn't recognize, faintly Gaelic, with a trace of French slur. The woman shrugged, the gesture carelessly eloquent. "Glamor is a skill I've had need of, on this world of mortals."

Miranda knew she didn't mean glamor in the sense of modern celebrity, but in the original meaning of the word: a spell to make one thing look like another.

Conal dipped his head in a gesture very close to a bow. "Maeve, this is Miranda Drake, the woman we told you about."

"Yes, I know." She shot him a glance laced with some impatience, before turning back to Miranda. "I am Maeve. Some call me the Mother of Fairies."

And I just acted like a total fool, Miranda thought, feeling her cheeks heat with scalding shame. *She'll never help us now.* "It's . . . ah . . . good to meet you."

"Ah, child, play no such games with me." Maeve's surprisingly callused hands fell away from Miranda's face and gave her shoulder a comforting pat. "Though I suppose it's no surprise you feel the need. That fool father of yours did his best to break you, didn't he?"

"And evidently he succeeded," Miranda muttered, frustrated at her own cluelessness. She promptly cursed herself for revealing weakness to this fairy . . . queen? blacksmith? goddess? She wasn't just Sidhe; Miranda had met purebloods, and they had not one tenth Maeve's power.

"No. No, he didn't break you, my dear." Inhuman eyes probed hers delicately. "The most he managed was a bend here and there. Apparently he has forgotten that the beat of the hammer in the flame's heart only strengthens a good blade. As to his other dubious gifts, we'll attend to them in time."

Miranda eyed her cautiously. "What gifts?"

"Patience, child." She'd turned her attention to Justice, who hovered protectively at Miranda's shoulder. "Now, as to you, my wolf . . ." Maeve's gaze took on that ferocious intensity again as she stared deeply into his ebony eyes.

Justice shifted under her stare, and muscle rolled in his broad shoulders as if he struggled with some aggressive instinct. Being the habitual protector he was, he was probably acutely aware that this lethal being stood a foot and a half shorter than he did. She was also female and at least old enough to be his mother. Most likely she was a great deal older than that. All of which added up to someone he could not take a swing at, though from the look on his face, he didn't care for her aggressive gaze.

Miranda suddenly remembered Daliya's prophecy: *She waits in her forge for the hero wolf to come for Merlin's Blade. Then will the Hunter Prince be free—then will he rule in bloody vengeance or bend his knee to his spirit's feral king.*

But what the fuck did all that *mean*?

"Ahhh," Maeve breathed. "You're no weak one, are you? But how will it end? That depends on just how strong you really are." She turned away. "Come to my forge at midnight on the morrow," she added to Miranda, as Conal fell in behind her, like a courtier attending a queen. "The moon will be high and full then. A good time for such doings."

"But I have no idea where your forge is," Miranda protested.

"I just told you, child." With a wave of a ringed hand, the Sidhe goddess crouched beside the woman's mangled corpse. "And now, you poor child, let's see what you have to say." With that, she touched a blunt finger to the pool of cold blood.

Maeve's eyes drifted closed, as she swayed over the corpse. "She was Vela Greer, a waitress at Mr. Pizza there round the corner."

Miranda straightened and shot a look at Justice. Maeve spoke with a voice that was suddenly completely different from the low Celtic music of a moment earlier. Her voice was higher now, her accent a slow Southern drawl. A chill skated down Miranda's spine at the uncomfortable conviction she was hearing the voice of a dead woman.

"She'd just finished her shift and wanted to get home to her babies," Maeve continued. "Mama was watchin' them, and she didn't like to impose too long." Her lip curled, and her voice took on a deadly hiss. "That's when Warlock's Beast came outta the dark like somethin' out of a horror movie. Vela's last thought was of her two babies, Carlos and Nala. Only three and four, brown-eyed darlin's. Vela'll never see them grow up, and they won't have a mama anymore. 'Cause of that *bastard*."

The Sidhe stood, all but leaping to her feet as she broke the magical connection she'd formed with the blood. She turned away, blinking tears from her iridescent eyes.

The goddess cries, Miranda thought, discovering some comfort in the idea. *You're more human than I'd thought.*

Conal frowned. "What will become of her children?"

Maeve shrugged and turned to pace a circle around the splattered puddle of drying blood, head down, concentrating on whatever message she drew from it. Her voice was back to normal now. "Their fathers have moved on to other women. And in any case, neither of them is suitable for the task. It will have to be Vela's mother, Charlene." Her eyes slid out of focus for a moment. "She worries why her daughter is late, when she'd have normally been home an hour past." Maeve shook herself and looked up at Conal. "Providing for the girls will be no easy task. Charlene will have to work, of course; children need food and clothing, and what government aid she'll receive wouldn't keep a cat in cat food."

"She'll have whatever they need." Conal stared down at the body, his strong jaw taking on a determined jut. "She's about to discover a wealthy relative has named her in a generous will."

Maeve arched one green eyebrow. Miranda was starting to wonder if the color was natural after all. "How fortunate for her."

"If you want to call it that." His fists opened and closed in an unconscious gesture that shouted of rage. "Vela Greer shouldn't have ended her life like this. This was not her war. Her children shouldn't suffer because she happened to walk by my building when a monster came hunting me and mine."

"And your security guards?" The question held an elaborately casual note, as if Maeve tested him. "The Beast killed two of them as well, did he not?"

He raked a hand through his dark hair in an unconscious gesture, pulling it free of its neat tail to straggle around his face in disordered curls. "They were both good men. I'm not looking forward to breaking the news to Amilo's partner and Daren's wife. Sheila and Daren's son Gabe is only seven." Conal sighed. "At least he still has his mother, and the insurance policy I maintain for my people is generous enough to take care of their needs."

Belle frowned. "But what cover story are you going to

use? 'They were eaten by a dinosaur' is not the kind of thing you put in a police report."

"Perhaps a drive-by," Maeve suggested, the modern jargon sounding odd spoken in that curiously ancient accent. "The police will investigate, of course, but there'll be nothing to find." She flicked her fingers. Vela's body was engulfed in a cloud of swirling green fireflies. When they vanished, the body was whole again, a plump, pretty woman whose expression was oddly serene. She wore jeans and a red knit shirt with the restaurant's flying pizza logo on one breast. The huge blood splatter that had surrounded her had vanished. Her only apparent injury was a gunshot wound in the temple.

Belle blinked. "That's impressive. I've cleaned up bodies with magic, but conjuring the upper half of someone you've never even seen . . ."

"Her blood told me how she should appear." The Sidhe contemplated her work with a certain grim satisfaction. "And this will haunt her children less than the truth. They will be left with a bitter mystery, but there is no help for that."

"Warlock has a lot to account for." Conal glanced at Tristan. "I'll give you whatever help I can. Somebody needs to stop that bastard before he makes any more orphans."

Andrew Vance made a very good spy. He'd Shifted to human formed and doubled back, wrapped in a shielding field so thick, not even the Sidhe goddess sensed he stood fifteen feet away. He'd even taken the extra precaution of standing behind a Dumpster, since the spell wouldn't stop the Slut's lover from seeing him.

This was a very big risk. If the wind shifted and the werewolves scented him, he was a dead man. Given that blazing power signature, the goddess could burn him to a cinder with one flick of her fingers. He wouldn't have a prayer of defending himself; she was far beyond his power class.

Christ, what an utter goat fuck this little adventure had been. The General had ordered him to kill his whoring daughter and her lover before they could fulfill this prophecy of theirs. Which he'd at first thought so ludicrous, Vance had wondered why Warlock was worried.

Then the goddess arrived, and suddenly the whole thing seemed a lot more believable—and dangerous.

To make matters worse, Vance had failed. Failed despite the spell Warlock had laid on the Slut, designed to make her freeze in terror the moment she heard her father's voice. That crucial instant should have been all the opening Vance needed to punish her treachery in the most agonizing way possible. Just as she deserved.

He'd so looked forward to her screams as he ate her alive, one bloody bite at a time. Feasting on her meat and magic. He'd even killed the three humans to determine the best technique to use when grabbing a victim.

He'd loved every minute of those kills. The sense of power he'd felt when he'd fallen on that stupid female had been particularly exhilarating.

He couldn't wait to do the same thing to the Slut.

At first, everything had gone precisely as planned. Miranda had frozen just as Warlock had predicted. But before Vance could finish her, her fucking ex-cop lover had leaped to the bitch's rescue. You'd think he had a cape and a big red S, the way he'd heroically knocked her out of the way.

So Vance had taken a big, juicy bite of hero instead, enjoying the crunch of bone and the taste of the bastard's magic.

That should have been that for the cop, but the Slut was a lot more resilient than Vance had expected. Her spell had cut right through his shield, and her spear thrust had damned near killed him. If he hadn't jerked aside a crucial inch, she'd have driven it right through his heart. Vance would have been dead before his massive corpse hit the ground.

Instead, Warlock was going to skin him like a rabbit for his failure, one flaming whip stroke at a time.

Unless he managed to come back with something useful.

So he flicked his wolf ears forward and listened hard, keeping his magical shield wrapped as close as a blanket on an icy night.

So the Sidhe commanded the Slut and the werewolf to meet her at her forge. Wherever the hell that was; Vance had hoped she'd actually mention a location, but she was apparently a bit too paranoid for that.

Huh. So this goddess intended to stick her nose into Warlock's business. The General wouldn't like that. Not at all.

And Warlock being Warlock, he'd find a way to make the Sidhe goddess pay.

Arthur Pendragon was pissed.

The Once and Future King glowered down at the iPad screen, watching the video of Daliya delivering her prophecy. He obviously didn't like what he saw.

He was not a particularly tall man, though his muscled build gave the impression he was bigger than he was. A black goatee framed the angry line of his mouth, and his dark eyes were narrowed in his broad, square-jawed face. His hair curled to his broad shoulders, currently clad in a Batman T-shirt.

Arthur did like to fly his geek flag.

Justice forked up a bite of the thick steak and chewed, eyes half-closed in pleasure. Guinevere was one hell of a cook. Which was a good thing, since he was starving. Between Shifting so many times and fighting that damned Beast, he could have eaten a buffalo.

Ass first.

When Tristan had contacted Arthur to brief him on the night's events, he'd ordered them all to gather at the Pendragon home. Gwen being Gwen, she'd promptly whipped up dinner.

Now Justice, Miranda, Belle, Morgana, and their hostess were demolishing rib eyes, salads, and crusty brown bread, still steaming gently from the oven.

Arthur and Tristan had already killed most of a bottle of Gwen's donated blood; apparently Justice wasn't the only one who was hungry.

"What the flying fuck does all that mean?" Arthur growled, pushing away from the table with a shove. He rose and began to pace the dining room. "Who the hell is this Hunter Prince? What has he got to do with this Merlin's Blade? Is it another Excalibur?"

Tristan poured himself another glass. "'The Hunter Prince' could refer to Warlock."

"No, because it says 'then will the Hunter Prince be free,'" Belle reminded him. "Warlock's obviously way too free right now."

"God knows I'd love to put the bastard in a cage," Arthur muttered.

"Then there's the bit about 'his spirit's feral king.'" Justice cut another bite of his steak with a single hard stroke of his knife. "Sounds like this king is the one who'll keep the Hunter Prince from ruling in bloody vengeance. Since bloody vengeance does not sound like fun to me, we're going to need the king. Question is, how do we find him before midnight tomorrow, when Miranda and I are supposed to meet with Maeve?"

"Maybe *you're* the feral king," Morgana suggested. She looked more than a little like her half-brother, Arthur, with the same aquiline nose and broad cheekbones, though the blunt strength of his features was softened into beauty by her more delicate bone structure. For once she was dressed casually—her tastes usually ran to suits with very short skirts in primary colors. Tonight she wore a silky scarlet top with a deep V neckline framing her bountiful cleavage. Her black jeans were tight enough to hug the curves of her hips. Scarlet stiletto heels made her long legs look even longer, giving her the look of a pop star instead of the most powerful witch in Avalon.

Morgana's gaze flicked to Justice, measuring the width

of his shoulders with obvious approval. She smiled at him with lips painted the precise red of her high heels. "You're obviously the hero wolf."

Justice cleared his throat and looked away. "Which brings up a good point." He glanced at Miranda, sitting beside him at the table, and blinked once in surprise. She was glaring at Morgana, her gaze hot with warning. *What the hell is that about?*

Miranda looked at him, realized he'd caught her snarling, and glanced quickly away, a flush rising to her cheeks.

He dragged his attention back to the topic at hand. "Why give the Blade to me instead of Arthur? I'm just an unemployed werewolf. And I'm sure as hell not a 'master of darkness.'"

"I, on the other hand," Miranda said, raising her glass of Riesling as if in a mocking toast, "am apparently the daughter of evil. Go, me." She drained the wine in one long swallow.

"Well, you've got to admit 'evil' is a pretty good description of Warlock," Justice pointed out.

"What does Grim say about all this?" Belle asked Arthur.

Merlin's grimoire was an enchanted book, a magical cross between the Library of Congress and a Cray supercomputer. He also talked, with an impressive intelligence that made him an invaluable resource when it came to any subject, no matter how esoteric.

"Not much. Grim's been damned weird through this whole werewolf thing." Arthur pivoted to pace another circuit of the room. "Apparently Merlin ordered him not to tell us a damned thing about the wolves, on the grounds that if we knew about them, we might take them out to keep them from interfering with whatever 'evil plot' I might have in mind." He shook his head in disbelief. "All these years, and he never mentioned them. Even with everything Warlock's done, all he'll say is that Merlin 'made arrangements,' whatever the hell that means."

"Maybe this Mother of Fairies is part of those arrangements," Gwen pointed out as she walked in with a plate of brownies. She put the platter down in the center of the table as the smell of chocolate filled the air. Everyone capable of eating grabbed one. She looked at her husband. "So don't mention Warlock at all. Ask him about Maeve and the Donovans, not to mention their little talking zoo. What are all these Sidhe doing on Mortal Earth? And what's with this Merlin's Blade? Why have we never heard of it?"

"It's obviously got some kind of magic attached to it," Morgana said thoughtfully. "Especially if it's the key to killing Warlock."

Miranda tore a chunk of brown bread off the loaf and began to spread butter on it, frowning. "That part about folding enchanted steel into blades and filling them with the souls of lost gods . . ." She took a bite, chewed thoughtfully, and swallowed. "Could this Hunter Prince be *inside* Merlin's Blade?"

"Of course." Arthur pivoted to stare at her, one dark brow lifted in interest. "Kel was trapped in Gawain's sword for fifteen centuries. They only got him out a couple of years ago."

"Which would explain the part about freeing this prince." Morgana contemplated the depths of her glass a moment. "On the other hand, if he's in the blade and we free him, we may end up in a worse mess than we're in now."

"And if that's not a chilling thought, I don't know what is," Arthur agreed. He gave Justice a tight, humorless smile. "It sounds like you're going to have to control this Hunter Prince if we don't want him 'ruling in bloody vengeance.'"

Justice damn near choked on his steak. "Arthur, I'm just an ex-cop. What the fuck am I supposed to do against a god, or whatever the hell he is? The only magic I can do is turning into a werewolf."

"You're also immune to magic," Miranda pointed out thoughtfully. "Even if he is a god, he's going to have a hard time doing anything to you."

"I wish we could send a witch with these two to visit this forge," Morgana said, leaning back in her chair. "Not to mention a couple vampire knights. Even up the odds a bit."

"Maeve told me she didn't want Magekind accompanying the wolves," Tristan told her.

"And considering the power I sensed in that woman, we don't want to piss her off. She'd make a very bad enemy." Belle bit into a steaming brownie and moaned in delight. "God, Gwen, these are good. I want the recipe."

"Only if you tell me how to make that lemon torte you served at the last Majae dinner. Talk about an orgasm on a plate . . ." She looked at her husband and grinned. "Well, maybe not quite an orgasm, but it was pretty damned good."

As the conversation swung to food, Justice pushed back from the table. Thinking about what he might face with Merlin's Blade had killed his appetite.

If they do fail, humanity will drown in blood under the white wolf's heel, and the crows will feast.

No pressure, though. Fuck.

Miranda shot another look at Justice from the corner of one eye as they walked back to her cottage. He looked so grim, she knew he was thinking about Maeve's coming test. Her gaze traced the straight line of his nose and the muscle flexing in his broad jaw, skipped to the curve of his lower lip and lingered. She was far too aware of the bulge of his pectorals against the soft cotton of the T-shirt she'd conjured for him.

She wanted to lay her hands on that hard satin flesh and feel his heart thudding hard under her fingers. She wanted to see his cock jut from his tight abdomen in a length of rosy lust, thick and veined, its round mushroom cap dewed with a gemstone drop of arousal.

Need clenched her belly as yearning flooded her blood. It had been months since she'd made love, and that had been to the most skinny, hapless human male she could find. Her fear had demanded a harmless partner, but her Dire Wolf body craved Alpha male strength.

Justice was nobody's idea of harmless, but he was definitely Alpha. Strong, decisive, fearless.

Big.

There was raw power in all that hard muscle, greater than she could claim even in Dire Wolf form.

He could hurt me if he wanted to, her fear whispered. *He could lay me open with his claws just the way Gerald did Mom.*

Images of that last lethal argument shot through Miranda's mind. Her stepfather's clawed hand knocking Joelle's small body flying. The horrific crunch as her mother hit the wall and slid to the floor, her head canted to the side like a sunflower on a broken stem.

Miranda's consciousness flooded with the memory of Gerald's snarling face as he charged, intent on ending her rebellion once and for all, smug in his certainty that she'd be easy prey.

She remembered the solid weight of the conjured sword filling her hand, the heavy jolt as it rammed into her stepfather's chest. Remembered watching the vicious life bleed from his eyes.

Gerald's gone, Miranda told herself. *He can't hurt me again.* She was no longer the victim Warlock had raised her to be. She'd proven her stubborn strength, first against a would-be rapist sent by Warlock, then again when she'd killed Gerald.

Justice is a hell of a lot bigger than Gerald, her treacherous fear whispered. *He knows what to do in a fight. If he wanted to hurt me . . .*

But he doesn't, she told herself firmly. *For God's sake, he risked getting* eaten *to save me. That's not the kind of thing an abuser does.*

But you've never defied him, the fear breathed. *Just wait until you disobey. The claws'll come out then. You'll discover he's just another Alpha, no more a hero than Gerald. Or Warlock, for all the ballads about his courage.*

Alphas kill. And Justice is Alpha.

But as Miranda wrestled years of engrained paranoia, her nostrils flared, drinking in the rich masculinity of his scent. Her gaze slipped down to the tight, working muscles of his ass, before tracking up his strong torso to round biceps easily the size of her head.

Her Dire Wolf body didn't give a damn about her fear. It only knew Justice called to her, male to female, cock to cunt, raw and blunt and fierce with elemental strength. Justice was everything her body craved—as he'd proven with that luscious, toe-curling kiss.

If her fear would let her have him, Alpha male dominance and all.

SEVEN

"What if I fuck up?"

Jolting in surprise, Miranda stared at Justice. It was the first time he'd spoken on the walk back. They'd almost reached her neat little two-story stone cottage, its stained glass windows glowing in the dim predawn light. "What?"

He headed across the neatly trimmed yard, his strides long, his dark gaze fixed on the distance. "What if I fail Maeve's test? What if she decides I don't deserve this magic blade?"

She frowned, trying to switch mental gears from dithering about his possibly hostile strength. "You're not going to fail Maeve's test."

"How do you know that?" He paused beneath the spreading arms of a magnolia and turned to face her, his gaze haunted. "We don't even know what kind of test it's going to be. I damned near memorized that prophecy, and I still can't figure out what the hell it's talking about."

"You're strong, Justice." Miranda met his gaze without flinching. Whatever her doubts about his capacity for violence, she had confidence in his strength. "Whether it's

Maeve or this Hunter Prince, you can handle whatever they throw at you."

He stared down at her for a crackling instant. Miranda felt the impact of his desperate gaze all the way to her toes.

She saw his self-doubt became abrupt, burning need. Big hands shot out and closed around her upper arms, hauling her onto her toes. His mouth covered hers, devouring, hot, and deliciously slick.

Oh, my God, his lips are every bit as soft as I remember.
And then she couldn't think anything at all.

His body crushed into hers without the armor to keep them apart. Broad, firm muscle flexed under soft cotton, arms wrapping around her in a powerful grip that dragged her close and drowned her in hot male animal need. His tongue stroked between her lips, drugging her with the taste of masculine hunger and Dire Wolf magic.

The blend of wild wolf heat and pure male heat hit her brain like a shot of Kentucky bourbon in strong black coffee. It jolted and dizzied, making the world swim and stealing her will to resist.

As if sensing that weakness, he swooped down and hooked one hand behind her knees, gathering her into his arms as if she weighed no more than a child. Carrying her toward the cottage, Justice stared down into her eyes, gaze hot with hungry need. When his foot hit the front step, she sent a wave of magic ahead of them. The door banged open and he swept her inside like something out of a fairy tale.

Miranda had quit believing in fairy tales when she was four years old—the day she'd realized her magical daddy was more devil dog than Prince Charming. But God, there was a different kind of magic in Justice's skillful mouth and strong, steady grip, and she let herself believe.

For the moment.

Justice kissed Miranda, losing himself in the velvety warmth of her lips, the curl and flick of her wet little tongue, her teeth tugging his lip in hungry demand. Her body felt warm in the cradle of his arms, deliciously soft in all the perfect places, firm and strong in others. Her scent flooded his head, sensual musk and the fresh green tang of deep forest. All of it spelled Direkind female to his growling libido.

His sexual need had grown stronger, darker, since he'd become a werewolf three years ago, and Miranda brought that hunger to quivering attention. But then, she could have aroused a plaster saint in a church niche with those soft, soft lips . . .

He wasn't sure he'd survive Maeve's test tomorrow. He wanted Miranda *now*.

Justice tore himself away from her mouth just long enough to scan the house for a likely place to seduce her. He knew damned well that if he waited too long, she'd start thinking about all the reasons this was a bad idea. He needed his hands and mouth on her *now* if he meant to keep them there.

Off to the left of the foyer lay the living room, with its fireplace and the semicircular conversation pit that curved around it. He carried her into the room and down the steps into the pit, where jewel-tone pillows lay in a tempting heap.

Lowering her into that soft, inviting nest, he shuddered at the heat flooding his cock. "God, I want you." He ached to see that pretty body spread for him in long-legged, exquisite nudity. "I've been craving you for weeks."

But as he reached for the hem of her T-shirt, he met her gaze. And froze.

She watched him as she lay sprawled across the pillows, her copper hair spilling in bright curls around her head. Her chest rose and fell in the quick rhythms of arousal, yet a trace of fear glittered in her magical eyes.

She's afraid of me? God, why? He would never hurt any woman, much less her. Hell, he'd almost ended up dino-chow for her.

I don't know what you're thinking, sweetheart, but I'm damned if you're going to think it for long.

Justice rose to his feet, grabbed the hem of his black T-shirt, and dragged it off over his head. Her eyes widened, the shadow of fear vanishing into surprised arousal. The tip of her pink tongue flicked over her lips.

He concealed a smile of satisfaction. During his human days, he'd logged a lot of hours running and lifting weights, but not out of the usual gym-rat vanity. For a cop, building strength and muscle was a survival strategy. If you got into a chase or a fight with some asshole, you wanted to make damn sure you won. Becoming a werewolf had only added to the size and density of the muscle he'd worked for years to build.

Judging from her dilating eyes, Miranda approved of the view.

His cock bucked against the fly of his jeans. Justice reached for his belt, unbuckling it with a metallic jangle. The zipper of his jeans whispered, erotically loud to his wolf senses.

Toeing off his running shoes, he caught the waistbands of both jeans and cotton boxers, to drag them down his thighs in one ruthless motion. Stepping free of the tangle of fabric, he kicked them away and straightened. His erection jutted in an unapologetic demonstration of his ferocious lust.

Then he simply stood there, letting her look as a bead of sweat ran down his spine.

By stripping first, he'd put all the power in her hands. Justice was good at reading people—another cop skill—and he knew if he didn't give Miranda this moment of control, she'd never trust him.

Jesus, the men she knew before me must have been real bastards.

Miranda stared at him in helpless, aroused amazement. Alphas didn't *do* this—didn't display themselves to a woman in silent offering, letting her make the choice. They seduced, they demanded, they overwhelmed with sheer

erotic skill. Just as Justice had been doing from the minute
he'd grabbed her shoulders.

When he'd put her down on the pillows, she'd figured
she was in for a dominance fuck designed to put her in her
place: that of a female who knew who her master was, and
obeyed accordingly. That realization had blasted an icy
flash of fear through her veins.

But now he stood there, magnificent in his nudity, and
waited. Waited to find out if she wanted him.

As if she could do anything else. Justice was armored in
delicious male muscle from wide shoulders to tight waist,
down long runner's legs to the big feet he'd planted wide.
Yet his build wasn't overdone, like some steroid-shooting
professional gorilla. Justice had a knife-fighter's body, the
perfect balance between mass, agility, and speed. Yet
despite his obvious potential for aggression, his powerful
hands hung open and easy, not balled in threatening fists.
And his cock . . .

Sweet Mother Mary.

It thrust from his furred groin, lust giving it a slight
upward angle despite its considerable length, rosy and
thick from the heart-shaped head to the broad base and
heavy balls. She felt a rush of heat deep in her belly as she
imagined him pumping it in and out of her with all the
power of that muscular ass.

Miranda licked her lips and lifted her eyes from that
meaty shaft. And got caught in his hungry black gaze as he
stared at her as if she was everything he'd ever wanted in a
woman.

Nothing like the Alpha Warlock had sent to breed her. That
one's stare had reduced her to the hole between her thighs.
He'd meant to rape her. Threatened to beat her mother if she
resisted.

So she'd killed him because Joelle Drake had been
beaten enough. Not that it had done any good. Her mother
was dead in less than a week. And having killed her murdering stepfather, Miranda had been forced to go on the run.

Two nights later in some one-stoplight town, she'd

picked up a twenty-year-old human in a bar, just to make sure her first time wasn't at the hands of one of Warlock's thugs. The human had been only four years younger than she was, but he'd seemed a boy to her. Yet he'd been sweet and surprisingly tender despite his clumsy inexperience, and Miranda had decided on the spot to stick to human lovers. She'd sworn then that no werewolf would ever occupy her bed.

But here was Justice, looking at her with those dark, hot, patient eyes. And waiting.

Miranda caught the hem of her T-shirt and pulled it off over her head.

As she tossed the shirt aside, he caught his breath, freezing as he stared at the round curves of her breasts cupped in her bra's black lace. The wolf heat in Justice's eyes should have made her feel like a mouse trapped under a cat's paw. Instead she felt powerful—and more profoundly female than she'd ever been in her life.

The front clasp sprang open under her fingers, and Miranda shrugged the bra off with a roll of her shoulders.

His tongue flicked over his full lower lip.

She dragged her boots off and threw them one by one across the room. They landed on the hardwood floor with a double thump and skidding clatter.

Justice's gaze remained locked on hers. Waiting.

Miranda tugged off her socks and sent them flying over the semicircular couch. Her heart hammered. Her zipper hissed. His powerful shoulders coiled. She took her time pulling off her jeans, adding some gratuitous hip wiggle just to make a muscle twitch in his square jaw. The jeans sailed after the socks. Miranda rolled to her feet, watching him watch her as she slowly slid the thin black silk panties down her thighs. Spinning it out, making them both wait.

She straightened, toed the panties aside, and stepped up to him, as naked as he was. Justice still didn't move, though those big hands had coiled into fists, as if he was fighting the need to grab and take.

He was six-three, maybe six-four, tall enough that she

had to tilt her head to meet his gaze. The wolf inside him flickered deep in his eyes, its ferocity caged by iron control.

That control gave her the courage to touch his chest, run her fingers over the curves and hollows of firm muscle under warm, tanned skin. His dark chest hair felt as soft and fine as fur. His heart thumped against her fingertips in a drumbeat of sexual need.

God, he was big. Even bigger than her stepfather . . .

Gerald towered over her in Dire Wolf form, his clawed hand drawn back, preparing to kill her the same way he'd killed her mother . . .

The memory disappeared back into the depths of her mind like a hit-and-run eighteen-wheeler, leaving Miranda dazed in its wake. *What the fuck am I doing? Justice is an Alpha Dire Wolf, just like Gerald. He . . .*

Justice lowered his head. Before she could obey a howling instinct to jerk away, his mouth touched hers, tender, soft, a bare brush of lip on lip.

Somehow, she found herself kissing him back.

Justice didn't grab her, didn't shove himself against her to make her aware of how he dwarfed her with all that muscle. Only his lips touched hers, the contact tender, questioning, reassuring. He'd carefully tamped his hunger down, though she could smell it in his scent, a dark male perfume growing stronger with every second.

Inside her soul, her werewolf nature stilled, protective rage draining. *Justice won't hurt me.*

A thought flashed through Miranda's mind, hard and sharp as a blade: *I can let Warlock and his thugs make a sexual cripple out of me, or I can prove I'm not a victim.*

She opened her mouth and let Justice in.

His tongue swirled around hers in sweet temptation, silently inviting her to play. She pursued it back into his mouth, letting his mint-and-male taste flood her brain and drown her ghosts. Passion began to heat her blood like a pot slowly coming to a boil.

Warm fingers discovered the stiff peak of one breast

and traced a tempting circle over the sensitive nipple. Pleasure flowed through her, lazy as a creek of poured honey. And just as sweet.

Miranda leaned into Justice with a soft, helpless little moan. And tried not to think about all the reasons this was a really bad idea.

Miranda's breast filled his hand like a sun-warmed peach, round and velvet-soft. Her nipple thrust into his fingers as her body swayed against his, tempting, long firm thighs brushing his as she kissed him back, licking and tasting. *Sweet. God, so sweet.*

His wolf wanted to pin her down and ride her hard, bucking into her as she knelt on all fours, submissive to his male beast, yet as juicy and slick as that peach.

But she still smelled of fear. The faint acrid tang of it lay under the sweet musk of need like polluting smoke. If he yielded to his wolf's instinct to dominate, the fear would build and build until it choked her desire to nothing.

So Justice collared his wolf and ignored its growls, his fingers careful as he worked to build need into passion. He stroked and teased her nipples into stiff demand with one hand even as the other drifted along the fine curves of her ribs, down the long, sweet dip of her waist to the rise of one hip. Tracing the shifting muscles in her round runner's ass with his nostrils flared wide, drawing in her scent, tasting it in his mouth, gauging the transformation of desire into lust.

Miranda's lust was what he wanted. Craved. Hot, animal, mindless, purified of fear and doubt so he could shoot her into orgasm like a bottle rocket into the night.

He drew back to read her hunger. A spark burst blue in the depths of her eyes, magic freed by heat. "Do you want to lie down?" he asked softly.

She blinked, and the tip of her tongue came out and touched her lip in a quick, hot little gesture. Need. Wanting. "All right."

Good. He'd begun to reach her.

Miranda walked to the pile of pillows, leading the way. Choosing to love him.

His eyes drifted down without his intention, taking in the long sweep of her back down to the sweet heart shape of her ass. Her legs were endless. His cock kicked upward as raw lust surged through him in a flooding jolt. His wolf growled deep. The sound rumbled from his throat.

She froze. Her head snapped around, eyes widening.

He shoved his wolf down out of his eyes and smiled at her. *I'm not going to hurt you, baby. I'd never hurt you. I don't do that.*

Something in his eyes calmed her, because she turned to face him and sank down onto the pillows. He dropped to his knees and pulled one of the pillows out from under her back.

Miranda frowned, bracing up on her elbows to watch him. "What are you doing?"

"I want you comfortable."

She helped him arrange the pile, positioning a huge square cushion under her body, piling the others around to support her arms and legs, sliding another under her hips to tilt it upward.

Justice had never been so *aware* of a woman. Her long, lithe body looked so lovely, all leg and smooth curves, her redhead's creamy skin a pale frame for the sweet fox-red fluff between those strong thighs. Her hair spilled around her head like a fiery copper halo, tumbling in thick curls over the pillows.

Her beautiful breasts tempted him, round as oranges, Celtic pale, their areoles pink, nipples darker, erect, round, and inviting as ripe cherries. *God, I want to taste her.*

His hand cupped one breast, and she stilled, eyeing him. "Sweet," he breathed, his thumb brushing the nipple back and forth. "You're so soft. So warm."

Justice lowered his head and took that little tip into his mouth, sucking gently until it hardened between his lips, inviting the tender rake of his teeth. Slowly, he moved his head, working the nipple between lips and tongue and teeth, varying the suction, first gentle, then hard, then gentle again.

His wolf shot him an image: Miranda on her hands and knees, that gorgeous ass lifted for him, submissive. The feel of her, tight and juicy, gripping his cock.

Foreplay was an alien concept to the wolf. To him, the chase should be enough to ready her. Once she accepted him, it was time to take her, driving dick into cunt until they both came.

No, he told it. *We're damned well not going to hurry her.* He could still smell fear, a faint bitterness souring the sweet musk of her need.

Justice was going to get rid of that ugly scent if it was the last thing he did. He wanted her wanting him with the same hot intensity he felt. *I'm not like those other bastards. You can trust me not to hurt you.*

So he cuddled her breasts in his hands, cupping, stroking. At last he felt her ease against him.

Miranda drew away. He managed to catch his wolf before it lunged for her.

Her eyes met his, and magic flashed in their depths like lightning in the clouds. Then she lay back on the pillows and lifted her arms to him.

She's still afraid, he reminded himself. And went into her tentative hold. Managed not to growl when he felt her tremble under him, all long, soft curves. So warm. So delicate.

How could anyone hurt her?

He felt hot, all hard muscle dusted with soft, tickling body hair that brushed her skin as he braced himself on his elbows so his weight didn't crush her.

As if it could. She was a werewolf. She could bench press his full weight. Yet he was treating her like a human. A woman who could expect—and receive—little human courtesies from her lover.

Justice bent his head to her breasts again, this time pleasuring the one he'd only caressed before. Little darts of heat shot through her as his teeth scraped over the hardening nipple, back and forth in arousing little rakes. She let herself loosen under him, muscles uncoiling with the realization that this one wouldn't hurt her.

Werewolf or not.

Justice braced on one elbow and used his free hand to stroke her as he made love to her breast. His big hand drifted over her skin, his palm tracing the line of her body, the delicate ripples of her ribs beneath the thin, sensitive flesh of her chest, the ticklish dip of her belly, the curve of her hip, the long sweep of her thigh.

She spread her legs, letting them part around his big body in silent invitation. Wanting to see how he'd touch her there.

But he didn't. Instead he continued those slow, gentle strokes, more like a man petting a cat than a wolf who wanted to fuck his way to a roaring climax.

Even her human lover hadn't been this careful, this sweet. Or, God knew, this skilled. Justice knew his way around a woman's body, knew just how to touch, how to use those long, warm fingers and that wicked mouth.

She slid her arms around him. His back felt so broad in her tentative hug, easily twice the width of hers, muscle lying in solid slabs that rolled and rippled under her palms as he moved so gently over her.

He could rip her apart with his werewolf strength, could beat her bloody even in human form. He could bite and claw. He could force her to do whatever he wanted.

But he won't.

Miranda blinked at the realization. Justice really *wasn't* like the others, Alpha werewolf or not. It wasn't an act. He knew she was wet—he'd be able to smell her heat just as she could smell his. Yes, he wanted her—the sharp tang of testosterone rolled off him, blended with his normal clean Dire Wolf scent of man and fur and forest.

Yet somehow he ignored the feral need to drive that meaty cock into her sex.

Justice was focused on *her*. Her arousal. Her pleasure. Even the human boy had been more interested in his own desires, doing just enough to get her hot so he could take her. Justice didn't have to work even *that* hard—she already wanted him, had wanted him for weeks now, even as she'd fought to ignore the attraction.

God, she was wet. She could smell the hot tang of her own arousal every time she took a breath, her musk blending with his. Experimenting, she slid a leg up the line of his hair-dusted thigh, caressing him with her body. He stiffened just slightly, but went on with his careful attentions to her breasts, pouring pleasure over her like a waterfall of delight.

Emboldened by his deliberate control, Miranda began to explore the body she'd admired with furtive interest for weeks.

Justice had always fascinated her. The shape of muscle lying under his warm, smooth skin, solid and thick as armor. His biceps rolled and jerked under her fingertips as she traced their round, warm contours. She looked down at the top of his head as he suckled her, admiring the dark gleam of his hair, curly, thick, and inviting.

After a moment's hesitation, she ran her fingers through his hair. It was surprisingly soft, more like silk than the coarser strands that curled on his chest. He didn't seem to notice, too focused on conjuring pleasure in her breasts with his sorcerer's tongue and teeth.

Miranda relaxed into the pillows and let the delight rise as her muscles finally loosened, no longer tensed to fight or run. No longer expecting him to inflict pain instead of pleasure.

Her wolf settled, knowing she was safe with William Justice.

Pleasure spun through her, endless velvet ribbons of it, conjured by Justice's magic.

At last he lifted his head and braced on one elbow, leaving her nipples standing hard and wet from his tongue. And looked down at her. Something in her face made wolf magic flare in his gaze, lust flashing across the dark irises like a lightning strike blazing across night-rolling clouds.

Miranda froze.

Justice lifted a hand toward her head, slowly, carefully. She jerked, and he hesitated before he touched her face. She managed not to flinch. His fingertips traced the arch of her brows, drifted down the rise and hollows of her cheekbones, found her mouth, brushed back and forth across her lips.

Pushing himself up with a flex of arms and thighs, he rose to kiss her. Slowly, asking permission to enter her mouth with gentle brushes of lip across lip. She opened for him. He sank against her with a soft moan edged in growl, slipping his tongue between her parted lips, tasting, swirling around her tongue, inviting her to kiss him back. So she did, closing her eyes to let the sensations of the kiss roll over her, absorbing the gentle warmth of his palm cupping her face.

His free hand slipped down between her thighs, brushed over the soft curls already damp with her heat. She caught her breath against his mouth as his fingers slipped between her vaginal lips, stroking up and down the length of them.

One finger slid inside her. A slow, testing stroke. She gasped, surprised at how wet she was. He groaned against her mouth.

He'll fuck me now. He'll lose control to his wolf and be on me.

His mouth opened wider over hers as he sank deeper into the kiss, letting his weight settle over hers as his tongue swirled around hers. In no hurry at all.

Lifting his head, Justice gazed into her face, studying her. Reading her gaze, gauging her arousal, his eyes dark, pupils huge with desire. Magic sparked in them, flashing like a swarm of fireflies as his lust called his power.

He lowered his head to her throat, his lips brushing over the beating vein, his tenderness calming the instinctive leap of fear at having his teeth so close to her jugular. He kissed his way down its throbbing length, stringing kisses between her collarbones, licking a trail between her breasts.

Down to the ticklish flesh of her belly, where he paused to nibble until she squirmed.

God, it felt good. He swirled his tongue in a teasing circle over her bellybutton. Miranda laughed, the kind of giddy sound any woman might make with her lover.

Victims don't laugh.

Justice went back to his erotic exploration, nibbling the jut of one hip bone, following its curve down to her thigh, then across to the triangle of soft hair between her legs.

Miranda caught her breath, this time in anticipation. She'd heard of this, but her young lover hadn't done it. Too busy seeing to his own pleasure.

Why had she thought that kid was so good? Was it only her wolf, craving any love at all?

But Justice *was* good. He licked down the top edge of her hair, following the soft little thatch to the plump curves of her labia. Tasted one of them with a long, lazy swipe of his tongue. Miranda twitched, waiting breathlessly for the sensation she'd only fantasized about.

Instead Justice caught the lip between his teeth and gave it a gentle nip, then licked it as if in tender apology.

At the bottom of the stroke, that wickedly clever tongue slid inside, finding her clit with unerring skill. The sensation burst inside her brain, all hot, shimmering pleasure.

Miranda inhaled as a bolt of raw lust shot through her. Her hands drifted down to tangle in his hair, unconsciously pressing him closer, silently begging for more.

EIGHT

He gave her exactly what she wanted. Licking back and forth between her labia, teasing first one side of her innermost lips, then the other, swirling and stroking the delicate, sensitive flesh.

Miranda squirmed helplessly on the pile of pillows, instinctively lifting one leg to rest a heel on his muscular ass, opening herself wider for him, the press of her foot urging him on.

He spread her sex with his fingers, still licking, until quivers jerked the muscles of her thighs. Her toes curled.

That clever tongue thrust inside her once, twice. She thought about his cock, about its demanding length and width. About how it would feel driving inside her. She moaned. "Justice. God, Justice."

"Yeah," he growled back. "You're so wet, so tight. I can barely get my tongue in you." He slid between her lips again, then retreated to swirl around her clit. Not quite touching it. Just tracing tempting little designs around the tiny nub.

Two fingers thrust into her sex as he flicked the tip of his tongue up and down her clit. His lips sealed over its eager jut, suckling gently at first, then harder and harder in time to the pumping rhythm of his fingers.

The orgasm exploded out of nowhere, fierce and bright and unexpected, shocking her into a scream of delight. Justice sucked more fiercely, fingers thrusting deep to touch some bundle of nerves she hadn't even known existed. The heat blinded her. She writhed in helpless pleasure as the climax thundered through her like a torrent.

When it passed, Miranda lay panting, helpless, one leg sprawled out to the side, the other still hooked over Justice's brawny ass.

He went right on licking her. Slowly. Up and down in thorough swipes, tender as a mother cat with a kitten. Miranda could only pant as inner muscles laced, readying for another orgasm.

Her wolf rose out of the depths of her brain, feral and growling, to drown her brain in wild instinct and stark, driving lust. Demanding to mate with this big werewolf male, this Alpha beast.

Miranda was on her hands and knees with no idea how she'd gotten there. "Fuck me." She didn't even recognize her own growling voice as she stared over her shoulder at him. "Fuck me now."

Astonishment widened Justice's eyes; he hadn't expected her wolf to surface. A flash of Mageverse lightning exploded in those black irises, and his own wolf filled them, all lust and feral heat. He growled back and rose onto his knees, moving into position behind her.

This time the deep rumble didn't frighten her.

Neither did the hard clamp of his hands as he gripped her ass. He promptly eased his hold as if fearful of hurting her. She watched over her shoulder as he positioned his cock between her slick lips. His thrust made her throw back her head with a cry that was damned near a howl.

Ramming right to the balls, Justice froze. Filling her perfectly, long, wide, stretching her almost to the point of pain.

Miranda had never felt anything so arousing.

Her wolf growled again, making her chest vibrate. "Fuck me!" She ground her ass back into his pelvis, then rocked forward, sliding along that endless length, gasping at the burning heat of it.

Justice rumbled back, caught her hips in both hands, and began to drive in hard, demanding strokes. Inner muscles clenched and released with every entry, every retreat, readying for another orgasm.

Her breasts danced as she rocked, fucking him as he fucked her, lost in instinct, in lust, in wolf. So close to animal that as her fingers curled into a pillow, her nails lengthened into claws. She wrestled the Shift back down and rolled her hips harder to the sound of flesh slapping flesh and the soft male growls of Justice and his wolf.

The scent of their mutual lust flooded her brain, raw sex blended with the earthy musk of fur and forest. He was as close to transforming as she was.

Justice rammed to his full length into her until his balls swung against her ass. Stuffing her full as he roared a lupine howl of pleasure. Coming hard, triggering her own climax as the pressure of his grinding hips on her sex gave her clit that last bit of stimulation.

Miranda screamed as the fierce clenching seized her belly, her sex, driving burning darts of pleasure up her spine right to her brain. Shuddering, she ground back on Will's cock, and came. And came.

And came.

The information Vance had risked his life for hadn't been enough.

Crack! Agony ripped across his back with the lash of Warlock's whip, a vicious, searing pain that tested his will against his body's animal panic. He clenched his jaws, forbidding himself to make a sound, trying to still even the involuntary flinch of his shoulders. He smelled burning flesh and knew the magic was branding him like a red-hot iron.

The relentless rhythm of the whip paused. Vance denied his traitor body's sense of relief, the hope that it was over, that Warlock was satisfied.

He wouldn't be. Not this soon.

"Are you trying to impress me?" the General snarled, his voice arctic cold. "Or just denying me the pleasure of listening to you scream?"

"I failed . . ." Vance broke off to clear his throat; he sounded hoarse, as if he'd voiced every one of the shrieks his abused body had demanded. Swallowing, he tried again. "I failed you. I didn't kill the Slut or her cop."

"No." The whip's bright lash struck the ground beneath his dangling feet with a savage buzzing crack of magical force. "She's a cunning little whore, isn't she?" The note of reluctant pride in Warlock's voice made Vance blink. "She's got far more power than any female should." The General snorted. "Never mind, I'll kill her myself."

Crack. The whip struck again, ripping so deep, Vance knew he was lucky to be a werewolf. Had he still been human, he would have been crippled for what little remained of his life, the muscles in his back eaten away until he would have been unable to breathe, much less lift his arms.

Another stroke, then another. Neither hurt as much as the ones that had gone before, probably because too many nerves had died to transmit the pain.

Warlock stopped. The magical bonds holding Vance in midair vanished, and he fell. He tried to brace for impact, only to discover his crippled body would no longer respond. His feet hit the cavern's stone floor, his knees instantly folding. He'd have slammed into the ground face-first had the General not caught him in a cradle of magic. Otherwise he knew he'd have been knocked unconscious, being unable to catch himself on his hands.

"Shift and heal yourself," Warlock ordered. "I'm going to need you Bastards to capture a few sacrifices for me." A snarl rumbled into his voice. "If the Slut thinks her Hunter

Prince can match my power, she'll discover she's dead wrong. And Arthur Pendragon is just dead."

The tub was huge, easily big enough for both of them. Miranda lay back in Justice's brawny arms, watching the candlelight dance on the tiled walls. Her gaze drifted to the stained glass window with its image of wolves running through a moonlight-dappled forest, eyes glowing gold in the dark.

Resting her head back against Justice's warm, slick shoulder, she savored the heat of the water, listened to the muffled pop of bubbles in the thick foam that surrounded them. She did love a bubble bath.

Justice hadn't objected, though it would probably make him smell of lilacs. He must be feeling mellow.

God knew she felt almost boneless, hot water to her shoulders, breathing the smell of lilacs and masculinity and fur.

For once, the scent of male werewolf didn't make her tense in anticipation of pain.

Justice ran his big hand over her wet skin, a cake of French-milled soap in his palm as he washed her as tenderly as a child. She let him do it, lazily enjoying the slippery stroke of the soap.

"Why were you so afraid of me?" His chest rumbled pleasantly against her cheek.

Miranda stiffened.

She considered pretending she hadn't heard him, but she knew he was too stubborn to let her get away with that. She considered her answer a long moment before admitting, "I haven't had a lot of good experiences with Alpha werewolves."

"Yeah." Justice slid the soap over the curve of her breast and across her nipple, then reversed the stroke and did it again, teasing the tip into full erection. "I kind of gathered that."

"Warlock sent a man to rape me once." Her eyes widened as she heard what she'd just blurted. Dammit. She hadn't intended to tell him that.

But now that she'd said it, she might as well spill it all. He needed to know why they'd never work as a couple. Assuming he even *wanted* it to work. *Maybe he just wants sex.* She could understand that. Sex with him was damned tempting.

Miranda suddenly realized he'd stopped washing her. Worse, the scent of rage filled the air. She flinched, expecting a blow.

Instead he asked a question. "*Your father* sent a man to *rape* you?"

He's not angry at me. She relaxed knotted muscles, managed a shrug. "It was my Burning Moon, and he wanted to breed me. That's the reason Warlock got my mother pregnant in the first place—he needed a female child he could get grandsons from. He wanted to raise my children to be his warriors." And God, what a horrific idea that was. Children—*her* children—at Warlock's mercy.

She knew too much about what it was like, being a child at a monster's mercy.

Justice slid the soap down her ribs, stroking slowly, thoughtfully. "Why not breed sons himself? He's immortal, right? It's not like he's too old."

"He did breed sons." Miranda shrugged against his wet chest, trying not to think of all the brothers she'd never known. "He ended up killing them all. Warlock's paranoid as hell, Bill. He's afraid sons with enough power would turn on him."

"Given his parenting skills, I can understand why." He ran the bar down between her legs, and she squirmed at the delightfully slick sensation. "Why isn't he afraid of you?"

Miranda snorted. "Are you kidding? I'm just a woman. He doesn't think there's any way in hell I'd ever be a threat to him. And he made damned sure of it."

"What do you mean?" He ran a soapy hand along her arm, stroking her absently.

She really wasn't in the mood to revisit that particular set of memories. "What do you think I mean?"

That big hand quit moving again. It seemed his entire body hardened under her as he tensed. "He beat you?"

"Among other things."

The muscles of his chest seemed to harden into rocks against her back. "What other things?" He spoke in a low, deadly growl.

Realizing what Justice was thinking, Miranda recoiled. God, the idea of Warlock . . . "No, it wasn't like that, thank Jesus, Merlin and all the saints."

He relaxed fractionally. "Good." Blowing out a breath, he said again, "That's good. When I was a cop Never mind, you don't want to hear about that shit. What did he do?"

Miranda shrugged. "Used magic on me. If I tried to fight back with my own power, he'd cut lose. And no matter how hard I fought, Warlock could kick my ass. If he hadn't healed the injuries he gave me, I'd have died more than once."

Justice tensed again, until his pectoral muscles felt as if they'd turned to granite behind her head. "Conditioning you not to use magic against him."

"Exactly." Miranda shuddered, memories rising despite her best intentions. "That first time . . . You've got to understand, when I was small, my mother taught me Warlock was this great hero. He was the prince in every fairy tale she read me at night."

"Why in the fuck would she do that?"

Miranda winced as he unknowingly prodded the worst of her psychic wounds. Not even Warlock's methodical abuse had hurt her like the realization that her mother had deliberately lied to her. "I asked her that once, when I was sixteen and feeling particularly bitchy. She told me she'd thought it would be safer for me to believe he was a hero. If I treated him that way, maybe he'd see I wasn't a threat and leave me alone."

"Well, obviously *that* was a total waste of time."

She sank deeper in the water, frowning. "Not at first. When I was really small, he used to work magic during his visits, conjuring toys and pretty fireworks to make me clap and laugh."

Justice snorted and began rubbing the soap over her body in soothing circles. When he spoke, there was grim comprehension in his voice. "Somehow I have a hard time picturing Warlock as the doting daddy."

"In retrospect, so do I." There was such comfort in the touch of Justice's big hands, she found that her memories seemed a little less painful. "But they'd always told me Warlock was my real father, even though Joelle was married to Gerald Drake. Gerald really was a bastard, so Daddy Warlock seemed like a knight in shining armor by comparison."

"So when did he come out of the kennel as the son of a bitch he really is?"

"When I started developing my powers. I think I was four years old or so."

"Damn." Justice stopped soaping again. She caught his hand and urged it into motion again, and he went back to caressing her. "But Direkind don't start Shifting until they're teenagers. How did you come into your magic so early?"

"Actually, I couldn't Shift until I was fifteen." She traced a lazy rune on his bent knee. "I got the power to work spells a lot earlier, though. That's when Warlock goaded me into using magic against him."

"*Goaded* you? He wanted you to attack him?"

"Basically. I had this doll I particularly loved—she had all this red hair and big gold eyes, just like mine. Warlock had conjured her for me a year or so before, and I carried her everywhere. I was proud my daddy gave me something so pretty."

"So he ripped her little red head off." There was a distinct growl in Justice's voice.

"Not quite, but that's the general idea. He told me I was too old for dolls and took her away from me."

"Wait, let me get this straight. You were four—and he said you were too *old* for dolls?"

"Yeah." She watched the soap slip out of his hand and disappear into a mound of foam. Justice didn't appear to notice. "Then he dangled her over my head and pulled her away whenever I tried to grab her."

"Pushing you into using your powers so he could punish you." His teeth ground together in rage, the sound grittily audible to her Dire Wolf hearing.

"Yeah. When I finally got tired of jumping after the doll, I tossed a spell at his hand. It wasn't much of a spell, mind you—just something to make his fingers go numb so he'd drop the doll. He blasted me. I mean, *blasted* me. With a fireball, the way you'd hit someone in battle."

"He fried a four-year-old child?" His arms tightened protectively around her, as if by unconscious instinct. "A little girl? *His* little girl?"

"I was never really his little girl, Justice. If I had been, he couldn't have done something like that."

"Good point." There was that protective growl again.

"I've never forgotten what it felt like when that blast hit my face." Lost in scarring memories, she ran soapy fingers absently over the strong tanned forearm around her waist. "My hair went up like a torch. I turned and tried to run, but he hit me with another spell that put the fire out. I was in so much pain, I just kept running."

"Oh, God." Justice sounded sick.

Miranda barely noticed, lost in brutal memory. "He grabbed me. God, the touch of his hands was agonizing. I looked down and saw some of my skin fall off. He'd cooked me like a chicken."

Justice began to swear, an impressive rolling blast of profanity that made her blink in surprise. She'd never even heard some of those words.

Finally he ran down enough to ask, "What did he do then?"

Miranda frowned. "I don't remember. I woke up in my bed at home. The pain was gone. I ran to the mirror to look at my hair—I loved my hair, and I knew it had burned away. I'd smelled it. But every hair was back, perfect, like nothing ever happened. I'm pretty damned sure he gave me third-degree burns, but he'd healed me completely. You'd never have known what he did to me."

"What did your mother say when you told her?"

Miranda laughed, the sound ugly even to her own ears. "That I shouldn't have tried to get the doll back. She told me Warlock was an Alpha, and when an Alpha gave you an order, you did what he told you to do. Or you'd pay."

"All Alphas are not like that." Justice's voice sounded as cold as dry ice, temper steaming like vapor from every word.

Miranda twisted her head to look warily up at him. His handsome face was set in hard lines, though the arms he'd wrapped around her were deliberately gentle. "I know, Bill. I'm starting to see that."

Justice lay staring up into the darkness, Miranda cuddled against him, one arm draped over the width of his chest, deliciously warm and smelling of werewolf and lilac bubble bath. He must have made some progress in convincing her he wasn't just another vicious Alpha, or she wouldn't have trusted him enough to fall asleep in his arms with the boneless innocence of a child.

Except he'd never met any child who'd suffered as much abuse as she had, because such a child would have died. A dozen times over.

What had Warlock's vicious treatment done to her mind? Especially considering he'd gone right on abusing her into adulthood.

It wasn't a comfortable thought. Any cop knew you couldn't turn your back on a criminal domestic violence victim. They'd call 911, you'd show up, see the bruises, the black eyes, the blood. You'd start to handcuff the bastard who had done all that—and his victim would promptly hit you with the nearest cast iron frying pan.

Or worse.

Justice was living proof you couldn't trust a CDV victim. He wouldn't even be a werewolf if he hadn't tried to save the wrong woman.

It was June 3, 2009. He was a lieutenant with the Greendale County Sheriff's Office, the same department where his grandfather had served two terms as sheriff and his father had gone down in the line of duty.

When he was twelve years old, his father had told him, *"Kid, your name is Justice. And don't you ever forget it."*

He hadn't.

So when 911 Dispatch radioed reports of a woman screaming at 425 Magnolia Avenue, Justice had responded to the call. That kind of thing was normally Patrol's job, and he was a detective, but all the patrol units were tied up with a multi-vehicle accident. Which made him the only cop available.

Besides, he'd just spent the last sixteen hours working a homicide; a husband had cut his wife's throat. *If I can prevent another woman ending up dead, it'll be worth a little extra overtime.* Unlike the scene of the murder—a doublewide out in the middle of nowhere—425 Magnolia Avenue turned out to be nothing less than a mansion. Not the kind of place you'd expect a man to terrorize his wife.

When Justice walked up to the front door, he noticed that its glass oval inset was etched with a stylized wolf head. He'd had no idea werewolves even existed then, or he'd have recognized the symbol of a Chosen household.

The Chosen were werewolf aristocracy who could trace their lineage back to the original twelve warriors Merlin magically transformed into the first Dire Wolves.

Chosen males demanded complete submission from their mates, and they liked to enforce their dominance the hard way. Since the women could heal damned near any injury just by Shifting, the men figured they could do whatever they wanted.

Justice hadn't known any of that. Not that he'd have cared, once he heard the pain and terror in the woman's scream. He'd been on the verge of kicking in the door when the couple's teenaged son finally opened it. He was questioning the kid when the boy's father barged in. "Who the hell are you," a male voice interrupted, "and what are you doing in my house?"

Justice pivoted, his hand going to his gun. He didn't draw it—quite. "I'm the police, sir. Who are you?"

"Christian Andrew Price." The man tilted his head so he could look down his nose at Justice. Quite a trick, considering he was three inches shorter. "I know you aren't getting ready to draw a weapon on me in my own home."

We'll see, asshole. "Where's your wife, sir?"

"Who are you again?"

Justice tapped the gold badge on his belt. "Lieutenant William Justice, Greendale Sheriff's Office."

Price smiled thinly. "Oh, yes. I donated to the sheriff's campaign."

"So did I." He took a single menacing step closer. "Where's your wife, Mr. Price? I heard her scream."

Price curled a contemptuous lip. "Carol screams quite frequently." He was a pale aristocrat of a man—blond, thin, and elegant in chinos and a sky-blue silk shirt open to reveal a wisp of chest hair. "She's a bit high-strung."

"Funny how people get high-strung when other people hit them." *And you're about to find out just how it feels, asshole.* "If I don't see your wife by the count of three, I'm going to assume something's happened to her. In which case I'm going to handcuff your ass, throw you in my patrol car, and go looking for her myself. One . . ."

"My wife is none of your damned business!"

"This badge says otherwise. Two. Thr—"

"Carol, get out here, you clumsy cow!"

The woman who stepped around the corner would have been delicately pretty, if not for the vicious cuts that raked across her face. The top slice ran from her temple to the corner of one green eye, while three others slashed her

cheek right to her nose and the corner of her mouth. The
bottom cut laid the length of her jaw open all the way to her
chin. Blood streamed from the wounds to mat her shoulder-length chestnut hair and soak her pink Polo shirt. Her
neat white pants were splattered with crimson flecks.

Shit, Justice thought in horror, *that's going to scar like
a bitch. What the hell did he use to attack her, Freddie
Krueger's claws?*

She smiled at Justice through the gore. One side of her
lip sagged oddly, as if the cuts had damaged nerves. "Hello,
Lieutenant. I'm afraid you've caught us at a bad time."
There was a curious light in her eyes, an odd blend of tri-
umph and revenge. Something that said, "I'm going to
show him for what he is."

"Mom!" The boy stared at her in shocked horror. "Why
in the hell didn't you Shift?"

"Dammit, Carol!" her husband spat, taking a threatening step forward. "I'm going to—"

"That's enough, sir!" Grabbing Price by one wrist, Justice swept behind him, jerking the bastard's arm back and
around to jam it painfully high against one shoulder blade.
Teeth bared, he used the arm bar to slam Price face-first
into the wall so hard, the watercolors shook with the
impact, their elegant silver frames rattling.

Price yelped in startled pain. "That hurts! Let go,
you . . ."

"No." Maintaining the arm bar with practiced skill,
Justice used his free hand to pull his handcuffs from the
leather case on his belt. "You're under arrest on charges of
criminal domestic violence, high and aggravated. Which
means you're going to jail, and your wife is going to the
emergency room. If you're lucky, a plastic surgeon will be
able to save her face."

"Don't be absurd!" Price snapped, and rammed back
against his grip, breaking free with effortless strength.

Astonished, Justice stumbled and damn near fell on his
ass. Breaking free of that kind of hold took a hell of a lot of
strength, far more than a skinny little bastard like Price

should have been able to exert against a man three inches taller.

"The little bitch is fine." Price glared at his wife, his lips peeled off his teeth. "All she has to do is Shift and her ugly face will be as good as new. At least until I slice her open again for bringing a human into Chosen business!"

Oh, great, the bastard's psychotic, Justice thought, and drew his gun. Swinging the weapon up into a two-handed Weaver stance, he aimed it squarely between Price's eyes. "You're not doing a damn thing except going to jail. Turn around and brace your hands against the wall, feet apart."

The blond rocked back in offended astonishment. "I'll do no such thing! You have no authority to . . ."

"I've got a badge and a gun, asshole. That gives me all the authority I need." Justice took three steps forward, until the nine-mil almost touched Price's thick blond eyebrows. "Lean both hands on that wall and stand with your feet apart. I will not tell you again."

"This is really not necessary." Carol wrung her hands, her distress obvious even through the mask of blood. "This isn't what I had in mind. I don't want you to arrest him. Just make him leave me alone!"

NINE

"Lady," Justice *had* growled at the woman in frustration and rage, "the only way to make an abuser leave you alone is to leave his ass and make sure he doesn't know where you're going. Which is what I strongly advise you to do. Get your kid to pack your shit while you're in the hospital and this creep is in jail. Then hop a flight to anywhere, and don't come back. Have your lawyer serve the divorce papers, and stay the fuck away from this lunatic."

She stared at him in shocked astonishment. "I can't divorce Christian! The Chosen don't do that."

Great, she was as crazy as Price. This is why I hate domestics. "Then I give it a month before I'll be working your murder." He glared into Price's furious eyes. They actually seemed to glow with sparks of insanity. "It won't exactly be a whodunit."

Carol lifted her chin. "Christian won't hurt me."

Justice kept his gun aimed directly at Price's skull. "Check the mirror, sweetheart. He already has."

"Carol, you stupid slut, look what you've gotten us into!"

Price exploded. "You've exposed us, you fool! When this human makes his report and the media gets involved . . ."

Green eyes narrowed. "He won't be making a report. I'll fix this, Christian. You'll see."

And Carol Price became a monster.

Light sparked around her as if she'd detonated hidden fireworks. Her body contorted, muscle and bone twisting beneath her flesh as her head shot toward the ceiling, dark fur rolling to cover every inch of her body.

Sheer reflex made Justice jerk his weapon toward her. In the instant it took to switch his aim from Price to his victim, Carol grew from barely five-foot-six to over seven feet tall. Her delicate female features transformed into a wolf's tapered muzzle and pointed ears, as her elegant manicure sharpened into three-inch claws. Her fur was the same rich chestnut as her hair, short and fine over most of her body, thickening into a long mane that surrounded her head and formed a ruff over her round breasts.

Justice wondered numbly where her clothes had gone.

"You . . . What did you . . . ?" He felt as if someone had hit him hard, right in the side of the head, disconnecting his dazed thoughts like a derailed toy train. "How did you do that?"

"I'm sorry about this," the monster told him in a deep, rumbling voice. "But you really shouldn't have tried to arrest Christian. The Chosen don't go to jail."

She lunged at him. He fired, but she ducked with impossible speed, wrenched the gun out of his hands, and bit his wrist with the speed of a striking copperhead.

Justice screamed as knife-blade fangs sliced into his skin. Blue sparks flashed around her jaws.

Hallucinating. He had to be hallucinating. *What the fuck did they drug me with? Gas? I didn't drink anything . . .*

Fire shot up his arms in blazing agony. Yelling, he jerked away just as she released him.

He'd have fallen flat on his ass, but Carol caught his elbow, steadying him. "I'm sorry, Lieutenant," she told him, regret in her glowing orange eyes. "I truly am. But now you're either one of us, or you're dead. Either way, you won't be taking Christian to jail. And you won't be making a report."

Bleeding, Merlin's Curse blazing through his veins in waves of agony, Justice could only watch as Carol's husband turned into a monster too. She'd fled, yelping, Price raging at her heels. The two Dire Wolves shot out the back door into the moonlit woods beyond.

The couple's teenage son, Peter, helped Justice make that first agonizing Shift. Otherwise the magic probably would have killed him.

Later, Justice returned to the Price home, driven by some stupid need to make sure Carol had survived. Her cheek unmarked by so much as a scar, she'd thanked him politely for his concern.

And shut the door firmly in his face.

He hadn't filed a report.

That wasn't the last time he'd dealt with the Chosen, either. After the Council of Clans appointed him wolf sheriff, Justice often dealt with aristocrats in one way or another. He'd soon found most of them were just as bugfuck crazy as Carol Price and her psychotic husband.

The only exception was Elena Livingstone Rollings, his ally on the Council of Clans. Elena was married to a cop, Lucas Rollings, who'd also become a werewolf after being bitten in the line of duty.

After Justice resigned from the Greendale County department, Elena had lobbied hard for his appointment as wolf sheriff. He hadn't been all that sure he wanted the job, but she and Lucas convinced him that his law enforcement experience would make him an asset.

"Kid, your name is Justice. And don't you ever forget it."

Maybe Dad had been joking when he said that, and the twelve-year-old Justice just hadn't realized it. It did sound a bit cheesy in retrospect. Yet those words had lodged in his brain like a cocklebur, and he couldn't seem to dig them out.

Maybe he didn't want to.

Justice curled tighter around Miranda's sleeping warmth and closed his eyes, trying to go back to sleep.

Until a chilling thought made his eyes snap wide.

When we go up against Warlock, will Miranda turn on me like that? And if she does, what the hell am I going to do?

A shrill scream of raw terror jolted Justice from sleep. Miranda jerked out of his arms and practically clawed her way from the bed. A sword appeared in her hand in an explosion of azure sparks.

Instinctively, Justice rolled after her, hitting the floor in a coiled crouch, scanning the room for whatever had frightened her. He was unarmed, not to mention buck naked, but he didn't give a damn. Something had scared her, hurt her . . .

Only there was nobody there.

"Miranda, what did you. . . ." He glanced at her and broke off, ice creeping along his veins.

Miranda's gaze was locked on *him*, her face twisted with fury and fear as she drew back her sword for a killing stroke.

Aimed squarely at his neck.

Oh, fuck. She's having a nightmare, and she has no idea who I am.

He'd read somewhere that you shouldn't grab a sleepwalker—she'd attack. You were supposed to call her name and speak calmly . . .*Yeah, right. Speak calmly to the naked woman with a freaking broadsword in her hand.* And unlike Miranda, he couldn't just conjure weapons out of thin air.

"Miranda, it's me. It's Justice." He retreated, desperately scanning the room for something to use as a shield.

"I'm not going to hurt you. I'm your bodyguard, remember?" *Among other things.*

Glowing eyes blinked as fury gave way to confusion. Then, thank God, to hesitant recognition. "Justice?"

He blew out a relieved breath and gave her a smile that was probably a bit too bright. "That's me, darlin'. You awake now?"

"Bill," she gasped, the conjured blade vanishing in a burst of sparks that winked out as they tumbled to the floor. "Oh, God, Bill, I could have killed you!"

"Must have been one hell of a nightmare."

"It was." Miranda dropped onto the bed as if her knees had given way. "I was dreaming about Mom's death. Again." Bracing her elbows on her knees, she buried her face in her hands. He tried not to watch her bare, pretty breasts sway. "When I woke up and smelled werewolf, felt your arm around me, I thought . . . Oh, hell, I don't know what I thought. That you were Gerald, that you'd just . . ."

"It's all right, sweetheart. It was only a dream." Dropping down beside her, he looped an arm across her bare, smooth shoulders and drew her close.

Miranda leaned into him with a sob. "He killed her, Bill. He finally killed her. I knew it was coming—hell, *she* knew it was coming, but she wouldn't leave him. I tried, God, I *tried* to get her to go, but she just wouldn't. *"Chosen women don't leave their husbands."* Miranda looked up at him. Her eyes were red, tears rolling silently down her cheeks. He wondered if she'd ever allowed herself to grieve.

Justice drew her head against his chest and cradled her in his arms. "Yeah. The Chosen are like that. Brainwashed all to hell."

Miranda took a heaving breath, half-laughter, half-sob. "Joelle definitely was. She'd lecture me about a woman's duty and honor and all that horseshit." Conjuring a tissue, she buried her face in it. The next words were muffled, as if she hated to admit the truth even to herself. "Sometimes I just wanted to shake her."

"I know." He kissed the top of her shining hair.

"Why wouldn't she go, Bill?" A fat tear hit his naked thigh and slid downward, leaving a cool trail that gleamed in the moonlight. Her skin felt hot against his chest. "Why wouldn't Mom leave that bastard? She never loved him. He was a complete jerk. He married her and pretended I was his daughter only because Warlock ordered him to. My father rewarded his obedience with construction contracts, business deals—he made sure Gerald got all kinds of gravy."

"Yeah, I heard Drake was connected." He'd been investigating the Drake murder case before the Council of Clans fired him for refusing to go along with Warlock's declaration of war.

Miranda straightened out of his hold, wiping her eyes. "Just hours before Gerald killed my mother, Belle offered to get us out. She said she'd take us to Avalon. We'd have been safe, dammit. Joelle said no. *Why?*"

That last word had the ring of a child's betrayed wail, stabbing him right to the heart.

Justice sighed, rubbing one hand absently up and down her back. "It was probably fear, Miranda. Fear of being alone. Fear of starting over. Fear the female Chosen would turn on her; that crowd can be pretty vicious. Fear Gerald would hunt her down and kill her. And he probably would have. Chosen Alphas are touchy about slights to their pride, and a runaway wife is one hell of a slight. Implies you can't control your own household."

"I killed him." The words seemed to hang nakedly in the air, stripped of all emotion except profound weariness.

"Good."

Miranda blinked at him in surprise, as if she'd expected condemnation. Justice caught a glimpse of the agonized guilt she probably didn't even realize she felt.

Gerald might have been an abusive bastard who'd murdered her mother, but she'd also known him her entire life. Called him "father," celebrated holidays and birthdays with him, shared meals, seen him in moments he was happy and sad.

Maybe there'd even been times when he *hadn't* acted like a complete douche bag.

Justice knew from personal experience that killing anyone, even a murderous stranger, put a burden on the soul. How much worse would it have been to kill a family member, no matter how much he may have had it coming?

So he met her gaze and told her the truth. "Gerald would have killed you, Miranda. You actually *saw* him break his wife's neck. Even Chosen Alphas aren't allowed to go that far. When I was wolf sheriff, I charged aristocrats with murder in situations exactly like that."

He grimaced, remembering some of the more miserably frustrating trials. "True, getting a conviction was a bitch and a half, since they usually bought off the jury . . ."

"Yeah, that sounds like something Gerald would have done." Miranda's sodden tissue disappeared, replaced by an entire box of Kleenex. Pulling out a fresh handful, she wiped her reddened eyes and sniffled.

"Of course, because he could have been put to death." The Direkind didn't have prisons. Depending on the crime, the Council of Clans either imposed a fine or ordered you beheaded. There was no intermediate sentence. No appeal process, either. The headsman's axe fell at dawn the day after sentencing. Over the three years he'd been wolf sheriff, Justice had swung that blade four times, always on bastards who truly deserved it.

Gerald damned well should have been one of them. Knowing the Direkind judicial system, however, Justice figured he'd have found a corruptible juror and beaten the charge. "But even if he'd gotten off, the social ostracism would have been merciless. No more lucrative Chosen construction jobs. No more membership in that gentlemen's club, playing poker with the upper crust and drinking expensive Scotch served by pretty young werewolves." Justice scooped her into his lap, settling her more comfortably against his chest. "So yeah, he'd have killed you. I'm just glad you got him first."

"He drew back his hand with his claws extended." Miranda gazed into the distance, as if reliving that night.

"His eyes were completely empty. It was like looking into a shark's. There was nothing human home." She wrapped both arms around herself and shivered. "I knew he was going to tear out my throat, so I conjured a sword and killed him first. Then I cut off his head, just to make sure he was really gone."

Justice sighed. "Miranda, it doesn't sound like he gave you a choice."

"I could have gated away." She turned in his lap to search his face with anxious eyes. "I had the power to do that even then. Gerald wouldn't have been able to follow me."

"Then he'd have gone to Warlock, who would have sent his assassins after you. You'd be running from all of them now." Justice stroked her hair until her body began to lose its defensive stiffness.

"Look, if you're waiting for me to tell you you're a sinner for killing that bastard, you're barking up the wrong tree." He gave her a smile. "If you'll pardon the expression."

"Aren't you worried about sleeping with a killer?" Miranda tried out a flippant smile, but the anxiety behind it peeked through her eyes.

Justice snorted. "I hate to tell you this, but you're about as frightening as Miss Piggy."

Miranda laughed, a little giggle of surprise and relief. Her amber eyes lightened as though the pain and fear had dropped away.

Just like that, Justice was abruptly aware he had a lapful of beautiful, naked woman who was no longer sobbing. One breast pressed against his chest, soft as a rabbit's fur, while the other displayed a tempting pink nipple drawn into a tight bud. Her ass felt just firm enough resting on his thighs, and her long, long legs draped over his, thighs slim and strong as a dancer's, her slender, endless calves sweeping down into pretty feet.

She painted her toenails. He thought about nibbling them, then working his way up to even more interesting territory. His cock stirred beneath her, hardening at the tempting images spilling through his brain.

Miranda, no dummy, purred at him. Apparently she was in the mood to be distracted from her troubles.

And I'm just the man for the job. Justice swooped down for a taste of that soft mouth, salty with her tears. She sighed and opened for him as he cupped one breast, toying with the little nipple until it grew nicely plump between his fingers. His tongue swept in to explore her luscious mouth.

Beep beep beep beep . . .

The raucous beeping of the bedside alarm made both of them jump.

"Oh, hell." Miranda drew reluctantly out of his arms and rose from his lap. "It's time to dress for our meeting with the Mother of Fairies."

Justice curled a lip as his arousal drained into cold apprehension. "And then there's whatever test I've got to pass to get my hands on Merlin's Blade."

And I'd better succeed, or we're all screwed.

Justice stopped shaving to meet Miranda's eyes in the mirror. He was frowning, though he should have been in a better mood, having teased her mercilessly in the shower. She could have cast a cleaning spell, but there are some tasks too pleasurable for shortcuts. And the chance to rub soap all over Justice's powerful body was one of them.

Even if a godlike fairy *was* waiting for them.

"How are we going to find this forge of hers?" he asked, his face half-covered in shaving cream. "She never gave us the address."

"I know where it is." She spoke automatically, though she'd been worrying about that same problem in the shower.

"You do?" Justice's dark brows lifted as he leaned forward and began shaving again, running the razor over one high cheekbone and down the line of his square jaw. "How? Since when?"

Miranda frowned thoughtfully. "I have no idea. But I

do." And wasn't that creepy? Had the Sidhe answer to June Cleaver somehow planted the knowledge in her head just now? And if so, did that mean Fairy Mom could poke around in her skull any time she wanted? And if *that* was the case, could anyone else poke his way in?

Like, say, Daddy?

Miranda and Justice spent the next twenty minutes arguing about what you wore to meet a goddess, or whatever the hell Maeve was. Miranda was in favor of dressing to the teeth, but Justice was afraid he'd end up fighting something, which he didn't care to do in the Armani suit she planned to conjure. He lobbied for blue jeans and a leather jacket, but Chosen werewolf that she was, Miranda thought that would look disrespectful.

Somehow he ended up wearing leather. Not tight, shiny leather—neither of them wanted him looking like a gigolo—but matte black pants and a leather bomber jacket over a black silk shirt, all loose enough to swing a sword in. The silk, she told him, would hold up to anything he needed to do.

Miranda conjured half a dozen outfits before settling on black slacks and an emerald-green sweater accessorized by a strand of antique pearls. With her fox-fire hair curling around her shoulders and her classical features flawlessly made up in shades of bronze, she looked aristocratically beautiful.

"You ready?" she asked at last.

"Whether I am or not, it's midnight." Justice coiled his hands into fists as his icy stomach flipped. "Open that damned gate and let's go." *God, I hope I don't fuck this up.*

Miranda grabbed his head between both hands, tilted his face down, and covered his mouth with soft, passionate lips that brushed and stroked, then parted to allow the teasing thrust of her tongue. Her body pressed against the length of his, soft breasts right down to long, firm thighs. By the time she pulled away, she'd turned his anxiety into sizzling lust. "You can do this, Justice," she told him softly. "You're the strongest man I've ever known."

And she meant it. Truth rode in her scent, in the steady gaze of those lovely amber eyes fringed in dark lashes. He started to reach for her . . .

She stepped back. "Now we're late—and I don't care." Flashing him a wicked little smile, Miranda turned away and gave her fingers a casual flick. A point of magic flared blue, then expanded into a shimmering dimensional portal.

Justice stepped through first, taking the bodyguard's lead and wishing he had a sword. Unfortunately, even he could see walking into Maeve's forge armed would not send the right message.

He wasn't sure what he'd been expecting, but it wasn't what he found. Scanning their surroundings, Justice felt his jaw drop in awe. He had to consciously close his mouth as Miranda joined him.

"Damn," she murmured, voicing his thoughts.

They were standing in a long corridor. On one side, antique walnut-paneled walls stretched into the distance, lined with paintings and objets d'art on pedestals. The floor was constructed of contrasting shades of oak and walnut, cut into intricate geometric shapes that fit together like a gleaming puzzle.

But what riveted his attention was the enormous window that ran the length of the corridor. Beyond the glass, the moonlit ocean crashed against the rocky shore, as in the distance, a long, slim shape leaped high into the air, only to plunge deep again in a burst of lacy white froth. For a moment, Justice thought it was a dolphin, until long hair and lush curves told him differently.

"Was that a mermaid?" He stared at Miranda in disbelief. "Sure looked like one."

"I didn't think there was any such thing."

"There's all kinds of weird shit in the Mageverse," she told him. "Where do you think all those myths and legends come from? Periodically, something gets through to our dimension."

A rapid thumping drew their heads around.

A cougar raced down the corridor toward them, going full out, its paws thudding on the expensive hardwood. In the ten seconds it took him to recover from his astonishment and consider shifting to Dire Wolf, the big cat raced right by them, without even stopping or giving them a look.

Gaping after it, Justice realized it was wearing something on its back.

Saddlebags?

The cougar sprinted through open double doors, turned a corner, and vanished, leaving behind the blended smells of musk and magic.

"I tawt I taw a puddy tat," Miranda said, in a sotto voce Tweety Bird imitation.

Justice took another sniff of that uncanny scent. "And I think Sylvester's been taking magic lessons."

The click of small claws emerged from the same doors the cougar had disappeared through. After what they'd just seen, Justice was a bit disappointed when nothing more exotic than a black Chihuahua rounded the corner. Watching the dog trot toward them on tiny white paws, Justice curled his lip. "I hate neurotic little dogs. They remind me of bug-eyed rats."

"And I hate rude, tardy werewolves," the dog said in a crisp voice as English as Prince Charles's. "But one must be tolerant of the lower classes, whose mothers apparently never taught them proper manners."

Justice damn near choked on his tongue, though considering the lizard leprechaun, he should have seen it coming.

"Three minutes," Miranda protested. "We're three minutes late. I wasn't sure what to wear, and . . ."

The tiny dog only stared at her coldly.

Biting off the rest of the excuse, she added weakly, "But we're sorry if you were inconvenienced."

The dog sniffed. "If you'll follow me, I'll take you to the mistress." Turning, he clicked away, his tail pointedly not wagging.

"How does something that short look down its nose at someone six feet taller?" Justice whispered.

"Shush!" Miranda gave the dog's back a wary look, but the little beast didn't deign to retort. They hurried after it.

The Chihuahua led them through a series of interconnecting rooms. If Justice hadn't been tied in a mental knot from sheer tension, he probably would have gotten more out of the tour. As it was, he had a vague impression of room after room filled with beautiful works of art cast in bronze, gold, and silver, enhanced with precious gems—everything from exquisitely tiny figurines and pieces of jewelry, all the way up to massive statues taller than Justice in his Dire Wolf form.

Every corner held antique furniture in satiny gilded wood, in styles he'd never even seen before. They walked across priceless hand-woven rugs—looped, soft wool in vivid shades telling stories of dragons slain, handsome young men wooing fairy queens, and beautiful maidens seduced by gods.

And there were animals everywhere he looked. Bright, curious eyes peered at him from beneath chairs or the spreading leaves of potted plants. Cats, dogs, birds, monkeys, ferrets, a couple of snakes, and a lynx.

And it seemed every last one of them could talk, calling greetings to the dog—they called him Guinness—or holding low-voiced conversations that included the words "Hunter Prince."

One bold chimp jumped down off the towering bronze of a naked warrior and loped to intercept the dog.

"So this bloke is the candidate for Hunter Prince?" the chimp asked, eyeing Justice before falling into step beside their four-legged guide. Judging by the voice, she was female.

"Yes." The word sounded even more clipped than the Chihuahua's snark about rude werewolves.

"Ain't you gonna int'a'doose me, Guinness?"

"No."

"Stuck-up git." The chimp glowered. "Drag the poker out of yer arse."

Justice decided the ape's accent was Cockney. Where the hell did Maeve find all these talking animals? "William Justice," he said, nodding to the chimp in greeting.

Mostly to piss off the dog.

Miranda's eyes flicked at him before she politely added, "I'm Miranda Drake."

The ape's pleased grin was all teeth and gleaming pink gums. "I'm Eliza. Maeve named me for . . ."

"Eliza Doolittle in *My Fair Lady*," Miranda guessed.

"Cor! Ain't you the smart one, then?"

Justice eyed the dog. "Guinness. After the beer?"

The Chihuahua paused long enough to direct a cold glare over one diminutive shoulder. "After the *actor*. Sir Alec Guinness."

Justice grinned in pure delight. "Obi-Wan?"

Miranda shook her head in pity. "You really shouldn't have told him that."

The dog's voice grew downright withering. "Yes, I'm sure he'll come up with something suitably *clever*."

"Considering the ears, I'd have gone with Yoda."

Guinness sniffed and turned away. "As I said. Clever."

Justice was amazed anything with legs that short could stalk.

TEN

Miranda stared in awe at the precious jewelry that filled the vast room—rings, crowns, necklaces, bracelets, in silver, gold, and some strange, iridescent metal she didn't even know the name of. Each piece glittered with every imaginable kind of gemstone as they adorned sculpted busts or torsos in gleaming black marble. Power radiated from them all, so the total effect was a storm on her magical senses.

"Miranda!" Justice hissed, snapping her out of her dazed admiration.

A massive oak door was swinging wide for Guinness, who trotted through it. She and Justice hurried after the little dog.

It was like walking into a furnace, but one that generated magic instead of heat. Power beat against her face, making her skin crawl and tingle.

The energy emanated from a waist-high stone fireplace in the center of the room that leaped with green flame—a type of pure magical plasma she'd never even seen before.

A spring bubbled up beside the fireplace in the center of a great stone bowl, the magical water spilling out to stream along a channel in the floor to an opening in the opposite wall. The stream didn't babble; it chorused, countless voices rising and falling in an aria Miranda couldn't quite understand. She tried casting a translation spell, but all she got for her trouble was an incomprehensible chant that sounded vaguely like a spell. One even more powerful than the magic blasting from the forge.

The room itself was built of gray stone blocks, each a yard square and mortared together with some odd black material that definitely wasn't cement. A quick spell revealed there was a great deal of lead in the mortar, while the stones themselves were enchanted. The whole arrangement was obviously designed to keep an enemy from sensing how much power Maeve was using—and tracking her down.

But there was more than simple paranoia at work. The vaulting ceiling twenty feet overhead was reinforced with massive wooden pillars as thick as entire trees. That plus those massive stones added up to a facility designed to withstand magical explosions.

Just what kind of forces does the Mother of Fairies play with—and how big a crater would you get if one of her spells went sideways?

At first Miranda thought Maeve herself wasn't even present. The woman standing beside the fire talking to the cougar looked nothing like the short, motherly person they'd met the night before. She was easily an inch or two taller than Justice, perhaps six-foot-six as opposed to the barely five feet Maeve could claim. She wore an emerald-green leather vest that hugged full breasts and bared the powerful biceps of her arms. Leather pants in the same shade hugged her long legs down to knee-high boots. Intricate symbols, possibly Celtic, were tooled into the thick hide. Miranda had taught herself to read the symbols the ancient Celts had used, but she couldn't read these.

The stranger wore her long green hair in a cascade of thin braids tied with feathers, gemstones, and charms that chimed as she moved. Her ears were elegantly pointed, and there was a regal beauty to her profile. Maeve's strong features weren't even pretty, though there'd been something about her that fascinated.

The woman glanced around at them, and her eyes hit Miranda's with a familiar magical punch that rocked her back on her heels. The Sidhe nodded, held up one finger as if to signal she'd be with them in a moment, and went back to talking to the cougar.

"Is that   " Justice murmured.

"The Mother of Fairies." Who damned well looked the part today.

"That's not some kind of glamor or illusion. Spells like that don't work on me," he whispered, his lips barely moving, his voice pitched for her ears only. "Neither was the way she looked yesterday. She's got to be a Shifter."

Maeve hooked the saddlebags off the cougar's back and reached in, scooping out a handful of gems that chimed like bells and blazed with magic. She nodded in satisfaction. "Please tell the Troll King that I accept his first payment. The rest will be due when I deliver the sword."

The cougar sank to the stone floor and rolled on his back, baring his belly and throat to Maeve. "It's an honor to serve the Lady of the Forge." The words emerged with a purring growl.

"Thank you, Erielhonan," Maeve said. "May thy game be ever plentiful and thy prey slow and fat."

"And may the magic ever flow to thy will." The cougar rolled to his feet and trotted out, nodding to the dog as he passed. "Guinness."

The Chihuahua dipped his chin. "Erie."

The massive oak door swung wide without anyone touching it, and the cougar slipped out.

Maeve walked over and handed the pouch of gems to Eliza, who flipped them across her shoulder and loped out the open door with them.

The Sidhe witch followed her out with long, regal strides. "Come, children," Maeve said. "It's time to seek your fate."

And damn, could she have picked a more chilling way to put it?

* * *

The great blue dragon flapped her wings in long, lazy strokes, watching with an indulgent air as her baby circled her in aerodynamic loops, darting through the air like a swallow. Assuming you could compare ten feet of scales and teeth to a swallow.

Vance glided along behind them, his wings spread wide to catch the wind. He'd Shifted into a California condor, though he was a bit larger than the actual bird usually was; seven feet from beak to tail, with a twelve-foot wingspan. Even at that size, though, he weighed less than fifty pounds.

Which made it problematic to bring down a thirty-five-foot, twenty-thousand-pound, fire-breathing dragon. But since the scaly bitch was unlikely to let him make off with her baby otherwise, that was precisely what he had to do. The blood magic sacrifice of a dragon child would be even more potent than killing a human infant. Just the thing to stoke Warlock's power to even greater heights.

And Vance didn't dare disappoint the General again.

Luckily, his invisibility shield was strong enough to keep even a Sidhe goddess ignorant of his presence. It was apparently just as effective on dragons.

Otherwise he'd be dead now.

The thunder of running hooves snatched him from his preoccupied obsession with the best way to kill the dragon. He glanced up to see her winging away, her magic riding around her like a bow wave, supporting her great weight far more than did her massive wingspan.

Vance increased his own speed with a magical push, soaring over the ridge of hills below to see a huge herd of buffalo racing across the ground, backs rolling like a woolly brown sea. The creatures' collective magic thudded against his senses, not so much an energy they could use as a projection of their life force.

In the Mageverse, *everything* was magic.

The buffalo raced along in an out-and-out stampede

now, panicked by the dragons winging overhead. The female dragon picked out a lone cow too slow to keep up with the herd, folded her great wings, and began a lethal plunge, all four legs extended to grab her prey.

Vance saw his chance. He shot forward like a rocket-propelled grenade, the wind tearing at his feathers with more force than they were designed to resist. Angling his talons before him, he conjured an energy blade and plummeted toward the diving female dragon. Condors had evolved for scavenging, not killing prey in the air.

He rolled as he dove, slicing the blade over the dragon's throat as he cut across her flight path, ripping through scaled flesh and muscle and great, pumping arteries. Blood flew, long, purple ribbons of it, sailing in oddly beautiful arcs.

The dragon hit like a crashing jetliner, twenty thousand pounds of meat and bones that crushed several buffalo and made the ground shake with a magical shock wave that damned near tumbled Vance right out of the sky. He barely managed to right himself and climb to safety with long, desperate flaps of his wings.

Above him, the dragonet screamed, so high it sounded oddly like a woman shrieking in grief. Vance looked up to see the child fold its wings and dive, as if trying to help its parent.

But the huge beast lay broken and still. If Vance's magical blade hadn't killed it, the impact with the ground certainly had.

The baby touched down beside its mother's bloody remains and called out to her in a musical babble of dragon-speak.

In its distress, it didn't even notice Vance land behind it, Shifting into the raptor form he'd taken to fight the Slut and her lover.

Opening his jaws, he breathed a spell over the dragonet, immobilizing it in loop after loop of magic. The baby shrieked, high-pitched cries of surprise and terror. The psychic cries could have echoed all the way to the Dragon-lands, had Vance's spell not squelched their magic.

Ignoring the dragonet, Vance set about eating its mother. There was a great deal of magic still lingering in the creature's huge corpse, and he needed to recharge the energy he'd expended over the past days.

As he happily gorged, he was distantly aware of the dragon child's piteous screams gradually dying away into stunned, agonized silence.

Miranda had never seen so many sharp objects in her life—and that included a visit to the Avalon armory.

Swords, axes, spears, shields, daggers, maces, bows and arrows, weapons she couldn't even name . . . Thousands of them, arranged in racks on the walls, displayed on tables, standing upright in bunches like deadly flower arrangements. They radiated magic just as the jewelry had, but this was a cold and deadly sort of enchantment.

The kind that killed.

Yet more than the magic, what drew her fascinated attention was the singer.

Over the room floated a single voice singing unearthly music, so beautiful the hair rose on the back of her neck. There was loneliness in the woman's voice, a sweet yearning, so beautiful and vivid it sounded as if the singer were standing right in the room. Yet there was no one there. It had to be some kind of spell.

"God, that song is beautiful," Miranda told Maeve, as the singer hit a particularly high, piercing note. "And heart-breaking. It's like listening to an angel grieve."

Maeve gave her a faint, pleased smile but said nothing.

Justice shot Miranda a sharp look. "I don't hear anything."

"You're not supposed to," Guinness told him coolly.

A chill replaced the delight. It *was* some kind of spell. And it was apparently aimed right at her. She'd read a lot of stories about mortals who'd been enchanted by

Sidhe magic—that's what the word "enchantment" meant, after all.

Those stories never ended well. At least, not for the mortal.

The thing that *ate* the mortal lived happily ever after.

Yeah, I don't think so.

Miranda dragged her eyes away from the corner of the room where her ears insisted the singer stood. *We're here for Justice, dammit. It's my job to help him obtain Merlin's Blade.*

As usual, he stood by her side, apparently in bodyguard mode. But when Miranda looked up at him, he wasn't wearing what she'd come to think of as his paranoid-cop face. Instead he stared into the distance with a distracted expression. "What's wrong?" She asked the question as softly as she could manage and hoped Maeve didn't hear her.

"Do you smell that?" His expression was odd. Longing.

Miranda sampled the air with her werewolf senses. The scent of ozone and power hung so heavy, she was surprised it wasn't visible, like smoke or storm clouds. "Hell of a lot of magic in here. Hard to tell what it does without a closer look at the weapons."

"No, not that. This smells . . . tempting. Like food or sex. Or freedom, if freedom had a smell. It keeps changing. I can't quite nail it down, but it's coming from somewhere over there." He nodded off to his left.

"Ignore it," she whispered, one eye on Maeve, who seemed deep in conversation with Guinness. "Some of the legendary blades are booby-trapped. It's the ones that try to seduce you that are most dangerous."

Maeve turned her face to the ceiling and went still, as if looking right through the roof to watch some heavenly object slide into position. "Ahhh, yes. It's time." She dropped her gaze to them, power flaring so bright in her eyes that Miranda had an impulse to shrink away. "Each of you may select one weapon."

Miranda wasn't sure she liked the sound of that. "We're here for Merlin's Blade. The prophecy said . . ."

Maeve waved that aside. "I know what it said."

"How? You weren't there." Justice frowned at her. "Did Branwyn play the video for you?"

She laughed, a hearty guffaw as deep as a man's. "Who do you think sent poor Daliya the vision to begin with?"

This is beginning to smell like a trap, Miranda thought, though the high, pure notes of the angel's song insisted otherwise. She ignored it.

Maeve's head snapped around, and she stared at Miranda as if she'd spoken the thought aloud. Finally the Sidhe nodded slowly. "It's well you don't leap to any lure that presents itself. But this is no trap of mine. Merlin gave me the prophecy from his own mouth these fifteen centuries gone, just as he gave the blade into my care."

Miranda frowned as the question that had always nagged at her rose to mind. "Did he know what my father would become?" *And if he did, why the hell did he let him have so much power?*

"Nay." Maeve sighed as she seemed to gaze into a past long gone. "The man who now calls himself Warlock was a hero once, a strong and clever man with courage and heart, who passed every test Merlin put to him. But the future is a tangle of choices, and no one can see where they'll lead." Her eyes shifted to Miranda's again, and hardened. "Unfortunately, the choices your father made carried him into madness. Merlin said that if Warlock grew corrupted, I should give the weapon to one worthy of becoming the Hunter Prince. When it became obvious that he'd gone mad, I looked into the fire of my forge." She nodded at Justice. "The face I saw in the flames was yours, boy. Go find your weapon."

His eyes, focused somewhere across the room, snapped to her face. "But which one is it?"

"That's for you to discover," Guinness told him. His upper lip peeled off his teeth. "If you can."

When Justice hesitated, Maeve snapped, "Well, boy? What are you waiting for? Find the blade."

He stiffened at her tone, staring at her for a beat that

made it clear she had no authority to give him orders. Then he turned and moved off, scanning the racks of weapons. Miranda was relieved to see that he walked in the opposite direction from whatever it was that had so entranced him.

"You, too, child."

Miranda turned back to Maeve, her brows climbing. "The prophecy said nothing about me."

The Sidhe witch shook her head. "There's no trick here, girl. My forge tells me there's something here you'll need if you mean to survive your father's attentions. You'd be well advised to seek it out."

Miranda hesitated a beat more, her instincts howling that it was insanity to trust anyone as powerful as Maeve.

As if to prove the point, the Sidhe's magic snapped over her mind like the jaws of a bear trap. "This morning when I looked in the fires of my forge, I saw your death."

Caught in Maeve's pitiless, infinite gaze, Miranda felt ice creeping over her chilling skin, her stuttering heart pumping the blood from her body. The crimson puddle of her life sank into stony, thirsty dirt and soundlessly disappeared. In the distance, she heard Warlock's howl of victory. An icy blackness drank her down as completely as the dirt . . .

Then Miranda was alive again, and gasping, back in the present. Her relief was so intense, her knees buckled. She had to steady herself against the wall.

"When I looked a second time, you stood over your father's body with one of my blades in your hand," Maeve continued coolly. "The path you follow is your choice, girl."

Chilled to the bone by the vision, Miranda turned up the nearest aisle of weapons and started to search. She might be stubborn, but she wasn't stupid.

Fifteen minutes later, Miranda was cursing Maeve for the number of weapons in her bloody damned armory, her own father for his psychopathy, and that fucking angel for her refusal to shut the hell up.

Again and again, Miranda stopped, picking up a sword there, a dagger here, even a couple of axes. But none of them felt right.

Instead it seemed her magic slid away from theirs, like one magnet being pressed against the same pole of another. A weapon like that would actually weaken her power instead of strengthening it.

Justice wasn't having any luck either. He prowled up and down the aisles of weapons, examining sword after sword with the kind of intense concentration he'd probably once used at murder scenes. Every breath Miranda took carried the scent of his growing frustration and anger.

Meanwhile the angel sang, her loneliness and despair growing. Until a faint note of hope sounded, threaded through a descant of pleading.

Automatically, Miranda glanced toward the sound— *and saw it.*

A dagger.

It lay on the black marble table beside her. Other weapons surrounded it, but Miranda barely noticed. She had eyes only for the slender blade engraved with ancient symbols of protection and power. Silver quillions formed an intricate swirl designed to curl around the hand, decorated with sapphires of varying sizes. Glowing blue sigils floated above the blade, rotating slowly in the air as if stirred by some magical wind. And the weapon *sang* to her, its voice impossibly pure, so inhumanly high it made the bones of her skull ring.

Miranda slipped her hand through the cupping quillions to curl her fingers around the engraved hilt. The quillions wrapped around her fist in a comforting grip—not cold as metal should be, but as warm as a mother's hand.

And as the steel cupped her, she felt a mental click, as though the athame slid into a slot in her magic, filling an emptiness she hadn't even known was there. Power surged through her as if the blade completed a circuit, enabling her to draw on the Mageverse with a new intensity.

"*Look,*" the blade sang.

Gazing down the length of her body. Miranda saw blue glowing chains coiled around her chest, binding her arms and legs. She caught her breath in astonished anger. Where the *hell* had that come from?

"Your father's work."

Miranda looked up to find Maeve standing by her side, though she hadn't sensed the woman's approach at all. It was as if the Sidhe had simply materialized.

Maeve leaned close, examining the chains "Judging by the age of the spell, he probably created it when you were a child—four years old. Perhaps five."

She remembered the fireball that had seared her hair away. "What does this thing do?" A chill stole over her at the thought of her father casting spells on her without her knowledge

Maeve shrugged. "From the looks of it, it acts as a governor on your power, preventing you from drawing on your full talent. I suspect he's trying to make you less of a threat. But the spell's primary purpose is to engender fear. Fear of all Alpha Male werewolves, especially Warlock. Whenever you hear his voice, you'll feel overwhelming terror."

Like the paralysis that had damn near gotten her eaten by Warlock's demonic dinosaur. If Justice hadn't knocked her clear, she'd have died. Instead, he was the one who'd damn near gotten killed. Fury pierced her fear with welcome heat. "That *bastard*."

Charms chimed in Maeve's hair as she tilted her head, appraising the magical chains. "The spell should have lost strength as you grew into adulthood, but he seems to have reinforced it recently." The Sidhe frowned, tracing a thoughtful finger through the air just above the glowing links. "Has your father hit you with an energy attack in the last month or so, something you thought you'd shielded against?"

Miranda blinked. "Well, the last time I fought Warlock in person was during a big battle between the Magekind and the werewolves last month. And . . ." Her eyes widened. "I wasn't afraid!"

She'd felt none of that paralyzing terror as she'd fired salvos of crackling electrical blasts at her father. In fact, she'd actually forced him to retreat. *"Fuck you, Daddy!" Miranda howled, shooting blast after blast at him. He'd barely shielded in time.*

"Traitorous bitch," Warlock spat as he backed away and hurled a fireball that looked less savagely bright than those he'd been tossing before. Miranda blocked it easily and fired back.

"That was it," Maeve said, as if reading the memory right out of her head. "You blocked the fireball, but it was only a carrier for the real spell."

"He suckered me." Miranda stared at the chains, her eyes widening in furious realization. "That's when I started being afraid of him, the way I'd been when I was a kid." Her lips parted in stunned realization. Warlock wasn't the only one she'd begun to fear then. Before that battle, she'd never been afraid of Justice. True, she hadn't wanted to get involved with him because she thought him just a little too dominant, but fear had never been part of it. *Is there any part of my life Warlock hasn't poisoned?* "How do I break this spell? I want it *gone*."

"Now that you know it's there, it will begin to lose its power." Maeve straightened, giving her a decisive nod. "You'll still feel the fear, but every time you refuse to give in to it, you'll weaken it. And now that you have my athame, you'll be able to access more of the talent it has blocked."

Intrigued, Miranda studied the Sidhe. "How much power are we talking about?"

Maeve shrugged. "That depends on your will—and how much you want it."

Miranda bared her teeth in a grin that felt downright savage. "Good. Because I really, *really* want Warlock dead."

ELEVEN

Justice watched Miranda and Maeve, heads together over her new dagger, discussing its powers. Despite himself, he felt a frustrated twist of envy.

He couldn't find that damned sword. And it was logical to assume it *was* a sword, perhaps something like Excalibur. Not that he thought himself the werewolf Arthur . . . Though it was for damned sure Warlock wasn't either, no matter what the wizard had suckered his fellow Direkind into believing.

But Justice had examined every freaking sword in the room, and none of them was it. No matter how much magic he smelled on them, every single one was inert metal in his werewolf immune-to-magic hands.

Meanwhile, all he smelled was that mysterious whatsit, which carried no scent of magic whatsoever. He couldn't even acclimate to it, the way he could adjust to even the worst reek, because the smell kept changing. Baking bread one minute, then honeysuckle, peaches, roses, apple pie, pit barbecue. The nape of Miranda's neck. Any smell he loved, the spell trotted out to tempt him.

But whenever he turned to follow it—just to make sure

it wasn't the sword—it vanished. Miranda was probably right. It was just some booby-trap fucking with him.

Dammit, can't you give a guy a hint? Justice thought in Maeve's direction, before squashing his resentment under a fresh layer of determined resolve. This was his test. If he couldn't find the blade on his own, Maeve needed to look into her scrying fire until she located the true Hunter Prince.

A sniff sounded from somewhere in the vicinity of his left boot. He looked down to find Guinness peering up at him wearing an expression of aloof disdain. "I knew you weren't the Hunter Prince," the dog said in that irritating, prissy, *smug* British voice.

"Shut up," he growled. *Must* not *boot the little bastard across the room . . .*

The Chihuahua curled his upper lip. "You don't even have the wit to see what's right under your muzzle."

Justice froze as an idea hit him. A grin spread across his face. "Yoda, I could kiss you!"

"Please don't." The dog sank down on his belly, horror in his bulging brown eyes.

Drawing in power from the Mageverse, Justice Shifted. Maybe he couldn't follow that scent in human form, but nothing could elude his Dire Wolf nose. The rippling pain of his shift hadn't even begun to fade when Justice sank into a crouch, putting his head at the level of the weapons tables, the better to follow that maddening scent.

"Oh, for God's sake, put on some pants!"

"Sniff my hairy ass crack, Muppet." He breathed in, pulling air deep into his lungs.

And smelled his mother's perfume: Obsession. It drifted through the heavy ozone tang of the other weapons' magic like a flute solo through a death metal guitar riff.

Still crouching, he worked his way down the aisle after the scent, slowly at first, then more quickly as he realized it lay in the air like a neon arrow, pointing clearly to its source. The smell shifted again as he passed swords and daggers and throwing stars and maces the size of cannon balls. It smelled like Miranda, like love and sex and everything he'd ever wanted but had never found . . .

Until he found it.

Merlin's blade wasn't a sword. It was a huge, double-bladed axe, forged of some alien metal that radiated magic with such intensity he could almost taste it. Justice wanted to pop himself upside the head. *Of course it's an axe, dumbass. Warlock carries an axe.*

But he'd seen Warlock's axe, and it looked nothing like this. Nor had the wizard's blade blazed like this, burning with a ferocious, seductive energy that filled Justice with a combination of awe, anticipation . . .

And fear. *What's it going to do to me?* Fighting to ignore that fear, Justice concentrated on the great weapon. Its steel shimmered in a wavering pattern that reminded him of a Japanese katana, as if the metal had been folded over and beaten flat hundreds of times as it was forged. Beaten and folded until its molecules aligned in impossibly thin layers, resulted in an incredibly strong, flexible blade. It would hold an edge no matter how you beat it against steel and armor and bone. And it would never break.

As Justice straightened from his crouch, rainbow patterns slid across the axe's twin blades, one on either side of the haft. They were etched with delicate symbols in some language he couldn't read, alien words that glowed to his werewolf eyes, blue as the huge gem blazing azure from the tip of the haft.

"Took you long enough," Guinness grunted, but Justice barely heard him. Distantly, he sensed Maeve and Miranda approaching, but he didn't even glance at them. He was focused completely on the axe, fascinated by the play of light over the blade, by the glowing spells engraved on its haft, by the magic he could sense roiling in the fist-sized blue gem implanted in the handle's butt. The smell that had drawn him had vanished, as if the axe knew seduction was no longer necessary. And it was right. He was completely entranced; it was the most beautiful weapon he'd ever seen. Curling both hands around the heavily engraved grip, Justice lifted it from the stand that held it upright. He pivoted, trying a practice swing. *The balance is perfect. Feels like a feather in my . . .*

Power blasted out of the Mageverse like water from a fire hose, knocking him flat on his back. Distantly, he heard Guinness's alarmed yip as the dog dodged his toppling body.

"Justice!" Miranda shouted, but he was too busy fighting for his life to reassure her.

The Mageverse raged and lashed in his grip as if the great axe had turned into a snake of fire, burning his hands, his eyes, his brain. He yelled, struggling to bring it under control, but it blazed like a forest fire, radiant heat beating his skin in waves. His connection to the Mageverse intensified as he clenched the burning haft, growing more powerful than he'd ever experienced it, even when he'd Shifted that very first time, balanced on the verge of flaming oblivion.

If I don't gain control of the magic, it's going to burn me alive.

"Bill!" Miranda fell to her knees beside him as he convulsed, screaming between clenched wolf jaws. Despite his obvious agony, he gripped the axe like a man who'd grabbed a high tension line that was now electrocuting him.

Automatically, she conjured a belt sheath and shoved the athame into it, then reached for the axe. She had to get it away from him before . . .

Maeve grabbed her wrists with both hands hard enough to grind the bones together. "No! The magic in that thing would burn you to a cinder."

"But it's killing him!" She coughed, choking on the smoke from his burning fur.

"If he can regain control, he'll survive." Maeve scooped Justice into her arms as if he weighed no more than Guinness. The Sidhe rose to her feet, lifting four hundred pounds of Dire Wolf brawn with ease. Carrying him with her arms stretched out before her, chest drawn in to avoid contact with the axe, she strode along like a woman carrying a live grenade. Miranda hurried after her, one hand unconsciously curling around the hilt of the athame sheathed on her belt. At her touch, the knife began to sing again, its magical voice calming, like a lullaby sung by an angel. Her terror eased.

"Is the boy going to make it? That's a hell of a lot of power flying around." The Chihuahua sprinted past Miranda to gallop at Maeve's side, his short little legs a blur, his claws clicking an anxious tattoo on the hardwood.

"I don't know," the Sidhe said grimly. "It all depends on the strength of his will." A set of side doors swung wide at their approach. Beyond lay a garden surrounded by oaks, dogwoods, and maples blazing with the fiery shades of fall. Maeve hurried through the doors and down a curving pebbled path, carrying Justice away from the house. As if he was about to blow up and take half the landscaping with him.

"The axe is flooding him with too much power." Trotting by Maeve's side, Guinness whined softly as he looked up at the man writhing in the Sidhe's cradling arms. "If he doesn't get it under control, it's going to incinerate him."

"What do you care?" Miranda snapped, too frightened now to listen to the knife's calming song. "You hate his guts."

"Me? Oh, no." They reached a thick pile of fallen leaves. Maeve lowered Justice into it, tender as a mother putting her child to bed as Miranda and the little dog watched. "Sometimes a nudge, the boy needs," the Chihuahua intoned in a dead-on Yoda impression. "Provide, I do."

Miranda snorted. "Oh, God, it's a Star Wars geek in a fur coat." Conscience gave her a prodding sting. *Mom raised me better than to take my temper out on a fuzzy Mini-Me.* She sighed. "Sorry I snapped, Guinness. I'm just scared out of my mind."

Rising to her booted feet, Maeve glanced at her. "You should be."

"Wow. Thanks for the encouragement. That was *just* what I needed to hear."

The Sidhe studied her. "You'd make a lovely toad."

Miranda gave her a deliberately wide-eyed look. "Oh, God, is that where all the talking animals come from?"

Maeve's eyes gleamed, but before she could retort—or turn Miranda into an amphibian—Justice gritted a strangled scream and began to convulse. Miranda forgot all about making semi-hysterical jokes and dropped to her knees, reaching for his lashing head.

Maeve slapped her hands away. "Damn you, child, don't touch him! Or do you *want* to burn to floating ash?"

His body arched, as he threw back his head with a long, ululating wolf howl of pain. His hands still gripped the axe against his chest, straining arms shaking with waves of tremor. He began to glow, the magic spilling from his body as the axe poured still more power into him.

Even standing well back from the big weapon, Miranda felt its power beat on her skin. The blade radiated magic like heat from a red-hot poker, growing more and more intense with every passing second. His eyes met hers, wide, wild and desperate, and she knew what he was thinking. *Justice isn't going to make it. It's too much power. I couldn't even control all that.*

The athame sang a single, calming note, sweet and high as struck crystal. Under its calming influence, Miranda felt her desperation morph into determination. *Maybe he can't do it alone, but I can show him how to gain control, just as I helped him Shift after that raptor bite. It's just a matter of channeling the magic . . .*

Yeah, right, some cynical part of her snorted. *Kind of like channeling Chernobyl.*

The knife sounded a cautioning note, deeper now, like the echoing *bong* of a great bell tolling. Miranda looked down into Justice's despairing golden eyes and realized what the weapon was telling her. You needed a cool head to control violent elemental forces. Strong emotion was the enemy.

Neither of us is calm enough. No wonder he can't control his magic. She searched for the right thing to say to help him regain his grip on his fear and his power.

Until suddenly she knew exactly what to say. "I love you." The stark sentence seemed to hang in the air, naked in its utter emotional truth. The athame chimed a triumphant note. Miranda froze. She'd never even *thought* those words before.

Which made them no less true.

Joy and hope flared in Justice's eyes an instant before they narrowed in determination.

She'd think about the implications of loving an Alpha after they were both safely on the other side of the Shift. Miranda threw herself open to the Mageverse, seeking the magic she needed to transform.

It was the mistake that almost killed her.

Power slammed into her brain as it blasted from the battle-axe like the wind from an F5 tornado. As the vortex tried to suck her in and rip her apart, Miranda instinctively grabbed the athame's hilt. The weapon steadied her against the raging energy as if it were the thirty-ton anchor of an aircraft carrier instead of a fourteen-ounce stiletto.

Because in magical terms, the athame *was* an aircraft carrier.

Change, dammit! Miranda told herself, clinging to the knife hilt grimly as magic raged around her. *Shift so he can Shift. We did it before. We can do it now.*

With the dagger anchoring her, she reached into the power vortex and drew out just enough magic to transform. She sensed Justice follow her example, drinking the rogue energy, using it as she did to reshape flesh, bone and muscle all the way to the cellular level.

All the way down to the DNA.

The storm died as if God had flipped off a giant fan. Miranda opened her eyes and sat back on her haunches with a sigh of relief. Feeling something cool and metallic in her hand, she saw she still held the athame, though the weapon should have disappeared with her clothing during the Shift.

Guess my pointy little friend wanted to hang around. The way things are going, I'll probably need it.

Rising to her Dire Wolf feet, she looked down at Justice. *Oh, hell.* Her heart plunged right to her clawed toes. He hadn't completed the Shift. The outline of his body still roiled with energy that rippled through every shade of werewolf magic, pale sapphire shimmering through peacock blue into deepest cobalt, then back again in an endless, deadly cycle. Miranda reached out with her magical senses, trying to determine what the problem was. And recoiled.

He hadn't completed the Change because his magic was trying to alter the ancient enchantment at the core of Dire Wolf power.

"Oh, my God," Miranda breathed, "he's rewriting Merlin's Spell!"

Fifteen centuries ago, the alien sorcerer known as Merlin had administered a magic potion to twelve Saxon warriors. Merlin's Curse, as it became known, turned the twelve into werewolves before copying its genetic coding into their saliva and sperm. As a result, anyone the warriors bit became a werewolf, just as their offspring Changed as teenagers. Those children then passed the Curse down to their children, and so on through generation after generation. And *that* was the spell the axe's magic was rewriting.

It had to be the axe's doing, because Justice wouldn't have known how to rewrite the spell. Hell, Miranda couldn't have done it either, and she'd been studying magic for years. Though come to think of it, the Curse had been rewritten once before. Eve, the third Dire Wolf ally of Avalon, had done something similar with the guidance of an elemental ghost. The changes she'd made had enabled her to work magic. *So why do I get the nasty feeling this is not the same thing?*

The last glowing sigil of the spell changed into something equally incomprehensible. The raging energy coalesced at last, forming a huge furry body curled up on the ground. *He did it.* A giddy grin spread across Miranda's face. *Justice did it! He's going to be okay!*

Then she got a better look at the massive shape, and her grin died.

"What the hell is *that*?" Guinness retreated behind

Maeve's boots and peered between them warily. "A woolly mammoth?"

It wasn't a Dire Wolf, that was certain, or even a gray wolf, which was the third shape Dire Wolves Shifted into. And it definitely wasn't human.

But the dog was right. Justice's new form was damned near the size of a mastodon.

The huge creature stirred, then rose stiffly on four legs before planting big paws well apart.

Even Maeve gaped.

Despite his enormous size, Justice's new body was much more elegant than an elephant's: long-legged, muscular, built for the hunt, with pointed ears, a bushy tail, and a long canine muzzle. Golden eyes blinked down at them, obviously confused. *It* is *a wolf*, Miranda realized, as Justice shook himself from head to tail, shedding a cloud of sable hair to float in the air. *It's just one hell of a big wolf.*

Mentally comparing this new form to Super Chicken, she decided the wolf was actually a foot or two taller at the shoulder. *Well, that'll even up the odds in the next fight.*

In fact, he was so damned big, those slender wolf leg bones should have shattered under his own weight. It seemed the same magic that had created him powered and protected his huge new body. Which probably explained why the axe had disappeared when her knife hadn't; its magic was hard at work sustaining its new creation.

Well, he had to do something with all that power. Better to turn it into eight tons of wolf than fry himself like a bucket of KFC.

Meeting Justice's golden eyes, Miranda gave him a smile. "Well, it looks like you pulled it . . ." She broke off, an icy hand clamping her heart.

There was no recognition in his gaze. In fact, the wolf's eyes held no human intelligence at all. His growl made the bones of her chest vibrate as he glared down at them, baring white teeth longer than the athame in her hand. *Oh, sweet Jesus*, Miranda thought in horror. *The lights are on,*

*but that's not Justice in there. And whoever it is, he doesn't
like us one damned bit.*

A burst of magic dragged Miranda's horrified attention
away from Justice.

Maeve had conjured a boar spear—a seven-foot oak
shaft tipped with a steel point more than a foot long. Two
crosspieces protruded from either side of the point, designed to keep an impaled, pissed-off boar from charging
up the spear and killing its hunter.

Miranda stared at the weapon, appalled. "Are you planning to use that on *him*?"

Maeve didn't take her grim gaze off the wolf as magic
flashed in his pupils, lightning arcing through menacing
hurricane clouds. His growl sounded like a Harley at full
throttle. The Sidhe had to shout over the bone-rattling rumble. "I have no desire to kill him, but I have even less desire
to be eaten." She frowned. "Normally, I can touch the
minds of animals—if not people—but that one refuses to
let me take control of him."

Justice snapped at them, and a ball of bright blue magic
flew from his mouth. Maeve threw up a shield to deflect the
fireball as the wolf jerked back, looking startled.

"I don't think he intended to do that," Miranda said
quickly.

Maeve threw her a cold glare. "Intent matters not at all.
The longer Justice remains lost, the more likely it is he'll become a threat to make Warlock look like a Buddhist monk."

A line from Daliya's prophecy ran through Miranda's
head: *"Then will the Hunter Prince be free—then will he
rule in bloody vengeance or bend his knee to his spirit's
feral king."* "There's never a feral king around when you
need one," she muttered.

"Which leaves you," Maeve retorted. "Best make him
bow, or by the Gods I'll skewer him."

Justice opened his jaws and huffed, inflating a ball of
blue fire like a kid blowing a bubble of pink gum. He
watched in pleased satisfaction as it drifted lazily toward

them, only to pop as it hit Maeve's shield. The wolf rumbled, as if disappointed it hadn't done more damage.

"Dammit." Miranda sighed. "All right, drop the shield and let me go talk to him."

"*Talk* to him?" Guinness stared at her, looking even more bug-eyed than usual. "How long have you had this masochistic desire to become a chew toy?"

"Justice won't attack me." *I hope.*

"No, he'll just huff and puff, and blow pretty blue fireballs at you," the dog said in his clipped Queen's English. "Then all he'll need is two graham crackers and a chocolate bar, and he can turn you into S'mores. I'll wager he likes his marshmallows extra crispy. Maeve and I can sing 'Kumbaya' while you roast."

Miranda winced. "Funny, Yoda. Ever thought of doing stand-up?"

"No. The pay *sucks*." This, delivered in that plummy accent, would have made Miranda snicker—if she hadn't been afraid he was right about the "extra crispy" thing.

"That is entirely enough." Maeve glared at the little dog until Guinness tucked in his tail and dropped his ears. She flicked her fingers, creating an opening in her shield. "Talk fast, child. Our furry friend doesn't strike me as patient."

Taking a deep breath and squaring her shoulders, Miranda stepped through the opening, her mind racing as she tried to think of every point she needed to make. Some of which she didn't want to say in front of the dog, who'd probably laugh his light saber off.

Without looking away from the wolf—she didn't dare—Miranda asked, "Give us a little privacy, please?"

"Yes, a mute field," Guinness drawled. "Just the thing so we don't have to listen to those distressing screams."

"Shut up, Guinness. I know you're worried about the child, but you're not helping." Gesturing an elegant spell, Maeve sent another wave of magic across the shield, closing the opening.

The Chihuahua's mouth moved, but despite her Dire

Wolf hearing, Miranda was spared his next words of snarky wisdom. *At least I'll have privacy while I spill my guts.* She looked up at the wolf. And up. And UP. *I just hope the gut-spilling isn't literal.* "Um. Hi, Justice."

Grrrrrrrrooooooooooowwwwwwl.

"Yeah, yeah, 'What big teeth you have, Grandma.'" She licked her dry chops and hoped she could get a shield up in time to avoid gracing a graham cracker. "Just don't blast me with a fireball, okay? I have enough PTSD about that as it is."

The wolf cocked his massive head. She prayed the impression he was actually listening wasn't self-delusion.

Tightening her clawed grip on the athame, Miranda began her pitch. "Justice, you need to come back. Maeve's got that magic spear, and if she thinks you're going rogue, she'll . . ."

The wolf's roar shook the trees. He lunged at her, gaping jaws revealing teeth that would probably star in her nightmares for the rest of her life.

If I live to have any.

Miranda leaped aside with all the speed and power of her Dire Wolf legs. Teeth snapped closed on empty air. Growling in frustration, the wolf wheeled after her, radiating so much raw magic, she damn near froze in Warlock-inflicted reflex.

The athame sang a long, sustained note in her hand, jolting her out of her paralysis. Freed, Miranda took off like a shot, dodging Justice's snaps, leaping aside from his lunges, bouncing around like a furry rubber ball. All the while, he kept after her, a starving wolf pursuing a particularly agile—and tempting—field mouse.

The knife chimed a sound her brain translated as *Running from a predator only makes him chase you.*

Yeah? And just how am I supposed to stop without getting myself chomped?

The blade didn't answer.

I don't even get a "Use the Force, Luke"? She spun like a bullfighter, avoiding yet another homicidal charge. *Some ghostly Jedi Master you are.*

Miranda was beginning to feel like Jerry to Justice's Tom. Or was it the other way around? She could never keep straight who was the cat and who was the mouse in that damned cartoon. But she *was* beginning to wish she had a giant animated frying pan to clobber him with . . .

Though a sword and armor would be even better. She considered conjuring them, then reluctantly rejected the idea. Armor would only slow her down. As for the sword, if she wanted Justice dead, Maeve was more than capable of doing the job with that god-awful spear.

What she really needed was to buy herself time to get through to him. Preferably before he could take a nice, juicy bite out of her backside.

An image from one of those old cartoons flashed through her mind: Tom glaring at Jerry through the arch of a mouse hole. *Just the thing.* Miranda shot a stream of magic at the ground ahead of her, conjuring a steel tunnel deep into the earth. She promptly dove into it, Bugs Bunny vanishing down a rabbit hole one cotton tail ahead of Elmer Fudd. Hitting bottom with a sigh of relief, she looked upward to watch Justice raging in frustration thirty feet overhead. *I seem to have cartoons on the brain. I can't imagine why.*

"Hey, Big Bad!" she shouted up at him. "If you'll pardon the expression, *pipe down!* I can't even hear myself think!"

He fell silent, probably out of sheer offended astonishment. *That, or disbelief I'd make a pun that bad.*

TWELVE

"Look," Miranda called to the huge werewolf staring down at her from the tube's mouth. "We're in deep shit—and sinking fast. If you don't get a handle on this Hunter Prince thing, Maeve will kill you. I know you probably don't think she can do it, but that woman is some kind of fairy goddess. You may be big, but that only means you'll make a really nice wall-to-wall wolf skin carpet . . ."

Golden eyes narrowed as they peered down at her. Then he disappeared from the opening.

Miranda frowned uneasily. "Uh, Justice?"

A furious scratching, scraping sound came from somewhere around the lip of the pipe, along with a rhythmic thumping. It took her a moment to realize she was hearing giant paws digging at the earth surrounding the metal shaft, sending great clods of dirt showering around him.

Oh, fuck, Miranda thought, picturing the wolf unearthing her pipe and spilling her out of it like an errant gumball. She supposed it could have been worse—he could have lobbed fireballs down the damned thing. This should at least give her time to get through to him before he figured out how to liberate her from her self-inflicted trap.

If push comes to shove, I can always gate the hell out of here.

Leaving Justice to Maeve's dubious mercy.

Yeah, I'm fucked.

"When did I fall in love with you?" Miranda mused, not really talking to him; she was just trying to think of some argument strong enough to get through his thick furry skull.

Scratchscratchthumpscratchscratchscratchthump-thumpthud . . .

"It must have been before the raptor almost ate you, because by then I didn't care if I got incinerated if it meant you'd survive," she said, working through the puzzle for herself more than Justice. "I rationalized it, of course. Told myself I felt nothing more than gratitude that you'd saved my life, but that was bullhockey. My life literally wouldn't have been worth living if you'd died. Not because of guilt, either."

Miranda let her head fall back to thump against the curved wall of the pipe, staring blindly up at the blue sky an infinite distance overhead. Outside the tube, the sound of digging paws began to slow. "Don't get me wrong, I'm good at guilt. I'm Joelle Drake's daughter; I'd have to be. Thing is, you make my life *more* than it was before I met you."

The wolf whined, the sound soft, questioning, even through the thick steel of the pipe.

"You're the first Alpha werewolf I've ever known who gave a rat's ass if I lived or died." She drew up her furry legs and looped her arms around them, then rested her chin thoughtfully on her knees. "Not because it would somehow inconvenience you if I kicked off. You actually *care* about me. About Miranda Drake, offspring of a nutjob and the woman who'd suckered herself into believing she loved the nutjob. The psycho and the dishrag. Some parentage, right?

Let me tell you, genetics like that have given me some sleepless nights."

Snorting, Miranda began to nibble on the curving claw of her thumb. "Yet you've saved my life over and over, risking yours to do it." She started ticking off those rescues, one claw at a time. "There was that werewolf councilman who tried to gut me during the first battle with Warlock. You broke his neck. Then came the three assassins in Paris. I got one, but the other two would have cut my head off if you hadn't minced them into dog chow. And the raptor . . . That was close. That was really close."

Brooding, Miranda looked down at her lupine reflection wavering on the blade of the athame. "When you killed the councilman, I figured it was just because you hated his damned guts. Not that I blamed you; he was *such* a bastard. In Paris, I told myself you were one of those guys who pride themselves on protecting the weak and helpless. And boy, did I hate the thought you'd think of me as weak *or* helpless."

Slowly, thoughtfully, she stirred the fur over her knee with the point of the athame, then absently started writing his name. "I think I began to fall for you when I finished that damned vaccine. I'd had to burn so much magic making enough doses of the potion for every agent in Avalon, I didn't have a damned thing left by the time I was finished."

Miranda sketched a frowny face. "I couldn't even lift my head. I just kind of lay there in the middle of my spell circle, barely conscious."

The wolf panted, deep gusting breaths somewhere outside her pipe. God knew what he was up to. Maybe he was listening. Maybe he was plotting the best way to turn her into Puppy Chow.

"You just walked into my circle, picked the cauldron up, and took the potion out to Morgana and Gwen, who were inoculating people. It was the fifth one I'd brewed." She drew a heart in the fur. "I knew you'd come back to check on me. You're that kind of Boy Scout."

Sighing, Miranda ran her free hand through her red

mane, only to encounter a garden's worth of leaves and sticks. Absently, she went to work plucking them out. "I started wondering how I'd get to the bathroom, because by that time, nature was calling. And she'd gotten pretty damned loud, since I'd just spent ten hours in that circle without a potty break. Which was when you walked in, picked me up, and carried me out. I thought, 'Fuck, he wants sex. How the hell am I going to fight him off?' "

"Boy, I really didn't understand you at all." With a snort, Miranda started picking at a particularly stubborn tangle wound tight around a twig.

"Thing is, I know what an Alpha werewolf smells like when he's horny, and I'd smelled that scent on you a few times since we'd moved in with Belle. I was trying to decide if I had the strength to yell for Tristan when you carried me into the hall bathroom."

The tangle was so stubborn, she had to put aside her athame and conjure a comb. "You seated me on the toilet and tugged off my jeans and my panties, but you didn't try to cop a feel. Didn't even leer. Then you turned your back and waited. So I did what I had to do. You turned around, dressed me again, and carried me up to my room."

Pulling the comb slowly over the tangle, Miranda smiled a little, remembering how flabbergasted she'd been at Justice's gentlemanly streak. "I thought, *Okay, either he's decent enough to help me with the bathroom, or he was afraid I'd pee all over him if he tried to rape me first. So I waited to see what you'd do. Not that I had much choice, because I couldn't have fought off a toy poodle humping my knee."*

The tangle refused to surrender. Growling softly in frustration, she cast a spell. The tangle vanished. Miranda hated doing things the easy way—it could become a bad habit—but it was that or cut the knot with her athame. She couldn't exactly go to the beauty parlor and get a stylist to fix the resulting gap in her mane.

"You put me down on the bed and you took off my shoes. *Oh, shit*, I thought, and waited for you to take off the rest of my clothes. Instead you flipped the blanket over me and asked if I was thirsty. When I said yes, you got me a glass of ice water. Even held it while I drank. You very politely asked if I needed anything else, and after I said no, you just . . . left.

"I lay there looking up at the ceiling, trying to figure out whether you were suckering me, the way Dad conjured all those pretty toys when I was little. About the third day you waited on me hand and foot, I realized you weren't running a scam. You really were that . . . kind."

She closed her eyes as the exhaustion of the chase suddenly caught up with her. "Please don't be gone, Justice. I need you. Come back." A tear rolled slowly down her muzzle. She wiped it away with the back of her wrist. "Great. Now I'm crying."

"Then you'd better get out of that pipe before you drown," Justice said.

Miranda jerked her head back so fast, she almost gave herself whiplash. He smiled down at her, handsome and human again. She'd been so lost in her misery, she hadn't even sensed his Shift.

"Justice!" Grinning in delight, Miranda grabbed the athame, stuck it between her teeth, and shot up the pipe, claws sinking into the steel like a squirrel's scrambling up an oak. Propelling herself into an arching leap at the top of the tube, she Shifted in midair.

Justice caught her flying human body as if she was as weightless as a Ping-Pong ball. Plucking the knife from her mouth with one hand, he hauled her into a kiss with the other arm. Dizzy with pure joy and relief, Miranda kissed him back, drinking in the taste of his mouth: mint, a hint of fur, and the sharp ozone tang of magic.

"Fuck, that was close," she gasped against his lips. "You have to quit doing that to me. I'm twenty-four. My heart won't take the strain."

"And I don't think I can take the humor." When Miranda rocked back and stared at him, Justice grinned. "Do you realize you make the most god-awful puns when you're under stress? 'Pipe down'? Jesus."

Miranda laughed. "You understood that?"

"I think it was the sheer appalled horror that brought me back." As he smiled down at her, her magical senses detected power rippling off him like heat from a summer sidewalk.

Good God, Justice's magic is even more powerful than mine. Maybe even greater than Warlock's. Miranda wound her arms around his neck and grinned up into his eyes. "You *are* the Hunter Prince now, aren't you?"

Something grim flickered in his gaze. "Looks that way."

"I've got powers of my very own, you know." She ran a fingertip over his velvety lower lip.

He nipped lightly at her fingertip and gave her a smile. "Yeah?"

"Yeah. I can even walk and everything."

"I gather that's a hint."

"Not that I don't enjoy getting carried around like a bag of Kibbles 'n Bits—but put my ass *down*."

"Oh, all right." Justice started to lower her to her feet, then paused. "Are you sure?"

"Biiiilll . . ."

"Because I'm feeling kind of insecure here."

"And I'm beginning to feel like Linus's security blanket."

"Has anybody ever told you you've got an obsession with cartoons?" He let her feet touch down. "Next you'll be dressing up as a Klingon at *Star Trek* conventions."

Miranda leaned into him and grinned. "Don't worry, darling, I won't be moving into Daddy's basement any time soon."

"God, I hope not. He's probably got a collection of body parts in jars down there."

"I wouldn't be at all surprised." Sensing something blazing magic at her feet, Miranda automatically glanced down. "Oh."

Justice grinned and did a very bad Scarface. "Say hello to my leeettle friend."

Merlin's Blade had evidently reappeared with his Shift; the huge weapon was half-buried in the ground beside their feet. *Probably stuck it there while listening to me emote.*

A wave of power rippled across the axe's Celtic engraving, sparks leaping between the symbols with a low electric crackle. Miranda had seen Warlock's great blade do exactly the same thing whenever her father was nearby.

And what a comforting thought that *is.*

Maeve had given Erielhonan leave to tend to his own needs before taking her message to the Troll King. The cougar stopped off in the forge's kitchen to beg a quick meal from the plump, good-natured brownie who was Maeve's cook.

After bolting the generous bowl of raw beef the little woman gave him, Erie padded out of the kitchen and through the ballroom beyond. Double doors swept open at his approach, and he ghosted out into the garden. Despite the season, Maeve's roses were in full bloom, great bursts of vivid color the goddess had coaxed into climbing elaborate wooden trellises. The end result left the garden brilliantly populated by rose unicorns, rose dragons, and dancing rose fairies.

Erie strolled over to one particular oval-shaped trellis and announced, "The Elemental Falls." The gems Maeve had sunk into the wood promptly generated a dimensional gate that expanded into a wavering oval in the air. The cougar leaped through the opening, which closed behind him with a soap bubble pop he sensed more than heard.

King Dovregubben was in a paranoid mood at the moment, as one might gather from his need for a sword forged by the Mother herself. Apparently he'd learned some young bull of a warrior intended to challenge his right to the throne, and the old troll felt threatened.

To keep the court gossips from learning of his intentions and alerting his challenger, Dovregubben had asked to meet at the falls. Where, no doubt, he hoped to dicker Erie down on the sword's delivery price. Maeve, knowing the trollish love for bargaining, had authorized the cat to negotiate in her stead. Erie fully intended to get every last magical gem he could out of the old cheapskate. After all, this was a blade crafted by the Mother's own hand. Selling it too cheaply would be an insult to both Maeve and the sword itself. Which Dovregubben knew as well as he did.

Still, one must play the game. That was half the fun.

A glance around the clearing told Erie the Troll King had yet to arrive. No surprise, that; Dovregubben was often delayed by the affairs of his kingdom. (Or, Erie suspected, by a willing female or a cold tankard of elvish meade.)

The cougar didn't mind his tardiness this time. It was rare enough that he had the chance to return to the Elemental Falls.

He padded through the thick screen of ferns and brush that surrounded the oval pool as it bubbled and roiled with the pounding energy of the falls. Technically, the water did not have that far to fall, as the black stone cliff was barely twenty feet high.

But just above the falls hung a wavering oval in the air— the Elemental Gate, the eternal breach between this universe and the Elemental dimension beyond it. The magic there was even wilder and more powerful than in this world, and those energies infused the water. The falls glowed to Erie's senses, burning with the warm light of home.

The cougar crouched at the edge of the pool and lowered his head to drink. With each lap of his tongue, the taste of the Elementalverse's magic flooded his senses, more intoxicating than any meade, elvish or troll or even Maeve's own.

The flavor of that ancient magic sent his mind dancing backward through centuries gone, back to the days before he'd become Erielhonan, the Mother's Cat. The days when he'd spread his great wings to the wind between the worlds, a being of pure, swirling magic.

He and his band had not been as powerful as others who'd come to the Mageverse even earlier. In those days, the Children of the Wind had been content to simply dodge the great predators who warred on one another and hunted those of lesser magic. Predators who ripped the life force from others as the sharks of this world tear flesh from a fish. Growing ever stronger with every life claimed.

And ever more viciously hungry.

The Great Predators hunted the Children of the Wind until only a handful survived, clinging to the edge of extinction in a thin, cold cosmic desert where there was little magic to feed them.

Until, starving and desperate, Erie and his herd found the Gate. Conscious of the danger of traveling to another dimension, yet knowing death was even more certain if they remained, the band streamed through the gate.

Only to realize they had only chosen a death more fleet. The alien energies of the Mageverse threatened to rip them apart. Would probably have done so, had not the Mother sensed their cries of pain and fear.

Maeve already maintained a menagerie of sorts, a collection of magical creatures who'd become her companions. Now she offered the dying aliens homes within her pets, allowing them to merge with the creatures, gaining protection from the forces that would otherwise have destroyed them.

In merging with her animal companions, the Children had discovered a new and fascinating world. Erie had never regretted the bargain. He knew he'd have been dead centuries since had the Mother not taken pity on the Children of the Wind.

"Ah, there you are, Maeve's Cat!" Dovregubben's voice boomed as the troll's dimensional gate vanished at his heels.

He was a big, barrel-chested creature, shaped more or less like a Sidhe, though much bigger, with skin the rich shade of jungle leaves and a beard that reminded Erie of moss growing on weathered stone.

The troll swaggered into the clearing on legs like oak

trunks, oddly graceful for all his bulk. The grace was not an illusion; Erie had seen him in combat. The constant challenges he faced as his people's king had made Dovregubben a skilled and wily swordsman, despite the layer of fat from his love of elvish meade.

Dovregubben grinned, the scar that ran the length of his face pulling at the shape of his mouth. Most of his left ear was ragged and missing, in contrast with the tall emerald point that was his right. Gold rings circled his thick green fingers, studded with gemstones like the armbands around his massive biceps. His leather armor was intricately worked with swirling trollish designs that curled around yet more gems, most of them enchanted with one spell or another. Spells for strength, spells for cunning, spells for endurance. Dovregubben apparently kept his people's wizards busy.

"So, what says the Mother?" the big troll asked, folding his massive arms. "Will she craft me my sword?"

"Aye, but 'twill not come cheap," Erie told him, and named a price that made the old troll sputter.

"Ridiculous!" Dovregubben snapped, waving away the sum, just as Maeve had predicted. "I'll give you fifty-six gems, and not one stone more. Twenty emeralds, twenty rubies, and diamonds for the remainder. Flawless stones, by my mother's dugs, ready to take any enchantment Maeve would cast on them. Far more valuable than a little worked steel."

"Bah," Erie spat, Guinness at his most lordly. "The Mother of Fairies forges the finest blades on this or any other world, and well you know it. The sword she'll craft for you will make your rival piss his breechcloth. Any less than sixty rubies, sixty emeralds, and fifty diamonds would be an insult to her honor."

"Would you bankrupt my kingdom?" Dovregubben demanded, rocking back on his booted heels as if staggered by Erie's presumption. "Why, I . . ."

Evil exploded around them, the stench of it so thick and vile, Erie instinctively flattened, hissing, ears drawn back and tail lashing as four dimensional gates opened around them. Dovregubben drew his great sword in a ringing sweep as he cursed in guttural Mountain Troll and readied himself for battle.

An enormous white werewolf was the first through the gates, towering on his massive bunched legs, hands gripping a huge battle-axe. Power radiated from him, along with waves of vile intent.

Three more Dire Wolves stepped through after him. One led a floating cage that imprisoned a dragon child lying in a heap of golden scales, as if flattened by despair. Another dragged a furious unicorn on the end of a magical chain, the beast rearing and fighting every inch of the way, horn glinting as it tried to stab its captor. The last wolf guided a ten-foot energy bubble filled with darting, madly circling demi-Sidhe, none more than six inches high, though they could assume human size when they had the room. Their glowing eyes shone out at Erie, huge with pleading in pale, terrified faces.

"Ahhhh," the white werewolf purred. "Look, boys— what luck. Two brand-new sacrifices, just waiting for the blade."

Erie snarled and prepared to fight, even as his heart went cold.

Justice and Miranda's moment of privacy ended as Guinness and Maeve emerged from the shielding spell. Thankfully, the Sidhe did not bring her boar spear.

The sun had just begun to rise, spilling red and violet light across the Mageverse sky; more time had evidently passed than Miranda had realized.

"I see you finally regained your wits," the dog told Justice. "I was beginning to think we'd have to get you fixed to keep you from humping the neighbor's Saint Bernard." The Chihuahua flashed his teeth in cheerful malice. "That, or Maeve would have to skewer you like a cocktail wiener."

"Yeah, that *would* have been unfortunate," Justice displayed all his own dentition right back. "Especially since it might not have been quite that easy." He reached down and pulled Merlin's Blade out of the ground with an easy jerk of his wrist. At his touch, the weapon flared as bright as an arc welder.

"Nicely menacing." The dog bestowed a judicious nod. "Very *Scarface* Pacino, with just a splash of *Shining* Nicholson. May I suggest a bit more Anthony Hopkins? The Hannibal the Cannibal Hopkins, not the Merchant Ivory butler." He gave Miranda a limpid puppy dog look, the effect slightly spoiled by those bulging eyes. "Would you like to play Clarice, my dear?"

"Not even for a nice Chianti."

"Whoever you decide to channel, save it for Warlock," Maeve said shortly. "In the meantime, I'd suggest more combat practice with your new powers. Those fireballs were pitiful."

A particularly brilliant spark exploded in the ebony depths of Justice's eyes. "I'll try to do better."

Guinness nodded like a gourmet at a wine tasting. "Just enough Anthony that time."

"Glad to hear it." Deadpan as a cobra, Justice lifted a brow. "I'd hate to chew the . . . scenery."

"As long as the scenery is the only thing you chew," Maeve shot back. "I would suggest talking to Arthur and Morgana about that training. Immediately."

"Yes, ma'am." In contrast to those zingers at Guinness, his tone was actually respectful.

"Come, dog." Looking at the blazing horizon, Maeve sighed in weariness. "I haven't seen the dawn after a night this hard since the Kennedy administration." Glancing back at Miranda and Justice, the Sidhe nodded. "Sleep well, children."

Chorusing good-byes, Miranda and Justice watched the pair disappear into the mansion. "So, do you think Maeve and JFK . . ."

"No," Miranda told him quickly. "And I don't want to, either."

"Oh, come on. All that supernatural power? I could definitely see Kennedy hitting that." Justice swung the axe up onto his shoulder with one hand and took her elbow with the other.

"So can I, but that doesn't mean I want to."

"Pussy."

"You never complained before. Anyway, I have enough psychic scars as it is." Raising a brow, she asked, "Shall I open the gate, or do you want to give it a try?"

Justice guided her around a rosebush that probably dated back to the Declaration of Independence, judging by its sheer leafy glory. Despite the crisp fall air, it was covered in blooms the same burning orange as the sky, each rose as big as her head. "It's a gorgeous day. Why don't we just walk?"

"Justice, Avalon is halfway around the planet from here."

"I didn't mean all the way back."

"Oh, God. Is this going to be one of *those* conversations?"

"Don't know yet." He cocked his head and studied her face. "Why are you still afraid of me?"

Flustered, she began, "I'm not afraid, exactly. I'm just . . ."

Justice didn't let her get the rest of the lie out of her mouth. "The fear scent is almost as strong right now as it was when you were diving down rabbit holes to get away from my teeth. Give it up, Bugs. What's wrong?"

"I'm neurotic. Would you like a back sheath for that axe so you don't have to carry it? Looks heavy."

He gave her a long cop look that told her he wasn't swallowing the act. "Sure. As long as I can draw it in a hurry."

Miranda relaxed and closed her eyes, picturing what she wanted to create. Drawing on the magical forces that always roiled in the Mageverse, she started conjuring. A moment later, the sheath appeared, black straps circling his chest, supporting the thick leather case for the battle-axe.

She showed him how to guide the weapon into its diagonal cradle. "You have to angle it at forty-five degrees, or it won't slide in." He adjusted his hold until the big weapon slid down his back into the grip of the leather case.

Miranda nodded. "Yeah, like that."

"How do I get it out?" Justice gripped the haft protruding over his right shoulder.

"Just pull down on the grip. The case is spelled to pop open to release the blade. Then it snaps closed again so it doesn't get in the way while you fight."

"But can I do all that fast enough with one of Warlock's beasts on my ass?" Justice practiced the maneuver a few times until he was satisfied he could free the axe with one easy jerk, then swing it up and around at his target.

"Nice work," he said at last. "But if you think I'm that easy to distract, you underestimate me. I repeat: what's wrong? And if you say nothing, I'm going to get pissed."

Miranda's pleased smile faded. Hesitating a moment, she stroked her fingers nervously over the athame in its belt sheath.

"Miranda . . ."

"Give me a minute!" Gathering her thoughts—and her courage—she launched into an account of what Maeve had told her about her father's fear spell.

"When I used the athame to look down at myself, I saw links of glowing chain wrapping my body. Maeve told me it's designed to weaken my power and make me panic whenever I confront Warlock. Or an Alpha Male, or *anybody* with a lot of power, like Maeve." She drew in another breath. "Or you. When I first climbed out of the pipe, it wasn't bothering me, but now. . . ."

He swore, using a couple of particularly creative phrases Miranda had to admire for their pure lyrical obscenity. They also sounded like good descriptions of Daddy. "What does the spell look like now?"

Drawing the athame, Miranda called on its magic as she looked down the length of her body. "Crap. It's worse. I'm wearing more chains than Snoop Dogg. Why the hell is it stronger?"

"Whenever you give in to it, you probably *make* it stronger. Wonder if I could see that damn thing . . ." Justice frowned in concentration. A wave of azure rolled across his eyes, and his head jerked as if he'd been sucker punched. "Fuck. You're lit up like Times Square on New Year's Eve. No wonder you keep freezing in combat. I'm amazed you can fight at all."

"It's not easy," Miranda admitted. "I've locked up a couple of times at really bad moments. If I don't find a way to get rid of this spell . . ."

"It'll eventually get you killed." He said the words with flat certainty.

"Yep. Any suggestions?"

"Do I look like I go to Hogwarts? All I know about magic is how to get furry." He shrugged. "But I'll give it a try." His dark eyes narrowed in concentration.

"Magic's not just a matter of will, Justice," Miranda began uneasily. "If you try to break a spell like this without knowing how it's constructed, you . . ."

She gasped as the chains abruptly tightened, flaring blue with blinding intensity. "Stop!" The loops jerked so hard, her bones creaked, her arms and legs howling a painful protest as their blood supply cut off. She barely managed to wheeze, "Justice, don't!"

THIRTEEN

He flung up his hands. "All right, I stopped! I'll . . ."

But the chains went on tightening, blazing so bright her skin began to burn. Curls of greasy smoke stung her eyes with the nauseating stench of cooking skin. Every link of the chain grew white hot. Miranda writhed, a scream tearing her throat, though she couldn't draw enough breath to give it voice. Her knees buckled.

Justice caught her, easing her down on the ground, one hand cupping her head to keep it from slamming on the ground with the power of her convulsions.

"Miranda!" His face looked as white as bone china. "Miranda, what the hell am I supposed to *do*?"

"Maeve," she wheezed, the sound barely audible. "Get . . ."

The pain died as if God had flipped a switch. Miranda sucked in a huge breath and collapsed in gasping relief. Her burning flesh cooled, only to ache and prickle as circulation returned.

"Naughty, naughty, traitor," her father whispered in

her brain. *"Leave my spell alone and stay out of my way if you don't want to die."*

He could touch her mind at this distance, all the way from Mortal Earth? Across dimensions? Fury and terror knifed her heart. *"If you could do this, why haven't you killed me already?"*

"Oh, I'll get around to it . . . eventually. At the moment, you're just not that high on my priority list."

"I'll give you a priority list, you ass-sniffing son of a bitch . . ."

But he was gone. The icy presence had vanished from her consciousness, leaving her numb to the bone.

God, Warlock was powerful.

"Miranda," Justice said in a low, careful voice. "What's going on, honey? Talk to me."

"Warlock. It was Warlock." She concentrated on breathing for a moment, gathering her strength. Realizing her right hand was empty, she grabbed his wrist. "My athame! Justice, where's my knife?"

He glanced around, then pounced on the bright blade lying in the leaves. When he pressed the hilt into her palm, Miranda curled her fingers gratefully around the cool metal. The weapon sang a note so pure and high, strength flooded her body, the last of the pain vanishing like a nightmare at dawn.

"We've got to quit doing this," she gasped. "It's kicking my butt." Miranda tried to sit up, but would have hit the ground again without Justice's supporting arms.

"Don't try to stand just yet," he cautioned. "Give yourself a little time."

"Okay." Cradling the athame in both hands, she sat dazed, watching magic dart across the blade in waves of Celtic sigils. "M'okay, Justice."

"Yeah, right," he said roughly. "Considering I nearly fried your pretty ass like a fish stick, you're just dandy."

The guilt in his voice roused her from her daze. "That wasn't you. That was Warlock." She described what her father had said. "He can kill me any time with this damned spell, and there's nothing I can do about it."

"Like hell." A muscle rolled in Justice's square jaw, jerking under the morning stubble. "I'm not going to just let him murder you, Miranda. Not with a spell, not with a sword, not with a fucking paper cut. That is just not an option."

She looked up. The concern in those beautiful eyes made her grapple for control of her temper. "The spell is booby-trapped, Justice. It's designed to cook me if anybody tampers with it. If I don't want to end up basted with an apple in my mouth, we've got to leave it the hell alone."

"If the spell was that damned powerful, how would you be able to get rid of *any* of it just by resisting your fear?" He ran a soothing hand up and down her back. His tone was so reasonable, she wanted to smack him. "It's got a weakness. We can break those chains if we just find the right approach."

Temper body-slammed her. Miranda surged to her feet . . .

. . . And almost fell on her face. She caught herself and snarled. "Yeah, well, you're not the one standing on the IED, waiting for some idiot to jerk the wrong wire."

Stung, Justice rocked back on his haunches to glare up at her. "So we just give up? That's your plan?" He rose to tower over her, taking a deliberate step forward to invade her space with raw masculinity. "I may be an idiot, but that doesn't sound like much of a strategy to me."

"You're not an idiot." Miranda shoved the athame into its sheath. The blade fluted a mournful protest. She sent it a mental apology and began to pace, raking both hands through her tangled red hair. "I didn't mean that, and you know it. This entire situation just pisses me off. Warlock *trapped* me when I was four years old. He didn't even give me a chance to defend myself!"

"He's an abuser, Miranda." Justice watched her pace, frowning. "That's what they do. Strip away the magical fireworks, and he's the exact same kind of bastard I dealt with as a cop."

Stepping into her path, he reached out to cup her face, forcing her to stop and meet his eyes. "Look, guys like that prefer prey who can't fight back. Kids. Vulnerable women. They condition you to believe you're helpless." Justice laughed, but it was the cynical bark of a man who'd seen too much and hadn't been able to do a damned thing about any of it. "They know if you ever realize you're *not* helpless, you'll shoot them in the back of the head and bury them in the basement."

Miranda moved away from him to lean one shoulder against the trunk of a nearby cottonwood—mostly to avoid face-planting in the grass from sheer exhaustion. Glancing down, she noticed the outline of chains on her bare arms, each link the same lobster red as a sunburn. "Well, if anybody ever deserved to rot in a crawl space, it's Warlock. How do you suggest we put him there—preferably *without* me ending up battered and pan-fried?"

He frowned thoughtfully. "Maeve said every time you refuse to give into your fear, the spell erodes. Sounds like your fear actually powers it. Which makes sense. Warlock wouldn't want to spend all that magic keeping it running for—what?—two decades?"

"Yeah," Miranda agreed slowly. "He's got other things he'd rather use his power on, like creating giant snakes that eat people." She frowned, processing the implications. "That makes giving into despair the worst thing I could do. Which is exactly what I just did. God, I'm a moron." She threw up both hands in self-disgust.

"No, what you are is a woman who was an abused child." Justice studied her, his normally warm gaze cool, assessing. Not the lover, but the cop. "Obviously, you're not a child anymore."

Miranda snorted. "Glad you noticed."

He ignored her attempt to lighten the mood. "But are you still Warlock's victim? Because if a victim is all you are, I can't save you. Not that I don't want to—I'd die for you." Justice didn't even blink as he said it; it wasn't braggadocio. "But it doesn't matter if I am the Hunter Prince of that fucking prophecy. *Nobody* can save someone who doesn't want to be saved."

Anger stung Miranda like a wasp, hot and quick, and she glared. "I'm *not* a victim."

"Then quit thinking like one, and start thinking like the woman who ran a twenty-foot wolf right into the ground. *That* woman is nobody's victim."

Miranda blinked, her anger draining away. For the first time, she felt a gleam of hope, like a ray of sunlight pouring into an icy room. "The spell didn't beat me that time, did it? I actually *won*."

"Yeah, you did." His eyes narrowed, as if he was examining the chain. "The thing I don't understand is all the juice the spell is putting out. It's not just your fear powering it, because at the moment, you're not afraid."

"No. I *am* starting to get pissed, though."

"You and me both." He moved in closer, examining her with that unnerving concentration.

Damn, he's tall. The thought pierced her concentration. Miranda's gaze flicked across the width of his shoulders, unconsciously assessing the muscular strength, the sheer power that poured off him, magical and otherwise. That awareness brought fear darting into her consciousness, like a wharf rat skittering into a kitchen. She forced herself to ignore its icy patter to concentrate on the shape of those delicious pectoral muscles under his black silk shirt. The fabric looked soft as it shimmered in the rising sun. *It'd probably be torn to ribbons,* she thought, *except his magic kept it whole.*

When a werewolf Shifted to human again, he ended up in the same clothes he'd worn to start with. She had no idea why. It was just how the magic worked.

Her mind drifted to the feel of his warm skin, like velvet layered over sculpted steel. Soft hair grew in a curling cloud on his chest, narrowing to that dark, inviting little trail that wended its way down the ridges of his belly . . .

"Maeve said the spell is decreasing your power, right?"

"Uh, yeah." Miranda's attention drifted to his lower lip. It looked plump, tempting. She'd fantasized about giving it a good nibble for weeks before their first kiss.

"I'd bet my next paycheck"—he grimaced—"if I got one—that the fireball he threw at you diverted a big chunk of your magic to drive that spell." Justice's brooding attention was obviously so firmly on the problem, he'd completely missed the scent of her mood shifting into desire. "The more power you try to use, the stronger the spell gets, and the stronger your fear becomes. *That* would set up a really nasty feedback loop in a hurry."

"Yeah, it would," Miranda murmured. "But if I concentrate on something else, I can stop the loop." *God, his shoulders are broad.*

Justice nodded. "Yeah, that might work." Pivoting, he dropped his gaze to the toes of his boots and began to pace across the leafy ground, obviously deep in thought. "It would have to take more than your lack of fear to break the spell. Otherwise it would die the minute you calmed down."

"Maeve said I could use the athame to crack it," Miranda said absently as the width of his shoulders led her eye to the broad supporting straps that held his axe angled across his back. His dark leather slacks were just tight enough to reveal the roll of his muscular ass and the powerful brawn of his long legs. He'd be fast, with legs like that.

"Did she say how?" Justice turned and walked back to her again, his dark gaze probing as he studied her face.

"No, not really." *His muscled ass had felt warm and delightfully brawny beneath her hands. She'd curled both legs around that strong back, seeking the leverage to meet his driving thrusts. His cock filled her with a delicious, burning pleasure as he worked it in and out of her slick inner grip. He'd had her so turned on, she hadn't even noticed the fear.*

His eyes stared into hers, velvet dark, magic rolling across their irises in waves of hot blue sparks. His nose flared as if he drank in her scent. His lips parted, displaying white teeth. "You're staring."

"I was wondering when you'd notice." Resting a hand in the center of his chest, she leaned into him, eyes shuttering as she enjoyed the warmth he radiated into the morning chill. "I was started to think I'd lost my touch."

"Oh, I noticed." That buccaneer's smile flashed as his cock hardened, lengthening against her belly. "I just didn't want you to think I'm easy."

Miranda laughed. "Of all the words I could use to describe you, Justice, 'easy' ain't one of them."

He purred at her, the sound rumbling through that broad chest. Long fingers brushed the line of her jaw, stroking slowly. His fingertips were just slightly rough with calluses, and she shivered at their delicate rasp. "Just what words are we talking about?"

"Let's see." She rose on her toes and kissed him slowly, thoroughly, brushing his lips with hers, slipping her tongue between his even teeth, tasting him with dreamy arousal. "Hot." Her hands explored his chest, discovering slabs of hard brawn and tight ridges that flexed as she touched him. "Strong." She drew back an inch and smiled as she slid a hand down to cup his erection with bold fingers. Miranda grinned shamelessly as his eyes widened in erotic surprise. "Big."

"Wicked," he purred back, as he reached for her, caressing the curve of her ass, the width of her waist, then sliding a hand up to one breast. He cupped her through the cotton of her shirt until her nipple rose against his palm. "And soft," he breathed against her lips. "You feel so soft."

Justice's free hand cradled her head as he kissed her as if savoring each tongue stroke, every brush of lip on lip. Miranda moaned against his mouth, her eyes drifting closed as she drank the clean rainwater tang of mint and ozone from his mouth.

His power began to rise in response to his desire, a slow spiral that rolled against her magical senses.

Bearing down. Grinding.

Fear shot through her brain. She tried to ignore it and concentrate on the delicious length of his cock pressed against her belly.

As if scenting her fear, he made a soothing sound and

pulled her shirt from the waistband of her jeans. One big hand slid under it, up the bare, sensitive skin of her ribs. Miranda shivered and relaxed against him as he tugged a bra cup down. Fingers plucked and rolled her nipple until pleasure made her forget everything else. The sensual musk of testosterone flooded her nose. Justice growled, a low lupine rumble.

The fear that had faded under his delicious attentions instantly rushed into her brain, chilling her warm arousal.

"Work with me here, darlin'," he murmured, and started nibbling his way down her jaw to the pulse that leaped with magic-stoked fear.

"That damned spell," Miranda growled in frustration. "Every time I think I've beaten it, it surges back. I wish to hell I could just . . . burn it out of my skull."

He paused. "Ah, I really don't think . . ."

A wild idea flashed into her consciousness, one that sent an icy chill up her spine. Which, perversely, made her want to do it, if only to prove that she wouldn't cave in to her father's spell. "Tie me up."

Justice lifted his head to stare in genuine alarm. "What?"

"Tie me up." Miranda gritted her teeth as mental voices howled in protest. Now that she knew about the spell, she could hear how alien they were. Warlock's nasty chorus, doing his bidding to weaken her.

"I really don't . . . ?"

"I'll conjure a bed, and you can tie me to the frame." She forced a smile despite the anxiety that clawed her at the thought. "Silk scarves and a big brass bed, right out here in the magic forest. We can be kinky in comfort."

"No." Justice's hot gaze chilled. "I may be an Alpha werewolf, but I am not a sadist."

The athame sounded a warning note—something about *'dangerous territory'*—but she ignored it. "Tying some-body up doesn't make you sadistic. Lots of people play bondage games."

"Yeah, they do. *I* have." He stepped away from her.

Some part of her instantly missed his warmth. "But that's not a game I'd play with somebody who's fucking terrified."

He jerked Merlin's Blade out of its sheath and buried the battle-axe in the dirt with a solid *thunk*. The gesture shouted of temper barely under control. A burst of power and dominance rolled off him, so feral, so Alpha, she longed to duck her head and drop her eyes . . .

. . . Or run like hell.

Instead, Miranda lifted her chin and forced herself to meet his gaze, though his irises burned blue with Hunter Prince magic. "I have to beat this, Justice. If I don't, it's just like you said. I'll never be anything but a victim. And I'm damned tired of being Warlock's victim."

"My torturing you is not going to solve the problem." A muscle in his broad jaw flexed his teeth ground. "It would only make the spell stronger. Your fear would hit it like gasoline on a forest fire."

"Justice, that's exactly how they *fight* forest fires. Starve the flames of fuel by running a flamethrower across its path, and the fire dies."

"Miranda, dammit . . ."

But she rushed on. "If you tie me up, it's going to scare me. Yes, I know that. But if you make love to me anyway, the spell will lose its power as we burn out the fear. And that will make it easier to kill the spell altogether, once we figure out how."

"Forget it." Justice slashed a hand through the air in a savage gesture of negation. "I'm not a rapist, and I'm not going to become one so you can resolve your daddy issues."

"Dammit, I'm not asking you to rape me. Merlin's balls, I wouldn't do that. I just want you to help me." She spread her hands, pleading. "Do you think there's another Alpha werewolf on the planet I'd trust to do this? No. But I trust you. No matter what this damned spell tries to tell me, the real Miranda knows the kind of man you are."

"Yeah—the kind who won't psychologically waterboard the woman he loves."

Miranda's train of thought instantly derailed. She must have misheard. "Loves?"

"Yeah—loves." He said the word like a challenge.

Her startled heart seemed to swell in her chest, joy inflating it like a balloon. "You love me?" *Me? Warlock's damaged daughter?*

"You think I'd have jumped between a dinosaur and just anybody?"

"Yeah, actually, I do. You wouldn't stand by while *anyone* got chomped by a monster."

Justice opened his mouth, closed it again, and shrugged sheepishly. "Okay, maybe. That doesn't change the fact that I love you. I've been in love with you from the first time I saw you throw a fireball at that raging psychotic you call a father."

Her chest ached with a sweet pain she'd never felt before. *Must be all that joy.* "I love you, William Justice."

He opened his arms so she could walk into them. "I know. I heard you say so from the bottom of your rabbit hole." Drawing her close, he rested his chin on top of her head. "Don't make me do this, Bugs. I can't stand the thought of hurting one hair on your cotton tail."

Miranda sighed and surrendered. "It would have worked."

"No. I never would have done it. Not as long as you're so terrified." Justice drew back to give her a satyr's smile. "Now, if you ever decide you've got a yen involving a pair of fuzzy handcuffs and a carrot . . ."

"You're a bad, bad boy, Elmer."

He winced. "Oh, God. No. Do *not* call me Elmer."

Miranda smirked. "If you insist, Foghorn."

Justice cringed. "Oh, Christ."

"What?" She batted her widened eyes, trying to fake innocence. "You'd prefer Deputy Dawg?"

"That's just damned *not funny.*"

"Daffy?"

"I'm beginning to reconsider the water-boarding thing."

"Porky?"

With a mock growl, he pounced on her, tumbling her backward. She conjured a mattress as they fell.

In its belt sheath, the athame trilled in delighted satisfaction. But deep within Miranda's brain, the spell pulsed, malevolence worked into its every magical rune.

Justice twisted as they fell, meaning to hit the ground on his back with Miranda in his arms, tucked safely against his chest.

Instead of smacking into hard dirt, they sank into eight inches of expensive mattress padding. Feeling slick fabric against his skin, he smiled at Miranda as she sprawled across him, all legs and arms and warm, sweet curves. "Silk sheets. You little perv."

"I am *not* a perv." She tilted her chin and sniffed with all the offended dignity of a Chosen aristocrat. "I just hate making love with sticks digging into my butt." Miranda wrinkled her nose, looking cuter doing it than any grown woman should. "Not to mention ticks. Disgusting little bloodsuckers."

"Actually, I can't blame them for wanting a bite of you. You're pretty tasty." Justice rolled over with her—damn, the bed was the size of Lake Michigan—and braced his weight on his elbows. Savoring the soft femininity of her body, he kissed her slowly. She gave as good as she got, her lips angling back and forth over his mouth, her tongue circling and flicking his in an erotic duel.

With a deliciously sensual moan, Miranda wound slender arms around his neck and slid a long leg up to hook her calf across his ass. The position nestled her belly against his erect cock with just the perfect pressure.

His wolf growled. Its mental rumble seemed to vibrate his skull right down to the spine.

Don't you dare start, he told it savagely. *She's not up to your shit right now.*

Justice had been a werewolf for three years, more than long enough to come to terms with his hairy half. Yes, his first weeks as a Dire Wolf had been a little rough, but he had learned how to control all that animalistic strength and feral instinct. They'd gotten along fairly well ever since.

Unfortunately, that was then. This was AMB—After Merlin's Blade. The battle-axe's magic had turned the wolf he'd managed to tame—more or less—into the Wolf.

A monster straight out of a torture porn splatter flick.

The vicious creature had come so damned close to eating Miranda, Justice went cold to the bone every time he remembered it. He'd had no control of the Wolf whatsoever, no influence over it, no power to restrain its savagery. He'd been forced to watch in grinding fear as the great monster hunted Miranda, ignoring his roared mental orders to back off. If she'd been an instant slower, a tiny bit weaker, the barest fraction less smart, he'd have lost her.

And if the Wolf *had* killed her, Justice would have put a bullet in its brain—even though it was also his own. Maybe *because* it was also his own. He couldn't have lived knowing he'd murdered the woman he loved.

Especially not like that.

Fortunately, Miranda was every bit as smart as she was lovely. When she'd dived down that rabbit hole of hers, she'd bought him the time he desperately needed to figure out how to get back in the driver's seat.

And when she'd artlessly confessed her love—even as the Wolf tried to dig her out of her hole like a gopher— Justice discovered the raw mental strength to regain control. He was damned if the furry fucker was going to get another shot at her.

The Wolf snarled, yellow eyes shining in the depths of his brain. With a rising howl, the monster exploded to the surface in a skull-rattling burst of magic that damned near broke Justice's hold.

Justice ground his teeth, fighting the Wolf's attempt to force another Shift. His eyes flicked open. Miranda smiled up at him, her wicked gold gaze bright with love as she cradled his body in the loving grip of her arms and legs.

That was all the help he needed.

As the Wolf charged again, battering at him, Justice caught it in a net of raw will and *shoved*, stuffing the thing back in its mental cage, locking it in, slamming the foot-thick steel bar into the massive brackets that braced it across the door.

The Wolf raged, slamming into the two-inch bars so hard the cage shook. Shook, but held. Bright, hard, and unyielding.

Justice smiled coldly into the thing's savage eyes. *Not this time, asshole.*

The Wolf snapped at him in frenzied rage, spittle flying, throwing its massive body against the door. *Slam slam slam!* The cage rocked like a sailboat in a hurricane.

But the bars held. And they would go on holding.

True, the cage was only a manifestation of Justice's will. But so far, it was working. He'd keep the Wolf caged as long as he had to.

If that meant he had to fight his inner monster every waking minute until he found a way to take Warlock's head . . . Well, fine. He'd do that. Then he'd figure out how to get rid of the Wolf.

Even if it meant becoming merely human again.

He didn't have much choice. Controlling the Hunter Prince his axe had created took too much concentration and willpower. He didn't know how long he could keep doing it.

Maeve would probably help disentangle him from Merlin's spell; he figured he'd have earned it by then. The Sidhe goddess certainly had enough juice for the job.

As for becoming the powerless lover of a werewolf lit up with more magic than the Las Vegas skyline . . .

Well, one problem at a time.

He opened his eyes again to find Miranda kissing him slowly, her lips like warm velvet, her tongue quick and clever in his mouth. Her hips rolled against his, spread legs curled over his ass, holding him deliciously close. His erection had softened during the struggle with the Wolf, but it instantly hardened, lengthening clear to his waist.

Miranda did that to him.

"There you are," she murmured, drawing back to search his face with far too much perception. "What's going on, Justice? For a minute there, you were gone. *Something* looked out of your eyes, but it wasn't you. And it scared the crap out of me."

FOURTEEN

Justice knew he was going to have to tell Miranda about the Wolf—she'd need the advance warning if it escaped again. He just didn't want to tell her *now*. The trust growing between them was too fragile. She'd start being afraid of him again. "Not now," Justice murmured. "Give me a little time."

Her eyes narrowed. For a moment he thought she was going to force him to spill the whole ugly thing.

Instead Miranda nodded slowly. "It can wait." A wicked smile broke across her face. "This can't." She rolled her torso, making him acutely aware of her body—those exquisite breasts, the legs that went on forever, the maddening scent of feminine desire . . .

"I need you, Justice." Honesty was stark as a blade in those golden eyes, sharp enough to take his breath. "I need your body. I need your strength. I need your love."

"You've got them." His voice sounded hoarse. "I love you, Miranda. Everything I am, everything I have—it's all yours."

Miranda grinned, wickedly sexy. "Glad to hear it." She

caught the hem of his polo shirt in both Direkind hands and jerked. The tough material ripped like a wet paper towel. "Because I've got plans for you, Fudd."

He laughed, enjoying the creamy heat that streamed into his blood. "Oh, Bugs—you do like to live dangerously." Her shirt had even less chance against his hands.

Laughing like loons, they went after each other's clothes, as gleefully ruthless as kids tearing into Christmas gifts. Shoes sailed off into the bushes. Slacks, boxers, her lacy black bra and its matching panties, even their socks—every stitch yielded to Dire Wolf strength, filling the air with ripping sounds and a confetti drift of shredded fabric.

They spared nothing but the sheaths of their weapons. Those they unbuckled and put carefully down beside the bed.

You didn't throw Merlin's Blade into the bushes.

Finally they were both naked . . . and just a little out of breath from laughter and wrestling. "What the hell." Justice settled down on top of her again. "We can always conjure more clothes." He flashed a grin. "Though quite frankly, I like the view just as it is."

"And you call *me* a perv." She stretched luxuriously beneath him, as if savoring the cool texture of silk against her back—and the warmth of his flesh against her chest. Her nipples had drawn into delicious pink buds riding the soft, full curves of her breasts. So impossibly sweet, so deliciously tempting.

She reminded him of some Celtic fairy, her skin creamy and perfect over lean, elegant muscle and delicate bone. Long runner's legs and slim, strong arms, wrapping around him, holding him close.

Her hair spilled over the bed's pale cream silk in flaming curls streaked with shades of gold and copper. The soft delta between her thighs was every bit as fiery.

The woman of his dreams.

Now if only I can keep the Big Bad Wolf from eating her . . .

He cut the thought off and bent his head to one peaked, rosy nipple. It tasted deliciously of clean forest air and woman and Dire Wolf musk. Closing his eyes, he licked and nibbled and sucked. And made himself forget everything but her.

Pleasure rolled through Miranda like shimmering streams of magic cast by every flick of Justice's tongue, every nibble, every strong, suckling pull of his mouth. Sliding her hands into the curling silk of his hair, she arched her back and sighed, surrendering to his erotic spell.

He felt so damned good against her. Hard, warm, a little furry here and there. Everything she'd ever dreamed of as a lonely young girl awaiting whatever demon wolf Warlock sent to breed her.

But as sweet as it was letting Justice make love to her, Miranda ached to explore. "I want to touch you."

Justice lifted his head, black eyes flicking up to meet hers over the curve of her breast. "You are touching me." He grinned like a devil. "And you're doing a damned good job of it, too."

"Glad you approve." She tightened the grip of her thighs around his waist and twisted with agile Dire Wolf strength, flipping him onto his back and landing neatly astride his hips. "But this time, *I* want to be on top."

Sable eyebrows rose. "I see that." One corner of his lip quirked, and he folded his arms beneath his head. "I'm all yours."

"Yes." Miranda grinned down at him in pure anticipation. "You certainly are." She nibbled her lower lip, considering all the gorgeous masculinity sprawled beneath her. His shoulders looked very broad against the cream silk sheets, brawny biceps bulging like grapefruit in his bent arms. Muscle lay in clear relief beneath the warm tan velvet of his skin and a soft cloud of curling chest hair. Small brown nipples peeked at her, and she wondered if they were as sensitive as her own.

She touched one, and he caught his breath. Miranda grinned in delight at the sudden sense of power she felt.

Not that power was a stranger, of course. She couldn't even remember a time when magic didn't leap to her will. What she hadn't felt was the purely feminine power of making a man respond to her touch. Especially not this man, this lethal wolf warrior.

Now, *that* was power.

Staring into the rich chocolate of his eyes, Miranda stroked her thumb back and forth over one of his hard little nipples. "You like that?"

"You have to ask?" Twin fireworks of magic flared bright across his ebony irises. From the corner of one eye, Miranda saw Merlin's Blade begin to glow, the huge blue gem in its haft spilling a neon wash of light.

But at the moment, the only shaft that interested her was his cock. It lay deliciously trapped beneath her, its width pressing between her inner lips, flushed mushroom cap pinned to his hard belly. A bright bead clung to its tip like a gem.

Miranda reached down and collected the pearl of liquid with a flick of her forefinger. Feeling wicked, she met his gaze and slid her fingertip into her mouth, sucking the salty little drop away. "Mmmmm. Distilled Justice."

He swallowed, Adam's apple bobbing in his muscular neck. "Anytime you want to taste anything else of mine, I can make a few suggestions."

"I believe my imagination's up to the challenge." God, had that purr come out of her? Miranda Drake, the repressed, emotionally scarred daughter of a psychotic sorcerer?

Fuck Warlock. This is for me. For us.

She stretched out on top of him, sliding down his body, savoring the hard pressure of the thick erection pressing against her belly. Taking her time, Miranda kissed him, drinking in the taste of his mouth, her tongue exploring the velvet warmth of his lips and the slick points of canines gone wolf-sharp; he was on the verge of Shifting.

Justice started to lower his arms from their folded position under his head. She gave him a mock glare. "Hands behind your head, cop, or I'll have to use the cuffs."

His brows winged up. "Oh, we are in a kinky mood."

"You heard me. Hands behind your head."

"Yes, mistress." A chuckle vibrating his chest, he obeyed.

"Good dog." Miranda went back to kissing him, slowly, thoroughly. Savoring the contrast between his soft mouth and his hard body. *He's like a hero out of one of those books I wasn't supposed to read.*

Curious, she started exploring, stroking her fingers along the contours of brawn, up ridges of tendon, through the soft tufts beneath his raised arms.

To her delight, he squirmed at the gentle brush of her nails. "Why, Justice—are you ticklish?"

Black eyes narrowed. "Are *you*?"

"Bad puppy." She gently raked her fingernails across both armpits. "No threatening Mistress Miranda."

He jerked in reaction and glowered. "Mistress Miranda is going to get a spanking if she tickles me one more time."

"You and what army, Fudd?" Grinning, Miranda ran her nails down his ribs, just hard enough to make him buck.

"I don't need an army." Fireworks detonated in his eyes like the Fourth of July. Not a little Dire Wolf burst, either. It was pure Hunter Prince, more howitzer than bottle rocket. Savagery followed, flooding his ebony eyes with feral animal rage.

Miranda froze, ice sheeting over her skin. Her father's spell choked her, cramming her throat with a knot of terror.

Justice blinked, and the ferocity vanished, replaced by stricken pain. "Miranda . . . God, I didn't mean . . ."

"Shhhh." She covered his mouth with a kiss, concentrating desperately on the taste of him, on the feel of his mouth as he kissed her back. An aching apology delivered with his lips. "It's all right."

Miranda focused on the hard, warm reality of his body,

until the last of her fear drained and passion began to rise again.

"I love you," Justice whispered against her mouth. "God, I love you."

"You do realize you're giving me psychic whiplash?" She lifted her head just enough to smile down into his worried gaze. "From abject terror to giddy delight in 8.2 seconds."

He winced. "I'm sorry."

"Don't be. You love me. I love you. That's all that's important. Not Warlock. Not the Hunter Prince. Not fairies or talking dogs or prophecies. None of it matters—except this." She kissed him again, slow and deep and passionate.

When she finally lifted her head again, Miranda found determination in his narrowed eyes. "I'm not going to let my Wolf hurt you again, Miranda. Ever."

He means it. Muscles relaxed between her shoulders, and she sank against his mouth for another slow, deep kiss. *And Justice always keeps his promises.*

His softened cock hardened beneath her, pressing against her belly, hard as the haft of his axe and damned near as long.

Which gave her a delicious idea . . .

Miranda's kisses heated his blood, chasing away the chill the Wolf had left behind. Marking its vicious territory in his brain like the stink of urine.

But he'd locked his monster away again, clanged the cage door shut, left it to glare out at him in frustrated hate.

And a hearty "fuck you" to you, too, ass-sniffer. She's mine. *I'm not going to let you scare her again—much less anything else.*

Then Miranda began kissing her way down his face to his throat, and he forgot all about his Wolf. Swirling her tongue over his throbbing pulse, she nibbled the tendons with gentle little nips.

Justice started to reach for her, but she shot him a narrow golden look. "I told you where I wanted your hands, Fudd."

"Okay, okay!" Lips twitching, he slid his palms under his head again.

With a satisfied sniff, Miranda began working her way down his body, leaving a trail of kisses and tiny bites and teasing little flicks of her tongue. She explored each rise and valley of bone and muscle, stroking him with silken fingertips until his nerves quivered like plucked harp strings.

Pausing over one small brown nipple, she demonstrated she had indeed been paying attention to everything he'd ever done to hers.

He'd never considered his male nips erogenous zones, but Miranda proved him wrong. Every flick of her pointed pink tongue, every rake of her teeth over those tiny points, every stroke and pinch sent darts of pleasure straight to his balls.

By the time she moved on to her next target, his mouth was dry and his cock lay across his belly like a lead pipe.

Miranda headed straight for it, drawing delicious little patterns on his skin with tiny licks and soft caresses, lighting up his nervous system like Christmas lights.

As she approached his cock, Justice tensed, his back unconsciously arching as he imagined her wet mouth closing over his cock, suckling hard, velvet lips tight around the sensitive shaft.

Almost there . . .

She stopped just before she reached his violently flushed glans, pausing to swirl lazy circles around his navel. His erection bucked as if to remind her it was waiting.

Miranda ignored it completely. She was far too busy playing erotic, maddening games with her mouth.

Good God, she's tongue-fucking my navel . . .

Beneath his neck, his hands curled into fists as he fought the impulse to grab the back of her head and pull her down where he wanted her. *I am not a barbarian.*

But dammit, she was pushing it. Hard.

"Mirrrrandaaaa . . ." The growl that vibrated his chest could have come from his Wolf.

Miranda slanted him a teasing glance, not intimidated in the least. "Yes?" She caught the skin around his navel between her teeth and nibbled.

Justice imagined her giving the same treatment to a far more sensitive body part. He almost whimpered.

Her lips curled into a smile that was more cat than wolf. "Is there something you wanted to say?"

Suck my cock! Somehow he swallowed that less-than-chivalrous demand. "You do have a talent for teasing." The words emerged wrapped in a deep, hungry rumble. "You might want to remember that I do too."

"Threats, Fudd?" She danced her fingertips over his belly, a fraction of an inch from his bobbing, violently flushed cock. "You sure you want to go there?"

"You're just begging for that spanking, Bugs."

"More threats." Smiling wickedly, Miranda reached out to run a slow fingernail along a vein that ran the length of his heavy erection. The bowed shaft danced under her touch. Justice gasped. She wrapped long, graceful fingers around his cock and tilted her head, contemplated its glans, once again pearled with arousal. "Not very smart, particularly considering what I'm planning to do to this big, juicy carrot of yours."

Justice managed a strangled laugh. "Consider me your personal vegetable patch, Bugs. Carrots. Cucumbers. . . ." He swallowed as she angled the thick organ toward her mouth. "Zucchini."

"Mmmmm. I have this urge to ask, 'Ehhhh . . . What's up, Doc?'" She lowered her head until her lips were a breath from his cock. "But that's kinda obvious."

"Yeah, I'd have to say I'm definitely up." He licked his dry lips. "In fact, I don't believe I can *get* any more 'up.'"

"Ya think?" Miranda smirked. "Let's find out." And in one breathtaking rush, she engulfed him in the snug, wet heat of her mouth.

His head was still spinning from that searing pleasure when she began to suck.

Hard.

So hard those strong, drawing pulls instantly sent salvos of pleasure blasting straight into the base of his brain. The heat she generated with lips and tongue and ferocious erotic suction had him teetering on the verge of climax in five minutes flat.

"God!" Writhing with gritted teeth, Justice throttled his reaction, clawing for control. "God, Miranda, you're driving me insane . . ."

She drew him and purred a laugh. "Oh, baby, I'm just getting started."

With that, Miranda slid his cock deeper into her mouth, angling her head down as she tried to swallow him to the balls. She couldn't quite manage it—he was a bit too well-endowed for that—but she got him deep enough to make his nuts feel as if they were about to blow like hand grenades. Dragging in a desperate breath, Justice grabbed the mattress with both hands, fingers digging into the silk.

She pulled her head up again, slowly. So slowly. Her mouth caressed every inch of his shaft until she reached its exquisitely sensitive glans. Pausing, she danced her tongue over the tight flesh, drawing mind-blowing swirls and runes over the mushroom head.

Probably sketching a spell to blast me into orbit.

Heat pulsed in the tight balls she held cupped in cool, tapered fingers. Each suckling pull and flick of her tongue built the fire higher, hotter, until it thundered in his skull.

Gritting his teeth, Justice fought his rising orgasm. *Dammit, not yet. I'm not going to come until I'm in her.*

Then she opened her mouth and swooped down again.

He twisted like a man on a rack, fighting his body's need to come. *For God's sake, you'd think I was a sixteen-year-old getting his first blow job.*

No casual hummer had ever felt like this. Yeah, some of his past lovers had been a lot more skilled than Miranda, who was clearly making it up as she went along. Yet she reached parts of him none of those women ever had—and he wasn't talking about his dick.

Miranda touched his soul.

Jesus, that sounds corny. Yet despite the instinctive protests of ex-cop cynicism, Justice couldn't deny the truth. She made something deep inside him reverberate like crystal singing to a tuning fork.

It scared the shit out of him. He'd never been this vulnerable to anyone or anything.

But blended with that instinctive fear was a reckless surge of excitement. Justice recognized it as the same adrenalin junky rush he'd once enjoyed as a homicide cop playing cat and mouse with killers. No matter how wild the ride got, he knew Miranda would be right there beside him, watching his back and protecting his heart. Despite her fear, despite his inner Big Bad Wolf, she loved him right to the marrow of her bones.

She deserves roses, he thought, with the tiny portion of his brain that still could think in the midst of such a storm of pleasure. *Candles and diamonds and romance.*

Then she started drawing him out of her mouth one throbbing inch at a time, and he couldn't think anything at all.

Miranda smiled around her mouthful of cock like the Cheshire Cat swan-diving into a vat of cream. Nothing had ever made her feel so deliciously powerful as watching Justice writhe in erotic delight, just from the flick of her tongue.

But as she listened to his deep groans, she reluctantly decided he was a little too close to the edge. It wouldn't do to let him climax just yet. She released his rosy cock, feeling more than a little smug at his heartfelt groan. *Not bad for a trick I learned from a romance novel.*

Before Justice could do more than open his stunned eyes, she rose to her knees, swung a leg across his hips, angled his cock upward with one hand, and sank down. Which was yet another move from one of the erotic romances her mother had forbidden her to read.

Unfortunately, the book hadn't mentioned that getting a cock correctly aimed was a little more complicated than it sounded. She had to fumble before she found her slick, swollen target with the head. "Ahhh . . . *There* you are."

"Yeah," Justice gasped, his eyes a little crazed. "*There* I certainly am."

Slowly Miranda began to lower herself, letting the thick shaft sink into her tight, slick depths. Stuffing her, stretching her, the sensation raw and overwhelming. He was almost too big, yet pleasure skated on the edge of that pain, shimmering delight following the ache.

The first time they'd made love, her wolf's hunger had blinded her to everything but her own erotic need. But now Miranda felt every inch of broad, endless cock as she sank lower. And lower. And lower. Until finally her ass nestled against his heavy balls.

She froze there, trying to get used to the feeling of being impaled, breathing in through her nose as she fought the instinct to *get the hell* off *him*. Gradually, as she breathed in the scent of roses and incense, the pain faded, replaced by the slow rise of arousal.

Biting her lip, Miranda blinked down at him. "God. You fill me so full."

"Well, you are a little . . . tight." He grinned like a devil. "Not that I'm complaining."

"Neither am I," she decided. And rose, sliding up his thick length.

Pleasure began to waft like smoke from the slow friction raking along her wet, snug grip. Arousal grew, burning slowly brighter, like the candles that blazed all around them in the gathering dark.

Until she forgot the discomfort of his size. Forgot everything but the sweet, keen delight that intensified with every jog. Warmth grew hotter, building degree by slow degree into burning lust.

Before she knew it, Miranda was riding with furiously rolling hips as Justice bucked beneath her like a half-tamed stallion.

Sliding a skilled finger beneath her sex, he reached up with his free hand to cup her breast. Circling and flicking her stiff clit, he simultaneously teased her nipple while she worked thighs and calves, riding hard, pleasure thundering through her like the beat of hooves.

Fire became firestorm.

Her wolf surfaced with a savage, delighted growl. Justice growled back, sounding every bit as feral.

Miranda ground down on him, the pain gone, loving the thick heat of his cock screwing its way within her wet grip, loving the bolts of delight his fingers teased from clit and nipple. A growl rumbling in his throat, Justice stoked her pleasure higher, higher, higher, a reckless arsonist spraying gasoline over a brushfire.

Her climax detonated, shooting blazing streamers down every nerve she had. Miranda threw back her head and screamed its blinding glory.

A heartbeat later, Justice bellowed in echo. Her body still quivering in the aftermath of her orgasm, she looked down, hungry to watch him come.

He roared again, deafening as a roll of thunder, impossibly deep, inhumanly loud as he soared like a rocket on a tail of flame.

Miranda sucked in a breath, an icy chill cutting through her heat as she watched Justice's wide, black eyes fill with fire.

And the Wolf.

The black terror of Warlock's spell choked Miranda like strangling hands clamped around her throat. All too aware of the Wolf looking out through Justice's eyes, she knew she had to get her panic under control. Fast.

There was nothing that made a predator hungrier than the smell of fear wafting from its prey. She'd have been in deep trouble had she been human. That kind of terror wasn't something most people could hide.

But Miranda was an old pro when it came to dealing with her emotions and their effect on predators. She'd been only eleven when she realized the scent of her fear brought out the sadist in Warlock. The barest whiff of anxiety or the sound of a heart's increased beat could inspire her father to acts of demonic creativity.

She'd never been able to avoid feeling fear altogether, though God knew she'd tried. In retrospect, that was no surprise, given Warlock's fear spell. She'd had to find another way to protect herself.

So Miranda had invented a spell to bleach the stink of adrenaline from her body, while keeping her heart thumping as slow and steady as a clock. She'd only been twelve years old at the time.

Unfortunately, she soon learned the contrast between her panicked brain and calm body was disorienting to the point of being sickening. She avoided using the spell unless she had no choice at all.

Yet Miranda cast it now, just as fast as she could mentally chant the words. She had no choice. If Justice Shifted, she'd be far too close to all those teeth.

So even as Miranda purged the fear from her scent and heartbeat, she smiled sunnily down into the Wolf's cold, fierce eyes. "I love what you've done with the place." She held her voice cool and steady, despite the howling fear Warlock's spell induced. "Very romantic."

The beast faded under a wave of confusion as Justice's human mind jolted to awareness again. Just as she'd intended. The savage struggle between Wolf and Man flashed across his face like shadows projected on a film screen. Miranda held her breath.

Justice won, thank God.

"You mean all this?" He gestured vaguely at the clearing around them. "I thought you did it."

"I did the bed," she told him, relaxing a trifle. "You conjured everything else."

Which was saying something. They were now surrounded by waterfalls of cream silk and huge silver vases of red roses.

Massive sterling silver candelabras illuminated Miranda's bower with the light from dozens of beeswax candles. A table for two stood a few feet from the bed, filling the air with wafting steam and the scent of blood-rare beef.

Miranda tugged free of Justice's body, controlling a wince. *I'm going to be sore as hell tomorrow.* As she remembered his explosive reaction, her mouth curled in a private, wicked smile. *But making Justice lose his mind was worth it.*

Right now, though, she figured she'd better put a little distance between them, just in case his Wolf gained ascendency over his human half.

FIFTEEN

She sauntered over to the table, keenly aware of his gaze. Two beautifully engraved silver domes sat across from each other, equally gorgeous silver place settings to either side, arrayed on red linen napkins. In the table's center stood a crystal vase bursting with two dozen crimson roses, surrounded by a cluster of tall, slim white candles. Beside the table, a magnum of champagne chilled in a sterling silver bucket heaped with ice.

Miranda lifted one of the domes to find a thick rib eye steak steaming beside a huge lobster tail and a small silver bowl of drawn butter. A baked potato and asparagus spears rounded out the meal.

Which was pretty damned close to perfect, at least from a werewolf's carnivorous point of view. Her mouth watered. "Damn, Justice, this smells delicious."

He rolled from the bed and padded over to join her, gloriously naked. Miranda paused to admire the view, at least until he stepped behind her to pull out her chair. A little nonplussed, she sat down, and Justice slid the chair into place, as skillfully graceful as any Regency buck.

"Are you sure you didn't do this?" he asked, turning to tug the champagne bottle from its nest of ice before popping the cork with an efficient flick of one thumb. "Because I don't have the faintest idea how to go about conjuring all this stuff. For God's sake, this is a Dom Perignon 1966." He eyed the front of the bottle. "At least, that's what the label says."

"Really?" Miranda watched in interest as he filled a crystal champagne flute with the foaming golden wine. "One of Gerald's magazines said that year goes for something like two thousand bucks a bottle."

"Ouch." He tilted the magnum up, obviously trying to avoid spilling any of it. "My tastes just aren't that expensive. Not that I'd even know how to conjure a Big Mac . . ."

"Justice, *not* knowing what you're doing actually makes you a lot more likely to do something like this than I would be." She cut a bite of her steak and moaned in pleasure. "God, that's good."

He frowned as he settled into his own seat. "What do you mean?"

Miranda chewed, enjoying the tender, smoky steak, cooked precisely as she liked it. "Because you don't think you know how to use magic, you give your subconscious an opening to do what it does best: create. Dream." She waved her fork. "Make your wishes come true." Miranda grimaced, remembering one or two magical misadventures she'd had as a child. "And that includes your nightmares. Which is why you'd better get the magic under control before you do something god-awful without meaning to."

Justice started, remembering the thought that had flashed through his mind as she'd made love to him. *She deserves roses. Candles and diamonds and romance.*

Now here they sat, surrounded by candles and roses.

And those dime-sized crystals glittering in the rims of the stemware and china? He had the feeling they weren't cubic zirconia.

"Damn," Justice breathed. His hands curled into desperate fists. "Miranda, what the hell do I *do*? How am I supposed to get control of this thing?"

"Well, first you need to create a solid mental image of what you want to conjure. The more detailed, the better. I'm talking the way whatever it is smells, tastes—the works. Then you reach into the Mageverse and gather the magic to conjure it . . ."

"Like you do to Shift?"

"Yep. Same thing. Then you . . ."

They discussed the fine art of conjuring something out of nothing while they worked their way through dinner. "You know," Justice paused to finish off his glass of champagne. "We haven't reported in to Arthur. He's going to be pissed."

Miranda snorted. "Tough. I was kind of busy trying not to get eaten."

Justice winced, managed a smile. "I'm not sure he'll accept that as an excuse. He doesn't strike me as . . ."

"My Wolf!" The voice blasted through his brain, so shatteringly loud, he instinctively clapped his hands over his ears. *"My Hunter Prince, he has killed them all. Help me!"*

"Maeve!" He reeled to his feet, the goddess's urgency driving him like a cattle prod. "She needs us—*now*. I hear her calling, and she sounds frantic."

Miranda rose so fast, she knocked over her glass of very expensive champagne. Neither of them noticed as the foaming liquid spilled across the table. "What happened?" A flick of her fingers conjured armor for them both, identical to the suits she'd created before.

Even as the gleaming steel materialized around her, Miranda hurried back to the bed to collect their weapons. Picking up the axe in its harness, she tossed it to Justice, who caught it neatly out of the air. "Did she tell you what's going on?"

"No. All I got was an impression of fear and rage." He slung the axe harness around his armored torso, shrugged it into place, and buckled the straps. "And I can't even imagine what would get that kind of reaction from the Mother of Fairies."

"Doesn't sound good, that's for damned sure." Miranda scooped up her athame and slid it into the sheath she conjured around her waist. "Do you know where she is?"

"Yeah, she sent me a . . ." Justice paused, groping for words to describe the magical knowledge now shimmering in his brain. ". . . Well, something like GPS coordinates." He gestured, creating a point of magical energy that instantly expanded into a wavering oval. "Through here."

It didn't occur to Justice that he had no idea how to create such a portal until they'd already stepped through it. "How did I do that?" Frowning, he stared over his shoulder as the gate vanished like a popping soap bubble.

"Oh, Jesus," Miranda whispered, such horror in her voice that he forgot the mystery and spun into a crouch, ready to defend her.

It should have been a pretty place: a leafy forest pool fed at one end by a foaming waterfall that tumbled down the black, rocky face of a cliff. Trees surrounded the clearing, bright with autumn glory in the golden spill of morning sunlight.

Warlock had turned the bucolic setting into a scene of mass murder.

Corpses lay curled on the forest floor surrounding the churning waterfall pool. Most of them had been bound, either with ropes or chains of enchanted steel. Wounds gaped in throats and chests, and drying blood in a dozen alien shades splashed the lush soil.

Just a few feet away, a unicorn sprawled on its side, cloven hooves hog-tied, its snowy throat slashed so deeply, its horned head was almost severed from its neck.

A nine-foot corpse sprawled nearby, brawny limbs lax in his bonds, skin the gray green of moss matching the bushy thick green beard. The—man's?—huge biceps bulged, his wrists manacled behind his back, a length of chain binding them to his chained ankles. Apart from a massive gold helm, he was naked, and was definitely a "he." Horrific wounds slashed his skin like gaping purple mouths, and a lake of violet blood surrounded him.

A small gold dragon—only about ten feet long, which made it a child by dragonkind standards—lay on the opposite side of the pool. Its scaled head had been hacked from its neck. Justice winced, imagining the grief of its parents.

All around the larger corpses lay tiny bodies he first mistook for dead dragonflies because of their shimmering, transparent wings. When he looked closer, Justice realized the bodies between those wings were unmistakably human, though only a few inches in height. These must be the Demi-Sidhe he'd heard Belle mention; magical beings who were genetic cousins to King Llyr's Sidhe.

Walking among the carnage, Justice saw each of the tiny bodies had been stabbed by a thin blade. An ice pick, maybe, or a stiletto . . .

"My God." Miranda sounded hoarse with horror. "Warlock has gone completely insane."

"I don't think so." Justice crouched on his heels to examine the huge green victim. "Look at how deliberately this one was stabbed. Each wound is roughly the same depth, the same width, as if they'd been punched by a machine. There's no sign of the crazed emotion you'd see in a serial murder. This killer was as businesslike as a farmer slaughtering a pig."

"But don't you sense the *evil* here, Justice?" She gestured at the bloody chaos around them. "The whole clearing reeks with it."

He shrugged. "Oh, this was definitely an evil act. But it wasn't an act of passion."

Justice rose to his feet and continued around the clearing, examining the scene with the analytical eye of the homicide cop he'd once been.

Had it not been for all the bloodshed, the clearing would have been breathtaking in its natural beauty. Huge mounds of blossoms surrounded the trees with flaming petals of crimson, orange, and gold. Their delicate perfume battled the smell of blood and the overwhelming reek of evil.

In the center of the clearing lay a pool ringed with flowering plants and foaming around the foot of a waterfall. The falls danced down the black, craggy face of cliff, filling the air with the thunder of falling water.

But just as intense as the sound was the sense of pounding power coming from somewhere overhead. Justice looked up, following the bouncing tumble of the water. Just above the point where the falls tumbled over the cliff, the wavering oval of a dimensional gate hovered like a ghost.

It was like no other gate he'd ever seen. Most portals were as unstable as soap bubbles. This one hung suspended in an energy lattice as solid as the crystalline structure of a diamond.

Energy poured through the opening, blazing with such intensity, it infused the water flowing past the gate with magic. But definitely not a magic native to the Mageverse. This was a force more primal than that, more alien—and far more powerful. It was as if someone had opened a gate to the birthplace of creation. Gazing up into the wavering oval, Justice felt the skin creep on the back of his neck with an almost religious awe.

By rights, a pool fed by such fantastic power should have blazed to his senses like a star. Instead, the water . . . *stank*. It wasn't a physical stench—more a psychic reek, as if the murders committed around the pool had polluted it with a flood of sewage.

"Death magic," Miranda said, her voice low, choked. "All these people were human sacrifices in a death magic spell."

Justice turned to find her crouching over something in the thick underbrush. Moving to join her, he looked down at the ground she stared at so intently. "I don't see anything."

"Not with your eyes." She shot him an impatient glance. "Use your magical senses."

Justice let his eyes slide out of focus and concentrated. Viking runes suddenly appeared, glowing blue on the rich black soil, following a long, curving arc that circled the entire clearing.

The smell of death abruptly intensified until he gagged, damn near losing his lunch at a crime scene for the first time since he'd been a rookie. "God, what *is* that smell?"

"Like I said, death magic." Miranda rose and wiped her hands on the leaves of a nearby plant, grimacing like someone who'd put a palm down in shit. "Going by the runes, I'd say the spell was designed to funnel these beings' power and life force into my father. Which would mean an exponential increase in the magic he can command."

Fighting his gag reflex, Justice breathed deep, trying to judge the degree of decomposition in the stench. "I don't think any of these poor bastards have been dead more than a few hours. If that's the case . . ."

Miranda nodded, her expression grim. ". . . Warlock is a lot stronger now than he was even a few hours ago."

"It's far worse than that," Maeve said, her voice icy with rage. "Warlock fed on more than just these innocents' pitiful lives."

Justice glanced around as the Sidhe goddess emerged from a stand of thick brush on the edge of the clearing. She wore the tall form of her goddess persona, now dressed in armor forged from emerald metal. The limp body of a cougar lay draped over her mailed arms. The cat's thick fur was smeared with blood from a slashed throat.

"Is that the cat we saw talking to you earlier?" Miranda asked, moving closer to look down at the animal. "The one you sent to the King of Trolls?"

"Yes, my messenger, Erielhonan. And that's King Dovregubben himself." Maeve nodded grimly toward the huge green corpse. "Apparently, Warlock's Beasts ambushed the two when they arrived here to discuss the new sword I was to make for the Troll King. When I felt Erielhonan give his life, I gated here hoping to avenge him. Unfortunately, I could not overcome Warlock's monsters."

"What?" Miranda gaped at her, horrified. "But you have so much power . . ."

"Not enough. Not since Warlock used some of these sacrifices to strengthen his Beasts." She gestured at the pitiful corpses. Her eyes glowed hot with magic and rage. "The sorcerer cut Dovregubben's throat as I fought to get through the shield he'd raised. I could only watch as he syphoned away not only Dovregubben's power, but the magic of his kingship."

"Oh, hell," Justice growled, his stomach sinking. *Yeah, we're fucked.*

"That's not even the worst of it." A cluster of ferns rustled behind Maeve, and Guinness emerged from the leafy emerald fronds. "The spell—and the sacrifices that fed it— were designed to augment Warlock's power with the pool's magical energy."

"Which for centuries has been fed by the Elementalverse." Maeve moved to kneel beside the pool, laying the cougar on the ground as tenderly as a mother putting her child to bed. "That adds up to a great deal of power for the thieves."

Justice gazed up at the gate. "What exactly is this . . . Elementalverse?"

She glanced around at him. "A dimension parallel to this one, a universe where magic is an even more powerful force than it is here. My familiars—"

"Me, for one," Guinness put in.

"—were creatures of pure magic who fled the warring gods there."

"I'm not sure I'd call them gods, exactly," the dog said thoughtfully. "But they were extremely powerful, and vicious as demons. They'd have killed us all if we hadn't fled through that gate." He wrinkled his muzzle in a grimace. "From the frying pan into the fire. We were all creatures of pure magic, you see, and the alien magic here threatened to tear us apart."

"I sensed their distress and took pity on them," Maeve explained. "So I summoned my pets to the pool and showed the visitors how to meld with them. In the process of fusing with the creatures' minds, the aliens enhanced the animals' intelligence and magic."

She looked down at the cougar's pitiful body. "Which has proved the death of poor Erielhonan."

"What about Smoke?" Miranda asked, referring to the powerful Shifter who was one of Arthur's allies. "Isn't he some kind of elemental too?"

Maeve shook her head. "Smoke arrived centuries before the time we speak of. He was one of a group of beings far more powerful than my familiars."

"We were among the last to flee our universe." Guinness rolled his bulging eyes. "Mostly because we didn't have the power to escape any sooner."

Tenderly, reverently, Maeve straightened the cat's limbs, then stroked its head in a gesture of farewell. Rising to her feet, she pushed her beaded hair back from her face with bloody fingers. The charms clicked and chimed as she spoke through gritted teeth. "Warlock stole these innocents' lives and magic. He's twisted and perverted them." She curled her gauntleted hands into fists. *"And I will make him pay."*

In grim silence, Maeve began the process of gathering up the victims one by one, and gating away to return them to their grieving kin.

Justice and Miranda offered to take some of the dead themselves, but the goddess told them this was a task she must perform.

So they said their good-byes and watched Maeve summon yet another gate. Her steps slow, solemn, she carried the little murdered dragon through it on a shimmering litter of magic. Guinness followed, his tail drooping in sorrow.

"I have the distinct feeling this is all part of some kind of ritual revenge magic she's casting," Justice commented, once the gate vanished.

"Probably." Miranda sighed, taking a last look around the defiled clearing. "We'd better get back to Avalon. Arthur needs to know about all this crap."

"I think I remember how to conjure a gate." Justice narrowed his eyes and concentrated on building an image of Avalon's central square in his mind, trying to re-create the steps he'd followed when Maeve had summoned them.

Just as he sent the magic streaming into the air, Miranda yelped in alarm. "Justice, don't! The city wards . . ."

It was like crashing headfirst into a brick wall—at a dead run. The rebound of his own magic knocked him flat on his ass so hard, he saw stars.

Miranda's pretty face appeared upside down over him, wearing a worried frown. "You okay?"

He blinked. "What the fuck was that?"

"Avalon is protected by powerful wards," Miranda explained, putting a hand down to help him stagger to his feet. "If the shield doesn't recognize your magic, it will give you a good hard swat. Keep digging at it, and it will assume you're a would-be invader and fry you like a mosquito in a bug zapper."

"Isn't that a little extreme?" He dusted off his armored backside.

"Not given the invasion of evil vampires a couple of years ago. From what I gather, several Magekind got killed trying to fight off the bastards. After that, the Majae combined their power to make the wards even stronger. Now nobody gets through unless the wards recognize your magical signature."

The light dawned. "And since I didn't have the ability to work that kind of magic the last time I was in Avalon . . ."

"The wards don't know you from Adam." Miranda flicked her fingers, creating a gate of her own. The city shone through it, wavering like a pale ghost in the moonlight. "Luckily, they do know me."

Justice smiled slightly, all too conscious of the bloody setting around them. "Show-off."

"That's me." Bowing with a flourish of an imaginary hat, Miranda gestured to her gate. "Milord, your carriage awaits."

Shaking his head at her antics, he stepped through—

and stopped in his tracks as several hundred people turned to glare at him. "Shhhh!" they hissed in chorus.

"Uh, sorry," Justice whispered as his face heated with a furious flush. He moved aside to give Miranda room to join him.

Turned out, they'd managed to crash the funeral of Kadir and Daliya, the first Magekind victims of Warlock's new Beasts.

Everyone in Avalon had turned out for the funeral, all of them garbed in their finest medieval clothing of deepest black. The air was full of the rustle of silk and the whisper of velvet, trimmed with jet beads and embroidered in intricate Celtic knots of black silk or metallic silver thread.

Justice felt horribly conspicuous in his armor, still bloodstained and probably stinking of the crime scene's corrupted magic. He tried to ignore the feeling and concentrate on Arthur, who stood next to the couple's bier in the center of the city square. The former king was well into one of his thundering Once-more-into-the-breach-style speeches. Henry V had nothing on Arthur when he was on a roll.

"By the time he gets done," Justice murmured to Miranda, "we'll all be ready to invade France."

"Shush!" she hissed, as several people turned to glare. Again.

Justice snapped his mouth shut and managed not to cower in embarrassment.

". . . gave his life in a heroic effort to stop Warlock's Beasts from claiming more innocents," Arthur was saying. Unlike the rest of the crowd, he and the Knights of the Round Table wore full ceremonial armor. Moonlight seemed to blaze off his broad shoulders and helmeted head.

"Kadir fought with courage, even in the face of a horrific death, just as his wife Daliya battled to save him. Neither stinted at giving that last full measure to stop the killers. We will never forget their bravery and sacrifice, and we will honor their memory as we do other heroes fallen in the battle to protect humanity."

"As for Warlock . . ." His black eyes narrowed, his mouth tightening into a grim line. "He will pay for the deaths of these good people—and for all the innocents he's murdered in his insane quest for power. We will defend Merlin's Great Mission, and Warlock and his followers will die, just like all the others who've pitted themselves against us these past fifteen centuries." Arthur paused, sweeping his hard, determined gaze over the crowd, who started back at him, just as determined.

"We are the Magekind, and Merlin did not create us to lose!" Arthur barked. "And we will *not* lose. We will *not* allow that madman to enslave humanity with his corrupted power. *This I do swear!*" The last sentence was a roar, as he drew Excalibur, its enchanted steel ringing like the call to battle.

As one, all the Round Table knights drew their weapons, echoing his words in a thundering shout. "This we so swear!"

All the other vampires followed suit, thrusting their blades heavenward. "We so swear!"

Morgana moved forward, all magic and rippling black velvet skirts. "The Majae join this oath as we send brother and sister home!"

"We so swear," the Majae echoed, calling their magic in one blazing rush of power. It exploded from their lifted hands, blasting into the flower-piled bier that held both Daliya's white silk–clad body and her husband's helmeted head. The platform flared white, glowing brighter and brighter until the raw magic raged in a hot, boiling globe.

The witches raised their arms, sending the globe blasting skyward. There it detonated, raining sparks of golden magic over the empty space where the bier had been. All of it—the bier, Daliya, Kadir's head, the mounds of flowers—had been consumed by the spell.

Daliya and Kadir were once more part of the Mageverse, returned to the source of all magic.

* * *

The service over, the black-clad crowd streamed off toward the Great Hall, where the Majae had prepared a funeral feast. "Let's wait and see if we can catch Arthur before he takes off for the Hall," Justice suggested.

Miranda nodded, swiping an armored hand across her reddened eyes. "That last part makes me cry every time."

Justice nodded, his own eyes stinging. "They were good people."

"You, on the other hand," Arthur growled from behind him, "are an asshole."

SIXTEEN

Miranda had heard of the legendary Pendragon temper, but she'd hoped never to have it directed at her.

No such luck.

Arthur was actually three inches shorter than Justice, yet somehow he seemed to loom over both of them, broad as a fortress in his ceremonial armor, his helm tucked under one arm. *The better to glare at us.*

"Where the fuck have you been?" Turning his black, burning stare on Miranda, he snarled, "Why didn't you answer Morgana's repeated calls? We thought that damned fairy had fucking *killed* you!"

Miranda blinked up at him. "What calls? Morgana never called me."

"Yes, I did." The witch appeared at Arthur's side as if she'd materialized there like a black-clad ghost. Her narrow eyes glittered with irritation, and her power beat against Miranda's magical senses like meaty fists. "I sent psychic calls to you no less than ten times today, but you blocked me completely. I couldn't even tell if you were alive, much less conscious."

"I tried to reach you, too." Guinevere moved up behind her husband, her expression concerned. "I got the distinct impression you were blocking me. Or someone was, anyway."

Morgana curled her lip. "Which was not well done of you, my girl. I realize you're not technically a Maja, but when you accept a mission of such import, you should at least have the courtesy to report in!"

Miranda wasn't sure if the suspicion she saw in their eyes was real or simply a product of her own paranoia, but suddenly she was acutely aware of being Warlock's daughter. Did they really suspect her of spying for her father? Despite the anger that thought inspired, she tried for patience. "Look, you're right—I should have reported in, but things have been a bit chaotic. Justice's control of his new Hunter Prince powers isn't quite . . ."

"So he did pull it off. Is that Merlin's Blade?" Arthur interrupted, his attention focusing on the haft of the axe, protruding beyond Justice's left shoulder as it rode in its harness. He frowned, cocking his head. "I assumed it would be a sword."

"You mean this?" Justice asked in a deep, rumbling growl that made the hair rise on the back of Miranda's neck. She turned to stare at him in alarm as he grabbed the axe handle and jerked, spilling the big weapon into his waiting hands. Reaching to his touch, its fist-sized gemstone rained blue sparks to the cobblestones.

Morgana actually took a step back.

Arthur studied the weapon with interest, his gaze flicking from its massive battle-axe blade to the Celtic engraving on its haft.

He can't sense the axe's magic the way we can, Miranda realized. *Or he'd be a lot more worried.*

"Well, it definitely has a little juice," he drawled.

"Oh, it does," Justice purred back, in a guttural voice that sounded nothing like his usual pleasant baritone. "In fact, it has more than a 'little' juice."

Arthur might not be a Maja, but he was damned well an

Alpha Male, and he knew when he was being challenged. His black eyes narrowed as he looked up into Justice's gaze—a gaze that at the moment was far more wolf than man. "You planning to do something with that blade, boy?"

Justice's nostrils flared. Miranda was pretty sure he didn't like being called "boy." "What do you think, old man?"

Arthur grinned, all teeth and ferocity. Excalibur sang as he drew it, its magic flaring golden as it flooded Miranda's senses with power. "You want to play, Wolf Boy, I'll be happy to oblige."

"Ahhh . . ." Miranda began, fighting panic. She didn't think the vampire seriously intended to hurt Justice—but she wasn't sure Justice knew that. And as for his intentions toward Arthur . . . "I don't think that's a good idea, sir."

The former king's lips peeled off his teeth. "My dear, I can take anything your furry friend can dish out. The question is, can *he* say the same?"

"Arthur, my 'furry friend' turns into a wolf the size of a mastodon," Miranda snapped, abruptly in no mood for idiot posturing. Especially knowing just how close to the edge her lover really was. "He damned near ate me earlier today. He didn't even know who I was. Getting his oars back into the water is the reason we're so damned late."

"*Ate* you? Literally? *Justice?*" Arthur's brows flew up in astonishment as he stared at her, visibly dumbfounded. "But the boy is crazy about you!"

Her cheeks heated. Damn, did everybody know? "His wolf half was in control, and it didn't recognize me. Jogging his memory wasn't easy, either. Justice's conscious mind is in the driver's seat at the moment . . . more or less." Miranda glanced at her lover, who, thank God, looked shamefaced. She'd apparently snapped him out of it. "But it's not a good idea to goad him, because if his Wolf gets out, things could get seriously ugly."

"She's right," Justice admitted roughly. "I'd rather cut my own arm off than hurt one hair on Miranda's head, but the Wolf . . . The Wolf is another proposition. If it escapes again, somebody could get hurt. Badly. And I don't want that someone to be Miranda—or any of the rest of you."

" 'Then will the Hunter Prince be free,' " Gwen quoted softly. " 'Then will he rule in bloody vengeance or bend his knee to his spirit's feral king.' Daliya wasn't kidding, was she?"

"No," Justice said. "No, she really wasn't." He shrugged, his expression almost defeated. "As to blocking Morgana's attempts to communicate, I probably did that myself. Not consciously, but Miranda tells me I sometimes do things with my power without intending to. I conjured a really impressive steak dinner and a magnum of Dom Perignon '66 earlier this evening, and I had no idea I'd done it until Miranda brought it to my attention."

Morgana frowned. "That's not good. Using magic unconsciously can be extremely dangerous. You need to gain control of it before you do something truly regrettable."

Miranda nodded. "Which is what Maeve told us. She said Justice needs to learn both control and combat tactics. And considering what Warlock has been up to, the sooner, the better."

Arthur stiffened. "Exactly what *has* Warlock been up to?"

"Killing people," she told him bluntly. "And using their lives to work death magic."

Arthur stared. "Oh, shit."

"Yeah," Justice muttered. "That's it in a nutshell."

Justice was working hard on a fireball when Morgana asked in a tone of polite interest, "Why do you think you tried to kill Miranda?"

He flicked his gaze up to stare at her in a blend of astonishment and rage. The fireball instantly inflated to the diameter of a basketball, a roiling blaze of blue werewolf magic. It had been a dim tennis ball a moment before, and he'd had to work his ass off to manage that much. Merlin's

Blade, tucked in its harness, spilled sparks down Justice's back as he spoke through gritted teeth. "I didn't try to kill Miranda. That was the Wolf."

"What do you think the wolf is, William?" She cocked her head, ebony hair spilling over one armored breast in a gleaming wave. Like Justice, Morgana wore light practice armor. "It's you. Perhaps a part you don't want to admit to, but still, it's you."

It took a real effort not to tell Morgana just how full of shit she really was. He'd never liked the arrogant leader of the Majae. She was just a little too convinced she was always right, a little too willing to use her considerable power to get her way.

He was hardly alone in his dislike. To his knowledge, Belle and Gwen were the only people in Avalon who actually liked the cold-blooded bitch—and that included Arthur. Her half-brother seemed to regard her with a kind of wary respect, but damned little affection. He'd apparently been the victim of her scheming a few too many times. True, she always acted out of the best of intentions, but that was little comfort to the many targets of her manipulation.

Which, apparently, now included Justice.

Unfortunately, Morgana also knew her stuff when it came to magic, which was why she'd appointed herself Justice's teacher in the use of his new abilities.

"Look, I *love* Miranda." He looked across the practice field where Tristan was working to teach her a new parry while Belle kibitzed from the sidelines. "I'd sooner cut my arm off than hurt one red hair on her head."

"And yet your wolf half tried to eat her."

"The Wolf is a creation of Merlin's Blade. He's that damned Hunter Prince Daliya talked about in her prophecy." His tone hardened. "What he definitely is not is some kind of projection of subconscious hostility."

Morgana lifted a dark brow. "Why not? Miranda's given you plenty of reason to be hostile. Up until recently, that girl treated you like the hired help, despite the fact you were obviously so infatuated with her, the waves of sweet longing threatened to send me into insulin shock."

His fireball grew so hot, it started giving him a radiant burn across his cheeks. "I'm sorry you found my passion so distasteful."

Morgana shrugged, somehow making even that gesture elegant. "I'm used to it. This town is full of people who exchange gooey glances. But that wasn't how Miranda treated you, was it? To her, you were just the bodyguard who sometimes made himself useful by saving her life. She didn't even notice how you felt. Or if she did, she didn't care. That had to gall a man so proudly Alpha."

Justice turned and tossed the fireball into the bushes around the practice grounds. They exploded into flame with a roaring *whoosh*. He froze, appalled. "Shit!"

Morgana gestured, and the fire winked out, smothered in golden sparks.

"I really didn't intend to do that," he told her, a flush climbing his face. "That spell was burning my fingers."

"I'm not surprised, I could feel the heat from here. I suppose I'm lucky you didn't throw it at me."

"I don't hurt women." Belatedly processing what he'd just said, Justice winced. "That probably sounds chauvinistic."

"More chivalry than chauvinism, I think. Which, God knows, I see a lot of around here." She examined him, her gaze so cool and analytical, he felt like a lab rat in an experimenter's fist. "But then, you were raised to be protective, weren't you? That instinct goes all the way to the bone with you."

Justice shrugged. "My dad was a cop. So was his dad. And we all worked for the same county sheriff's office, even if it was years apart." Old grief stabbed him with a bitter, familiar ache. "My father went down in the line. Surprised two armed robbers trying to knock over a convenience store. One of them grabbed the clerk and put his gun to her head as he dragged her toward the door. Dad shot him, but he had to take his eyes off the other robber to do it. And *that* guy had a sawed-off. The funeral was closed-casket." He fell silent, lost in dark memories. "Granddad was in his second term as sheriff at the time. Dropped dead at his desk three weeks after we buried Dad."

Even Morgana winced at that. "I trust they at least caught the killer."

"Oh, yeah. He got the death penalty for killing a cop, though I was pushing thirty before the state managed to carry out his sentence."

She studied him, one dark brow winging up. "How old were you when your father died?"

"Thirteen." He absently conjured another fireball, this one even bigger and brighter than the first. "My sisters were five and seven at the time. Dad's death benefits got socked away to send us all to college. Mom had to work two jobs just to keep us in peanut butter and Ramen noodles."

"Son of a hero with two little sisters." Morgana rocked back on one armored boot, watching him like a particularly entertaining lab rat hard at work in a maze. "I'll wager you did a great deal of babysitting."

"Yeah. In between mowing lawns and delivering papers. And pizzas, once I was old enough to drive."

"I didn't realize Ramen noodles were that expensive."

"They're not." He shrugged. "But add in orthodontist bills and school clothes . . ."

"I see your point." She fell into a contemplative silence. Just as he conjured a second fireball and started juggling the two, Morgana observed, "Raising a hero can't be easy. Your mother must be ruthless as hell."

Both fireballs swelled and grew considerably hotter. "My mother's dead. Pancreatic cancer. Three years ago, not long before my Bite." At least he hadn't had to tell Deborah Justice he'd become a werewolf. Nor had he been forced to explain why he'd quit the department. Which was a good thing; he'd never been able to lie to his mother worth a damn. Deceiving his sisters and their respective families had been bad enough.

But after he damned near Shifted during a fight with the murderer of a five-year-old girl, Justice realized he couldn't remain both a homicide cop and a werewolf. Too many killers attempted to resist arrest, which never failed to piss him off. And when Justice got pissed, he tended to get furry.

He realized he'd eventually out himself—and drag the rest of the Direkind along for the ride. The world just wasn't ready to learn some people actually *could* turn into seven-foot wolves.

Fortunately, not long after he'd quit, Justice discovered the werewolf Council of Clans was looking for a new wolf sheriff. Elena Rollings, who was both a cop's wife and a councilwoman, persuaded them to give him the job.

At least until they'd decided to go along with Warlock's plans. Justice had disagreed so violently, they'd fired his ass and replaced him with Galen Vandenberg. Vandenberg was a member of the Chosen with no law enforcement experience whatsoever, but he had known how to follow orders and keep his mouth shut. That was apparently all they required.

"So there you are," Morgana said softly, watching Justice add a third fireball to the pair he was magically juggling. "In love with a woman who not only won't give you the time of day, she's actively afraid of you. You, everybody's big brother, protective man of the house from the age of thirteen. No wonder you tried to eat her. And no wonder you can't admit it to yourself."

"Dammit, I didn't try to eat Miranda," Justice snapped, concentrating furiously on his fireballs. He was afraid of what he'd do if he let any of his attention drift to the witch. "That was the Hunter Prince. *Not me*."

Morgana sighed, an expression far too close to pity in her eyes. "It *was* you, Justice. And until you come to terms with that, you'll never be able to access the full power of the Hunter Prince. Which means you'll never be able to take Warlock, no matter how big your battle-axe is."

She gestured. All three fireballs went out like a trio of snuffed candles.

* * *

Justice and Miranda decided to go for dinner at the Majae's Ladies' Club, despite the fact that Miranda wasn't a Maja and Justice sure as hell wasn't a lady.

As a rule, both werewolves would rather eat a big slab of protein than anything else, especially if it was still mooing. Yet the neurochemical demands of magic could give even a wolf a ferocious appetite for something either made from pasta or covered in chocolate. Or both.

The Ladies' Club was Avalon's top choice for anyone suffering from post-combat munchies. Actually, it was the only choice, since half the city's population was on a liquid diet and ignored anything that didn't come out of a bottle— or a throat.

However, the other half had to eat, which was why the Majae rotated serving and cooking duties at the Ladies' Club. Being female and thus viciously competitive, the witches took pride in seeing who could serve the club's most delicious, elaborate meals.

Miranda considered the Ladies' Club the primary perk of living in Avalon. Well, aside from the landscaping and architecture, both of which were also expressions of that same vicious witch competitive steak.

The club combined all three witch obsessions. The long, low Mediterranean-style building was stuffed with wrought iron furnishings, enough plants to populate a jungle, and marble statues of Roman gods and goddesses. Food was served cafeteria style around the clock, to accommodate the Majae's erratic, vampire-influenced schedules.

The two werewolves strolled in and headed straight for the nearest serving line, where they loaded their trays with happy greed. Justice located an empty table half-concealed in a cluster of ferns. He took a seat with a sigh of anticipation and contemplated his huge plate of spaghetti and a tall glass of Scotch.

Miranda slid in across from him, her tray dominated by a piece of lasagna large enough to feed a family of four.

According to the calligraphied card on the serving dish, Gwen Pendragon herself had committed the felony yumminess in question.

Miranda refused to feel guilty about eating it, either. Belle and Tristan had given her such a relentless asskicking, she figured she was entitled to a plate of sin covered in cheese and tomato sauce.

She'd inhaled half the meal before it dawned on her that Justice hadn't said a damned thing since they'd sat down. Miranda glanced up to find him picking unhappily at his spaghetti. The Scotch was gone.

Fuckity fuck fuck, she thought, knowing exactly what was bothering him. The question was, should she bring it up herself or wait for him to broach the subject? Glancing down at her remaining meal, Miranda decided in favor of cowardice. She wouldn't feel like eating once the fight started, and her magic-using brain was still carb-starved. Forking up another bite, she moaned, at length and with considerable volume. Maybe listening to her have a simulated orgasm would snap him out of his funk. "God, Gwen knows her way around lasagna. But then, I guess if you've been cooking since the fall of the Roman Empire, you'd have to pick up a thing or two . . ."

"Do you think that damned witch was right?"

"Ahhhhhh . . . *Oh, hell, here it comes.* "Which witch?" She tried out a grin. "Sounds like the beginning of a tongue twister."

"Who do you think I mean? *Morgana*." Enunciating, he bit out, "*Do you think my wolf tried to kill you because I'm pissed about the way you treated me?*"

"Oh." She put down her fork with a sigh of resignation. *So much for cheesy goodness.* "That witch."

"Yeah. *That* witch. Do you agree with her that the Wolf is the evil part of me?"

"I wouldn't say *evil* . . . exactly."

"Dammit, Miranda . . . !"

"Look, I realize you're one of the Bitten, so you didn't grow up with this stuff." She took a deep breath and decided it was time to quit pulling her punches. "But everyone raised Direkind knows the wolf part of a werewolf isn't something separate. It's *part* of you. And if you're not strictly honest with yourself, it can express emotions you hide even from your conscious mind. Kind of like a dream does. You know how you do things in dreams you'd never do in real life?" She gave him a too-bright grin, knowing she was babbling, but completely unable to stop. "Go to school naked, or bang the pretty secretary in the break room in front of the boss . . ."

"Miranda, dammit, I love you!" he thundered.

Dead silence fell as every woman in the room turned to stare. Miranda felt a furious flush roll to her hairline, and silently cursed her redhead's coloring. "Well, gee!" she chirped. "Thanks!"

As she'd intended, everyone cracked up and went back to eating.

Once they were all safely occupied again, Miranda leaned forward and hissed, "Can we not do this in front of half the witches in Avalon?"

Justice shot to his feet and growled, "Fine. Morgana gave me a grimoire she wants me to study. When you're ready to come home, call me on that magic cell phone of yours and I'll walk you." A gesture left his dirty dishes stacked on his tray and sparkling clean.

Of course he'd insist on walking me home. Miranda watched Justice stalk off to deliver the tray and its now-clean contents to the serving line for reuse. *Dad might beam in and try to eat me on the way.*

But she wasn't that lucky. Warlock would never appear when she was actually in the mood to kick his ass.

Miranda scrubbed a weary hand over her face as her temples began to pound in slow, deep throbs.

Cool fingers caught the sides of her head from behind, and the pain instantly vanished. Startled, she glanced around as Guinevere fell into the chair Justice had just left. Arthur's wife gestured. "Eat, child. I love watching a woman do justice to food I worked my ass off to cook." She snorted. "Most of the wenches around here like to pretend they're too dainty to feel an appetite."

"When you turn into a seven-foot werewolf, dainty's pretty much a lost cause." Miranda picked up her fork and took a dutiful bite.

Only to discover Justice had turned all Gwen's wonderful lasagna into sawdust without so much as casting a spell. Her gaze flicked over to find the immortal still watching her. Miranda took another bite.

The witch sighed. "Don't bother." One corner of her lip twitched. "Men. Can't live with 'em, can't fry 'em with a lightning bolt." She paused as Miranda snickered, before adding blandly, "Of course, one can fantasize . . ."

Miranda was still laughing when Gwen asked, "*Do* you think Justice tried to kill you?"

She stared, incredulous. She'd have expected a question like that from Morgana, but not from Arthur's wife. "Eavesdrop much?"

"Justice has a fine, deep voice," Gwen observed coolly. "Which tends to carry over a room full of chatting women, even when he's not bellowing like a bull."

Miranda thought that one through and her anger cooled. "Point taken." She shrugged and sat back in her chair, conjuring a badly needed cup of coffee. "At the time, I'll admit I was scared out of my mind. But I've been thinking about it since then. And I realized something."

Gwen lifted a brow. "And what would that be?"

"He stopped." Miranda met the woman's gaze. "I think he would have stopped even if I hadn't given him time to calm down. He'd have stopped even if he hadn't been in love with me. He's a very strong, intensely moral man. No matter how peeved he was, he would never hurt me. He'd never hurt anybody he considered an innocent. He's just not wired that way."

"He did chase you with enough homicidal intent to scare you silly."

"He'd also just had his DNA rearranged by Merlin's Blade." Miranda waved her spread fingers as if conjuring.

"When you've never been able to work any magic beyond turning fuzzy, getting that kind of power dumped into your brain would throw anybody for a loop. Most people—especially men I'd been such a flaming bitch to—would have done more than chase me down a rabbit hole."

Gwen lifted a blond brow. "A rabbit hole?"

Miranda grinned. "More a pipe into the ground, actually. I think I saw too many Bugs Bunny cartoons as a child. The Wolf was right on my ass, so . . ."

"Rabbit hole."

"Worked, too. I talked to him while he tried to figure out how to dig me out. Gave him time to calm down and Shift back to human."

Gwen settled back in her chair, her expression thoughtful. "You're right about his power. And the magic is not only in the axe—it altered his genetics, unlocking Merlin's Gift in ways I've never even seen before." Correctly interpreting Miranda's puzzled frown, Gwen explained, "I scryed his DNA for Arthur, before and after he obtained the Blade. And I don't mind telling you, what I found knocked me for a loop. First, he's a multiple carrier of Merlin's Gift . . ."

Miranda stared at her in disbelief. "But . . . He's Direkind. The Bite doesn't work on Latents." Latents were the mortal descendants of those who'd drunk from Merlin's Grail. They never gained powers unless Merlin's Gift was activated by a member of the Magekind, who had to make love to the Latent at least three times.

Gwen looked up at her, interested. "What makes you say that?"

"Daddy dearest."

"I didn't realize you did that much chatting."

"We didn't. I was a nosy little kid with a taste for eavesdropping."

"Given your father's homicidal tendencies, that was probably a survival characteristic."

"Pretty much. Anyway, he told a bunch of his Chosen buddies that he'd experimented with Biting Latents, but the spell didn't work. His exact words were 'They might as well have been bitten by a Chihuahua.' I gather he was hoping to create some kind of Magekind/Direkind blend."

"Which he probably intended to use in one of those endless plots of his. But yes, the bastard was right. The Bite and Merlin's Gift normally cancel each other out."

"But not in Justice's case."

Gwen nodded "Not in Justice's case. Damned if I can tell you why, either. It may be because he holds an unusually strong Gift, probably because both his parents were Latents."

Miranda shook her head hard, wondering if she'd misheard. "Wait—what?"

"We see that sometimes. Say Lance stopped at some little medieval town a few hundred years ago and sired one of his many bastards. Now, there may have been no more than a couple hundred people in the whole town, especially if you're talking post–Black Death. So within a few generations, half the people in town carry the Gift. Now, say Bors comes through, and he gets some wench pregnant . . ."

Miranda sat back in her seat, fascinated. "So before long, everybody in town has the Gift, and they're all crossbreeding like mad, since none of them have any idea about the Gift, Merlin, or that there are Knights of the Round Table in their collective family tree."

"Exactly. And considering the Magekind have spent fifteen centuries siring bastards all over the planet—well, eventually *everyone* will carry the Gift. Which I suppose would mean the Direkind will no longer be able to make more werewolves by biting people. You'd only become Direkind if you were born to Direkind parents."

"Makes sense." Miranda chewed her lower lip, thinking it through. "Even then, nobody would have more than two copies of the Gift in his DNA—one from the mother, and one from the father. And you might not get it at all, since you get only half of each parent's chromosomes."

"Justice, however, *did* get two copies of the Gift. Then some idiot werewolf Bit him, which added still more weird genetics. Now, if the Gift had been active, he'd have gone into anaphylactic shock, but his magic wasn't 'live' yet."

"But why did he Shift at all, when the magic shouldn't have worked on him?"

Gwen leaned forward and braced her elbows on the table, her expression intense. "It's got to have something to do with the two copies of the Gift. There are probably other wolves with two copies, but unless you've got the magic to detect it, you'd have no way of knowing. And since it's relatively rare, Warlock may not have seen it before."

"Why would he look? You don't go running around gazing at people's genetic code."

"Which someone probably has, except none of the labs knew what they were looking at." Gwen's expression turned grim. "Once they figure it out, we're all in trouble."

SEVENTEEN

Miranda and Gwen fell silent, considering the chain of events.

"Chocolate," the witch announced. "This is a discussion that just cries out for chocolate." Her agile fingers flashed, and two slabs of pie appeared on the table. She picked up the fork that had materialized alongside hers and took a large, gooey bite.

Miranda eyed the pie with its towering cloud of whipped cream and thick, chocolate core, and picked up her own fork. Her first bite made her moan. "Oh, God," she whimpered, not even caring that her mouth was full. "If Brad Pitt were a pie, this is the pie he'd be. All three thousand calories a slice. I might as well apply it directly to my ass. And you look like such a nice person, too. Evil, evil woman."

"You're a werewolf." Gwen forked up another bite. "You'll burn it off the next time you Shift. Quit whining and eat."

They devoured pie in semi-orgasmic silence for the next several minutes. It was close to dawn and most of the Majae had gone home, so they could gorge in peace.

"Merlin obviously suspected Warlock would go bad. Otherwise, why give the axe to Maeve?" Gwen said at last, scraping her fork across her barren plate in hopes of collecting any remaining molecules of chocolate. "So why did he choose such a raging jerk to receive so much power?"

"Merlin also suspected *Arthur* would go bad, or he wouldn't have created the Direkind to begin with," Miranda pointed out. "Which suggests Merlin was one seriously paranoid wizard."

Gwen considered that point. "I think I'd describe him as more 'wary wizard idealist' than actively paranoid. He hoped we'd all remain as heroic as we seemed when he tested us fifteen centuries ago, but he also knew people change. The longer you're alive, the more changing you do. An immortal can change one hell of a lot."

"Hmmm. Well, yeah."

Gwen glanced down, and a cup of coffee appeared at her elbow. "When you've got this much power and you've spent years watching all the really creative ways humans invent to brutalize each other, you start getting the urge to slap the evil out of them. But there's no such thing as coerced decency. Either people are moral, or they're just . . . not. The best you can do is educate them about why they should be moral, and make sure you can stop them if they choose another course. Otherwise you can become a tyrant really, really fast."

"That's what happened to my father," Miranda said slowly. "I found one of his journals once. It must have dated back centuries. I had to cast a spell on it to keep it from crumbling every time I turned a page."

Gwen's brows rose. "That must have been interesting reading."

"It totally floored me. The man who wrote that book was nothing like the utter asshole he is today. He wrote with such eloquence about the Direkind's responsibility to humanity, and how guilty he felt because he couldn't prevent the casual viciousness he saw every day. He even said he admired Arthur and the Knights of the Round Table. But when Arthur went to war with his own son . . ."

"Mordred." Gwen spat the name, her voice as flat and chill as a frozen lake.

"Right, Mordred. There was one passage where Warlock wrote, 'This is not what Merlin would have wanted. Arthur has failed by letting Mordred's mob kill his people.' "

"It wasn't a question of 'letting' him do anything. Mordred was a tactical genius. No surprise there; he was the son of Arthur and Morgana. Just imagine what you'd get with *those* genetics, inbred or not. We had a hell of a time stopping him once his rebellion got traction. Arthur has always said he made his worst mistakes against Mordred."

"I think that was the beginning of Warlock's fall." Miranda stared out across the darkened garden. "That's when he started hating your husband. He'd thought Arthur was the perfect warrior king—until Arthur failed to keep Mordred from destroying Camelot. Then he felt . . . betrayed."

"That's the thing with heroes," Gwen observed quietly. "Once you convince yourself your idol is more than human, the minute he fails to live up to your expectations, you feel stupid for believing in him. Hero worship always rides the razor edge of disgust. Nothing will turn an acolyte into an assassin any faster."

Miranda grimaced. "Especially if you're nuts to begin with." She glanced around to find Gwen staring at her, a frown on her pretty face. "What, do I have chocolate on my nose?"

"That's a really ugly spell Warlock cast on you—and it's gotten worse. When you arrived in Avalon, I only caught glimpses of it. Shadows. I wasn't even sure it was there at all. Now it's all but solid," Gwen told her bluntly. "You need to get rid of it before you go into combat again, or it's going to get you killed."

"Believe me, I've tried. It damned near cooks me every time anyone messes with it."

"Given the way it's set up, I can believe that. I'd be afraid to touch it, too." Cocking her head, Gwen studied her. "But there is one thing that might work . . ."

"Which is?" Miranda prompted when she fell silent.

"Are you in love with Justice?"

She blinked in surprise at the blunt question, but she nodded. "Yes."

"In love enough to consider a Truebond?"

"Direkind don't Truebond," Miranda said automatically. "We have something called a Spirit Link, which is similar." She frowned. "Unfortunately, our version still kills you when your partner dies, which is why it's not all that popular. Warlock went so far as to outlaw it for the Chosen, because he didn't want Chosen males dying for the love of anything female."

"He should just call those guys the 'He-Man Woman Haters Club' and get it over with."

"Yeah, well, he's afraid people would think he's gay."

Gwen snorted. "Yeah, that sounds like him. But you still didn't answer the question."

Miranda shook her head. "I don't see how a Spirit Link would break the spell."

"Justice has power enough to shatter your chains like peanut brittle. You don't, even with your new athame."

"Justice *tried* to break them. And I almost ended up a crispy critter."

"That's probably because his counter spell was coming in from outside your mind. Warlock knew the first thing we'd do is try to break the spell, and one or the other of us would have the juice for the job. If *you* applied the force from the within, I'll wager those chains would shatter like a Victorian teacup. It's impossible to build a spell that can resist *anything* coming from *any* direction."

"All right," Miranda said slowly. "That does make sense."

"But . . . ? And there is a 'but.' I can almost see the thought bubble over your head."

Miranda sighed and sat back in her chair. "I'm not comfortable asking Justice to take a risk like that just to get me out of a bind."

Gwen considered her. "Somehow I don't think he'd see it that way."

"No, of course he wouldn't. If he were any more heroic, the *Star Wars* theme would play whenever he walks into a room."

"You really *are* a nerd, aren't you?"

"Bite me."

"*So* not my type. Look at it this way: Justice doesn't have the knowledge to use his new power to its fullest, and he doesn't have time to learn. Not with Warlock breathing down our collective necks. If you Truebond—or Spirit Link, or use the Force, or whatever you lot call it—you'll be able to help him. And Darth Warlock will find it a lot more difficult to kill us."

Miranda closed her eyes and sighed, knowing an argument she couldn't ignore when she heard one. "Oh, crap."

Gwen smiled.

Justice looked up from the big grimoire he held in his lap as Miranda walked in. His eyes narrowed.

Which was when Miranda remembered. "Crap! I was supposed to call you so you could walk me home. I'm sorry, I started talking to Gwen and . . ."

"Do you *want* your father to kill you?"

So much for discussing Gwen's psychic meld idea. The angry tension in his voice told her they were on the verge of a really memorable fight. "Given Avalon's wards, it's damned unlikely even Warlock could find a way in."

"You forgetting what we saw at the falls? Fifteen Demi-Sidhe, a unicorn, Maeve's cougar, a yearling dragon, and the King of the Trolls . . . Who knows what he could do with the power from that many sacrifices?"

Miranda grappled with her rapidly heating temper, trying to ignore the chill claws of Warlock's fear spell that had already begun raking at her consciousness. The last thing she needed to do was cower—that would definitely set off Justice's werewolf instincts—but she did owe him an apology. Especially since a note of genuine worry echoed behind the rumble of his rage.

"Look, Justice, I really am sorry . . ."

"I'd expected to hear from you an hour ago." The dark light she associated with his wolf flashed in his eyes. "I was on the verge of heading out to search."

"You could have just called my cell." Everybody in town had a phone spelled to work in the Mageverse.

On her hip, the athame sang a trill of discordant notes that sounded distinctly like a warning. As if in agreement, Merlin's Blade spilled blue sparks from its harness, as it leaned against the arm of Justice's chair.

The wolf light brightened into true fury, flashing against the darkness of his eyes. *Damn, he really was worried*, Miranda realized. *He didn't even think about the cell.*

That was why at least half his anger was directed at himself.

Unfortunately, that made no difference whatsoever to Warlock's damned spell. She could see the links beginning to glow as they wrapped around her body, increasing the beat of her heart, double-time, triple-time, as adrenaline spilled through her blood, tainting her scent with the acrid stink of fear.

Not good.

Miranda reached into the Mageverse and pulled power, knowing she needed to disguise her physical reactions before they goaded his wolf even more.

Too late.

"I'm not going to hurt you, dammit!" He shot to his feet, towering over her even tall as she was. His big hands curled into fists. "I would never hurt you!" He didn't even seem to realize just how irrational he sounded.

Miranda flinched before she could contain the reaction.

His dark eyes widened and his lips parted in a soundless gasp, and she knew he'd have looked at her with just that expression of wounded surprise if she'd conjured a sword and rammed it into his heart.

Stop it, she told herself savagely. None of this was in character for the strong, controlled man she knew. *I've got to help him regain control.*

"Justice, it's really late." Ignoring her rising fear, Miranda reached up to rest a hand on the bunched muscles of his chest. She held her voice steady despite the spell's efforts to catapult her into outright, screaming panic. "I'm sorry I kept you up so long. We'll both feel a lot better after we get some sleep."

"You're afraid of me." The anguish in his eyes was even stronger than his wolf's anger. "Are you sure you even trust me enough to occupy the same bed?" He curled his upper lip, as if trying to hide that vivid pain behind sarcasm. "Since the Wolf is just an 'expression of my subconscious,' I might hurt you in my sleep."

Miranda gazed up into his handsome face, and this time she didn't have to work to do it. Fuck the spell. She knew what she knew. "You would *never* hurt me. Wolf or no wolf, axe or no axe. You're William Justice, and you don't hurt women. Not in your sleep. Not ever."

Something new flashed in his eyes, a brilliant magical flare that definitely wasn't wolf. Pain and anger vanished, burned away in an instant. "I sure as hell wouldn't hurt the woman I love." He pulled her into his arms as tenderly as a man lifting a newborn infant. Wrapping her in cradling warmth, he sought her mouth.

Justice's kisses started out gentle, but they didn't stay that way. In seconds, he began kissing Miranda the way a half-drowned man pulls in oxygen, in starving, desperate gulps. Suckling her lips, biting first one and then the other with tiny nibbles, he alternated swirling his tongue around hers with deep, suggestive thrusts.

But there was more to his kisses than lust. They tasted of love, fear of rejection, and the need for forgiveness, stripped bare of pride and disguise, as naked as an erection. She'd never dreamed an Alpha wolf would be willing to reveal himself so utterly. Especially not a man as proud as Justice.

Even if he'd never told her he loved her, those kisses demonstrated just how he felt, told her how important she was to him.

Miranda gasped against his mouth. Kissing Justice, she forgot Warlock's spell, forgot her own anger and distrust. Forgot everything but her need to show this vulnerable, powerful man how she felt. Show him so vividly, he'd no longer doubt either of them.

He dragged his mouth away from hers, breathing in pants. "There's something . . . something I need to tell you. Someplace Maeve said we had to go. Now."

"Now?" Miranda laughed against his lips. "Somehow I think it can wait thirty minutes." She kissed him again. "Or an hour." Another soft, brushing kiss. "Maybe two."

Justice pulled away with visible reluctance. "No, she said as soon as you got back. I offered to call you then, but she told me to wait for you to return on your own. But by then, I was pissed . . ." He shrugged, wincing.

"Wait—she specifically told you to wait until I got home?" Miranda drew away from him, frowning. Frowning still harder when she realized her arousal had given way to worry.

"Yeah."

And that confirmed it. "She saw something. Scryed something. Anyway, she's had some kind of vision."

"That was my thought. Which was why I got so pissed off and worried when you were late." He grimaced. "Then I jumped you like an idiot, instead of just telling you we had somewhere to be."

Walking to his chair, he picked up his axe harness and shouldered into it, then buckled the straps around his torso. The big weapon shed sparks the entire time, as if urging them to greater speed.

"I am sorry." Miranda stared at him with blatant longing. "And I'm even sorrier we don't have time to make love."

Justice paused as if a thought had just occurred to him. "Maybe not," he murmured, before looking up at her with a wicked grin. "Then again, maybe we do. Let's find out." He gestured, opening a dimensional gate as easily as if he'd been doing it all his life.

"You do learn fast." Miranda gazed through the portal, getting an impression of a large room so dimly lit, she couldn't make out many details.

"I did some practicing while I waited for you. It helps that Morgana's set the city wards to recognize me so they don't knock me on my ass whenever I try to go through." He drew his axe and stepped into the gate, leading the way as usual.

Miranda took a deep breath and followed, wondering what the hell Maeve had in mind this time. *But if Justice thinks I'm having sex* anywhere *Guinness is likely to walk in on us, he's out of his furry werewolf mind.*

Stepping through the gate, she stopped, eyes widening as she stared around at their surroundings. "Damn. I mean . . ." Words failed her. "Damn."

There might be a more sybaritic bathroom somewhere on Mageverse Earth, but if so, she'd never been invited there.

The room was huge, large enough for an Olympic-sized pool—which the sunken rose marble bath was damned near big enough to be. The walls were white marble, shot with veins of rose and carved with bas-relief images of gods, goddesses, and animals. Pillars supported the soaring dome ceiling high overhead. A fresco that could have been painted by Michelangelo himself depicted Sidhe warriors in battle. Plants surrounded the circular bath with an explosion of vivid blossoms, many so exotic, Miranda couldn't identify them at all.

But what riveted her attention was the tiny dimensional gate, not much larger than her hand, set high in the wall, just above a nozzle gushing a spray of water. At the tub's opposite side, a drainage catch carried away the overflow.

Despite the gate's diminutive size, the alien magic it

radiated seemed to pound at her awareness. "Does that gate . . ."

"Lead to the Elementalverse, like the one at the falls? Yeah." He looked up at the wavering hole located some fifteen feet up the wall. "She said the gate was here before the house. Apparently, it's why she built this place here to begin with. A system of pipes pumps the magic-infused water throughout the house. Apparently, this room is a hell of a long way underground. I gather it was some kind of cavern or something until she converted it."

Miranda stared up at the opening. To her magical senses, it seemed to blaze with magic so intense she couldn't feel anything else. "It feels even stronger than the falls."

"It is." Justice sat down on a padded marble bench and started unlacing his shoes. "She had to close the gate at the falls. Said the death magic spells there had polluted the pool to such an extent it had to be drained, or it would have started poisoning everything for miles around." Pulling off his socks, he tucked them into his running shoes and stood to unzip his jeans. "Because that gate closed, more of the Elementalverse's energy began flooding in through the one here."

Miranda blinked. "Wait—she closed a gate that had existed thousands of years?"

He shrugged. "Seems that way. I really don't think she had much choice."

"Well, no, but the power that would have taken . . ." Miranda shook her head and eyed him. He'd taken his shirt off, and the breadth of his powerful chest made her heart beat a little faster. "And she wants us to bathe in it?"

Justice grinned. "I think she wants us to do more than that." His smile faded, and he continued more seriously, "She told me she wants us to form a Spirit Link."

Miranda stared. "You're kidding."

Justice stiffened. "Look, I know it's a lot to ask, but Maeve told me . . ."

"No, I'm not objecting," Miranda told him quickly. "I

just think it's odd because that's why I got delayed at the Club. Gwen was trying to convince me to ask you to do the same thing."

"But you didn't want to." He said the words in a tone of utter neutrality, no expression at all on his face.

"No—I mean, yeah, but not because I don't want that kind of connection with you. She argued a Spirit Link would make it easier to break Warlock's spell, but I told her I didn't want to ask you to do something that could endanger your life."

"It would also endanger yours."

"Did you miss the part where I told you I love you—*how* many times now?" she demanded. "I just don't want to die knowing that I've cost you your life."

"And I don't want to live without you." Again, he sounded almost emotionless, but a deep breath revealed the acrid scent of rage and fear: his violent response to the thought of her death.

"I don't want to live without you either," Miranda said, stepping over to him and taking his hands. "But what if we have kids, and something happens? Who'd take care of them with both of us dead?"

He frowned so deeply, she realized he hadn't even considered that angle. "Yeah, that's a point. Thing is, Maeve said we need a Spirit Link, or neither one of us is going to survive . . . whatever the hell she's seen coming."

"And she didn't say what that is?" Miranda released his hands and reached for the hem of her shirt.

He watched her pull it off, desire flaring hot in his eyes. "No, but apparently our hanging out under that spray for a good long while will definitely help. And we're supposed to take our weapons with us."

"Naked. In the water. With our blades." She flashed him a grin. "Sounds kinky. Good thing magical steel doesn't rust."

"You know, I was right." Miranda eyed Justice as they waded hand in hand into the gently steaming waist-deep bath. He had stripped down to the intricate leather straps of his axe harness. An impressive erection cut the water in front of him. She herself wore the athame's strap wrapped around one bare thigh; like Justice, she'd had to strip before putting the sheath on again. "This *is* kinky."

"Not yet." He gave her a very wicked grin and pulled her into his arms. "But it's going to be if I have anything to say about it."

The kiss was slow, gentle, a teasing brush of lip on lip. He felt so damned good standing against her that Miranda found herself forgetting everything else.

Including the very nasty question of what exactly it was Maeve had scryed when she'd looked into that forge of hers. *I'm not thinking about that*, Miranda told herself firmly, focusing on the velvet texture of his lips against hers.

One callused thumb found her nipple and began to brush back and forth. Sensation jolted through her as though her every nerve vibrated like a plucked violin string. "God!"

He stopped, eyes widening with alarm. "What?"

"No, I mean . . ." Miranda wrapped one hand around his cock for a slow stroke.

"Jesus!" He jerked in astonishment. "The water . . ."

"Yeah. It *so* does." She gave him another slooow stroke, mostly for the pleasure of feeling him quiver against her as the magically amplified sensation raged through his body.

"You'd . . . probably better hold off on that for a while," Justice murmured, and swooped in for another kiss, stroking both nipples with wickedly clever fingers. Pulling, squeezing, he rotated the stiff points until she gasped, writhing in his arms.

His lips curved, and he murmured, "I wonder what would happen if I nibbled certain sensitive little bits?"

"Not sure I'd survive." She threw back her head, shuddering, though a smile curved her mouth.

"Oh, let's find out." He swooped down and lifted her into his arms until he could reach a nipple with his mouth.

His tongue drew a hot figure eight, flicking over the erect pink tip with each pass. Every teasing circle sent electric pleasure buzzing right into her sex. Miranda crossed her ankles under his ass and hooked her fingers into the straps of his harness. Leaning back in his supporting arms, she let Justice do whatever he damn well chose as bright comets of delight shot across her closed eyelids.

God, he loved the way she tasted. Distilled femininity flooded his tongue, salt and woman with the faint undertone of fur. The skin of her long legs felt like silk as she gripped him. The pool's magical water swirled around his thighs, teasing fingers rolling over his flesh, stoking his arousal as his cock bobbed in the current. The warm flow teased his balls, his shaft, the drum-tight flesh of his glans.

He lifted his head to admire Miranda as she lay back in his arms, her lovely eyes closed, her lips parted and dewed with water. Her full breasts danced in the current, droplets beading her tight, flushed nipples. Her wet hair streamed down her back and across the pale flesh of her breasts, fox fire darkened to bronze. Fine muscle worked in her tight waist as she clung to him, contours thrown into relief by her strong grip on his body.

He let his eyes slide out of focus until he could look at her with his magical senses.

And frowned as Warlock's chains became visible, blue and glowing, so tight as they looped around and around her slender body that it was surprising she could work any magic at all. He could almost feel them feeding on her, diverting her power into Warlock's spell.

Fuck you, you bastard. I'm going to kill that spell today if it's the last damned thing I ever do.

His gaze flicked up to the spray pouring past the dimensional gate. His eyes narrowed, and he started toward the rear wall and its tumbling supernatural shower. Cradled in his arms, Miranda opened her eyes to gaze up into his face, her expression pleasure-dazed. "What . . ."

"Hold your breath," he told her.

Her eyes widening, she obeyed just as he stepped into the tumbling fall of water.

Magic slammed into them, pounding down on their heads with a force much greater than the water spray itself, so hard Justice's knees almost gave. He fell forward, snapping one arm out, barely managing to catch them both on a braced palm in time to keep from rapping Miranda's head on the marble wall.

She stiffened against him, staring up into his face with wide, startled eyes. As he stared down into them, they began to glow with magic, brighter and brighter, building into a brilliant amber blaze as her body absorbed the alien energies of the Elementalverse.

"Justice . . ." she whispered hoarsely.

"Yeah," he gasped back. "Yeah." He could feel Merlin's Blade raining sparks down on his shoulders, each individual flash of energy stinging his skin, then shooting straight into his brain with an intoxicating power that made him shake.

Desire became blinding lust. He jerked her upright in his arms even as she started climbing him, her lips peeling off her teeth. He reached down, found his cock, and somehow got it pressed against her wet velvet lips as her legs tightened their grip. They both cried out in mingled shock and delight as she impaled herself in a rush of deliciously tight flesh over his aching cock.

He braced her back against the wall, wrapped both arms around her thighs, and began to drive against her. She met every fierce thrust, rolling her hips, her breasts bouncing.

As if from a great distance, he felt her athame spilling stinging sparks on the skin of his arm, though the little weapon had never rained energy as his so often did.

But all he really cared about was Miranda. Her eyes burned solid blue from corner to corner, so bright they cast shadows over his body. She stared up at him through those glowing eyes, her lips parted with her desperate, heaving gasps for air, her expression twisted with a delight so intense it seemed to verge on agony.

"Love you," he gritted, as heat shot from his balls in the first fierce pulses of orgasm. "God, Miranda, I love you!"

"Loveyou . . . loveyouloveyou . . ." she panted back, the words fusing, growing louder with every repetition, building to a yowl.

Even as they came in screaming unison, the intensity of the magic built into a burn so bright, so viciously intense, Justice instantly realized it was too much. They'd incinerate themselves if this kept up. "Shift!" he roared at her. "Shift *now*!"

With that, he let the magic rip, tearing him from his human form even as Miranda simultaneously poured herself into the magic. Their bodies disappeared into a blinding glow.

Acting out of pure instinct, he reached for her, trying to create a Spirit Link.

And for a moment, they touched. Mind to mind, heart to heart.

He could *feel* Miranda: feel the wounded strength he'd always sensed in her, the courage she'd built resisting the will of a vicious killer from the time she was four. The strength that had refused to let Warlock break her, refused to bend to his evil despite all his power, despite all his centuries of magical skill. Despite everyone—including her own mother—who'd always insisted yielding to her father was her duty.

Most of all, though, Justice felt the way Miranda loved him. Loved him with a pure and shimmering power he'd never known anyone could ever feel for him. To her, he was her hero, her unflinching protector.

And *she* touched him. Touched his power, his darkness. Touched his Wolf.

For a moment panic stabbed him. *What if it scares her? What if she stops loving me? What if I lose this before I even have time to have it?*

"*Idiot,*" she told him. "*I'll never stop loving you. That's not the kind of love we have.*"

But even as they reached to seal their mental union, a savage presence thundered into their minds, alien and evil. "*No, Goddamn you!*" Warlock roared into their joined mind. "*I've worked for centuries for this day! I will not allow you to ruin it!*"

EIGHTEEN

There, Warlock thought in satisfaction as a ringing mental silence fell. The thundering power he'd sensed from his traitorous bitch of a daughter and her idiot lover had vanished. *Did I kill them?* He could no longer feel them at all. Maybe the death magic he'd sent knifing into their joined consciousness had slain them both.

Pleasant thought.

No matter what, he'd kept them from forming a Spirit Link. They'd have posed a very real threat to his plans had they managed to complete the psychic union. Miranda could have shown Justice how to use the full power of Merlin's Blade, while the cop could have broken the containment spell Warlock had cast on Miranda as a child. Now, even assuming they'd survived, Justice would not have the skill to use Merlin's Blade to its full potential. Meanwhile, Warlock's spell would keep Miranda's power contained.

Too bad his assassins had failed to kill the little bitch sooner. *Still, maybe she's finally dead. Even if she's not, she won't be a problem after today.* Warlock swept his satisfied gaze over the ranks of warriors awaiting his next command.

Two thousand fanatical armored werewolves made an impressive sight. Especially with an additional five thousand foot soldiers—not as well trained or well-armed, perhaps, but more than enough to provide whatever cannon fodder he needed.

Pleased, Warlock studied the faces revealed by raised visors as they stood in neat columns in the narrow, wooded valley. To either side of him stood his Beast lieutenants, also in Dire Wolf form.

The Beasts and the Chosen Knights wore full armor, the magical steel gleaming bright enough to blind in the morning sunlight. The armor's broad shoulder paldrons and long, swinging tassets made each knight appear even bigger and more formidable than usual.

That was saying something, considering each fighter's seven-feet-plus of fur, fangs, and claws.

The ornate armor had been handed down from father to son for generations, its enchanted plate steel segments designed to magically alter to accommodate each new wearer.

Warlock had spent centuries building his Cult of the Chosen in preparation for this day, handpicking the most physically fit and aggressive Alphas in the Direkind aristocracy. He'd personally taught the first cultists the blade skills his army would one day need, when he eventually went to war on Arthur. After that, each generation trained the next.

He'd demanded superior strength, skill, and cunning from his worshippers, quietly eliminating any who did not make the grade, in ways that would appear accidental to the rest of the Dirckind.

But the cultists had known. And just as he'd intended, the knowledge of the death that could await them had motivated them to still greater efforts to please.

The only thing they hadn't done was rebel.

Warlock had carefully taught his Chosen to believe he was a god. As a result, they never blinked at anything he did, even as they fought to meet his exacting standards.

He'd been forced to kill only a handful of failures in

recent years. Just as well, because there were barely enough in the Cult as it was. Arthur's Magekind outnumbered his warriors, even with the additional foot soldiers he'd recruited to round out their numbers.

Luckily, he knew exactly how to get around that problem.

Now he only needed to ensure they were in the proper mood for the mission.

Warlock began to pace before his men, in long, deliberately theatrical strides. His black armor gleamed dully as he moved, flashes of silver catching the light of the rising sun. He'd given variations on this speech before, during the recruitment drive, and he'd perfected every gesture, every nuance of tone and word.

"Today we will avenge our people, my brothers," Warlock began, his voice deliberately soft to force his men to listen even harder. "Today Arthur will pay for the murder of our three councilmen, along with the deaths of all the others who fell that day in August."

Never mind that Warlock had known the werewolf councilmen would die, just as he'd planned on the martyrdom of the stupid Direkind civilians who'd been trampled in the panic. They'd deserved death for panicking in the face of Arthur's knights.

Which was why he'd held back the bulk of his forces that day. He'd known it wouldn't be the final battle. He'd only intended to test Arthur's strength, perhaps steal the vampire's precious Excalibur. In the end, however, his first Beast, Wayne "Dice" Warner, had failed to escape with the sword. Instead the big werewolf died at the hands of Tristan and his magic-using whore, Belle. His loss was the only one Warlock had really regretted that day.

Yet Warlock had not considered the battle a defeat, because he'd learned exactly what he'd needed to know.

This fight would be the end of the Magekind.

He had to suppress an inappropriate grin at the thought of his enemies' dying screams, the shrieks of the Majae his werewolves would rape, the magical riches he'd loot. Excalibur, Merlin's Grimoire, the Round Table itself . . .

Ahhhhh, yes. He'd treasure the spoils of Avalon, and smile at the memory of this day for centuries to come.

But there was work to be done before he could know that pleasure.

Warlock swept a cool, even stare over the ranks, and began working to whip them into a suitable frenzy. "But most of all, Arthur will pay for failing Merlin. Merlin, the alien wizard who trusted the Magekind to guide humanity into a utopia of peace and prosperity."

He snorted in contempt, his magic ensuring his followers heard every sound he made. "And how did Arthur fulfill that mission? The evening news tells that story: assassins, terrorists, religious fanatics killing in the name of false gods. Yet Arthur does *nothing*!"

He pivoted to face them. "Is this the world Merlin would want?"

"No!" The deep chorus of werewolf voices shook the trees.

"Of course not." Warlock pivoted and strode in the other direction, lacing his clawed fingers together behind his back. "Wars rage while thousands starve, even as others die of obesity. Fools and madmen lead captive countries, slaying their own civilians by the thousands when they dare demand freedom. And what does Arthur do?"

"Nothing!" his army roared.

"Yes. Nothing. Despite the fact that his witches could make the humans turn aside from their fanatical faiths, could force them to abandon crime and hate." Never mind that even Morgana Le Fay lacked the power to so twist a human's belief. All that counted was that his men believed the witches could. "His Majae could use their power to feed the hungry and cure diseases like AIDS and malaria. His vampire warriors could exact justice on tyrants, and free whole countries from the leadership of madmen. Yet what does he do?"

"Nothing!"

"Wrong!" Warlock whirled, curling a lip in an expression of contempt. "Oh, he does something, all right. He sends his killers to murder our children, then blames *me* for his crimes. Me!"

They howled at that, the mass roared fury of fanatics reacting to blasphemy.

"Arthur blames me because I have strength where he has nothing but weakness." Warlock curled a hand into a mailed fist, lifting it high. "He knows I could lead the humans into the lives of peaceful order Merlin intended. He *knows* that under my guidance, war and dissent will cease as humanity turns away from the teachings of false gods."

While turning toward the worship of Warlock himself, not that he needed to say as much. His Chosen understood him perfectly well, just as they knew teaching humans to worship Warlock would require shedding a great deal of blood over generations.

But it was, after all, only human blood. Spilling was what it was *for.*

Warlock spread his clawed hands in a gesture of benediction. "Humanity will finally know peace after all these bloody centuries. They will come to enjoy the prosperity I will create through the order I will maintain."

Now to appeal to his Chosen Knights' sense of greed and entitlement. He scanned the ranks, his level gaze conveying confidence.

"But to accomplish this, I will need lieutenants, trusted Direkind to help govern the six billion I will rule. I will find that capable aid in you. You, the descendants of those first bold Chosen Knights who fought at my side so many centuries ago. As the most loyal and deserving of my Direkind, you will know riches beyond your dreams, and power beyond comprehension. Humans will learn to worship you as heroes, and generations to come will revere you as gods."

Warlock paused, letting that intoxicating picture reach full bloom in his warriors' collective imagination.

When the moment was exactly right, he pulled Kingslayer from the sling across his back. As the magical blade spat sparks in reaction to his touch, Warlock lifted the great axe as he spoke in a triumphal roar. "Together, we will lead Humanity into the shining future Merlin intended!"

His warriors knew a cue when they heard one. Steel rang as every single fighter drew his blade and raised it high. "For humanity! For Merlin!" They finished the traditional chant with the thundering bellow of the truly devout. *"For Warlock!"*

Warlock smiled. *Now* they were ready.

Stunned, Justice floated in darkness, only distantly aware of the patter of falling water.

Miranda.

The thought of his lover—possibly unconscious and drowning—slapped him to full consciousness. He flailed around, somehow got his feet under him, and surged upright, sending waves slapping against the marble sides of the bath. "Miranda!"

"Here," she groaned. "Damn, don't yell like that. My head feels as if it's about to split."

Justice scanned for her frantically. The lights flashed on, obeying some mental command he hadn't consciously given. Miranda was already on her feet less than a yard away, cradling her head in both hands. Her dazed eyes were slits of misery.

"Jesus!" He sloshed over to pull her into his arms, gentling his grip at her pained gasp. Sweeping a quick magical scan over her, he sought signs of bruises or blood. But, thank God, saw nothing. "Are you all right? Did I hurt you?"

"No, but Daddy sure as fuck did," she growled, slumping into his supporting arms. "Son of a bitch tried to fry both of us with a death spell."

Justice frowned, a hazy memory surfacing of Miranda recognizing the incoming attack for what it was. At the last moment, they'd thrown up a shield with their unified power. The block had worked—more or less—but the effort had shattered their fragile connection.

The Spirit Link was broken.

"Now what the fuck are we supposed to do?" Justice growled in frustration. "Maeve told me we had to link."

"So we'll try again." Straightening, she winced as if muscles protested the move. "*After* we've had a little more time to recover."

"Assuming we get a little more time to recover," Justice growled. He sighed. "We'd better gate back to Avalon."

The city of Avalon glittered in the morning sunlight, an elegant sprawl of castles, chateaus, villas, and neat little cottages surrounded by the blazing shades of fall. Its cobblestone streets lay quiet, without the morning bustle of a mortal city at this hour.

That was no surprise. The vampires were all asleep, along with most of their women, recharging their magical batteries for the next battle in Merlin's Great Mission: protecting humanity from its own worst impulses.

Warlock meant to see every last one of them dead.

He flexed his clawed hands and spread them wide, reaching out with his magical senses to probe the city's powerful shields. Shields that had to fall if Warlock's invasion was to succeed.

He was acutely aware of his knights as they waited in disciplined ranks, his magic rendering them undetectable to Arthur's witches.

They made an impressive sight, towering and muscular in their armor, clawed hands gripping axes, swords, and spears, all enchanted to kill Magekind. Their thick fur ranged in shade from pale gold to a black so dark they seemed carved from darkness.

He was the only white wolf. The sun seemed to tip his fur with a metallic glint so that that it blended with his black armor, as if he *was* a weapon. Exactly what Merlin had created him to be, all those centuries ago.

More than a match for the Magekind.

Still, his enemies weren't fools. The spell that protected Avalon swirled in a complex of lethal energies that would kill anyone without the proper magical signature. Unfortunately, it was a signature Warlock didn't have. Worse, the shield was designed to alert Morgana Le Fay, Guinevere, and the other senior witches if it was tampered with. If Warlock triggered that alert, they'd all be ass-deep in witches before he could blink. Though he had seven thousand fighters at his back, plus his three Beasts, he had no desire to be locked out of Avalon with his plans laid bare. Arthur would see to it he'd never get such an opportunity again. The success of his battle plan hinged on cutting through the shield without being caught.

He'd briefly considered a nighttime attack. Defeating Arthur's full forces would be far more satisfying than a simple slaughter.

Unfortunately, he knew his people were no match for Arthur's vampires, especially not under the leadership of the Knights of the Round Table. There might be only twelve of Arthur's bastards, but given that each one had more than fifteen hundred years of combat experience, they'd butcher his wolves like sheep. And Warlock might as well die with them.

He was damned if he'd live as a failure.

So Warlock probed the city's shield with exquisite care and an immortal's patience. He didn't need a large opening, only one wide enough for a single werewolf to slip through at a time.

Then he'd send them raging after the knights, drag them from their beds, and . . .

Ah, what a sweet, sweet thought.

More than an hour passed before Warlock's claws sank into Avalon's great shield as if thrusting into warm dough—or cooling flesh. He grinned. *And there's the pattern. I knew no woman could craft a spell I couldn't crack.*

The spell surged against his claws in a sudden crackling electric blaze, sending agony sheeting up his fingers. Smoke curled upward, carrying the smell of singed fur and burning flesh.

Swearing, Warlock forgot smug satisfaction in favor of reestablishing his control before Morgana sensed what he was doing.

Long, sweating minutes passed before the spell subsided in the grip of his will. Blowing out a breath in relief, Warlock went to work increasing the size of the opening, prying it open inch by inch until he had a wavering oval four feet high. The lethal golden energy of the shield hissed and crackled in sullen threat, smelling of ozone and burning dust.

"Go," he snapped to the nearest werewolf. "And if you value your hide, don't touch the edges. I have control of the shield now, but it would cook you like a lightning bolt if you aren't careful."

"I thought the Direkind were immune to magic," Tom Addison said, a piece of impertinence Warlock would see he paid for. As one of his Beasts, Addison should damned well know better than to question orders in front of the troops.

The would-be scout paused, looking back at Warlock in frowning question.

"Do you think you're immune to a hundred thousand volts of electricity?" Warlock growled. "Then by all means, touch that fucking shield and see." Immunity to magic didn't mean immunity to natural forces *generated* by magic. Fortunately, tossing around that kind of power was beyond most witches.

"What are you waiting for?" Warlock snarled, jerking his head toward the opening. "Go, damn you."

The Dire Wolf flung himself through the opening, rightly fearing his leader more than the spell. The spell would only kill him.

With the example set, the rest of the Dire Wolves ducked cautiously through the opening. None of them suffered anything worse than singed fur, judging by the reek and occasional high-pitched yips of pain.

The Beasts hung back with Warlock, awaiting orders. Only Addison looked uneasy, having finally realized his mistake. He fingered one of his prized daggers nervously, not quite daring to meet Warlock's gaze.

Deliberately, the wizard turned his attention to Jack Ferraro, currently in the form of a deceptively wiry form of a blond-furred werewolf. Ferraro watched his face with a fanatic's unwavering attention, but Warlock didn't believe the act for an instant. "I want you to take care of my daughter. Make sure the traitorous little bitch suffers."

"But you promised I could . . ." Addison began, before hastily swallowing the rest of his protest. The little bastard might love to use his knives on women, but he had no desire for similar attention from Warlock.

"I'll take care of it," Ferraro announced, one corner of his lip twitching in pleasure at being one up on Addison. Turning, he slipped through the opening, agile as a ghost, transforming into his full Beast form the moment he was clear. The ground shook as the huge centaur broke into a gallop, hooves biting into the hill's rocky flanks.

Warlock turned his attention to Andrew Vance, who promptly came to attention like the former marine he was. A disgraced Marine, true, with an unfortunate tendency to murder civilians, but loyal enough for Warlock's purposes.

"You will be my guard in the city square." Warlock flicked a glance at Addison. "You. Provide a diversion for the squad I've designated to capture Arthur. Kill anyone who opposes you, with the exception of Morgana Le Fay or Guinevere. Those two bitches, I want. And don't fuck up again tonight if you don't want to feel your own knives. I'm better with them than you are." Addison dipped him a carefully respectful nod and followed Vance through the opening.

Warlock eased through after them, before sending another wave of power through the shield to prevent the witches from conjuring gates to safety.

That reminded him. He gathered a spare bit of power and sent a psychic cry ringing over the streets of Avalon:

"And now, Miranda, my dear traitorous bitch of a spawn, get ready to die!"

* * *

Miranda's shout of rage and fear catapulted Justice out of a sodden sleep. His eyes snapped open as she jerked from his arms and threw herself off the bed. She was changing before her feet hit the floor.

"Miranda, what the hell?" Remembering she'd almost attacked him the last time this happened, he rolled off the opposite side of the mattress and eyed her warily.

"It's Warlock! He said he's coming to kill me." Her clawed hands swept in an intricate gesture, sending magic swirling around her werewolf body in a glittering fog. "The bastard's *here*, Bill. In Avalon." Her grim gaze met his, glowing with power—and tainted by fear. *That damned spell.*

The swirl of magic vanished, leaving her armored in magical plate, the athame sheathed at her hip next to a five-foot great sword sized for a Dire Wolf's hand. The silhouetted head of the Pendragon covered her breastplate, enameled in red and gold. "You'd better grab the axe and Shift," she told him.

"How the hell did he get past the city shields?"

"All that death magic apparently came in handy." Her lip curled, revealing fangs. "One thing is for damned sure: my father's primary objective is killing Arthur. And since the bastard's attacking at seven in the morning, Arthur won't be conscious to defend himself. Neither will any of the other vampires, including the Knights of the Round Table."

Justice swore at the sickening implications. "Leaving no one to save them except a city full of women whose main weapon is magic—to which the Direkind are immune. Merlin was too damned smart for his own good." He called the energy of the Mageverse and Shifted.

The magic responded with a ferocity he'd never felt before, a blazing roil of force that engulfed his body and brain in fire, trying to reshape him into the form it chose.

And it wanted to be the Wolf.

Oh, yeah, that's just what we need—the Big Bad Psycho. He'd really turn this mess into a goat fuck. Justice clamped down hard, exerting his will, forcing the magic to take the Dire Wolf form he wanted instead. Muscle and bone twisted, lengthened, taking on heavier contours as fur grew over flesh in a racing, itching tide.

When the fiery ache of transformation subsided, Justice glanced around for Miranda, only to find her looking up at him, wolf brows lifted. Her head was much lower than he'd expected, as if she'd shrunk. Or he'd grown a lot more than he'd expected.

She swept a glance the length of his body. "My, Grandma. What big . . . *everything* you've got. Guess the Hunter Prince spell wanted to upgrade more than just the wolf."

"Damned axe," Justice growled, shooting a glance at the full-length mirror opposite the bed.

She was right. He was easily nine feet tall, with the added muscle to go with the height. At a guess, he'd weigh a thousand pounds. About the size of a full-grown grizzly.

A grizzly who needed armor if he didn't want some giant whatever to eat his hairy ass. Justice concentrated, dragging another flood of magic from the axe. Seconds later, he was dressed in a suit of enchanted plate emblazoned with Arthur's Pendragon's dragon head. A glance at the mirror made him grunt in approval as he hefted Merlin's Blade. He looked like a tank with fur.

The floor creaked in protest beneath his feet as he turned to look down at Miranda. "Let's go save the Once and Future King," he said, and blinked at the sound of his own voice. It rumbled a full octave deeper than normal.

Miranda nodded shortly and gestured, conjuring a gate to Casa Pendragon. It was only a mile or so away, but every second was critical; they didn't have time to hoof it.

The moment the portal wavered into full existence, a female voice screamed, "Put my husband down, you furry bastards!"

"Damn it to hell," Justice growled, and jumped through the portal with his axe raised and Miranda at his heels.

NINETEEN

Crap, it's worse than I expected, Miranda thought, as she and Justice hit the cobblestones on the other side of her gate.

She'd expected to see Guinevere fighting a running battle with a trio of armored Direkind. She *hadn't* known one of them would be carrying Arthur slung over a shoulder like a bag of dog food.

The former king wore a pair of blue jeans, and not a damn thing else. His brawny back was already turning red in the morning sun. Thank God Magekind vampires only got radiation burns from sunlight, rather than, say, bursting into flames, as Hollywood insisted.

To make matters worse—no easy task—a seventy-foot cobra currently exchanged fireballs with Morgana and five desperate, sword-swinging witches.

Of course Dad would bring the snake that ate Daliya's husband, Miranda thought in disgust. *What else have I been having nightmares about for the past week?*

"We go for the snake," Justice rumbled at her, his Dire Wolf voice about an octave deeper than James Earl Jones doing Darth Vader. "Free up Morgana and her witches, so they can help Gwen get Arthur away from those damned werewolves." He flicked a look at her from glowing golden eyes. "That sound right to you?"

The two of us? Alone against that snake? Hell no. Miranda swallowed and coiled into a crouch, her athame in one hand, the great sword in the other. "Yeah."

Dropping her voice to a level hopefully inaudible to giant snakes, she added, "I'll distract him, see if he's using the same spell Super Chicken used. If I can get the counter spell to work, you can cut his ass in two."

Justice flashed his teeth at her in a wolfish grin. "Do snakes *have* an ass?"

"You're the Hunter Prince. Hunt it." Miranda took a deep breath. *If I don't do this now, I won't do it at all.* "For Arthur and Avalon!" she howled as she leaped at the Beast's swaying head, just in case seven feet of flying were-wolf wasn't enough to attract its attention.

At the top of her arc, she swung the great sword in a diagonal stroke with every ounce of Direkind muscle behind it.

Just as she'd expected, the thing's spell shield flared blue as a neon sign the instant before it reflected the full force of the swing right back at her. Somersaulting like a poker chip, Miranda sailed ten yards to land in a three-point crouch—on a palm and both feet, neat as an anime character.

Yep, that was definitely the shield spell Super Chicken had used—which was in turn the same one Warlock had been using since she was a kid. *Thank God he's a creature of habit. And that he underestimates me.*

Miranda looked up to find the witches—including Morgana—staring at her as if she'd lost her mind. Even the snake looked taken aback.

"Go!" she screamed. "Help Gwen, or Arthur's dead! We've got the snake." *Yeah, right. Want some swampland to go with that?*

As one, the witches looked from the snake to the

werewolves—and decided they'd rather fight werewolves. Because, hey, they weren't stupid.

The werewolves finally started running. They apparently *were* stupid, since they should have been long gone, despite Gwen's efforts to stop them. Must have found something appealing about the idea of watching a giant snake eat witches. Dad would have turned every last one of them into fur coats if he'd known they'd fucked around like that on a job.

Which was when, out of the corner of one eye, she saw a huge, dark shape flying toward her.

"Miranda!" Justice roared, and she jerked around to realize the shape was the snake's open mouth. Thirty-five feet of giant reptile shooting through the air right at her head, propelled by the other thirty-five.

Miranda flung herself sideways in a convulsive surge of frantic strength. The Beast flashed past so close, she felt the hot wind of its passage like an eighteen-wheeler on the highway. Except instead of diesel, the thing reeked of reptile—and death magic.

"Wake the fuck up!" Justice bellowed, sounding well and truly pissed as he charged the monster, his axe spitting sparks in his big hands.

Damned near got myself eaten. Miranda hit the ground and almost fell on her face when her trembling knees buckled. She forced them to straighten. *Get. Your. Head. In the* GAME*!*

Justice was taking his temper and fear out on the snake, slamming the axe into its spell shield over and over, sparks showering around him like the Fourth of July. The snake retreated, hissing furiously as it coiled away from his assault, its body language all but screaming, *I'm being attacked by a giant crazy werewolf!*

Which would have been groovy, except Miranda knew all his magic and muscle wasn't really *doing* anything, not with the snake's spell shield protecting it from Justice's attack.

And yeah, that was definitely the same spell from the

Super Chicken fight. All she had to do was craft the same counter spell, and she could spear Snakey like a fish. Apparently Super Chicken hadn't realized *how* she'd hit him through that spell, or Warlock would surely have created a new one she wouldn't know how to break.

Finally, a little luck. God knew they were due. She lifted her hands and started chanting . . .

Which was when a new spell snapped into place around her like a bear trap closing. Spinning as her heart shot into her throat, she found yet another Beast smirking, this one the massive armored centaur with the battle-axe. Its blue gem sparked from the center of its forehead, probably recording the entire thing for Warlock's later enjoyment.

How the hell can anything with hooves move that quietly over cobblestones . . . ? Oh. Muffling spell, twit.

"Hi, baby," he purred. "Daddy says hello." With that, the centaur reared to smash those dinner-plate hooves down at her head. The blue gem in the center of his head blazed, radiating malice—and her father's death magic.

Miranda sprang away, avoiding the hooves only to smash face-first into a new shield he'd put up around them both. Light exploded in her skull as the field picked her up and threw her into a helpless tumble.

The centaur laughed, a rolling, evil chuckle of delight.

Bastard, she thought, desperately scrambling to her feet as she heard his pursuing hooves clattering against the cobblestones. *You bastard.*

She ducked an axe blow and swung her own sword in a chop toward the centaur's torso.

Warlock's fear spell clawing at her, she'd forgotten about the Beasts' shielding spells. The thing's magic shot the force of her own blow right back at her, slamming her into the cage field again. She hit the ground on her knees, half-blind and tasting blood.

Dead, Miranda thought, as the athame chimed desperately at her. *I'm dead. Good thing Justice and I didn't manage to Spirit Link . . .*

Justice.

As if from a great distance, she heard that deep voice of his roaring something through the cage spell. She looked up to watch helplessly as he raced toward her and the centaur, Merlin's Blade lifted.

He'd either forgotten about the snake, or he didn't give a shit. Either way, the thing reared and hit him, snapping loops of gleaming three-foot-thick black coils around his armored body, immobilizing him.

Trapping his axe arm.

"Stupid slut," the centaur said, with that evil laugh. "Looks like you just got your lover killed."

Miranda turned and stared at him for one savage, vibrating second. She had never in all her life felt such blind fury.

The athame chimed again, an insistent, belling note. Afterward, she would never be sure whether the knife somehow told her what to do, or whether she'd realized it on her own. Either way, Miranda tightened her grip on the athame and began to pour power into it.

The flow of magic lit the length of her arm with snaking forks of magic and flashing sparks. The knife glowed brighter, then brighter yet, raining sparks to the cobblestones.

"And what do you imagine you're going to do with that?" the centaur sneered. "Scare me to death with a fireworks display?" He laughed and lifted his axe. "Well, mine's bigger, bitch."

She backed away, her eyes locked on his mocking face, still spilling her power into the athame. He reared over her, pawing the air above her head before slamming his hooves down at her face. Miranda leaped back, narrowly avoiding the strike, then danced aside again as he plunged at her, whipping the axe left, then right, then left again, cutting vicious figure eights in the air. Fear bit into her, blunting her magic as Warlock's vampire spell diverted her power.

Miranda ducked, feinted at him with the sword, spun. And kept pouring magic down her arm and into the blade. The athame began actively drawing on her power, speeding up the magical flow until the light grew so blinding that even the centaur threw an arm up to shield his face. *What the hell am I doing?* she thought, but she kept right on doing it anyway.

Until she hit some kind of critical mass. Miranda's legs gave under her, and she fell to her knees. Her enchanted armor vanished. So did the great sword.

And they weren't the only things. *Everything* sustained by her magic vanished, including her enchanted armor, leaving her naked except for her fur and the athame in her hand.

"Ha!" the centaur shouted with a grin of delight. "Miscalculated, didn't you? You fucking drained yourself! You've got nothing left—no magic at all!"

Miranda looked up at him, her eyes burning as she stared into Warlock's gem. She hoped the bastard heard her. "No. None whatsoever." She watched him draw the axe back over one shoulder, preparing to swing it at her like a batter going for a home run. By now, Warlock's spell should have her in a state of howling terror—but it didn't. "And you know what, Budweiser? For the first time in decades, I feel no fear at all."

"Then you're as stupid as Warlock always said you . . ." He broke off, his eyes widening. "The spell! What happened to Warlock's fear spell?"

Miranda grinned like a shark. "It broke."

Then she reached into her athame and called her magic back.

The knife responded with a single chiming note, high and pure as the sound of angels singing. The power slammed out of the knife and up her arm, staggering her like a blast from a fire hose. She had to lock a scream behind her teeth; it felt like the raging influx was searing every nerve she had.

Yet the power kept coming. *What the hell? This is more than I put into it! What's it . . .*

She could feel herself Shifting with no conscious control at all. Just as Merlin's Blade had changed Justice, the athame itself was changing her, making her a conduit for still more magic, expanding her limits even further now that she'd shattered the Warlock's crippling spell. Her skull ached as though it were being blown up like a balloon, and she could have sworn her skin was swelling over her burning bones.

Until, at last, it stopped.

God almighty, that hurt, Miranda thought, moving toward the centaur in a crouching slink. *But it was worth it.* Under her breath, she began chanting the spell to break through Budweiser's shield.

"I don't know what you just did, you little whore," Budweiser growled, though the hand holding his axe shook. Apparently the light show accompanying her transformation had been pretty damned impressive. "But it's not going to save you."

He surged at her like a race horse exploding from the starting gate, raising his axe over his head in both armored hands.

Miranda leaped straight up in an effortless bound, flying right over Budweiser's desperate swing. She hit the ground directly behind him, then bounced backward an additional yard when he bucked and tried to kick her with his rear hooves. Gathering herself, she started to lunge for his back, only to realize the athame was getting a hell of a lot heavier. Miranda automatically grabbed her knife hand with her left, meaning to steady the little blade . . .

Only it wasn't a little blade anymore. The athame was *growing.*

A blink later, it was a six-foot-long two-handed sword that glowed like a flipping light saber. *What the hell? She* hadn't done that.

The athame blew a warning note, sounding more French horn than flute. Hooves rang on pavement as the centaur whirled on her, his muzzle drawn into a vicious display of teeth. "I don't care what magic you jerked out of your ass, you're still dead, you little slut."

Miranda snarled back, "I'm not a slut, Budweiser."

They swung their weapons simultaneously. Miranda

had intended to block his axe blow and drive her sword into his chest. Instead, the athame hit the axe's long handle and cleaved it cleanly in two.

The now-haftless axe cartwheeled at her face. Miranda ducked, and it sailed harmlessly over her head to hit the cobblestones with a metallic ringing clatter.

Budweiser began to curse in a vile stream of filth. He was in the middle of calling her a slut yet again when she bounded straight up and swung the two-handed athame with all the considerable strength in her werewolf body.

The sword cleaved through the assassin's armored neck, slicing through the steel like a stick of butter. His head hit the ground near the lost axe as Miranda landed in a knife-fighter's crouch. She watched with a blend of nausea, horror, and grim satisfaction as the centaur's decapitated head rolled to a stop with a sodden, uneven *thump thump thump*.

Budweiser's body collapsed with a rending shriek of tortured metal as three thousand pounds of armored monster hit the cobblestone street.

She didn't stop to gloat. Budweiser's death had shattered his containment spell, so she started chanting as she launched herself toward the snake still wrapped around a desperately struggling Justice. Thank God for sadistic bastards; it was apparently taking its time about killing him. *Probably hoping to make Justice watch Budweiser kill me before it ate him. Well, tough luck, Cobra Commander.*

The monster's head whipped toward her, blue gem shooting sparks as it reared high over her werewolf head, hissing. Miranda reached the mass of coils that held Justice. *Dammit, I'm not close enough to decapitate it . . .*

Shifting her target, Miranda swung the athame greatsword with both hands. The magical blade sank into the snake as if she were cutting into a tomato. Apparently, whatever the athame had done had also increased her Direkind strength every bit as much as her magic. Which was saying something; she hadn't exactly been a wimp to start with.

The giant reptile threw up its head and shrieked at the

blade's bite, an oddly human cry of agony and rage. Whipping its upper body toward her, it reared to strike. It didn't seem to notice Justice's massive Dire Wolf form disappearing in a blaze of blue light.

Miranda leaped aside, avoiding the cobra's strike even as she swung her blade at its head. It jerked back, and she missed. But she didn't give up, spinning the sword with a showy rotation of her wrists, keeping the snake's black eyes focused on her below the blue gleam of its gemstone. The thing hissed, huge hood spreading. The gem shone like a star, emitting a reeking blast of Warlock's magic.

Justice leaped from the beast's coils as easily as a man shrugging out of a coat that was six sizes too big. Which they were, because he'd Shifted into human form, while she distracted the snake.

Hissing, the cobra jerked its head around as it finally realized he'd vanished. It plunged its open maw downward, aiming for the human Justice trying to get the hell away from it.

He jumped back and swung, burying the axe in the side of its head like a meat cleaver into a watermelon. Its upper third fell to the stones, boneless and limp.

Just like the snake it was, the huge creature began to convulse, its seventy-foot body whipping. Justice barely leaped clear in time to avoid getting crushed by the Beast's death throes. He hadn't taken more than a single step before a furry arm wrapped around his waist.

Miranda jerked him right off his feet, tucked him under her arm and kept running, the athame in her free hand.

"Put me down, dammit!" he yelled, all deeply insulted Alpha Male. "I can save my own ass!"

"Oh, shut up!" She spotted a building she thought was far enough away and raced toward it. "You're quick enough to cart me around like a bag of dog food whenever the urge hits. Sauce for the gander, Fudd."

Reaching the potential shelter, she put him down with a grateful sigh; he was heavier than he looked.

Justice glowered at her and straightened. "Yeah, well, I

also need to get my axe back. It's still in Captain Cobra's brain."

"Oh, hell." She stuck her head out from behind their shelter. Snakey's convulsions seemed to be winding down. And Justice was right; there was the axe, one blade gleaming in the morning sunlight, the other deeply buried in the side of the snake's head. "Well, looks like the devil is cooking up a little Sweet and Sour Reptile right about now."

"With a side order of horse meat . . ." Justice broke off in mid-word, staring at her. A grin of delight spread over his face. "How the hell did you break Warlock's spell? Every last chain link is gone! There's not so much as a whiff of his stink anywhere on you."

She grinned right back at him. "Poured all my power into the athame and de-powered myself. Since the spell is sustained by my magic . . ."

Justice whistled. "Smart. Risky, but smart. Once you were powerless, the spell couldn't sustain itself, so it collapsed."

"Yep. And once it was gone, the athame gave my powers back. And then some."

His pleasure faded into a frown. "I saw a flash of light, but I'd ducked down into the coils trying to pry my axe free and missed the rest."

Miranda shrugged. "That was probably when the athame did its thing, whatever the hell that was. Anyway, I seem to have picked up a lot of power." She lifted the sword, displaying it. "Then the athame turned itself into this . . ."

"*That* is your little dagger?"

"Yeah. Put it to good use, too, making sure Budweiser and his head came to a parting of the ways."

Justice lost his pleasure in a flash of incredulous anger. "You drained off all your power *while that thing was still alive*?" His voice went very low, very soft. "Locked in a containment spell with a thirteen-foot-tall armored monster who could have stomped you into roadkill?"

"What the hell was I supposed to do?" Miranda demanded

hotly. It occurred to her that she'd normally be shaking in her boots in the face of Justice's Alpha Male anger. But the spell was history now, and she could give him all the hell he had coming. "Yeah, I knew it was a risk. Unfortunately, a certain giant snake was about to eat the man I love, so I didn't exactly have time to fuck around."

"And if you'd failed, you'd have died while I watched. Then the damned snake would have eaten me, just like the scaly bastard told me it was going to do."

"Well, I *didn't* fail, we're still alive, and both assholes are dead." She stalked toward Budweiser. "Go get your damned axe. There's something I need to do before we rescue Arthur. I just hope Morgana and Gwen managed to stop those damned werewolves before they took him to Warlock."

Unfortunately, given the way things were going, she figured they just weren't that lucky.

She dropped to one knee beside Budweiser's head and went to work on the gemstone implanted in his forehead. Grimacing in disgust, she popped the gem free. Her father's magic rolled over her skin, feeling greasy. *If evil were a tactile sensation, this would be it.*

Miranda hesitated. This was the kind of thing that could bite her on the ass—or save it. Licking her lips, she conjured a pouch and dropped the gem into it, then threw a quick spell over the pouch to shield the gem's power.

Wouldn't do for Daddy to sense she had his little rock. Not at all.

Not that Miranda had any damned idea what she was going to do with the stone. *I'll blow that bridge when I come to it.* "Hey, Justice?" she called. "Got your Ginsu back yet?" She turned to find him levering the blade free, one foot braced on the snake's head. "Well, that's certainly one way to do it."

They created a gate to take them to wherever Gwen was, emerging to the sound of women screaming. Screaming in agony, in terror, in rage. Screaming spells, screaming curses, screaming orders. Yet those cries were barely audible over the thundering booms of spell blasts.

Every protective instinct in Justice's psyche went on quivering alert. Then he got a good look at what was going on, and wanted to scream himself.

The witches of Avalon fought an enormous blue dragon, forty feet of wings and scales and lethal teeth roaring and blasting away at them. They circled it, each woman's protective shield igniting in bursts of light in response to its blasts, flicking off only long enough to let her fire back.

"Is that *Kel*?" Miranda shouted over the insane racket. "Can't be," Kel was one of the Knights of the Round Table, though he was a shape-shifting dragon rather than a vampire. Before that, he'd been trapped in Gawain's sword for centuries, the victim of a Dragonkind uncle's magical plot. Kel and Sir Gawain had formed a partnership as tight as brothers; he would never turn on his fellow warriors. And he sure as hell wouldn't attack Gawain's wife, Lark, or his own mate, the Sidhe princess Nineva.

Yet there the two women were, side by side, blasting away at the blue beast every time they saw an opening. And the creature blasted right back.

No wonder. Just beyond the prowling dragon, Kel lay unconscious, along with the other Knights of the Round Table. Gawain, Lancelot, Tristan, Galahad, Percival, Marrok, Kay, Cador, Lamorak, and Baldulf.

As well as Logan, who was not a Round Table Knight, but Arthur and Guinevere's son. Warlock had probably taken him to replace Sir Bors, who had been murdered by his first Beast, Dice.

Twelve men lay on the ground in a great circle, arranged a yard apart like the spokes of a wheel, their feet pointing outward toward the circle's rim.

Arthur lay in the circle's center, Excalibur floating just above his chest, its point aimed down at his heart. Like his men, he was naked.

Each knight's sword floated over its owner's heart, bound in a glowing web of magic.

And the spider at the web's center was Warlock.

The werewolf stood by Arthur's still form, lips moving in a chant Justice couldn't hear over the thunder of combat.

"Bill, that's a death magic spell." Miranda gripped her athame so hard, her knuckles were white and bloodless. "When he finishes, it will—"

"—Drive those swords into their hearts and feed their collective life force to Warlock." Justice broke off to swallow the lump of raw fury that threatened to choke him at the thought.

"Along with the lives of Gwen and the other Truebonded wives. A little twofer for the bastard." Miranda glared at her father through the containment shield that protected him and his victims. "We've got to stop him."

She jolted forward, but Justice grabbed her arm, dragging her to a stop.

"We've got to figure out how to kill that fucking dragon first—*and* get through the shielding spell around Warlock's circle." A witch's spell blast hit the hemispherical shield, lighting it up with a blast of rolling energy.

"Yeah. But what the hell do we do about it?" Frustration edged her voice. "And how are we going to kill that fucking lizard?"

"To start with, we think a minute before we go off half-cocked."

The dragon took to the air, circling around the shield to blast fire down at the witches. Luckily, they erected their own shield wall in time—interlocking magical barriers stronger than any separate spell.

"*Another* Beast. How many *are* there?" Miranda said, watching the thing with narrowed eyes. "Look, he has the same gem in his head Budweiser and the Cobra had." Sure enough, a blue crystal burned on the monster's forehead, making him look as though he had three eyes.

Justice watched the creature a moment—and saw it

make a gesture he recognized. "No, it's Super Chicken. See how he tilted his head just now?"

"But his magic—he's one hell of a lot stronger than he was the last time we fought him. How did . . . ?"

"That yearling dragon." Justice curled a lip. "Warlock used its life force to juice him up. And he's drawing more power off Kel." The energy around the dragon shifter was much brighter than that surrounding the other knights. Which was probably why Kell was unconscious; unlike the vampires, dragons didn't have to sleep during the day. "I wonder how the hell Warlock trapped him."

"Doesn't matter," Miranda told him grimly, glowing eyes narrow. "One way or the other, I'm killing Daddy today. He's got to die."

"On that, we are in complete agreement!" Morgana Le Fay shouted from behind them.

Luckily, Justice had scented the witch's approach, so he didn't take her head out of sheer reflex. He still gave serious thought to telling her not to sneak up on a werewolf.

The witch's eyes burned hot and gold with magic. Not to mention sheer, feral desperation. Morgana's armor was her signature blood red, decorated with ornate swirls of metallic gold: spells of protection and strength. She'd scraped her mass of black hair back, emphasizing the stern, cold purity of her features.

"That damned dragon is beating us." As Morgana spoke, blood began to pour from her nose; God knew what her blood pressure was, but she was obviously courting a stroke from sheer magical effort. "Grace is down. We've stabilized her, but I'm not sure she'll make it. A fireball . . . She reinforced my shields when she should have been shielding herself. Dammit, I told her . . ." Morgana's voice cracked, and she clamped her lips closed.

Justice blinked. He'd had the impression Morgana's granddaughter hated her guts—and he hadn't thought Morgana gave a rat's ass about the girl one way or another. Apparently he'd been wrong on both counts.

"Lancelot . . ." Miranda broke off, shooting Justice a glance. He knew what she was thinking. Grace and Lance were Truebonded. If the young witch died, Lance was lost even if they prevented Warlock from carrying out the spell.

Guinevere wove across the battlefield to join them, followed by her daughter-in-law, Giada. Like Morgana, both women wore armor emblazoned with the Pendragon—Arthur's Dragon's Head. The younger blonde's face was marred by a second-degree burn, a thick blister running across one cheek.

Gwen's lips moved, but a thunderous blast drowned her out. She jerked one hand in a sweeping, impatient gesture, and the howling screams and booms abruptly muted, as if someone had hit the volume control on the war.

"Listen, boy, that bastard has my husband and my son," she growled, a note to her normally sweet voice he'd never heard before. Suddenly Justice could believe she'd been a queen rather than the soccer mom she usually pretended she was. "We need the Wolf. You have the power to put the dragon down, but only if you stop holding back. Quit trying to be human and kill that Beast. Kill him fast, or we're all dead. Along with every man we love."

Justice fought the instinct to obey her no matter what she wanted him to do. She'd been giving orders to Alpha Males a hell of a long time; no surprise that she knew how to do it. He also knew he had to warn her. "If I let my Wolf go, he could kill more witches than the dragon."

"He *is* you, you fool," Morgana snapped. "Stop being so fucking blind."

"And I'd rather *you* kill me than let that thing feed Arthur to Warlock," Gwen snarled.

She meant it. But she didn't *know*. She'd never seen his monster hunt Miranda like a fox chasing a field mouse.

Miranda caught his shoulder. "Do it," she said quietly. "They're right. And you won't lose control. You're better than that." She leaned in and kissed him hard, her mouth fierce and hot with promise. Giving him a reason to survive.

Miranda stepped back. "Go."

TWENTY

Justice nodded wordlessly and backed away from Miranda and the witches, trying to give himself plenty of room to Shift without stepping on anyone. The women turned away and went back to blasting Warlock's shield, trying to pound their way through.

Only Miranda was left, watching him with calm certainty, as if she knew he wouldn't fail. Tightening his grip on the axe, Justice looked down into the swirling magic of its gem. Letting its magic flow into him, *through* him.

The Wolf exploded from its cage deep in his inner darkness, all hunger and animal rage, craving blood. Justice clamped down tight, controlling its savagery with all his strength of will even as the power of his Shift transformed him.

No matter what the witches said, he damned well wasn't going to just let go. He didn't dare.

When his transformation finally completed, Justice shook himself and stretched, trying to adjust to his own sheer size. Glancing at the dragon, he realized the monster looked much smaller than it had just seconds earlier.

He could feel Miranda watching him, not even a hint of fear in her mind. Some echo of their failed Spirit Link must linger after all. They'd have to try again after this was over.

If we live long enough. He banished the doubt. They weren't going to lose, and they damned well weren't going to die. He wouldn't allow it.

Justice's instincts screamed a warning, and he bounded twenty feet straight up. The dragon exploded past just below his feet, and he fell on it, landing on its thick scaled shoulders to sink his teeth into the base of its neck. Roaring, the dragon rolled, trying to crush him beneath its vast weight.

Nice try, asshole. Justice leaped clear and darted in again, trying for its throat. All he got was a fireball in the face. He barely shielded in time, recoiling as it threw him off with a convulsive heave.

The dragon rolled to its feet, snarling viciously, tail lashing. Justice began to circle it, watching for any weakness.

Miranda's every instinct screamed at her to follow the two huge beasts, in case Justice needed help. Too bad she couldn't afford that luxury. Warlock could not be allowed to complete that damned spell. If he pulled it off, Justice would be just one of the thousands he'd kill. Miranda refused to have that on her conscience.

She moved in close to the shield, approaching from Warlock's rear. Delicately, carefully—hoping none of the witches would blast her by mistake—she began to analyze the magical patterns in the hemispherical shield.

It wasn't one she recognized. No surprise. Her father might be an overconfident misogynist but he wasn't stupid. But a pattern in the spell did remind her of something . . .

Miranda reached into the pouch around her waist and pulled out Budweiser's gem. The minute it was in her hand, she sensed the containment field thin slightly.

Of course Warlock's shielding spell would be designed to let his Beasts through. That meant . . .

She concentrated, drawing on the gem's energy, trying to make her own magic mimic the same pattern, the better to fool the shield. Making contact with her father's magic was like plunging lip-deep in raw sewage, but she ignored her instinctive reaction and began to chant, reaching out for the field with her free hand. Only to hesitate.

If she got this wrong, the spell would fry her so fast, she'd never know what hit her.

Miranda drew the gem's magic tight around her and stepped into the field . . . and passed through like a ghost. For a moment she just stood on the other side, her knees shaking.

Warlock was still chanting, and she listened absently, her heart pounding in her chest with a kettledrum thump as she recovered. *God, I can't believe that actually worked.*

Then she realized what her father was saying, and her heart rammed right into her throat. *Fuck, he's almost finished! If I'd been thirty seconds later . . .*

Get the fuck out before I kill you, Warlock snarled in her mind. He didn't stop chanting, didn't even look around. She knew he didn't dare. The spell was too close to fruition.

When he finished the next sentence, Arthur and his Knights would die, along with all their ladies. Warlock and his wolves would kill every living thing in Avalon. *I don't have time to panic*, she told herself savagely, throwing Budweiser's stone aside. *I have to stop him now, or he won't* be *stopped.*

Warlock's voice rose to a shout as he completed the chant. All thirteen swords began to drop.

Miranda threw up both hands and blasted a wave of force across the containment spell, sending every one of the weapons spinning aside.

The blades clattered harmlessly to the cobblestones as the energy of the death spell drained away.

"You *bitch*!" Warlock roared, his voice thunderous in the stillness of the containment field. "You'll die for that!"

Miranda laughed. "So? You'd have killed me anyway, you sadistic fuck. You've been trying to kill me for months."

He whirled on her, seeming to swell in his rage, radiating such lethal power Miranda's instincts screamed for her to fall on her face and cower.

"You think your little stunt has saved you? Idiot! Once you're dead—in about a minute and a half—I'll just begin again. And this time there will be no interruptions."

He stalked toward her, moving so slowly, so deliberately that every step communicated his confidence. "Arthur and his damned knights will die, and all the Magekind with them. Their deaths will give me the power to put humanity where it belongs: on its knees." He laughed. "Hell, half of them are there already. Why shouldn't I rule instead of some human dictator?"

"You know, when you laugh like that, you sound like the villain in a Bond movie," Miranda drawled. "One of the really stupid Roger Moore ones from the seventies. Except their dialogue was better." *Yeah, piss him off. Make him stop thinking.*

Growling, his eyes bright with fury, Warlock jerked his axe from the harness across his back and charged. She knew from the arrogant confidence in his eyes that he expected her to take to her heels in panic. Then he'd slice her apart with no effort at all.

He didn't know she'd broken his fear spell—or that she'd been drilling with the knights and Justice on a daily basis.

Unfortunately, Warlock was still far stronger than she was, not to mention a foot taller, with a much longer reach. Too, he'd been fighting for centuries. Miranda had no idea how long she could hold him off.

But just beyond the containment field, Justice battled the dragon. If she could only hold Warlock off long enough, maybe she'd come up with a way to drop the field. Then she and Justice could kill him together.

If she didn't, they were all screwed.

As Warlock reached her, Miranda whirled as though to run. He laughed, a contemptuous bark.

Miranda spun, whirling the athame at his head with every ounce of speed she could manage. Warlock barely swung his axe up to block in time.

The clash of the two blades rattled her teeth, but she managed a sneering grin anyway. "I broke your spell, *Daddy*. I won't be running from you anymore. And why *did* you cast that spell, anyway?"

His orange eyes narrowed and seemed to burst into flame. "Oh, slut, you're going to regret mocking me." He moved after her in a slow, relentless stalk, lips pulled back to reveal gleaming teeth.

"Me? Regret mocking a man so fearful, he'd cripple a four-year-old?" She smiled, slow and poisonous. "Just imagine what Merlin would say."

He didn't roar this time. He just whirled, swinging his axe in a scything circle. She knew better than to attempt a parry—not against a swing that hard. Instead, she ducked.

The wind of the blade's passage flipped up a lock of her hair. An instant later, the hairs floated past her eyes, neatly severed.

Miranda swallowed.

Blood rolled down Justice's head from one torn ear, and the claw marks on his chest and back stung fiercely, as did the bites on his right foreleg and left rear haunch. But he'd done just as much damage to the dragon in their battle, getting through its shield as often as it had his.

As he stalked the big monster, he glanced past its winged shoulder. And froze.

Miranda was inside the containment field—*fighting Warlock.*

Fuck. Oh, fuck. I have to end this now. I've got to get to her before the bastard kills her.

There was no more time to fight his animal instincts, no

more time to screw around being cautious. Caution would get Miranda killed.

So Justice let go. Released his tight, careful hold on the Wolf and the clamoring need to kill the dragon that had hurt him.

With a belling howl of rage, the Wolf leaped, slamming into the dragon so hard, the impact bowled the bigger creature right off its feet. The wolf swarmed up the dragon's body and latched onto its throat just below the jaw. The dragon wrapped its clawed forelegs around his torso and ripped, trying to slash him open. The Wolf barely even felt the pain.

All he wanted was to kill the Beast and save Miranda.

For the first time, Justice felt his animal half's true emotions. He'd been so busy fighting the Wolf before, so busy struggling to control him, he'd been blind to the truth.

The Wolf wanted to save Miranda every bit as much as Justice did, because the Wolf loved her as much as he did.

Miranda had been right all along. The Wolf had chased her because she'd hurt him, but he never would have hurt her. Hell, he'd been trying to *prove* himself to her as any male animal would. Prove he was worthy to become her mate by defeating her, then releasing her unharmed.

But because he was so damned much bigger than she was, neither Miranda nor Justice had realized that at the time. She'd freaked and hid in her rabbit hole, while Justice had . . .

Roaring in pain, the dragon grabbed the Wolf in clawed forepaws and flung itself into the sky, its great wings beating hard as it carried him higher, then higher still. The bastard obviously assumed Justice wouldn't rip out his throat if it meant falling to his own death.

Except Justice was no longer in control, and the Wolf didn't give a damn. The huge creature braced his legs against the Beast's chest and jerked his fanged grip on the dragon's throat, ripping it wide. Blood sheeted across his face, blinding him as the Beast shrieked in mortal agony. Its huge wings stopped beating.

And they fell.

The dragon's limp forelegs dropped away, and the Wolf tumbled, free-falling toward the ground that was much too far away. In a flash, Justice realized that even the Wolf wouldn't survive a fall from this height.

So he opened a gate in midair and dropped right through it.

The other end of the gate opened barely fifteen feet above the ground, and a comfortable distance from the impact crater the dragon was about to make. Thanks to his magic, Justice had only fallen about thirty feet. Which was definitely preferable to his enemy's five hundred yard plunge.

He rolled to his feet ready to cast a shield around the surrounding witches. Only they were already long gone, having gated clear themselves as they realized what was happening.

So when the dragon hit the ground with a bloody crash that shook the earth, no one else died in the impact. Even Miranda and Warlock were protected by the wizard's containment shield.

Justice shook off the dirt thrown up by the monster's landing and loped back toward the shield, wondering how the hell he was supposed to get in to save Miranda. He was vaguely surprised the Beast hadn't Shifted as it had when Miranda had come so close to killing Super Chicken before. Ripping out its throat must have deprived its brain of needed oxygen just a little too long. That, or it had panicked and never thought to transform at all.

"Justice." The voice echoed in his mind, startling him enough to bring him to a skidding stop.

Miranda? But no; the mind that brushed his own was someone completely different.

Maeve.

That's right, the Sidhe goddess had told them she could speak to the minds of animals, though she could barely read humans at all. At least, unless she'd touched you long enough to cast a communication spell on you, as she had with Miranda.

"I thought you'd never free that damned Wolf long enough for me to reach your consciousness," Maeve said, sounding peeved. *"Tell Morgana to let me through the city wards. I have a plan."*

He spotted Gwen and Morgana heading toward him, bloody faces grim. Justice moved to meet them, taking care where he put his big paws. Wouldn't do to step on a witch. *I hope Miranda can hold off that bastard until we can stage a rescue.*

Her father was a fucking sadist.

Miranda had known that before, of course; it had been appallingly obvious for a long time. But she'd never really felt the brutal truth of it until she'd watched him stalk her, smiling slightly, vicious pleasure in his eyes as she scrambled away. Every little bit, he'd spring at her, swinging that axe in a lethal arc that just barely gave her time to duck or retreat.

She was so damned exhausted, she could barely keep moving. Blood ran down her arms and legs from countless cuts, though fortunately none of them had cut through her armor deeply enough to cripple.

Weary fury surged through Miranda. He could have killed her long before now. Hell, she'd thought she was finished when the dragon slammed into the ground. Warlock had gone into a ranting frenzy at the death of his precious Vance.

Vance. Super Chicken's real name had been Andrew Vance. Warlock hadn't given a damn that she and Justice had killed his other Beasts, but Vance's loss pissed him off. Evidently the prick was supposed to be Warlock's trusted lieutenant during his conquest of humanity. Warlock raged at her that the former marine was supposed to be his second in command in the new order.

She'd thought he'd kill her then, but he'd calmed down. Calmed down, and started to smile. And play with her.

God, she *hated* that smile.

"Miranda." It took all her willpower not to start as Jus-

tice's voice spoke in her mind. *"We need to Spirit Link. Now. Maeve is here, and she and the witches have a plan. But I need to be in there with you, or it won't work."*

"You can't get through the containment field, and I don't have any way to open it," Miranda told him. Besides, if they linked, he'd only die when she did. Miranda knew she couldn't survive much longer. Sooner or later, Warlock would get tired of playing with her. Presumably, when he grew bored with watching her fight to survive.

We're still linked from that attempt we made before, Justice insisted. *Maeve said she can help me use your mind as a conduit through Warlock's shield. Then once I'm in there with you, I'll kill the fucker. But you have to reach out to me and help me link.*

But . . .

Now, Miranda. Or a lot of people are going to die who don't deserve it.

Every instinct rebelled at the thought of letting Justice risk death this way. But if she died *before* he got through the shield, Warlock would still have more than enough time to sacrifice Arthur and his Knights; they couldn't wake from their magical sleep until nightfall.

Then all of this would be for nothing. Too many people had fought and suffered—too many people would suffer. Even if it meant death for both herself and even Justice, if they could only save the others . . .

All right. Are you ready?

Yes! Miranda, for God's sake . . .

And she Shifted, reaching for him along the link they'd come so close to completing before. But this time, Warlock's fear spell wasn't there to keep them apart.

Maeve *was* there. Miranda felt the Sidhe goddess add her power to Justice's, helping him ride the forming link between them and slide *through* the shield.

She re-formed from her Shift holding Justice's clawed hand in her now much smaller human one.

"What the hell is this?" Warlock stared up at the towering Dire Wolf warrior.

Justice only grinned. "Your death, you bastard."

Roaring in rage, the wizard swung Kingslayer at them both. Justice stepped forward and met the attack with Merlin's blade, weapon ringing on weapon. A chain-saw snarl ripping his lips, he advanced on Warlock, driving the smaller werewolf back with his greater mass and reach.

Ha, Miranda thought. *See how* you *like it, Daddy*.

The blades beat together, each ringing impact spilling sparks around the two warriors like a blue rain.

Miranda watched, tensed and ready, the athame in both hands. She only hoped she'd get the opportunity to give him a little taste of his own poison.

Suddenly Warlock's head snapped back, his jaws gaping in astonished shock as he stared at the sky. "What? No! No, you bitches, you're not going to get away with this!"

He leaped at Justice, whirling Kingslayer up and across in a savage diagonal arc intended to cut his enemy in two. Justice blocked the blow, chopping downward with Merlin's Blade, muscling Kingslayer down and trapping Warlock's axe against the ground.

Miranda saw the chance she'd been waiting for. Stepping between the two men, she slashed the athame downward into the big gemstone embedded between Kingslayer's double blades. Her sword hit the gem . . .

And shattered it.

The magical blast knocked Miranda flat on her ass and slammed Warlock across the spell circle to slam hard into his own shield. The barrier winked out. His body flared with light. For a moment, Miranda thought he was about to detonate like a bomb . . .

Then the glow faded, and Warlock reeled to his feet like a drunken man, cursing in a vicious roll of Saxon obscenity. The axe was gone, vanished completely, but that wasn't why Miranda stared at him with her jaw dropping in astonishment.

He was human.

Warlock stopped swearing, his expression shocked, as if

the relatively high-pitched sound of his own voice had penetrated his rage. He looked down at his fully-human hands, and an expression of horror rolled over his face.

"No . . ." Looking up at Miranda, Warlock's face twisted in a snarl. "You bitch! What did you *do*?"

Oddly, she'd never really thought of her father as having ever been human, probably because she'd never known of him to Shift. Hell, this was probably the first time he'd been anything but a Dire Wolf in centuries.

He was a tall man, surprisingly wiry considering his werewolf bulk, built more like a marathon runner than a Dark Ages swordsman. His white hair was so long, it dragged on the ground behind him.

She was still adjusting to that reality when darkness fell. Fell between one heartbeat and the next, as if someone had turned out the sun like an electric light bulb. Miranda barely noticed, too busy staring at her father as another shocking fact penetrated her consciousness.

There was no sense of magic around him at all.

"I asked you what you did, you little bitch," Warlock shrieked, jolting toward her, his voice shooting high in helpless fury. "What did you do to my power?"

"I would imagine, you idiot," Arthur observed, his voice utterly calm, "that when she destroyed your blade, it took your power with it." As he stepped up behind the wizard, his armor swirled into being around him, apparently thanks to his wife. Gwen stood watching with the other witches, standing in a circle around what had been Warlock's shield.

Arthur grinned at his foe. "Unfortunately for you, I still have mine." The vampire's fangs flashed white in the golden glow Excalibur cast as he raised the great sword.

Warlock whirled to face his enemy, backing away, strain obvious on his face, as if he was trying desperately to Shift. And failing.

Arthur merely smiled, the expression every bit as menacing as the one Warlock had turned on Miranda. She grinned in delight.

"So it's to be an execution, then?" Warlock snarled. His eyes sought escape with the desperate flicks of a trapped rat.

"An execution is certainly what you deserve for the innocents you've slaughtered and the death magic you've worked." One corner of Arthur's lip lifted, revealing the tip of a fang. "Trouble is, I just don't want to kill you that fast." He raised his voice, not taking his eyes away from Warlock. "Give the bastard your sword, Tristan."

Without a word, the blond knight tossed Warlock his blade.

No! Miranda jolted forward instinctively. *You don't know what he's capable of!*

But as she opened her mouth, Justice caught her forearm and gave her a head shake. *He has to, baby*, he said in the Spirit Link. *These men live by different rules of honor than we do.*

Despite the sick anxiety in the pit of her stomach, Miranda knew he was right. With a strangled sob, she subsided to watch the two men square off.

And prayed her father wouldn't find a way to kill Arthur.

Justice slid an arm around her waist and drew her close. Despite the armor they both wore, she could sense his warm strength, and her fear abated. Despite everything, she and Justice were together—and alive. They could face whatever happened. Even if Arthur lost.

So held in the comforting circle of Justice's arms, Miranda watched her father battle Arthur Pendragon.

The two men tested each other, blade touching blade in faint scrapes, their gazes locked in a test of will and patience.

Warlock suddenly bellowed and disengaged, chopping his sword at Arthur's head. The vampire parried, took a step forward, and slashed Excalibur across his foe's chest. The wizard's eyes flashed to the blood rolling down his torso, widening in shock.

"First blood to me," Arthur said.

Warlock snarled a Saxon curse, all Germanic consonants. Arthur ignored the obscenity, cool in the face of his foe's rage.

"I took an oath to Merlin," Arthur said as casually as if they spoke over drinks. He didn't even sound winded. "I wonder—did he bother asking the same of you?"

Warlock's head jerked up, lips peeling off his teeth at the deliberately insulting implication that Merlin wouldn't have asked for his oath because the alien knew he'd break it. "Yes, I took his bloody oath!"

He lunged, slamming his borrowed sword into Excalibur, before spinning to ram the pommel of his weapon at the vampire's face. Arthur jerked his head back, avoiding the blow, and drove his knee into Warlock's gut.

Bent double, the werewolf spun away. He straightened painfully and began to circle his foe again.

"I swore to Merlin that I'd keep you from betraying mankind and becoming a tyrant." Warlock bared his teeth. "Evidently he expected you to betray your precious oath. And you have, you bastard!"

Arthur laughed in a bark of contempt. "I'm amazed you have the gall to question my honor when you reek with death magic." He glided closer, Excalibur spilling sparks. Warlock retreated warily.

The former king padded after him, all lethal male grace. "Killing an infant dragon, a dozen little Demi-Sidhe, a troll king, and Maeve's Cat, simply to gain the power to attack Avalon?" Arthur bared his fangs. "I can well imagine what Merlin would have said." His eyes narrowed with lethal fury. "Right before he told me to kill you."

The vampire whirled Excalibur up into a smooth, supremely controlled attack that forced Warlock to scramble away, his sword flying to parry the great blade. "The humans starve and wallow in their brother's blood, while you sit in your fortress city and do nothing!" Warlock charged, only to spin aside at the last instant and slash at the vampire's left thigh, trying to cut his hamstrings.

Arthur twisted, blocking low, then swung Excalibur up again in a hard diagonal slash. The great blade sliced across Warlock's throat, just enough to spill the werewolf's blood. A fraction deeper, and the sorcerer would have bled out in minutes.

Warlock leaped back, his face paling at the close call. "You could have guided the humans to an era of peace and prosperity," he shouted, "but you don't have the balls!"

Arthur beat aside the werewolf's furious swing at his right arm, entangled the point of his foe's blade with the guard of his own, and drove it downward to rake over the cobblestones. His left fist shot out, punching Warlock in the face with a short, hard left.

"I swore an oath, you Saxon bastard," Arthur snarled. He rammed Excalibar's jeweled pommel into the werewolf's mouth. Warlock reeled. "I looked into Merlin's eyes and swore to respect the right of humanity to find its way."

The wizard spat a tooth and wheeled, panting, his eyes wide and wild. Blood streamed from his mouth and broken nose. His voice sounded slurred and congested when he spoke. "Oh, spare me the sanctimony, you son of a bitch."

Arthur ignored that and circled him. "I pledged to keep humanity from destroying themselves, and that's exactly what we've done. No more, no less."

Warlock charged, blade swinging hard at his foe's gut. Arthur went for the block, but the werewolf suddenly reversed the arc of his swing, driving his sword point at the underside of the vampire's jaw.

Arthur threw himself backward, his body arcing into a somersault. Warlock missed by inches. The vampire landed on his feet and instantly launched into a whirling attack, forcing Warlock into frantic retreat, parrying desperately as Excalibur flicked around his face, spilling sparks down his chest.

"I never violated the oath I swore, even as I cursed human greed, stupidity, and cruelty," Arthur told Warlock as the werewolf retreated so fast, he almost tripped over his own feet. "You *did*. You misused every gift Merlin ever gave you."

"You're such a bloody hero," Warlock snarled, kicking out to catch the back of Arthur's ankle with a foot, jerking it out from under him. The vampire went down, and Warlock swung up his blade with a wild cry of victory . . .

Arthur launched himself upward, driving Excalibur into the werewolf's unprotected belly with one hand as he caught Warlock's descending wrists with the other.

Convulsing fingers lost their grip on the borrowed sword, and it tumbled from Warlock's grasp. He stared down at the great blade buried in his gut, eyes wide with disbelief. "No. That's not what's supposed to happen."

Arthur kicked him off Excalibur. Warlock fell hard as the vampire regained his feet with liquid grace. "You broke your oath to Merlin, Warlock of the Direkind," the vampire said in an icy voice. "You sacrificed innocents in acts of death magic, and you struck Avalon during the day to make war on our women." He flicked his eyes to the small group that watched from the edge of the crowd of witches. "What say you, wolves?"

The Magekind parted, revealing a group of Dire Wolves stripped of their armor and weapons, surrounded by a group of witches and vampires who had obviously taken them captive. Smoke and his wife Eva stood close, watching the prisoners with grim attention.

A hulking Dire Wolf stepped forward, his dark fur shot with silver. Beads, feathers, and silver charms clicked in his braided mane. No aristocrat, he had the broad features of a descendent of the Bitten; werewolves who, like Justice, had been transformed by a bite. "Warlock led us here promising revenge for our fallen—like my brother, dead in the last battle." The wolf stared at the wizard with utter loathing on his face. "He didn't say we were to slay sleeping men and the wives who sought to protect them."

"But I . . ." Warlock began.

The wolf spat a thick glob that struck him in the face. The sorcerer flinched. "I grew up hearing ballads of your heroism, Warlock," the big werewolf growled. "From what I've seen today, they were nothing but lies."

Arthur scanned the other captives, one black brow climbing. "Do you hope to gain mercy from me by forswearing your leader?"

A wiry red-furred wolf spoke from behind his evident leader. "You'd be a fool to grant it, after the way we've dishonored ourselves. Hell, I wouldn't trust us either."

"Warlock is an oath-breaker, and he's made oath-breakers of us all," the first wolf agreed. The others growled assent. "Kill him. Execute the murdering son of a bitch."

Arthur nodded and lifted Excalibur. Warlock's lips parted as if he meant to protest, but the king didn't give him time to speak before he brought his blade slashing down.

Miranda watched Warlock die with a sense of profound and utter disbelief. She stood staring at his headless corpse long after the triumphant Magekind had begun to greet one another, lovers walking into each other's arms, knights grouping around Arthur for intense low-voiced conversations and shoulder slapping.

"Are you all right?" Justice asked her softly.

"Fine," she told him absently, trying to believe it was really over. Some part of her was convinced that any moment now, blue magic would flash and Warlock would leap to his feet, head on shoulders again. Evil reborn.

"No, Miranda, you're not all right." She was abruptly aware of Justice's warm presence in their Spirit Link once again. *"But we'll work on that until you are."*

He drew her around to face him, waiting patiently while she dragged her eyes from Warlock's corpse. When he had her attention at last, Justice lowered his head.

The heat of his kiss thawed her icy disbelief. To her appalled mortification, she began to cry against his lips. "I always thought he'd kill me." She gulped in a shuddering breath. "I knew it. *Knew* those vicious orange eyes would be the last thing I'd ever see."

"That was never going to happen." Magic flashed in Justice's gaze like a salvo of launching missiles. "I'd never let that fucker take you away from me. Not as long as I drew breath."

Miranda sighed against his mouth and felt her terrified disbelief begin to drain. *Warlock really is dead.*

"Yep. Arthur doesn't screw around when he decides somebody needs killing," Justice told her.

They drew apart just as Grace du Lac threw herself into Lancelot's arms, both of them gasping in relief. "I thought I'd lost you!" the blond witch said just before their mouths met in a kiss so passionate, Miranda looked away, her cheeks hot.

"I do love a happy ending," Maeve sighed, strolling over to join Justice and Miranda. She carried Guinness cuddled in her arms. The dog's eyes glowed bright green, like a matched pair of alien moons.

Without looking around, the Sidhe goddess gestured, an offhand, almost casual sweep of one hand. Warlock's corpse burst into flames.

When the fire went out, a gust of wind caught the ashes and swirled them skyward. Miranda drew in a breath, watching the last gray flakes vanish.

My God, she thought, incredulous joy sweeping through her at last, *he really is dead*

TWENTY-ONE

"Thank you for my grandchild's life," Morgana told Maeve, gratitude and joy blazing in her eyes. "I tried to heal her, but the burns . . ." The witch broke off, shaking her head.

"Think nothing of it." Maeve shrugged gracefully, though she looked a bit uncomfortable at the witch's gratitude. "I know more about healing the results of a werewolf magical attack than you do. Especially given that Direkind power is antithetical to yours."

Morgana angled up her chin. "Either way, I owe you a debt."

"We all do," Gwen put in from the circle of Arthur's arms, where the two stood leaning together in an obvious blend of exhaustion and joy. "If you hadn't shown us how to filter out the sun once we regained control of the city shield . . ." She shook her head. "I would never have thought to use the wards that way."

"It's not a trick I'd make a habit of, were I you," Maeve cautioned. "Your vampires need the Daysleep as much as they do your blood. They'll grow weak without it."

"We know, Maeve," Arthur told her over his wife's head. "But it's still a useful trick to have. Especially in this case."

Maeve gave him a regal nod. "Believe me, boy, it was my pleasure."

Boy? Miranda heard Justice choke. But then, to a Sidhe goddess, perhaps even Arthur's centuries were the blink of an eye.

"As for you two," Maeve turned to Justice and Miranda, "you did well, children. I am most pleased."

In her arms, Guinness spoke up. "Ripping out the dragon's throat was particularly well done." He smiled in a broad canine display of teeth. "He definitely had *that* coming."

"We couldn't have done it without you," Justice told Maeve.

Her lips twitched. "No, probably not. But I couldn't have done it without you, either."

"Perhaps, but we owe you a debt, my lady." Arthur watched indulgently as Gwen pulled out of his arms to throw herself into her son's hug. "Avalon would have been lost if not for you."

"But it wasn't." She studied him with cool eyes. "Now. What of your Direkind prisoners?"

Arthur frowned. Miranda found herself tensing. She realized suddenly she didn't want to see her fellow wolves die.

"I understand that the ones who survived were all foot soldiers, not Warlock's Chosen Knights," the vampire said cautiously, as if feeling his way. "Judging by their scents, I'm inclined to believe them when they say they didn't know this invasion was supposed to be a massacre rather than a war. And they did help Smoke and his wife fight the Chosen . . ."

"They switched sides?" Miranda asked, startled. "That took guts. My father doesn't—didn't—deal kindly with those he considered traitors."

"Apparently they weren't kidding when they repudiated his leadership." Arthur shrugged.

"In any case, you may safely release them," Maeve told

him, green sparks dancing in her eyes. "In fact, you must. These wolves will tell the others what they saw this day— about Warlock's actions and your own. The Direkind will sing no more ballads in praise of the one they'll call Oathbreaker." She smiled slyly. "I suspect instead they'll sing of Arthur Pendragon and the Knights of the Round Table."

"What about the Chosen?" Miranda asked, frowning. "They've always worshipped Warlock. It's going to be hard to get them to stop."

Maeve snorted. "Most of the Chosen lie in heaps of dead around Avalon. Those who yet survive will find their power base destroyed. Elena Rollings and her mate will see to it that the old traditions die a well-deserved death. The days of blind female obedience and casual abuse will end at last."

Maeve blinked the fireworks from her eyes. "Now, if you'll excuse me, I must return to my children. We will be quite busy soon."

"Busy?" Justice demanded in alarm. "What do you mean, busy?"

Guinness just grinned a toothy dog grin at them as his mistress opened a gate. The two disappeared through it in a tumble of green sparks.

"Well fuck," Justice grumbled. "I wonder what the hell she meant by that."

Miranda leaned into him, suddenly tired to the bone. *"Knowing Maeve, we'll find out one way or another,"* she told him in their Link. *"Though I kind of hope we don't."*

They turned to find knights and ladies, vampires and witches in passionate embraces, lips sealed in ravenous kisses.

Only Smoke and Eva seemed to be thinking of something other than sex. The couple had opened a huge dimensional gate and were herding the surviving Direkind through it. "Come on, folks, let's go," Eva told them, her ghostly antlers glowing above her werewolf head. "Smoke and I have better things to do than provide you lot with taxi service." She exchanged a wicked grin with her mate.

See what I mean? Justice told Miranda. *Knights of the Round Table Gone Wild.*

He opened his own gate with a flick of his fingers, and reached out a hand. Miranda took it, not particularly caring where they were headed, as long as they were together.

They stepped through the gate directly into her cottage's spacious bathroom. The filled tub steamed gently under a layer of foaming bubbles, as candles burned around it. Their dancing golden light illuminated vases of flowers of every conceivable species and color.

"Oh, God, that's perfect," Miranda moaned "I so need a bath."

"As it happens, so do I." He grinned, gesturing again. Their armor melted away like mist.

"You're getting good at this." Miranda looped her arms around his neck.

"I'm highly motivated." Scooping her into his arms, he walked down the steps into the tub. Pausing in the waist-deep, deliciously warm water, he kissed her slowly.

Miranda's eyes slipped closed as she sank into the kiss, drinking his passion. His tongue swirled lazily around hers, and she chased it with her own, then caught his lower lip between her teeth for a gentle nibble.

Warlock's dead. The thought flashed through her mind, bringing another jolt of incredulous joy. He would no longer cast his black shadows over her life. She could love William Justice without looking over her shoulder, fearing that Warlock would plunge them into tragedy.

"Don't think about him," Justice murmured, his lips brushing hers. "He's dead now, and I'm damned well not sharing you with his ghost."

"You won't have to," she told him. "Because I'm going to forget the son of a bitch."

Justice grinned wickedly. "Let's see if this helps." His mouth left hers and started trailing nibbling kisses down the length of her neck, along her collarbones, down the delicate line of her sternum.

When he reached her nipples, she went limp, enjoying the sweet, rising delight of that hot tongue swirling around one tight pink peak. Her pleasure echoed into their Spirit Link, and he hummed in delight, the vibration of his lips making her shiver.

Which gave her the most delicious idea.

Miranda reached below the water to find the rigid thrust of his cock angled just below the surface. She stroked down its length with her fingertips—and gasped at the jolt of pleasure that leaped from his body to hers.

"Oh, now this Spirit Link thing has definite possibilities," Justice growled.

Miranda laughed. "Just what I was thinking." She tightened her grip on the big shaft, purring at the creamy pleasure of her own hand. Justice suckled her, one hand cupping and squeezing her breast, the other thumbing her nipple.

"I always wondered how this felt." He angled his head up to smile into her eyes. "I can definitely see the appeal." He drew back, cocking his head as he considered her breasts. "Suddenly I have this urge to experiment."

Miranda grinned into his eyes. "Feel free."

"Don't mind if I do." He cupped both breasts together in his big hands. The pale mounds were just generous enough that he could press her nipples closer together. With a rumble of anticipation, he started suckling first one, then the other, swirling patterns over and around them with his tongue.

Catching one hard tip, he rolled it between his teeth, suckling with carefully increasing intensity.

Miranda, both legs curled around his waist, slipped her fingers into his hair. The pleasure he felt at her touch intrigued her, and she started doing some exploring of her own. Leaning closer, she started nibbling his ear, then began working her way down the strong cords of his throat. She felt him shiver, and it was easy to see why. He apparently had a cluster of nerves just under the skin there that hummed in iridescent response to her teeth. Stroking her tongue up and down the jutting cord, she savored the delicate sensations she felt in her own neck, almost as if she nibbled on herself.

Justice, meanwhile, was discovering all kinds of new and fascinating things to do to her breasts: tiny bits that vibrated in hot pleasure with every clever flick of his fingers across whichever erect peak he wasn't currently suckling. Exquisite little twists and tugs that should have hurt but didn't; he knew exactly how much pressure to apply.

Finally he reached under her backside, stroking a finger between her vaginal lips to find her clit. He caressed it—and jolted in surprise at the white-hot intensity of the sensation. "Oh, now," he purred against the nipple he was sucking, "that *is* nice."

Miranda threaded her fingers deeper into his hair and shuttered her eyes. "It certainly is. You know what I'm thinking?"

"Sixty-nine," they said in chorus.

"Problem is," Miranda said, one hand idly toying with his furry balls, "we'd have to get out of this nice, warm bath to go drip on the bed. And then we'd have wet sheets all night."

"I've got a better idea," Justice told her, with a flash of a wicked smile. Magic began to swirl around her, thickening in support like a warm, glowing cushion. Miranda yelped in alarm, instinctively tightening her hold of him. Which didn't do her much good, since by now his magic was lifting them both clear of the water.

Wide-eyed, she clung to him as they floated two feet above the bubble bath foam, water raining from their bodies to patter into the bath. "Jeeez, Justice!"

"I'm not going to drop you." His hands swept, drawing patterns in the energy, sculpting glowing mounds of it around her, piling some here for a pillow, still more here under her ass to tilt her hips upward.

Still clinging to him, Miranda looked down. Even she had to admit they only had a couple of feet to fall, right into all that warm, soapy water. They'd probably flood the bathroom, but that was about it.

"Trust me, darling," Justice murmured, his dark eyes crinkling at the corners, magic flashing in their ebony depths. "I'll never let you down. Not very far, anyway."

Miranda smiled into those dark, beautiful eyes. "Well, you haven't so far." And she relaxed, letting herself sink into the cushion of energy. He leaned in and kissed her again in another slow, sensual exploration of the Spirit Link's erotic potential.

When he finally drew away again, he swept an appreciative glance down the length of her body.

"Oh, I do *not* look like that." Miranda blinked at the creamy warmth of her skin in the candlelight. She'd always felt self-conscious about her belly—she'd been trying to lose five pounds since she was fourteen, but her stubborn bathroom scale refused to cooperate.

Yet in Justice's eyes, her torso stretched long and elegant, her breasts full, delightful curves that stoked his appetite. And her legs—including the calves she'd always secretly considered too thick—were long and slim and graceful.

He met her eyes, and she felt a moment's dizziness. It was like looking at a mirror, but not quite. She'd never looked at her reflection the way she looked at him, with magic flickering in her glowing eyes and her lips parted, inviting a kiss. He didn't think her nose was too big or her mouth too full, and he loved the color of her hair. Though, to be honest, she'd always thought her hair was her best feature anyway.

"God," he said with a blink, "is there *anything* you like about yourself?"

"Hey, I'm female. Neuroses come with the territory."

He snorted. "Come here and let me give you something else to think about."

A moment later he was kissing her again as those big, warm hands cupped her breasts, thumbs flicking back and forth across taut, erect nipples.

His cock lay along the line of her hip, trapped between their bodies, offering all kinds of exotic possibilities. She reached down and cupped his balls.

"Damn," she breathed against his mouth at the lush pleasure. His body was so beautifully sensitive, each stroke of her fingertips sent racing flares of pleasure up his spine. "It's definitely time for a blowjob."

"You talked me into it," he panted.

But maneuvering in his cloud of magic proved a bit more tricky than she'd expected. First her knee punched through one mound of semi permeable energy that felt a bit like Jell-O, followed a moment later by the palm of her hand.

"Let me," he murmured, and suddenly she was moving, her body rotating in the air until she stretched head-down along his body. He brought her in closer with another wave of power, rolling her onto her side as he bent one knee. "Pillow your head on my thigh. That way you won't get a crick in your neck."

Miranda obeyed, finding him a firm—if slightly hairy—cushion. So she bent her own bottom leg to offer him the same support. He rested his head there, and she smiled in pleasure at the cool, fine silk of his dark hair curling against her leg.

She lost the smile when he hooked her upper thigh over his forearm, spreading her deliciously wide. She got a sudden close-up image of her own labia as he spread them with two fingers and leaned in. *So that's what that looks like,* she thought, and jolted with a gasp as he licked her in one long, delicious pass.

Curiosity spurring her, she leaned in and sucked his furry balls into her mouth to gently roll them back and forth over her tongue. The wave of silken pleasure he felt made her shiver.

Tonguing them, she sucked lazily for a while, then decided to go to new territory. Releasing his balls, Miranda started working her way up the length of his cock. There was a long, thick vein snaking up its underside to the flushed glans, and she licked her way along it. Shimmering waves of pleasure rewarded every flick of her tongue.

She wasn't the only one exploring. Justice was evidently trying to find out just how to lick to make her lose her mind. He slipped his tongue back and forth across her clit in precise, even licks, pausing periodically to seal his lips around the little nub and suck. Back and forth, up and down, twisting his head this way and that.

Until each tiny, delicate gesture shot jolts of raw heat up her spine.

Miranda wanted to make him feel that good, so she wrapped one hand around his shaft and drew it into her mouth. Sucking hard, she rolled her tongue over its warm, nubby head.

Oh, Holy God. The blazing delight of her own tongue hit her building lust like a shot of lighter fluid on a campfire. Heat blazed through her, so furious she didn't think her need had *ever* been so hot. Not even during her Burning Moon.

After all, then she'd had no one to share it with.

Like most women, it normally took Miranda far more time to come to this kind of raging boil when it felt as if any little thing at all would shoot her into orgasm like a comet. But between the exotic eroticism of the Spirit Link and sharing Justice's arousal—which built to a savage burn much faster than her own normally did—it wasn't long until she realized she just couldn't take it anymore.

Miranda didn't even have to save the words before Justice started moving. Rolling over with her, somehow maintaining their floating support cloud even as he scooped up her legs and locked her knees over his shoulders.

His cock slid into the slick, ready grip of her sex. Miranda caught her breath.

Justice instantly eased back until the penetration wasn't quite so uncomfortably deep. He drew out another fraction and began to ease in again, carefully controlling his thrusts to let her adjust to his width.

Not that she needed much adjusting, considering the lust burning up her spine like a flame along a fuse. Sensing that, Justice picked up the speed of his rolling thrusts, settling over her until they were close enough to kiss. And they did, meeting thrust with slow, rolling thrust as their lips slanted together, suckling deeply, tasting each other.

His cock hit something, some bundle of nerves she hadn't even known was there, and they both convulsed in delighted shock at the sensation.

And they were grinding, no longer careful, hips surging and twisting, his cock plunging deeper as her inner muscles relaxed. Justice stopped for a moment, ignoring her groan of frustrated need, and sat back on his heels, pulling her knees together to tighten her already delicious grip on his cock. Lifting her ass in his free hand, he rotated his hips, rocking over her clit at just. The. Right. Angle . . .

Later Miranda decided she had started coming first, swamped by blinding flashes of orgasmic delight. He followed her over the edge with a howl that sounded far more wolf than man.

Coming, coming . . .

And still coming when Justice's cushion of magic suddenly dissolved out from under them. They hit the water with a tremendous splash and came up sputtering.

"Dammit, I *knew* you were going to do that!" Miranda palmed water off her wet face and coughed.

He swept his wet hair out of his eyes and grinned at her. "Yeah, we won't be trying the magic bed thing again. My concentration just isn't that goo—"

Justice broke off, staring at her as if stunned. Miranda froze. She could see her own astonished face in the candlelight throwing shimmering reflections off the drops on her wet skin. The way her red hair was slicked down over the curves of her breasts as foam lapped back and forth.

His lips didn't move, but she heard the question in his mind. She had to force herself to wait for him to actually ask it.

And then he did. "Marry me."

"Yes! Oh, yes, yes, yes!" Laughing, she threw herself into his arms, sending another wave splashing out of the tub to flood the bathroom.

It was a long, long time before either of them even noticed.

EPILOGUE

Maeve tilted her head, contemplating the new sword she was making for Dovregubben's son. After all, the Troll King had paid her for the blade; the least she could do was ensure his family received it. Especially since a vision had shown her young Hrungne meant to fight for his father's throne—and that he could well win it, with the right weapon.

She didn't look up at the click of her familiar's claws on the stone floor. "Maeve?" Guinness said. "The petitioners are here."

Reluctantly, she dragged her gaze away from the huge blade to watch Danu, Finvarra, and Essus enter—the Phoenix eagle winging in to perch on her anvil, the cat and the Faedragon following more slowly.

Essus dipped his brilliant head in a bow. "Thank you for agreeing to hear our petition, Milady."

Maeve kept him in that bow while the others scrambled up the great stone to join him. The cat shot Essus an irritated glance, presumably for his refusal to wait for those who traveled by foot.

Fin, Maeve noticed, looked too worried to participate in the trio's usual sparring. That bothered her, for the Faedragon was always ready to fight anyone, anywhere. Particularly his fellow familiars.

"What has my children in such a tizzy, eh?"

"We are concerned for our changelin's," Danu said. "Our branch of the Sidhe has been too long from the Mageverse." As she spoke, her Georgia drawl dropped away. "Their blood grows weak, as do their powers. We want to find them suitable mates of Sidhe descent."

Maeve lifted a green brow. "From Llyr's kingdom?" Oh, Siobhan would not like that. Not at all. That in itself was a good enough reason to do it.

It would give Maeve great pleasure to irritate Siobhan as she so richly deserved . . .

But Essus shook his feathered head. "No, milady—that is, if it pleases you. We would ask for suitable matches from among the Hidden Ones." His clear, clever gaze met hers.

Maeve frowned. "You are aware I do not command the heart. Not even of those I consider my own dearest."

"We know, milady," Finvarra said, sitting back on his haunches with his tail curled around his toes, its frilled tip flicking in agitation. "But Branwyn . . . She faces greater danger than she knows, and I can't make her see sense. I fear for her, milady, I fear for her a very great deal."

The Sidhe studied the little dragon, reading his anxiety for his changeling partner in every flick of his tail.

Faedragons had a talent for sensing the future. If Fin thought the child was in danger, she probably was. Maeve sighed. "Very well, my dear ones. I'll see what I scry in my forge fire." She shot them a hard look. "But any matchmaking is your task, not mine."

All three familiars visibly sagged in relief. "Of course, milady," Essus said.

Danu nodded agreement. "We'll set affairs in motion as soon as you identify the candidates."

"And we'll find a way to bring them all together, none

the wiser." Fin's great golden eyes met hers, and his voice dropped to a despairing whisper. "Only . . . please, milady. Find my Branwyn a warrior, or she'll not survive. None of our changelin's will."

Turn the page for a preview of a new
Angela Knight story

ENFORCER

Appearing in Unbound,
coming in March 2013 from Berkley Sensation!

Dona Astryr paused on the dark, narrow wooden stairs, listening with the instinctive caution of a woman who has been betrayed one too many times.

Outside, a crier read the American Declaration of Independence in a fine, rolling baritone. The Philadelphia crowd hooted and stomped for some of the more incendiary lines, bellowing support for the Continental Congress. If there were any Tories among them, they had the good sense to keep their snarls to themselves. Dona didn't blame them; she'd seen a man tarred and feathered once. Judging by the screams of the victim, it hadn't been much fun, though the crowd had thoroughly enjoyed the spectacle.

Temporal natives could be a bit sadistic.

An evidence bot darted past Dona's shoulder, finding its way through the darkened house with the skill and silence of something programmed not to attract attention. The fist-sized robot anti-graved around a corner at the top of the stairs and vanished into the room beyond.

Outside the house, some hapless pedestrian apparently stepped into the path of a wagon rumbling along the narrow brick street. The wagoneer speculated—loudly—that the man's mother had formed an unnatural romantic association with a mange-ridden beaver. Dona's lips twitched. Probably the only smile she'd get tonight.

She continued up the stairs, only to pause just outside the bedroom door to do battle with her gag reflex.

The one thing Dona had always hated about time travel was the smell. All those romantic commercial trids never mentioned the reek of the horse manure piled everywhere, added to non-existent sanitation that often meant raw sewage running down the street.

This smell was worse. Much, much worse.

No surprise. It had been ten hours since the murders. Some of the bodies had spent nine of those hours ripening in the July heat before a courier bot arrived at the North American Temporal Outpost with the news that a tour group was under attack.

Two and a half minutes after the bot delivered its message, a team of ten Enforcers arrived in eighteenth-century Philadelphia, hoping to save lives. One deep breath told them they were too late. Though the call had seemed to come from a frantic temporal tourist, those poor bastards were all dead when the courier was launched. That meant the killers themselves had sent the bot.

Whatever their reasons for notifying Temporal Enforcement, the murderers hadn't been in any hurry to do so. Probably too busy playing with the female victims.

The women in the bedroom had been the last to die.

Squaring her shoulders, Dona stepped through the open door. Her cop's eyes automatically tracked the arching patterns of blood-splatter marking the walls. The rug squelched under her booted feet. No way to tell whether it had been an Aubusson or just hand-hooked wool.

The rug's owner was just as unidentifiable. Or would have been, if the nanocomputer implant in Dona's brain hadn't started a simulation based on her sensor readings. Its calculations stripped away the blood, reconstructed what was left of the face, and located the missing bits scattered across the room.

A DNA scan reveals there is a ninety-eight-point-five percent chance the victim is Lolai Hardin, the comp whispered in Dona's mind. *She was a licensed temporal guide and owner of Hardin's Independence Tours, using this house as her base of operations. I have a recording of her last trid commercial in my files.*

Play it.

Like a ghost, the woman's three-dimensional image faded into view. Lolai's oval face had been delicately beautiful, despite the fine lines that radiated from the corner of her blue eyes. According to her file, she was eighty-two, though someone from this time would have believed her no older than thirty. She wore eighteenth-century dress; a flounced floral petticoat and green silk gown covered by a lace apron and matching kerchief. A jaunty hat decorated with flowers covered her blonde head, tilting rakishly over one eye. She looked as comfortable in the historical garb as if she wore it every day. Which she probably did. When not ferrying tour groups back and forth through time, most guides lived wherever they conducted their tours. It helped them blend in with the temporal natives.

"I'm Lolai Hardin," the woman announced, speaking Galactic Standard with a faint Colonial Philadelphia accent. "I have sixteen years of experience as a temporal guide specializing in Colonial America in the year 1776, particularly in and around Philadelphia, Boston, and New York." Hardin's smile was bright, her manner calm and confident. Dona tried not to wonder how she'd looked when she'd realized she was about to die—and how that death would come. "If you'd like to live as our ancestors did, Hardin's Independence Tours will show you an experience you'll never forget."

"I'm certainly finding it pretty damned unforgettable," Dona muttered.

"What?" Chief Alerio Dyami glanced over at her. There

was no expression on his handsome face, though his black eyes gave him away. Glacial rage burned in those dark pupils, flecking them with crimson light.

Dyami wasn't just an Enforcer. He was a Vardonese Warlord, a genetically engineered warrior bred to protect, with the superhuman strength and speed to do the job. His eyes glowed whenever his emotions grew especially strong. Everybody on the Outpost knew that when the chief's eyes went red, you'd better duck.

The deaths of fourteen innocent people were more than enough to make Dyami's eyes burn. Especially since there wasn't a gods-cursed thing he could do about it.

You can't change history.

Even if Dyami traveled back in time ten hours and attempted to prevent these killings, he'd fail. The victims would still die, no matter what he did. Thirty years of time travel had proved that all time is simultaneous. Past, present and future are an illusion. This made the concept of predestination and time paradoxes equally meaningless.

Temporal Enforcement existed to protect the innocent by preventing time travelers from committing crime. But sometimes you were simply too late.

Then there was nothing you could do but clean up the blood.

"What have we got?" Dyami asked, the impatience in his voice suggestion he'd been waiting for her report on the situation downstairs a little too long.

Dona jolted to automatic attention. "All fourteen victims are accounted for. We've got a total of ten tourists downstairs, including a ten-year-old boy, along with three support staff who posed as house servants."

The chief grunted, his brooding gaze drifting to what was left of Hardin. "At least the bastards didn't kidnap anybody."

"Yeah, you definitely wouldn't want to be a victim they could really take their time with." Dona looked at the narrow bed under its flowered canopy. "It's bad enough as it is."

The woman's wrists were bound to the canopy posts

with mag cables. Loops of the metallic rope-like restraints circled the posts at the foot of the bed, but the ankles they'd bound had vanished.

Dona's comp helpfully informed her that Hardin's right leg was that red lump she could see half-under the bed, while the left one had somehow ended up against the wall across the room. She swallowed hard. *Don't you dare let me toss.*

Beginning anti-nausea treatment. Her stomach stopped bucking. "It appears the killers were Xer," Dona told the chief, once she was sure she wouldn't decorate his boots with her lunch. "The wounds are consistent with those inflicted by Xeran Sevaks." The fanatics' weapon of choice made a Bowie knife look like a toothpick. "Preliminary scans indicate the presence of Xeran DNA. They gang-raped one of the staff and a female tourist between butchering the other victims." When she met his gaze, she sensed he was just as concerned as she was about the sheer viciousness of the attack. "Chief, this isn't normal behavior even for Xeran priests. The simulations we've run indicate they hacked at these people in some kind of frenzy. Maybe religious, maybe sexual. Either way, it was ugly as the seven hells."

A muscle rolled in Dyami's genetically engineered jaw. "Lolai wasn't killed by Xerans. Her murderer was human—more or less."

Dona stared at him, feeling her stomach drop to her boots. Technically the Xerans were human too, but over the past couple of centuries, genetic engineering had changed them into something . . . else. Something faster and stronger and light-years meaner than any mere human.

To the Xerans, humans were inferior primitives, heretics who refused to worship the Victor, their so-called god. Dona could think of only one man they'd trust to help them slaughter a houseful of innocent time-travelers. "Ivar Terje."

It was a damn good thing her comp's anti-nausea procedures were so effective.

"Yeah, Ivar. Again." The chief curled a lip. "The DNA scan I just ran was conclusive. Ninety-nine-point-eight percent chance Terje raped and murdered Lolai Hardin."

"Gods." Dona's eyes slid reluctantly to the dismembered torso now drying to a shade of dark brown in the middle of the bed. "How could he have done something like this?" *And why in the name of all the hells didn't I know he was capable of it? I slept with him. I thought I loved him—at least until he tried to beat me to death and murder my friend.*

As if reading her mind, Dyami shot her a compassionate glance. "I didn't know what he was either." His lovely male rumble dropped to a mutter. "I still can't believe he sold us out for a handful of galactors."

Actually, Dyami's own internal investigation put the figure at 1.3 million galactors. But the chief wasn't the kind of man to turn traitor for any amount of money; to him, more than a million galactors might as well have been pocket change.

Which was why they were in this mess. If Dyami hadn't been so relentlessly honorable—not to mention inhumanly handsome in that Vardonese way of his, all height and muscle and hard black eyes—maybe she wouldn't have turned to Ivar as a distraction.

Oh, beefershit, Dona thought, suddenly impatient with her own rationalization. *You wanted to believe you were in love with the sociopathic bastard because he said all the right romantic tripe. You ignored the evidence that was right in your face.*

Her sensors had warned her Ivar used his comp almost continuously, controlling his body's normal emotional reactions at all times. You only did something like that if you were lying every time you opened your mouth. But no, she hadn't seen the truth until his fist hit her face.

Turns out, she'd gotten off lucky.

Her sickened gaze once more tracked to the corpse. *Fourteen, seven Gods love us. They killed fourteen people, and Ivar helped them.*

"Would these people be dead if we'd managed to capture Ivar six months ago?" She caught herself rubbing her aching chest and forced her hand to drop.

"Probably." Dyami shot her a twisted grin. "Though Goddess knows I hate to interrupt your wallow in guilt, Ivar is nothing to the Xerans. They don't think much of traitors."

"I'm not real fond of the dickhole myself," Dona muttered.

Dyami shrugged those impressive shoulders. The dim light from the evidence bot rolled over the dark blue scales of his armored T-suit, making its silver piping gleam. Her eyes helplessly followed the rolling line of light as it played over powerful muscle barely concealed by the tight-fitting suit.

"So the teams completed the evidence collection downstairs?"

Guiltily, Dona snapped her gaze back to his face. If not for her computer, her cheeks would be blazing beet red about now. "Uh, yes sir."

"Good." He gave her a decisive nod, beads clinking in the braids worked into his shoulder-length black hair—actually combat decorations on his home planet. "We need to finish the cleanup before one of the temporals decides to investigate."

No, they definitely didn't want some eighteenth-century good Samaritan walking in on an Enforcer team in all its armored glory. "I checked before we left the Outpost, but I didn't see any record of a mass slaying on this date," Dona told him. "If somebody'd found this mess, they'd have talked about it."

Dyami snorted. "Assuming any reports survived the ensuing five hundred years."

That was the trouble with time travel. You might think you knew what happened, but you really didn't. Records were lost, to fire or mold or other ravages of time. Those who reported the events at the time could have lied to protect their reputations, to make their cause look better, or just for the hell of it. Ever since temporal exploration began thirty years ago, humanity had been shocked to learn how much "history" was pure beefershit.

You never really knew what had happened during historical events until you went back and watched them occur. Otherwise, the past might as well be the surface of an alien planet.

"Coming through!" A body tube floated through the door, the blue glow of the two-meter-long cylinder's anti-grav field shining on the floor. Dr. Sakuri Chogan followed, her face grim and pale under her topknot of iridescent green hair. A swarm of evidence bots trailed her, ready to process the scene.

Chogan stopped in the doorway and stared around at the arching patterns of blood splatter. "Seven hells."

Dona automatically took a step closer, concerned by her sickened expression.

"Oh, back off." The Outpost's doctor shot her an impatient glower. "I do autopsies for a living." Then, as if against her will, her gaze drifted around the room again. "Though whoever did this ranks with the sicker psychopaths I've seen."

"DNA scans say it was Ivar," Dona said flatly.

"Oh." Chogan, being no idiot, winced on her behalf, and promptly changed the subject. "We'd better get her tubed." Revulsion crossed the human's expressive face. "As soon as we can *find* all of her . . ."

Grim, unspeaking, Dona, Chogan and Dyami went to work at the gory task. Luckily, temporal armor was as effective at blocking biological contaminants as it was at protecting the body from time travel.

As they worked, faint slurps and thumps signaled that the evidence bots were at work, removing every last blood cell from the plastered walls, every hair and bone fragment and stray bit of tissue from the bed and floor. Every last alien *anything* that didn't belong in the eighteenth century.

By the time they were through, you'd never know anyone had died here.

Dona lifted the stiff brown pillow that had lain under Hardin's head. A courier bot popped out from beneath it, darting into the air with its anti-grav spilling blue light. She barely managed to bite back a startled yelp.

"Alerio Dyami!" the bot thundered in a surprisingly deep voice. "I seek Alerio Dyami, Chief Temporal Enforcer of the North American Outpost."

"I'm Dyami." Alerio studied the device with narrow-eyed intensity. "My sensors say it's a Xeran bot," he murmured to Dona.

She backed off, one hand falling to the shard pistol holstered at her hip. Luckily, the fact that the courier had traveled in time meant it was unlikely to be armed with any really interesting energy weapons. Anybody or anything attempting a temporal jump armed with a tachyon beamer would only blow itself to all seven hells.

Unfortunately, there were a lot of other ways to kill, even a target as formidable as Alerio Dyami. Dona watched the bot with hard eyes, ready to fire if it made one move toward the chief.

"I have a message for you," the courier announced. "Would you like to take it privately?"

"Chief, don't!" Chogan began urgently.

Dyami shot her a cool look. "Give me a little credit, Doctor. I'm not stupid enough to smear anything from that thing on my skin." To the bot, he said, "I'm not concerned with privacy. If you've got a message, play it."

"As you wish," the bot said cheerfully.

And just like that, Ivar Terje stood in the middle of the room.

Dona damned near drew her pistol before logic kicked in. *It's just a trid, idiot.*

"Don't shoot the bot, Dyami," the three-dimensional recording said with a smirk. Ivar was inhumanly handsome in the way of the genetically engineered—at least until you realized his eyes were as cold and gray as the ice on a frozen planet. He'd cut his hair since she'd seen him last, buzzing it so short it covered his head in a red bristle. The style was apparently designed to call attention to the silver implants jutting from his skull.

"Look who's wearing horns!" Chogan curled a lip. "Looks like Terje's pretending to be a priest of the Victor now."

And I slept *with* that? Dona thought, even more revolted.

"What do you think of my handiwork, Chief?" Ivar's image flashed a vicious white grin. "Hells, that Lolai was a squealer. If not for the mute field, every primitive for miles would have come running." The grin widened still more. "It'll take a lot more work to get a scream out of Dona, but I'll manage—eventually."

To Dona's surprise, Dyami stiffened, his dark eyes flashing red, his lips pulling back in a snarl. "You won't get the chance, shiteater."

Ivar chuckled, almost as if he'd heard the chief. "I'm sure you're growling manly Warlord threats right now. I'd be impressed—if I were there. Instead I'll just give you a choice. Surrender yourself to the Victor's . . . justice. Along with Dona, Galar Arvid, Jessica, Nick Wyatt, and his whore Riane."

Every trace of humor vanished from his face, leaving nothing but vicious intent. "Otherwise, my team and I are going to butcher every temporal historian, every trid crew, every tourist and guide we can get our hands on. And that's a long list. Your choice, Dyami. Surrender now like the hero you are, or let innocents pay for your cowardice."

The image winked out.

Dyami lunged for the bot in a blurring surge of cyborg muscle, but before his fingers could close over it, the thing darted away. A flare of blinding light and a thunderclap sonic boom signaled the bot's Jump back to the Xeran home world.

When Dona's ears quit ringing, Alerio was still pacing and cursing. "Courier probably recorded our reactions to Ivar's little ultimatum. He'll want to gloat." He bared his teeth in something light years from a smile. "Glaciers will claim the Seven Hells before I surrender any of my people to those Xeran dickholes."

That reaction didn't surprise Dona in the least. "He meant it about the civilians, sir. They'll slaughter every tourist and historian they can."

"Then we'll just have to make sure they don't get the chance." His eyes were solid sheets of flame now.

And she was staring at him again. Her longing was probably written all over her face. *Fool*, Dona thought, dragging her eyes away. *He's your commanding officer. Didn't you learn a damned thing from what happened with Kagan?*

The temporal journey back to the North American Outpost was as grueling as always. The Enforcers Jumped from the house's great room in teams of two, accompanied by body tubes.

Alerio kept watch as was his habit, covering his team's retreat. As much as he could, anyway, having gone half-blind and deaf from the temporal flares and their accompanying sonic booms as they left. Luckily the suits' dampening field kept anyone more than ten meters away from feeling the effects. No temporal natives would wonder why there was a thunderstorm *inside* the house next door.

Finally only he and Dona were left. For a moment, Alerio let his gaze linger on the cool purity of her profile, with its high cheekbones, striking violet eyes, and the mouth that seemed gene-gineered for sin.

He looked away just before she Jumped with a deafening boom.

His ears were still ringing as his comp started reciting the familiar string of coordinates back to the Outpost.

Coordinates confirmed. Engage temporal warp, he told it.

Engaging temporal warp in three . . . two . . . one.

It felt like being hit by lightning. His mind blinked out . . .

Then he was back again.

Temporal warp to the Outpost successful, his comp announced.

Alerio made no answer, half-blind, stomach knotting in a violent rebellion, his muscles jerking from the temporal warp. Bracing his knees, he stayed upright by will alone until his comp could compensate. *My team?*

All members of the investigation team present and accounted for.

Alerio breathed a silent prayer of thanks to whatever Vardonese goddess happened to be listening.

He'd almost lost a Jumper once. Riane Arvid's sabotaged T-suit had bounced her back and forth across Terran temporal space before finally dumping her in the twentieth century. There she'd encountered Nick Wyatt, half-breed Xeran and superhuman guardian of an alien race called the Sela.

Nick and Riane had returned to the Outpost desperately in love.

Still, almost losing an Enforcer was an experience Alerio had no desire to repeat. Especially considering Ivar's threats.

It'll take a lot more work to get a scream out of Dona, but I'll manage—eventually. Sickened, Alerio shoved the memory aside.

Blinking the spots from his eyes, he glanced around the cavernous room. Its heavily shielded walls a soothing blue, Mission Staging was lined with evidence and equipment lockers as well as regeneration tubes for treating the injured. Most temporal missions began and ended here, especially those featuring a large Jump team.

Alerio spotted Dona deep in an animated conversation with Riane. The young Warfem and her cyborg wolf partner had been with the crew working the house's ground floor.

Enough mooning, he thought, suddenly impatient with himself. He had work to do—and he wasn't the only one.

Alerio lifted his voice to a command bark. "All right, let's get the body tubes stowed. The evidence bots are to be logged in and their contents transferred into evi-stasis. And make damned sure they're all *our* bots. Last thing we need is to give the Xerans another opportunity to sabotage our central computer."

Chogan stepped over to him. "I'm headed for the infirmary." She grimaced. "I've got fourteen autopsies to do."

Alerio winced on her behalf. "I don't envy you that job."

She snorted and headed out, followed by her med crew and the pitiful parade of body tubes.

Meanwhile the Enforcers began scanning and decanting each bot. After sealing the biological evidence in stasis tubes to prevent further decomposition, they logged everything in with the Outpost's main computer. If the Outpost's investigators—or the Galactic Union's Temporal Court—decided they needed any of that evidence later, it would be instantly available.

The procedure was one his people had done hundreds of times before. They didn't need Alerio hovering over them like a Soji Dragon with one egg. Especially since he was only putting off a job even more onerous than the one they were doing.

Somehow he was going to have to persuade Colonel Bevera Evetti to order a moratorium on temporal tourist visas. At least until Ivar was captured—or Alerio twisted the traitor's head off his shoulders.

That action would not be legal under Galactic Union law, his comp informed him primly.

I do not give a stinking pile of Soji shit. Especially if he even thinks about going after my team.

Particularly Dona, who'd become Alerio's obsession over the past two years. As Ivar damned well knew. The cyborg had been violently jealous of her even when he was still pretending to be a loyal Enforcer.

It had driven Alerio into a frigid fury, watching Ivar watch Dona's every move while shooting little verbal barbs her way. There'd been times Alerio had literally ached to kick his subordinate's ass from one end of the Outpost to the other.

Unfortunately, being Ivar's commanding officer made that impulse impossible to carry out. Especially since Dona never reported her lover for his conduct. Alerio wasn't sure whether she just didn't notice—which strained belief, Dona being pretty damned observant—or whether she just had a very thick skin.

Even though it looked so incredibly soft . . .

He pulled his gaze away from her yet again and started mentally composing his report.

Fifteen minutes later, the evidence was logged in and the bots stowed. The Enforcers headed out, either to their quarters or in search of a meal at the Outpost Mess. Normally they joked and laughed after a mission, but tonight's bloodbath had left them all in a grim mood.

Dyami followed, still wrestling with the report's wording. He stepped into the corridor just in time to see Nick Wyatt pounce on Riane.

Alerio watched with an involuntary smile as the big man pulled his Warfem lover into a passionate kiss, ignoring her startled squawk. She melted against him an instant later, her long body curving into his, her arms twining around his broad back.

The chief frowned at his sudden stab of bitter envy. Despite himself, he flicked a glance at Dona, who watched the pair with a pained smile.

Remembering Ivar? God, he hoped not.

"Pheromones!" Frieka gasped, staggering on his big wolf paws, his vocalizer's indicator lights flashing blue from the thick black fur on his neck. "Choking . . . clouds of lust! For the Goddess's sake, go find a bunk before you reek up the entire Outpost!"

Nick pulled his mouth away from Riane's to smile down at the big cyborg beast. "You're just jealous."

"And you're still not married," the wolf grumbled. "Get it together, would you? I want another cub to spoil."

Riane laughed and reached down to ruffle his thick fur. "We're working on it, fuzzy."

"That's the Goddess's own sweet truth." Frieka rolled his vivid blue eyes. "Sharing quarters with you two is like being trapped in a porn trid."

Dona held up both hands in a warning gesture. "Okay, that's it. I just don't need to know any more."

Her gaze slid toward Alerio, then darted away. Was it his imagination, or had longing flashed across her face?

Seven burning hells, he didn't have time for this. He had a report to make if he wanted to keep anybody else from dying.